Peter –
Here is the final cut.
Appreciate your kind
words.

Best regards,

SWAMPOODLE

The Life and Times of

Jack Hennessey

A NOVEL

by

P. D. St. Claire

Cover art – Pat Leibowitz

Jacket Design – Peggy Carr

"Swampoodle – The Life and Times of Jack Hennessey," by P.D. St. Claire. ISBN 978-1-60264-552-3.

Published 2010 by Virtualbookworm.com Publishing Inc., P.O. Box 9949, College Station, TX 77842, US. ©2010, P.D. St. Claire. All rights reserved. No part of this publication may be reproduced, stored in a retrieval system, or transmitted in any form or by any means, electronic, mechanical, recording or otherwise, without the prior written permission of P.D. St. Claire.

Manufactured in the United States of America.

to

Bink

The dead were everywhere

Laying in fields and ditches
Clustered in mud huts and caves
Crumpled and kneeled in churches
Eyes blackened and lungs caved

There were to the eye more dead
Than ever seemed to have been alive
And for the living who could
It was time to leave…

CHAPTER ONE
Coffin Ships

C offin Ships is what they called them and sure coffins they were, going down, some of them, not a full week at sea. Aboard each and all, the ships that made it and them that didn't, the castoff and wretched of famine and want making west for America on short rations and foul water. Sick from the roll of the ship, they were, and soon the typhus too, dying by the score of its fever and pain, all in air fouled by their own vomit and waste.

Barely getting by in the good years, the blight of 1845 took their pratties that year, and three of the five that followed. And they was all there was to eat, the pratties were. Not owning their own land because they was Irish, they was turned out by the thousands when they couldn't pay their rents. Ach! Away, now! We've heard it all before, at the knee of das and grand das, and uncles too, and why speak of it again? 'Breeding like rabbits on land wanted for grazing,' them in charge would be saying. 'So let it come and be done with 'em. 'Tis nature's way to clear the land of them unfit to tend it. Dead where they lived and dead where they dropped and who's to care? They're not of our own, they're not, so be done with 'em now and good riddance.'

An inconvenience is all, that's what Ireland was to England. Its poor rents and trouble to keep. Ach! If it wasn't there, it'd never been missed. But there it was, all the same, with the Queen's ministers taking care that it not fall to hostile hands, it being so close and all. But that was all the caring they did, and sure none for them native to it. And as the crop failed again and again, the small holders in the west, where the blight struck the worst, were driven from their places, threatened with jail or paid short to ship out. And ship out they did, a million or more, first for Liverpool and then the New World, with Mary Mulholland among them, her son Jack at her breast.

She'd got passage with the promise of more from an overseer who'd taken a fancy to her. Aye! Mary with her high spirit and flame-red hair! She and hers being so desperate, and all, and there being nowhere to turn... Ach! T'was the times, you know, none harder. Folks falling dead in their rotting plots, hard times, and that's for sure. So it come to this, it did, Mary with her Jack and needing to leave, getting three months food for her family and gone for America in her shame, an overseer's son never to know his da, his name neither, that being the bargain.

Mary, poor girl, she never looked back, fearing to see her da's face, him torn by the fates and the needing of food for the rest. Sure hunger's a terrible thing done at God's own hand, him having his reasons why and who's to question? But hunger done at the hand of man? 'Tis a crime it is, and a sin, too. And sure it wasn't to heathens in the ocean isles they'd done this to, neither. No. T'was to Christians they done it – Christians of a different calling, no doubt, but Christians all the same, and they turned them out to waste and die by the tens of thousands with nary a thought about it.

It was at Fells Point that they landed in Baltimore, weak and wracked from two months at sea, some wandering off to die in a wood. And the orphans, their das and mas dead at sea of typhus or hardship and put over the side, and who's to care for them now? Erin's poorhouses, that's what they called the cities where they landed, Boston and New York, Philadelphia and Baltimore. Thousands by thousands they come, near half the city by some's counting, and what to do with them all?

Now Mary Mulholland had come by the name of a man, and the street where he lived, too. It was got aboard ship from a woman dying, his sister by her telling, and would Mary call on him and tell him what's done? 'Don't know if he's living or dead, but the street's name is Lemmon and his name's O'Connell, and bless you dear lady for trying.' Living or dead, Mary Mulholland had a name and a place and that was more than most of the rest. And money, too, the overseer as good as his word, four fresh five pound notes that she'd kept safe from the thieving of others and the damp of the ship.

There were greeters come down to the docks, you know, helping poor souls find a place and some food. *The Ancient Order of Hibernians* is what they called themselves, and God's own help they were, too. One such, a lawyer named Larkin, took Mary Mulholland from her ship and its stench. A fine summer's morn it was, the sun full on her face and the air clean to breathe. It was first to a bank for her notes to be put, her taking a portion in cash for her needs. From there to West Baltimore they went, Lemmon Street running east to west above the rail yards, house upon house, shelter and home to the men who built the B&O and come later to work it, them and their families.

The home of Patrick O'Connell being found, Lawyer Larkin mounted the three steps of the stoop. Two raps on the door with the butt of his cane and soon it soon come open. Mrs. O'Connell, her eyes in a squint and her chin up in an aire, sure telling her mind at the sight of them. More off the boat, she's thinking, no doubt, and looking and smelling for all of it.

"Good day to you, Mrs. O'Connell," says Mr. Larkin. . "We've news for Mr. O'Connell, if he's to home?"

"He's not," says she. "Gone to work, don't you know."

"May we call on him later, then?"

"If it please you."

"A time convenient to him, then? And, of course, to you, kind madam?"

"Make it seven, if you wish," the door coming shut and them in the street.

"Ah, 'tis a start, Mrs. Mulholland! 'Tis a start, indeed!"

Now never being 'Mrs.' anything to anyone before, Mary Mulholland took well to the sound of it. 'Mrs. Mulholland,' indeed. And who's to know, aye, who's to know? Stepping back from the door of the house, she took in the two stories of it, brick at the front and the basement below. And now to the street she was on, its cobble stones warming the bare of her feet, the toes and dirt of them hidden by her dress. Wide it was, wider than that of the village she'd left, her mind counting what she'd seen to here from the ship and all the same, street upon street, row upon row, house upon house of it. 'Now, where's it we've come to, young Jack Mulholland?' says she to him at her shoulder, him looking about in the morning sun. 'Tis heaven, I think true enough. And right here on God's good earth!'

"Mrs. Mulholland?"

"Yes, Mr. Larkin, yes. I'm sorry, now, my mind's just drifting with it all, you know." She hiked Jack up a measure at her shoulder and smiled. Mr. Larkin, his top hat and kind face with whiskers of white, sure he seemed to her St. Peter himself at the gate on such a day as this.

"Mrs. Mulholland," says he, "might I suggest McMurphy's Dry Goods? I know him well and he'll be treating you fair." He stepped back a measure to view Mary better. "I think a fresh dress for you and something for the lad, there, as well. And shoes, now, Mrs. Mulholland? Will you be wanting a fresh pair of shoes?"

And so it come that Mary Mulholland and young Jack were to board at the O'Connells. Though saddened to learn of his sister's passing, Patrick O'Connell took some consolation in the three dollars rent for a basement from which he was expecting nothing but another mouth to feed. And in time it was to be her place, Mary Mulholland's, that is, she learning to read and to write and doing her fine stitching for the better ladies about, and buying the place when the O'Connells left for Ohio. *Mrs. Mulholland*, it was. Aye! Mother to Jack and widow to poor Sean, him gone in The Hunger, shot for a rebel! Mary Mulholland of Lemmon Street, landlord herself with boarders in the basement and people asking her opinion of this and that, and even taking some account of it!

But a fever had been on her now, two weeks and more, coming and going, but just as sure. 'Watch her closely,' says the doctor in the kitchen to Jack for his dollar. 'Keep her cool with water to hand, and plenty of it.' And who wouldn't be knowing that? thinks Mary Mulholland in her bed, up and down in her spirits, but sure weaker by the day. Neighbors nearby and ready to help, as she'd done them before. But a fear was coming to her, now, a darkness at night she'd not known before. 'Tis it time for the priest?' she's wondering.

But it's Jack on her mind now, joined with the railroad just four weeks before and gone to West Virginia, so far away. Sure it's two days now and not a word of him or a whisper. But word of war, aye, there was that, and that all about! The Rebels across the Monacacy and making for Washington with folks telling of cavalry north and east of Baltimore, scaring people half out of their wits, taking horses and tribute. What's to come of it all? 'And where's my Jack lad, now? Where's my Jack?'

CHAPTER TWO
At War

They'd been at it three full years and more, from Gettysburg to Mobile Bay to Vicksburg and beyond. The whole lot of it. Come June of 1864, Grant had Lee in a pickle near Richmond, things going back and forth with heavy killing since April. Guns and bombs all about, and arms and legs, too. Then the dead, blue and gray, young and old, lying about after a fight, roasting in a summer's sun, bellies swelled to near bursting. Grant was Lincoln's newest general and he'd said to him, he said 'Get it done, now, and done quick.'

Lee was holding his own but working hard at it and not knowing to where it was all to lead. Something needed deciding and he decided it. He sent near a quarter of his strength west to Charlottesville and from there up the Shenandoah. Under the command of Major General Jubal Early, they were to clear the valley of Yankees and then cross the Potomac east into Maryland and attack Washington City from the north. Mean of spirit and gifted at war, Early drove his men near 250 miles in the summer's heat and by July 7 stood outside Frederick, Maryland, barely thirty five miles northwest of Washington City itself. Taking $200,000 in tribute, he spared the town and made ready for Washington, only a scattering of Union forces and the Monocacy River standing between him and glory.

Now there's nothing like 16,000 marauding Rebels relieving a town of $200,000 in cash and gold to get the attention of a captain of industry. And sure enough, John W. Garrett, President of the Baltimore and Ohio Railroad, passed what he'd learned of the goings on in Frederick to Major General Lewis Wallace, commander of Union forces in Baltimore. There was a bridge there, you see, a railroad bridge, and Mr. Garrett was after having General Wallace mount a defense of it.

A man of high purpose and great courage, Wallace rounded up 2,800 irregulars which, on the afternoon of July the 8th, the B&O was pleased to deposit at Monocacy Junction, just south of Frederick, forty miles west of Baltimore. Setting up headquarters on the south side of the river, Wallace was quick to confirm that he was outnumbered at five to one and working hard on what to do about it. And then, as if sent by the angels above, a train load of Union regulars, 3,000 in all, appeared at two o'clock on the morning of the 9th. Under the charge of Major General James Ricketts, they'd been sent by Grant to reinforce Harper's Ferry, forty miles again to the west, against Early's raid. On learning from Wallace that Early was only across the river and making ready for battle, he placed himself under Wallace's command and ordered his men off the train.

It being the middle of the night and black as pitch, there was more than the usual confusion attending the disembarkation of 3,000 troops rousted from a hard sleep on a rolling train. There were horses and wagons for two weeks fighting, the whole lot to come off and be put some place safe. And then there's them to be sent forward first, stumbling in the dark, shouting at one another, ordering who's ever about to lift this or shove that and sure doesn't young Jack Mulholland find himself caught up in it all. Just four weeks now with the railroad, he's doing whatever he's told on old Engine 428, glad for his new situation and charged by the danger of battle near to hand.

Come morning, though, Jack Mulholland is on the north side of the river and brought up short by the sound of the train's whistle as it starts chugging west, great belches of smoke and steam from its stack as it begins to roll. Quick as a snap, he's on his toes, making for the covered bridge he'd crossed from the south, his arms pumping and his chest filling for the run. Not three full strides taken, though, and he's struck by a horse, a cavalryman making for the front. Knocked clear aside, he lands hard in scrub brush like a sack of mail off a train.

It was the bite of a horse fly that roused him, slapping at his own neck to kill it. Laying on his back in the broken shade of the brush, Jack Mulholland brought his hands to his head hammering inside, his eyes hurting and all of him wanting to be sick. Working the sides and back of his neck with his hands, and turning his head left and right, his brain come slowly around. And there were sounds now, too, horses and men moving about, some shouting, orders given and taken, and the heavy wheels of a wagon rumbling by, its driver calling its team on. Struggling to his feet, Jack Mulholland rose to a crouch, reaching to steady himself on a nearby tree, cowering as he looked about. By the sun he could see it was midday. He'd been out for...

Thud...Thud, Thud, Thud...Thud. Artillery! Low and distant, full runs of it, now, above the hammering inside his head. Ducking, Jack Mulholland looked for cover, the shells screeching in, a piercing scream in his ears, his head splitting from the pain of it. Falling to his knees, he presses his face against the side of a tree, hugging it like a lad at his mother's legs, shells striking the ground, quaking it beneath him, shattered bits of trees flying about, and shrapnel, too. "They're a-coming!" was shouted from the north, and then again and again from every side. "Ready arms, men, ready arms! Steady! Holding fire! Holding!"

Rising a measure, Jack Mulholland could see the Rebel's colors advancing. "Line to the fore, rise and fire!" A line of men rose before him and a fusillade of rifle fire roared left and right and center, men shouting, oaths taken, and a return fusillade in. There were screams now, words shouted of mothers and gods. A second fusillade out and more shouting, officers yelling. "Fire and withdraw! Holding ranks...Fire and withdraw...Holding your ranks, men..."

More artillery crashed in and about, Jack Mulholland looking out from behind the tree, and sure the Unions are in retreat. Backing to him, holding ranks, loading and firing, and soon some starting to break, three or four, then others, taking cover behind a tree here or a wagon there, holding in small groups around an officer. "Hold your ranks! Withdraw *in your ranks!*" The Rebs were on them now, some charging, breaking ahead, others reloading as they advanced and then firing and now charging, their rifles lowered and bayonets pointed. Then the Unions coming nearest to him stopped dead in their tracks, five of them abreast, staring beyond him, their mouths agape, one shouting "The bridge's on fire. *They've fired the bridge!*"

Jack turned. The covered bridge was ablaze on its south side. The Federals had done it to keep it from the Rebs, but had trapped their own men in the bargain! It was a rout now. The officers trying to hold the men in formation, their sabers held and pointed at the Rebs but without effect. The Federals were dropping their weapons and making for the railroad bridge to Jack's right, running by him now, rifle balls whizzing by, coming off the trees, striking a nearby shed, shards and bits of wood in the air, and all about him men falling when struck, some dead where they landed, others stumbling forward. Reb officers up and coming now, calling their soldiers forward, their side arms leveled at the Unions, firing as they ran.

It was every man for himself with Jack Mulholland on his toes passing the slower among them, darting left and right, in and around them, a blow at his left shoulder and over he goes and rolling up as quick, the bridge not fifty paces and him passing the others still, officers at the bridgehead and others firing at the Rebs in pursuit, waving Jack and the rest on now with Jack slowing a step to gauge the rail ties, then up at speed, leaping every two and landing the third, darting left and right around those stumbling and quick as that he's across, breaking left on orders from those in front, the roar of a battle to his right, now, hundreds of Federals standing their ground, artillery again but even more, and fusillades sounding, the river now to his left and him running along it, the sounds of war less with each stride and him now like the wind through trees and fields and then rails…Tracks! And it's every third again and again for as long as his legs would carry him, slowing in time to take the shade of a tree just off the rails, stepping carefully down the stones of the track bed and under its shade, leaning against it, breathing heavy and free.

Alert to sounds about him, his eyes darting in every direction, he was away from it all…then a dampness at this left hand…Blood! Crimson and deep, and his own, no doubt! Standing straight, he felt for its source, grabbing and feeling up his arm, finding a hole just below his shoulder, wet and tender to touch, and one behind, as well. Shot clean through! Loosening his bandana, he tied it off quick, pulling the knot tight with teeth and hand, only to see blood on his right hand and his sleeve as well, the run coming back to him now, men stumbling and falling, a soldier's head shot through, the spray of blood and brain from it on Jack's hands and face. Shaking his head to pass the memory, he left the shade of the tree and mounted the rail bed, making east on the tracks for Baltimore.

Covering two miles by dusk, maybe three, Jack Mulholland had come to a cluster of trees by a stream, a cornfield and apple orchard nearby. Stepping down to the stream, he found a sand flat in a bend and knelt by its edge, palming water to drink as parts of the day came back to him. Running was what he remembered most clearly, the sound of rifle fire and men shouting with others falling around him, a man's head... Feeling his face and neck, there were still bits and pieces... Jack buried his head in the stream to his shoulders, rubbing himself clean, back to front, his eyes closed, the coolness of the water a comfort against the heat of the day. Holding down till his breath was gone, he came out of the water, shaking his head like a dog in the sun and for the moment clean of it all and calmed.

Rising from the stream, he climbed the bank and gathered an arm load of corn and a half dozen apples. These he placed at the base of a tree, nearby a bit of flat ground to sleep on. The holes in his arm were next. Stepping back down to the stream, he eased off his shirt and loosened the bandana. Dried blood had crusted at each hole and black in the failing light, holding the bandana fast to the skin of his arm. Squatting, then kneeling, he palmed water to it and in time the bandana came free, the jagged edges of the hole in front not so clean as he'd thought. He set the bandana in the stream to soak as he remembered what he'd been told on the docks about the care of a wound. 'Piss in the dirt,' they'd said, 'and make a bit of mud with it. Mix it, now, like a lad in a puddle, and slap it on and cover it over. And if there's a bit of spider web nearby, put that in, too, to keep the paste of it together. That'll do for till you get to a doctor and proper care.'

Pissing would be easy he thought as he palmed water on the holes, front and back. Big as the holes were, though, he was going to need something for webbing, but how to find it in the failing light? His eye then caught the corn he had picked, its silk sticking out, fine as any baby's hair. Husking two ears, he took a handful of silk to a bit of flat dirt where he pissed himself empty. With a stick, he made a mud of it and dropped in the corn silk, mixing a paste of it all. Going back to the stream for his bandana, he squeezed it dry as he knelt by the mud.

Placing the bandana close to hand, he spread the paste to the back and front of his arm, catching it quick with the bandana as he pulled it tight and tied it off.

Holding his left forearm in his right hand to steady it, he came up out of the stream to the tree where he had placed the corn and apples. For all the horror of the day, Jack Mulholland had come to a certain calm, biting into an apple and making ready to husk the corn. He had seen war and gotten through it, tended his wounds and found this safe place to rest, the last reds of the sun now gone to the blue black of the night. He would walk the rails tomorrow, east for Baltimore. New Market was ahead, three miles, maybe five, and a railway siding there with a water tower. If Engine 428 was coming back through, it'd be stopping there, or maybe another train headed for Baltimore.

Lying out beside the tree, Jack Mulholland found a troubled sleep, memories of artillery roaring and rifles firing and men screaming and dying all gone to the call of crickets against the quiet of a summer's night. A day at war done, come and done, as quick as that, now, as quick as that…

CHAPTER THREE
The Confession

P *atrick's of Pratt Street* faced south on the rail yard. Home to the men that worked the B&O, it was here that Jack Mulholland had got to by seven the night following. Good as his guess, Engine 428 had come by New Market at three the next afternoon, stopping for water and wood. Aboard were the wounded and dead from battle, on their way home to those they'd left. There'd been great sobs and wailing at the station with a muffled drum to honor the fallen. But the crew of the 428 would have none of it. Their Jack had been to war and back with a hole in his arm to prove it, reason enough to lift a pint at *Patrick's*!

And wasn't Jack Mulholland feeling grand, now, drinking beer with the men, shaking hands with one and all. A grand day indeed, it was, him telling again of the battle, the roar of the fusillade and crash of the cannonball and everyman for himself to the railroad bridge, holding up his arm for others to see, freshly bandaged by a nurse on the train, the blood of others and his own still about his shirt and pants. Quite a lad, that Jack Mulholland, aye, quite a lad!

Not four pints into it, though, comes Michael Shannon, blacksmith at the yards and neighbor on Lemmon Street. Taking Jack by his good arm and away from the others, he speaks close and direct. "Your Ma's worried sick, now, Jack, and taken a turn, too," says he. "You'd best be getting to her, lad, and quick about it, too. Mrs. Shannon's been with her all this day, and most of last night. Hurry now, lad, she may be slipping by. It's the worst I'm fearing and there mayn't not be much time…"

Jack Mulholland sprinted the one block north and one east on Lemmon Street, the beer cleared of his head from the shock of it all and him not feeling the summer's heat that had the street on their stoops working their hand fans for air. Up he comes to a small cluster at 934, talking quiet, their heads low. Mrs. Burke was the first to speak, her voice hushed but certain. "Jack, lad. Good on you, now. You're back." She directed him by his shoulder. "In you go. We've got poor Mary on a bed in the kitchen, nearer the water and the air. She's been going in and out most of the day, but your voice will be a tonic, I'm sure."

Jack Mulholland stepped to the door, hesitating, making way for two others coming out so he'd be alone. Careful, now, up the steps and through the front room. He could see her in the shadows of the kitchen beyond, her head back and her mouth open, cheeks sunken and her eyes closed and gone in. He took a deep breath, his heart pounding and his stomach gone weak. By the look of her he's wondering if she's not gone already. Going to her side, he went down on a knee, taking her hand to hold, putting his face to it. "Ma, ma...It's me, Jack...I'm home..."

There's a stirring, now, her hand moving in his, the other rising and finding his head, cupping it, closing on his hair.

He lowered his head to her side. "Ma, Ma, I'm back. I didn't know..."

Her eyes opened, fixing on him, a smile coming her face. "Aye, Jack lad, it's good to see ya, now, so good..."

"What can I do, Ma, what's to be done?"

"Naught's to be done, now, Jack, I'm fearing, naught to be done at all. I'm here in my bed with you at my side, and what would I be needing past that? Aye, Jack, my son come home, safe and so..." Her eyes froze with the words she'd just spoken, her head twisting quick to the wall, her hand broken away from Jack's, a cry of anguish from her mouth. "Ach! A priest!" says she, "Get me a priest! In the dear name of God get me a priest!"

"Ma, ma…"

She was crying now, away from him, near curled in a ball. "A priest, I tell you, I need a priest…"

Jack rose and was quick to the door, looking about among the women at the stoop, fixing on Mrs. Burke. "She wants a priest…"

"Aye, now, Jack, and he's coming, too, he is. Already sent for, now. Before you got here. It'll be soon, Jack and don't be worrying. You just get yourself back in there, now, by her side. You're all she's got and you got to be near."

He stepped back to the kitchen and kneeled by her bed, taking her hand in his, palming her forehead and smoothing her hair.

"Aye, father, 'tis you, now? Come you have, father, praise the Lord." She turned on her back, her eyes open but blank, unseeing. "Listen close, now, and listen clear…."

"Ma, it's me, Jack…"

"Damn you now. I don't need your name, it's your listening I'm needing, I need you to listen…"

"Ma…"

"It was in the Hunger, now, and the worst of it. Dead all about, and others dying still. And this man and I, well, he being the overseer and all, and taking a liking…well, father, you'll be taking my meaning, I'm sure. And I come down with his child, I do, and tell him about it and he comes up right, he does, and we get some food. Aye, food! We were starving, now, like the others, and all soon to die, and there was food now, and later he gets me passage on a ship, and there's money to come, too, says he…" She stopped, breathing short, eyes away, struggling to go on.

"And I have the baby, I do. A boy it was, so small and so sick. Hadn't the strength to suckle, he didn't. And doesn't he die, now, in two days more… And there I am with breasts a bursting and nothing to hold, and him, the overseer, coming by to be sure I'm off and gone, but not a child to show him...And sure doesn't Bridget Hennessey come by...All rags and bone, is what, her just-born sucking at her dry teat and her hardly breathing herself...Aye, Bridget Hennessey, turned out, she was, living in what sheds and cover she could find, her and her two little ones at her side, they hanging about her, the lot of 'em, turned out since her Jack had been shot for a rebel, her babe crying for milk...

"T'was God's wish, father, I knew it was, God's wish it was, sure and true..." She brought her hands to her chest, joined, her eyes opened, wide and afraid. "I took him father, I took that boy from her, and gave her my own child, poor dead thing that it was, so cold to the touch. And she knew, now, didn't she, father? She must've done, now, so cold it was? And we gave her food and some for her own, so they'd maybe be taking her in. No one, sure, was asking anything of those that had food to share...And the overseer, now, he come by and saw that boy and gave me my passage from that corner of hell, and I took it, father, I took it...And I raised that lad right, I did, so don't be asking me, now, father, if I'm sorry because I'd do it again..."

She turned away, back toward the wall, the sound of her sobbing so low you'd miss it if you weren't listening for it. Jack was about to speak when he come under the shadow of man, a hand now at his shoulder to hold him still. Fr. McColgan put his full finger to his lips, offering a nod of his head to reassure, then reached his hand across to Mary, stroking her head and cheeks, caressing her.

"There'll be no penance for you this day, Mary Mulholland," says the good father, "child of God that you are." He made the sign of the cross over her. "Of all your sins, Mary Mulholland, I absolve you, in the name of the Father, and of the Son and of the Holy Ghost." Bending near, he cupped the side of her head, whispering. "God bless and keep you, now, Mary Mulholland, your rest is near…"

CHAPTER FOUR
The Letter

J ack Mulholland lay on his bed as dawn finally broke, wondering if it wasn't all some long, crushing dream. Where to start? Who to ask? Who *am* I?

In her every breath Mary Mulholland had spoken of family and blood, those lost and those left behind. It was Sean Mulholland's family she'd spoken of–uncles and aunts by name and grandmothers and grandfathers, too. But they weren't *his* family – none of them. He was a *Hennessey*. His *real* mother's name was Bridget Hennessey and he, Jack *Mulholland,* was taken from her by Mary Mulholland to get passage to America, to save her own life. And his father, Sean Mulholland? Shot for a rebel in the hunger..? There never was any such man. Anytime. Anywhere.

'Raised that lad, right, I did…' That's what she'd said, and that's what she did. Her eyes watched him and kept him from harm, but now it seemed as might any herdsman. All the parts and pieces that never seemed to quite fit to Jack Mulholland were coming together, his life seen in a new light now, and darkly. There was a hardness to her, like them all that came out at that time, the Hunger, but different in Mary Mulholland still more. Did she love him? That's what he was thinking to himself and asking all that night and into the morning.

It was summer and hot and the waking and burying of Mary Mulholland was to get done quick. Mrs. Shannon had taken charge, alerting Michael Mulcahy that Mary would soon be passing and telling him as soon as she did. Ice was the first necessity with Michael Mulcahy's son, Dennis, by the place at sun up, and Mrs. Mulcahy with him in the wagon. They were to measure for the coffin and figure the ice and boards and buckets needed to lay poor Mary out all right and proper. Making his calculations, Dennis was off to Baltimore Ice and Feed for the ice and to go by their shop for the boards and buckets. Mrs. Mulcahy stayed by, putting Mary in her best, and tending to the other needs of the newly dead.

The wake was set for six, with the rosary to be said at seven by Fr. McColgan and some kind words from him, too. Mrs. Shannon oversaw the getting ready of it all, the food and the drink and the fixing of the rooms. First was moving the furniture out of the house, across to the Murphy's to make room for all those to come. The doors would be open, front and back for the air, and tables set outside for the food, praying the whole time there's no rain to come. The bar was to be set out back in the garden with an alley beyond for an overflow.

Jack spent the morning looking to help where he could. There's a way to such things, though, and the women knew it well, moving among themselves and knowing who's to cook the corned beef and who's to bake the soda bread. Seeing him standing about with nothing to do, Mrs. Mulcahy took him aside and gave him her husband's card. "Here, now, Jack, off you go to the shop for your fitting. A good stretch of the legs will do you fine, now, it will."

It was a fifteen minute walk to the shop by Charles Street. Mr. Mulcahy, all five foot four of him, was out and brought Jack Mulholland into the fitting room with pats on the back to comfort and direct him. Standing him straight, "...chin up, now, lad..." and turning him face on, he ran his hands from Jack's shoulders down along his arms to his waist and out with his tape to measure the legs. Going to the back room, he was out as quick with the goods. "A mourning suit, with a top hat to match," says Mr. Mulcahy. "All part of the service." says he.

Jack put the suit on and turned to the mirror.

"Aye, it's grand you're looking, now, lad. She'd be so proud, your Mary would. Stand up, now, to make the fit. Ah, there's a lad! Tall and straight, just like Mary showed ya."

The midday heat was on him as he walked back to Lemmon Street, the sun high with little shade in the near empty streets, his thoughts of the night before. Would it have been better to be her bastard? At least he'd be of her blood, of someone's blood. There'd be some meaning to him of the stories she'd told, of brothers and sisters and cousins, the father she'd spoken of, something to be part of. But no, there was nothing. He was alone. An orphan, and without an orphanage. And Bridget Hennessey? What became of her? Might she somehow have survived? Lived? And his sisters? Or did she say what they were? His mind ran back, searching for her words, 'little ones' is what she'd said. Brothers? Sisters? Did they live? Who's to know? Then her eyes came to him, Mary Mulholland's eyes, blank as she passed, her breathing stopped, her face fixed and turned hard in the shadows and dark of the kitchen…

It was early afternoon by the time Jack got back to the house. Now empty of furniture and people, all was in readiness for the wake, quiet and still in the summer heat. With hardly any sleep in the last three days, he made his way to the second floor. Coming to the top of the stairs, he paused at Mary's room, now leaning against the door frame. Looking in, he studied the bits of paper at the mirror over her bureau. On it were lithographs of this and that, some framed and standing with others set against the wall. The lace at the windows broke the full heat of the midday sun. Mary Mulholland of Ireland, yes. But of where in Ireland? Of who in Ireland?

Since she'd bought the place from the O'Connell's, he and Mary each had their own room, and he was never to go into hers, ever. And he never did, until now.

Stepping in, his eye caught sight of a small desk and chair to his right, behind the open door, its seat of woven straw and slats up its back. His mind flashed to the table in the kitchen where she kept her books and accounts for business and property. This is something else. He pulled the chair back and sat down. There were no papers on the desk, not even a pen. Its surface, though, hinged up and he raised it, squinting into the shadows for what it held. There was a pen and an ink jar, a box of stationery and in the far right hand corner a single letter, folded to post. Touching it, he knew it be old. Sliding his fingers under it, he eased it up and out.

Going to the window, he carefully held the letter at a corner, letting its folds fall open as he held it to the light. The script was tight and clear, almost as if printed in a shop, the date of it being July 18, 1850, and a note beside the date in another hand – 'Read to Mary Mulholland, this day, September 3, 1850. Raymond O'Keefe, Baltimore County.'

Dearest Mary –

It was glad we were to hear from you, near two years passed since you're gone. And well it seems that you are. There's no telling of what's done here, girl. Aye, we'd all be gone as well but for the food you left us. Olmstead may have been of them, but he was as good as his word, for as long as he stayed. that is.

Aye, it broke your poor Da's heart, fine man that he was, to see you go. But he was happy for your prospects, and your name was on his lips when he passed. His heart was broken, it was. Like so many about, he just stopped fighting it all and slipped away.

And your brother Michael, as well. He was never strong, you know, and the consumption came on him and he was gone not three months later. It was in my arms that he died, a smile on his face, the miracle of a happy passing! 'I'm going to a better place, ma' said he, and

God's grace that he did. Forgive me, girl, but he was my last, and my favorite. His eyes would light my heart so, don't you know, and there was never a day he didn't see something good in it. I miss him so.

Brian, now, he's the lucky one! Always was, now, wasn't he? By the market, he was, and three blackguards fell upon a gentleman and doesn't Brian drive them off with a stick come to hand, and just for the sport of it! "Didn't like three beating on one" says he, helping the poor man to his feet and before you know it he's off to London in his lordship's service and, by his last post, soon to make for Australia! A lucky lad, that's my Brian, and none better!

The place is gone, now, you know, and that's for sure. They're tying them all together, they are, our bit of ground and those about. Grazing cattle for London is what, the blackguards. Think of it, now, Mary. T'is starving we are here in Ireland, and they're packing cattle off to London! And fat, they are, too, on our good green grass. There'll be a reckoning, I'll tell you that, Mary Mulholland, there'll be a reckoning! Here, or in the hereafter! But mark my words, it's to come! If there's a God in heaven, and I know there to be One, these sins will not go unpunished!

And don't be worrying about Rose and me, now, neither, Mary. We've found shelter and work at a manor house outside Galway. Rose is slow, you'll remember, and always will be, but she has a pleasant manner and a good soul, and sure she's stronger than most men hereabouts, them that remain! She does what she's told, and does it well, she does. And she gives them no trouble, neither, that being her special gift.

The missus of the manor, now, has a good eye for my stitching and fine needle, and has taken to my company, as well, I'm thinking. Lonely she is here, and why not? Aye, in such times as these and away from her own. So,

I'm happy to give her a smile when it might do her some good. A small price to pay, it is, for a dry place to sleep and food enough for both Rose and me self!

I hope this letter has found you well and happy in America, Mary. You're in my prayers always, each morning, noon and night, my flame-haired beauty!

All a mother's love,
Mary Catherine Mulholland

P.S. And you were asking after Bridget Hennessey , now, poor girl. She and her little ones were found huddled at the base of a tree, not a full mile from where we last saw them, all passed to God's mercy. There'll be a reckoning!

Writ this day by Daniel Morrison, County Galway, Athenry Parrish
July 18, 1850

CHAPTER FIVE
The Leaving

S t. Peter the Apostle was the parish, Fr. Liam McColgan now raised to pastor with Fr. Madigan having moved on to Annapolis in the spring. Like most about, Fr. McColgan had fled the Hunger, the Irish now counting more of the city than any other group, more than enough for the town fathers, even the Catholics among them. He'd taken his Orders in Galway just as the famine struck and like a good many priests, them that lived that is, he'd come to America. In the west, anyway, with the burying all done and the churches all closed, there was none to lead in their faith, so off they were to where their flocks had fled.

And for all the horror of it all, he'd found a fullness to life in Baltimore of which he'd had no anticipation on his leaving for it. It wasn't being out from under the Queen's law and her ministers, though glad he was to be free of them. No. It was a sense of self he'd come to here and saw in others about, that's what it was. He, Liam McColgan, priest or stone mason or whatever the calling, had come to be of account. A free man is what he'd become, and a free man he was.

He'd felt it first on a warm spring day, an April afternoon of some years back. It was a fullness to lungs and heart that broke him free of the shadow of repression that had so marked a nation for more generations than anyone knew to count. There'd come a shame to it all, you see, even to guilt, for not being free, as they knew they should be. It was the guilt of living in repression and not pressing harm or death to be free of it. And for all the slights and slurs from those born here, Liam McColgan was freer than they because he and his like had known the lack of it, freedom that is. It was by this that he knew himself to be an American, maybe even more than they.

And St. Peter the Apostle, with its grand pillars and fine murals, what more could a priest from County Sligo be asking? And for them still coming, St. Peter's was a welcoming parish. Fr. McColgan spoke the Irish and settled them in and with those of their home county where he could. Next was finding work for them with the railroad or in the crafts and trades, maybe on the docks or even the steamers that plied the Chesapeake, Baltimore being its capitol of sorts, certainly of its commerce. Aye, Fr. Liam McColgan had come to a place in life where his contentment and happiness was of such a measure that it started him to wondering might there not be some sin in it? And it was for just such times as these that he'd found some use in the passings of those he ministered. The hands of sickness and death are never stilled, and always a sadness, calling and touching us all, rich and poor alike, and longest on those left behind.

Mary Mulholland's wake and funeral had done as well as such things can do. There was a proper number about with heartfelt words of her glad company, and her good works, too. She'd led a good life, Mary had, and with some measure of success, owning her own place and three others nearby to let. But in his years as priest, Liam McColgan had never shared a final confession with another, let alone with the dying's only son, this being on his mind since mass this morning.

Jack Mulholland had been proper at the wake and the funeral, but away from it all, as well, not talking with the others as he might, and not a word to Fr. McColgan but a passing 'Thank you,' for the kind words at graveside. Here's a lad who needs watching, Liam McColgan is thinking this Monday evening, the summer's heat heavy in the rectory. And as by cue from the angels above, there's a knock at the door and who should it be but Jack Mulholland himself, kit bag in hand.

"Jack, lad!" Fr. McColgan at the door, his arms open wide. "Now wasn't I just thinking of you? Come in, now, lad, come in, come in." He took Jack's hand for a good hard shake, and such a big hand, it was, too, he's thinking, all bone and knuckle.

"Thank you," says Jack, his head bowing a bit, stepping in, careful to wipe his feet.

"I'll be taking that, son." Fr. McColgan reached down and took Jack's bag, resting it on a chair nearby, his arm over the lad's shoulder, guiding him into the sitting room all done with pictures of praying saints and statues, large and small, each and all under the fixed gaze of a dark crucifix put high on the far wall.

"Sit down, now, Jack, and make yourself at home. Would you be needing some water, now?" He turned and raised his voice. "Mrs. Fitzgerald…"

Jack waved his hand and shook his head 'no', Fr. McColgan leaving it be with Mrs. Fitzgerald, good woman that she is, not hearing him, or maybe just not choosing to.

"So, Jack, welcome." Fr. McColgan took a chair opposite, settling in the tight fit of it as he spoke across a low table. "Now, how can I help you, son?"

Jack was mum, his eyes down at his hands folded on his lap.

"Come, now, lad, it's been a hard time, and so quick, too, and then there was her last night…" He let his words hang to see if the lad wanted to speak of his mother's confession, but no, nothing, only a lad mum in his sitting room, not knowing what to say, maybe not even why he'd come.

"And your arm, Jack? Shot through and lived to tell of it! God's mercy you weren't killed." This brought the lad's head up at him, and just as quick away. "Is that it, then, son, the killing you saw, is that why you've come?"

Jack turned back to him, now, his head left to right, ever so slow, then a swallow before speaking. "No, father, that's not why I've come. It's who I am, that's why I've come."

"Aye, lad, yes." A clearing of his throat. "Well, we're all God's children to start, you and me, all the same, and all the rest as well. It's with each of us He is, through thick and thin…"

"No, father, no. I mean, Who am *I*? Who am I *now*?"

Fr. McColgan sat back. "The same as you were before, lad, and will be tomorrow. And who else, now..?"

"Who else? *Who at all*? You were there. And you knew her, too. '*You are your blood, Jack lad*,' that's what ma *always* said. 'It's your *blood* is who you are,' that's what she taught me. 'We're all Irish, true enough,' she'd say, 'but through a family's blood' and the blood I had was Mulholland. I was Mary Mulholland's son, that's where I started! But I'm *not*, don't you see, father? She took me from another, from *my* blood. Hennessey blood is what I have. That's what I *am*, but there's no Hennesseys that I know, that I'm any blood to…It was all lies! Don't you see, father? Everything she told me about me was a lie! Sean Mulholland wasn't shot for a rebel. And he wasn't my father. *He never even existed!* He was a lie like all the rest of it! All *lies*!" Jack's hands went to his head, his palms hard against his forehead. He started to cry but fought it off, sat up looking away, wiping his hands on his sleeves and pants.

Fr. McColgan waited for it to settle, it now being said. "They were hard times, now, son. God willing you'll never know the like of them. I lost all my own, you know, the lot of them. One is all that's left, and that's me."

Jack's eyes looked over, fixed on the priest. "But you know who you *are*. Don't you see? Can't you understand?

30

It starts with family, that's what *she* told me, it all starts with family, with blood, that's who we *are*. But I'm not her blood, so who *am* I?"

"She saved your life, son, she..."

"Yes, to save her own! She stole me to save *her* life! She swapped the dead body of an overseer's bastard–her bastard!–for food and a ticket out, that's what she did!"

Fr. McColgan stared across, his own mind and memories back to it all, burying his own, kept fed by the bishop to minister the dying as they died. 'And who's to bury them, then, father, if you're to die among them? There's not enough food, just not enough...And what's to be said of us in heaven if we're to let them die without the sacraments? So here, my son, here's a week's food. It's for you – to do God's work." His mother and father, two brothers and a sister, he buried these, with three others, all lads, wandering off to die in places unknown, prayers said by him to the wind and the mist that shrouded the land in its misery.

"Jack, lad..."

"No. There's nothing to say, there's just nothing." He stood up and started for the door. Fr. McColgan was up as quick, wanting to keep the lad at hand. Jack went to his kit bag and took out an envelope, they both now in the hall.

"This is for you, father. Mr. Larkin came by yesterday and read the will and it's all here, the four houses, her accounts, it's all here." He held the envelope out. "Fr. Madigan had been the 'executor' or something like that, but he's gone now, so Mr. Larkin thought you'd agree to be it. So that's how he wrote it up. All you have to do is sign it and bring it over to him, the note says where, and it's done."

"I don't understand, Jack..."

"She left it all to her *son*, don't you see? To *Jack Mulholland*. Well, the only son I know she ever had is *dead*, died in Ireland sixteen years ago, two days old and gone. *Dead*! She gave his corpse to Bridget Hennessey in exchange for me. I'm not Mary Mulholland's son, I'm Bridget Hennessey 's son."

"But Jack…"

"Here, take it. He's put it all in a 'trust' or something." Fr. McColgan took the envelope. "I don't understand any of it. It's all a bunch of words to me. 'Talk to Mr. Larkin,' that's what he told me to tell you. He can explain it all." Jack took his bag and turned to the door as Fr. McColgan reached for his shoulder to hold him.

"Jack, let me help you, now, son. You've got to give it some time, lad, to give yourself some time, time to understand…"

"No, father. I already know what I've got to do and that's to leave, to go."

"But to where?"

"I don't know yet."

"How, then?"

His face went blank, his head moving left to right, his eyes away.

"Then *why*, Jack? Tell me why, why do you *have* to go?"

This brought Jack's eyes up at him, alive, fixed and sure for the first time since he'd come. "Because, father, I'd rather be no one than someone I'm not…"

Jack Mulholland pulled the door open and offered his hand. "Good night, father. Do what you want with it all. It's nothing to me – none of it."

A quick shake of the hand and he was gone.

WASHINGTON, D.C.
1936

CHAPTER SIX
The Squires

J ack Hennessey stood in the morning sun at the middle of three windows in the office of Fr. William Murphy, president of Gonzaga College High School, his eyes fixed on the Capitol Dome. Oak molding, stained dark, lined the floor and ceiling of the office, marking the doorways and windows, as well. The desk was to his right, beneath a large portrait of St. Ignatius Loyola, founder of the Society of Jesus. Before the desk were two arm chairs, both oak, also stained dark, no cushions. A forest green leather couch was at the wall opposite the desk, a matching arm chair and a mahogany coffee table in front of it. On the table rested the room's only sculpture – a bronze eagle, the school's mascot, its wings spread and talons down in attack.

The windows extended from just below Jack Hennessey's knees to well above his head. Like the man, they were of an earlier time, designed to capture as much light and heat as the sun might offer on any given day. Jack Hennessey's eyes tracked down from the Capitol dome, just off to his left and a brilliant white in the early sun, to the trees ringing Union Station Plaza, and from there to the Post Office at Massachusetts Avenue and North Capital Street. Moving closer to the window glass, his cheek almost touching it, he looked for Kaneally's Drug Store at the corner of I and North Capital, but it was at too close an angle to be seen.

His gaze shifted back to the right, falling on the row of town houses facing on I Street. A slight shrug came to his shoulders and a grin to his face. He knew several of them to be bawdyhouses, and had been for years. Just across the street from a Catholic boys school and not a full mile from the Capitol Rotunda itself. Washington at a

35

glance, he thought, saints and sinners and everyone in between. In more prosperous times the houses might have raised a scandal, and had in the past. Not now, though. The country was in a depression that refused to end and there was more to worry about than a few ladies doing what they could to get on.

And especially in Swampoodle, or what was left of it, anyway. Swampoodle extended up North Capitol on both sides of the street, the lion's share of it to the east and falling in the Northeast quadrant of the city. A swamp with puddles when the city was founded, it didn't take much imagination to come up with the name. And what better place for the Irish to squat, especially those over from the famine? At its best, on a bright spring day such as this, it had been a shanty town. Come summer, though, after a heavy rain, it was more an open sewer than anything else. Tiber Creek had been its natural drainage, but the Washington City Canal had been built in its course and its locks would dam the run off and waste that in an earlier day would have found its way to the Potomac.

This morning was Jack Hennessey's annual call on Bill Murphy to discuss candidates to be his 'squire' for a year. When he had first approached Fr. Murphy about the idea, he had had in mind an apprenticeship of sorts. It was Bill Murphy who had suggested 'squire', explaining that the word comes from *scutarius*, Latin for 'shield bearer.' 'You see, Jack, in medieval times, a young noble or other worthy would attach himself to a knight, binding himself for three or so years. It was more than carrying another man's shield, though, or learning how to mount a war horse, or swing a broad sword, or other marshal skill. No. It was the age of chivalry, the lone knight on a sacred quest, righting the wrongs of the world, duty and honor above all. And the squire's ultimate quest was just that, to become a man of honor, a soldier of Christ. It's what we Jesuits today might call a man for others.'

And so each June, for the last seventeen years, Jack Hennessey, President and owner of the Hennessey Construction Company, would take the smartest, hardest working Gonzaga graduate not going on to college to be his *squire* for a year. It meant living in his house and being on call 24 hours a day – driving him wherever he needed to go and whenever he needed to get there. It meant fetching his laundry, delivering packages, picking up contracts and briefs from the lawyers, dropping off drawings at construction sites, backing up his office staff on his calendar, all the things he used to do for himself when there was less to do and he was young enough to get them all done easily.

While a squire, there were to be no girl friends and there was only one day off a month, with the occasional night out, but in and done by midnight. Alcohol was forbidden, no exceptions. For Thanksgiving, Christmas and Easter, there was a 36-hour furlough. And during slack times–waiting for Jack Hennessey at lunch or a meeting, or the occasional slow night or day–there was *The List*. Fr. Murphy had drawn up the first, but he and Jack Hennessey had made changes over the years. The squire could pick any book off the list, but the list was all the book reading he was allowed, and he had to read at least ten of them in the year. Newspapers were different. The squire could have the run of these, but *The Evening Star* was required, front to back every day, especially notices of public tax sales, bankruptcies and governmental appointments. On these latter, the squire was to report the previous day's listings each morning on the drive to the office. It was a 14-month commitment, one month to overlap the squire leaving, twelve months on the job, and one to train the squire coming in.

Fr. Murphy would pick two candidates each May. Jack Hennessey would meet with each and make his choice. Nothing but good for the one chosen, and one hundred dollars for the one not. By the July of the following year, a squire would have learned how Jack Hennessey thought, how he did business, how he made decisions, how he sized others up, what he looked for and expected. And of what Jack Hennessey looked for in people, the squire was to learn, patience was first. To Jack Hennessey , nothing was more important. For him, it meant having the strength to give things time to go your way. He looked for it in others and marked well those who had it, and even more those who did not.

Over the course of a year, each squire would have met or learned something about every player in the Washington construction community, most of the bankers, and heard all the lies about all the lawyers in between. Each graduate of the program had found some measure of success, some going on to college, the rest getting on by their wits. And nothing gave Jack Hennessey greater pleasure than to find himself doing business with one later on. One thing sure, no one in the program had ever regretted having gone through it. And they all met once each year, in June, at a private dinner in a downtown restaurant where the new inductee was to be introduced.

"Good morning, Mr. Hennessey ." Fr. Murphy strode in the room, offering his hand. "All is well, I trust?"

Jack Hennessey turned, a smile coming to his face. "As well as can be expected, father, in a six year depression and an 88 year old body."

"I should live so long." He smiled, motioning Jack Hennessey to the couch. "Here, Jack, have a seat. Rest your bones." Stepping to the desk, Fr. Murphy picked up a file and took the arm chair. "Did Mrs. Rourke offer you coffee? It's fresh…"

"She did, and, thank you, no."

"Very well." Fr. Murphy opened the file on the surface of the coffee table, laying two academic transcripts before him, each clipped to several pages beneath. He was about to begin when Jack Hennessey sat forward.

"Tell me, Bill, how much is tuition at Georgetown these days?"

Fr. Murphy sat back, his eyes fixed on Jack Hennessey . "About four hundred dollars. With books and fees, it comes $500 or so."

"Five hundred dollars...as much as that..."

"All of that really, but I'm sure we could get you some help if you're thinking of applying..."

Jack Hennessey smiled and nodded, his eyes turning to the two transcripts on the table as he put on his reading glasses. He picked up the nearest. Martin Jude Barry of St. Dominic's parish in Southwest. A familiar name. The address? 422 Third Street. Yes, he knew the family. Lifting the transcript, he scanned the record for grades, then detentions. Can't have too many, now, but a few showed spirit. Then a history paper, which he read quickly. Activities were next. Football. Jack Hennessey liked football players, especially linemen. He had a Packard and it took some muscle to turn it tight.

"You'd like Martin, Jack. A good kid and a hard worker. He has some size to him, too, but doesn't throw it around. And he's smart. Works at his father's warehouse most days after school and weekends. He'd have had better grades if it wasn't for that."

Jack Hennessey nodded as he put Martin Barry's papers down and picked up those of Timothy Alston Reagan. The grades were better, and it was a better term paper, shorter but more in it. Packed tight, nicely done. Track and basketball. He looked at Fr. Murphy. "Any size to him?"

"Not much by weight, but he's nearly six feet tall. And tough, Jack. Hard bones. Wiry. Just plain *tough*. No one messes with Tim Reagan."

"How do you rate them, Bill?"

Fr. Murphy sat back. "Rating this pair's difficult. Some years we've really only had one." He looked at Jack Hennessey , nodding. "And I'm happy to say you've picked him every time. But this year? These two? They're both really good. I have them equal. Don't see how you could make a mistake. It's going to come down to how they strike you the day you meet them."

Jack Hennessey nodded, placing Regan's papers on top of Barry's and putting them both in the file, closing it over. He sat back, looking at the file and then at Fr. Murphy. "I'm not sure whether I ever asked you this before, Bill, but do they know they're being considered?"

Fr. Murphy sat back, as well. "No. Don't see how they could, really. I never talk to them about it. Some figure out who you're *likely* to meet with. It's more than 15 years now and each year one bright, hard working kid gets to be your squire for a year. By March or April, when everyone's sorted out whether they're going to be able to go to college, there'll be three or four looking to be asked to have lunch with you. That's about it, really."

Looking away, Jack Hennessey fixed briefly on the portrait of Ignatius and then out the window. "Can we wait on this one for a couple of weeks, Bill?" He found himself avoiding the priest's eyes.

"Any which way you want to play it, Jack. It's your program. Graduation's not…"

"It's *our* program, Bill." Jack Hennessey fixed on Bill Murphy, holding his eyes, reaching over to grip his forearm softly. *"Ours,* Bill, yours and mine, and I appreciate your understanding." He rose, fixing on Bill Murphy's eyes again, now shaking his hand, finding himself gripping it more firmly than usual. "I'll be in touch." He nodded at the file on the table. "I like them both, Bill." He fixed on the file tag – *Hennessey Squires.* "I've liked them all, really." Some faces and names came to mind. "Loved them in a way, I guess…"

He forced a smile and made his way out.

CHAPTER SEVEN
Mt. Olivet

D own the front steps of the school, Jack Hennessey made his way to the car, his knees feeling strong in the warm weather. Michael Byrnes, this year's squire, had been waiting and pulled the Packard up to the curb. The rule was that Jack Hennessey sat in the front seat and let himself in and out of the car. If there was anyone with him, then he and his guest would sit in the back and the squire would open the door for them when it seemed to make sense. Getting this sort of thing right was part of the program.

"Where to, Mr. Hennessey ?"

Jack Hennessey heard the question, nodding, not certain what he wanted to do. "What's on the pad, Michael?"

"Three stops, then lunch at O'Donnell's with Mr. Riordan. You've got your lawyer at 10:00, the property at 7th and U…"

"The tax sale piece?"

"The same. Just a 'drive-by,' you said. Then you've got Mr. Riley at the Ag site on Independence. You said you wanted to be there by 11:15."

Jack Hennessey took a deep breath. It was early May and warming. The car windows were rolled down. He felt the air on his hands and face, filling his lungs. His eyes closed, he held the air for a moment, letting it out slowly, almost tasting it. Gleason, the lawyer, could wait. So could the drive-by. He looked at Michael Byrnes. Though average in just about every physical way and measure, there was a force building in this young man that Jack Hennessey had sensed when they first met and had watched grow and form in the year since. He'd been one of the best. More than anything, he listened, and not like

41

he was a walking stenographer's pad. No. He listened for what people meant, not just what they said. "Where's the nearest phone, Michael?"

"North Capitol and H."

"Okay." He reached for his change purse as Michael Byrnes started west on I Street to take two lefts to get them to North Capitol and H. "Here's a nickel. Tell Mr. Gleason we'll be delayed. See if he has a time this afternoon."

"You're free between three and four."

"Okay, see if that works."

Jack Hennessey waited in the car while Michael Byrnes made the call, looking east on H Street, thinking of a girl he once knew. Was it 204 H? Michael Byrnes broke his gaze, returning with a confidence in his step and determination in his eyes, opening the door and getting in behind the wheel. "Three's fine. Mr. Hennessey . Where to now?"

"The Mount."

The Mount was Mt. Olivet, a cemetery in Northeast, a few blocks up North Capitol to a right on New York Avenue and east for about two miles. And it was *Irish*. If there was an Irish name not on a tombstone in it, Jack Hennessey couldn't imagine what it was. Michael Byrnes signaled left at North Capitol and headed north, through the heart of Swampoodle. They passed Kaneally's drug store on the right, "To Let" signs hanging in most of the other store fronts, each and all dingy and faded, and too long there to be seen or noticed.

K Street was next, and Jack Hennessey twisted in his seat to get a clear look down its length. This was his first home in Washington. He'd come down from Baltimore on the B&O and found work in *Brady's Pub*. He started as a barback and took his pay in meals and a cot to sleep on in the store room. What money he had was found sweeping the floor and what he could make in odd jobs around the neighborhood.

Turning front and settling back, he looked at his hands, scenes from his years at Brady's rising and falling in his mind. His knuckles seemed even larger now with the backs of his hands all wrapped and lined in blue gray veins, marked with age spots and the nicks and scars of a life at work. At Brady's Pub he'd learned how to lift heavy things, oak barrels and tables, cases of liquor and whatever else needed moving. And then there were the fights.

Every man working at Brady's was on bouncer detail, and a fight could break out at any time, for any reason, or no reason at all. But whatever the reason, the rule was to get whoever started it down, and down fast. That's how you stopped a fight. And there was no room for standing off, throwing round house rights and pounding on a man. Not at all. Men being crammed in and pushing on one another was usually the reason a fight started in the first place. Everything was close quarters, especially on a Saturday night, so you had to get in tight with short, quick ones to the nose or chin, or whatever else you could get to. And in this, Jack Hennessey soon came to a place, of sorts. He'd developed a crushing right hand, a trip-hammer Skeets Skillen had called it, and the instinct to use it.

Prize fighting was illegal then and, like other things illegal, common to Swampoodle. Tom Brady owned the warehouse behind his bar and, when there was room, he would promote prize fights. There wasn't even a roped square, just a circle painted in white on the floor twenty feet across that the customers had to stand behind, and the fighters had to stay inside of. Tom Brady was the referee, and that's all there was to it. Brady, over from Killarney for twenty years, pushed Jack Hennessey into a few preliminary bouts. He won all of them. The idea wasn't to make him a prize fighter, though. At seventeen, Jack Hennessey hadn't built full out yet. The idea was to toughen him up for the bar work, and to mark him as someone on Tom Brady's crew who could take care of himself–and anyone of a mind to step out of line.

The original Brady's Pub was gone now, and the warehouse, too. Tom Brady was a man who knew his luck. He'd bought up the lots around the bar, and the warehouse, too, and in time put them together and razed near a quarter of the block. In their place he put up an apartment house and an office building, the latter having a bar and restaurant on the first floor, *Brady's Irish Rose*. The bar was the same as the original, even as to where is set on the street. It was Jack Hennessey's luck, too. The original contractor went under in 1893 and Tom Brady brought him in to finish the office building. It was Hennessey Construction's first genuine commercial building and he got it done right, and it had made all the difference.

The traffic on New York Avenue was light and soon Mt. Olivet rose to Jack Hennessey 's right. It was one of the highest points of land in the city and he tracked it as Michael Byrnes turned right on Montana Avenue and right again onto Bladensburg Road to the main entrance. Stone pillars and a gate house to match marked a small half circle, all linked by heavy, wrought iron gates and fencing, just painted and glossy black, shining in the morning sun. Michael Byrnes knew the routine. Go through the gates and up several hundred yards to a path on the right. Jack Hennessey would let himself out, motion silently to him to wait, then start alone up the lane that curved along the south face of *Mt. Olivet*.

It seemed a steeper climb this morning as Jack Hennessey made his way up the asphalt path and among the stones of those gone. Excepting June 3, there was not a set day to visit. He came when he needed or wanted to, and he wondered which of the two had brought him here today, need or desire, the pain in his abdomen rising as the hill steepened. Looking up, he could see the stone and this lightened his step and quieted the pain. "Yes, yes," he heard himself say and a freshness came to him as his eyes looked left, south toward the Capitol and the Potomac. The river sparkled amid the broad reaches of green and patches of buildings and homes, his focus turning back up to the shade tree and the bench he had had placed there. It was stone and simple, but it allowed him to visit longer, something he found himself doing as the years had passed.

Broad and polished on its every side, the stone itself now stood before him, not yet in the shade of the tree behind him. *Here lie Christine McCarthy Hennessey and her son, Gone to God, July 19, 1892.* He removed his hat and blessed himself, and, for the first time in some years, felt a great sadness come over him. He stepped backward to the bench and sat, grateful for the shade of the tree. Resting his hat beside him, he bent forward with this elbows on his knees and thought of her, her smile and her spirit, the raven black hair off her forehead and about her shoulders and the brightness of her eyes. She was twenty-eight when they met and, in four short years she was gone.

But Jack Hennessey had not come here to cry this day, and would not allow himself to now. Sitting up, he looked left and right about her stone and the perimeter of the plot he'd bought just before they married.

"A plot, is it, now? A burial plot?" She had laughed out loud, startled by the very thought of it. "Just before we marry? There's a queer thought, Jack Hennessey , if ever I heard one. Is it to be my wedding present, then?" She laughed again and he laughed back, explaining to her that just like they needed a place to live when they were alive, there had to be a place where they could rest when

*they've passed on. "A person should be buried right," he
had said, "not left in a field...or by a tree..."*

*"Well, Jack Hennessey , now at last I know the secret
of your success–planning ahead! That'll do it every
time!" She laughed even harder now, her head back, her
pearl white skin gone flush in the excitement, then her
eyes, quick and back at him, expectant and eager. "Can I
go with you, then?"*

"Where? To buy the plot?"

*"Of course to buy the plot. What've we been talking
about, now? And can I go? If it's to be where I'm to end
up, I think I should have a say in it, don't you, now?"*

And now the tears did come to Jack Hennessey .
They were not of sadness, though, but of the purest joy.
The memory of her walking about Mt. Olivet, looking at
this plot and that, taking the views, smelling the air. And
then coming to this tree, barely a sapling at the time,
standing beside it, looking left and right and then down
the hill to the river. "By the time I'm gone, Jack
Hennessey , this will be a mighty oak and our shade,
don't you see? Yours and mine, up here, looking down
across this land to the river. Aye! This is the place, now!
This is the one! How big is it?"

He'd checked the plat. "Twelve. It's as big a plot as
they have."

"And it's a big family we'll be having, now, too, Jack
Hennessey . Let's make it an even dozen, then. I'll fill it
for you, Jack Hennessey, I will. God's word, I will!"

He could remember holding her now, so many years
ago, his arms around her and her holding him tight, her
breasts at his chest and her breath at his ear, the warmth
of her. "Christine, Christine, how I've missed you...how I
miss you even now." He cried into his hands and, as his
breathing eased, he felt her close by, sensed her being,
there coming now a fullness to him, a completeness that
brought him to his feet, and to her stone in the full sun.

"Christine McCarthy Hennessey ..." As he said her name, the sound of her laughter came to him again, deep and full. "Aye...yes." The tears were gone now and he felt a smile come to his face. He looked up and over the stone and down the green of the fields to the river and then the sky above and all before and about him, closing his eyes and shaking his head in an easy grace. "My God, what a woman you were. What a *woman*..."

He stroked the stone, smooth and warm, and as he started down the hill, there came from deep within him a voice, certainly words, soft and caring... *Your hat, now, Jack...*

CHAPTER EIGHT
Paddy Riley

"**W**hat have I told you about Tim Riordan, Michael?" Jack Hennessey sat back in the front passenger seat, his eyes ahead as the Packard made its way south from Mt. Olivet on Bladensberg Road. They were circling back toward the city and the 11:15 meeting with Paddy Riley at the Department of Agriculture construction site.

"I'm not sure you've told me anything." Michael Byrnes slowed the car to a stop light. He had reddish hair combed back off his forehead above green eyes that looked right at you, listening.

Jack Hennessey thought about his answer. "That's surprising...but maybe not, really." He looked forward as the car passed into the intersection. "Anyway, I've known him for years. First met him when he was in building supplies – lumber, plumbing, whatever. Somewhere along the line he linked up with the building trades." Jack Hennessey turned to Michael Byrnes. "He's a 'tweener', you see, Michael. Keeps his head down most of the time. Looks for ways to be of use. Sets things up, makes introductions, helps people move into and out of places they're new to, or not sure they want to be seen in."

Jack Hennessey looked away, tried to remember a joke Tim Riordan had told the last time they were together. "He came down here on the 'Orphan Train', long time ago. Can't remember the year." He turned to Michael Byrnes. "Ever hear of the 'Orphan Train', Michael?"

"No, sir." Eyes ahead, he guided the Packard around a line of produce trucks on the right curb.

"Well, they came out of New York City, between the Civil War and the turn of the century, mostly. There were

49

more orphans up there than anyone knew what to do with. Hell's Kitchen and Irishtown and places like that, just all over the city. Broken families, fathers getting killed in a tunnel or on some other job, or just taking off, with mothers not knowing what to do, some just giving up. The kids would end up with the New York Foundling Hospital or something like it and they started shipping them out of town, out west mostly." The traffic opened up and the Packard picked up speed with Jack Hennessey watching left and right.

"The Church was big in it. They set up a system where parishes would find families on a farm or some other outfit to take the children. Some were looking to adopt and others just to help out if they could. Others, I'm sure, had in mind an extra hand to work their place. Anyway, these kids'd be assigned to a family before they got on the train in New York. The priest or someone from the parish would meet them at the station and introduce them to their new family, try to get them off on the right foot and all. After that, they'd just go off to their new home. Most were Irish and, from what I read, most got on well–worked their way into the family or community and lived good lives." Jack Hennessey shifted in his seat, resting his arm in the open window.

"Some of them, though, well they were just loaded on to a train and sent out with an escort from the agency to keep them fed and make sure they didn't get in any trouble. Priests and others along the line would have been alerted that a group of orphans would be coming through with a date and time and the number of the train. Then they'd do what they could about getting out folks looking for children, getting them on down to meet the train. When the train pulled in, the kids were lined up on the platform, shoulder to shoulder. Any one showing up, got their pick." He turned to Michael Byrnes.

"And they had to be quick, too, Michael. The train, you see, would only be there for a few minutes, just to discharge and pick passengers, drop off the mail, that sort of thing. So they'd line up on the platform in Princeton or Philadelphia or wherever and the picking and sorting got started. They'd be looking at the kids' teeth, feeling their arms and shoulders for heft, asking them to walk or run a bit. Could they read? What happened to their parents? Are you Catholic? Do you say the rosary every day? That sort to thing. Those picked were signed for with whoever was escorting them. Those not picked got back on the train and hoped for better luck at the next stop."

They'd turned southwest on Maryland Avenue with the Capitol now dead ahead.

"Well, when he was a little kid, three or four or something, Tim Riordan got his leg broken in some family scuffle. They took him to a clinic and the nurse there set it crooked and it stayed that way. It was a sight to look at, I'll tell you that. Saw it once fishing with him. Anyway, it gave him a limp. Not exactly the sort of thing people were looking to take home with them, especially if they had a choice. Now, most kids in the deal never got past Baltimore. They'd all be taken by then. Tim Riordan, though, well, he set a record of sorts. He got past Baltimore and Washington and right on through Fredericksburg, all the way down to Richmond! An Irish Catholic cripple in Richmond, how about that?" Jack Hennessey laughed, slapping his knee, Michael Byrnes laughing along as he turned west on Constitution Avenue.

"Well, a Jewish lumber merchant took him off the platform there. Taught him numbers and inventory and financing and the all the rest. In time, Tim worked his way into the family and ended up running the place! How about that? Taken unknown off a train platform and ends up heading the whole outfit. Pretty much starting from scratch, I'd say." Jack Hennessey looked at Michael

Byrnes and winked, then ahead again. "Anyway, his luck ran out in '93." He turned to Michael Byrnes. "Have they taught you anything about the Panic of '93, Michael?"

"Not really. Just a little in History class."

"How about '73? Anything?"

"The same."

"Well, you be sure to learn about them. They were tough times, I'll tell you that. Neither as bad as this, now, but it was bad. They're in one of the books on the list. Read that one next."

"Yes, sir."

"Well, anyway, the company got wiped out. Lock, stock and barrel. All the money was tied up in a bank and when it went under, it took Tim Riordan's company with it. Type of thing that happened back then all the time, just like now. Tim, though, he'd been good with his own money and moved up to Washington. Somehow or another he got involved in the labor movement. However he did it, he was always the fella in the middle, the go-between, the man everyone else looked to sort things out. Has a real knack for it. Puts in the time, looks for a break and then gets it done. A good man, Michael. I'll be sure you get to shake his hand after the lunch."

"Thank you, Mr. Hennessey ."

"It's all part of the deal, Michael, you being a squire."

The Packard had turned left on Third Street, Northwest, crossing the Mall with the Capitol building now on their left. Michael Byrnes took a right on Independence Avenue and headed west, the Smithsonian Castle coming up on the right and Agriculture straight ahead. 'Got to know your luck' Jack Hennessey thought to himself. Commercial construction is one of the worst places to be in a recession, not even to mention a depression. But not so much in the Washington, DC of Franklin Delano Roosevelt and his *New Deal*.

Loyal Democrat that he was, Jack Hennessey had voted for Roosevelt. It wasn't for any particular liking of the man, though. What he wanted was Hoover out. But he did like the way FDR came in, guns ablazing and getting things started and done, certainly changed. It was 1933 and for the first time in his life Jack Hennessey wasn't so sure how things were going to work out. He read what he could about what they wanted to do and served on some panels with the building and trade associations. The idea of the government spending what it didn't have, though, borrowing heavy against an uncertain future, well, this went against his grain. But being in construction, it did mean more work, especially in Washington DC, and he had no problem with any of that. The New Dealers were pouring in by the thousands and needed places to live and to work. And then there was the Public Works Administration.

'Know your luck, Jack' that's what Tom Brady taught him. It was the difference between just getting by and winning. It meant keeping your eye out for a break and getting what you can from it. In FDR's New Deal, this meant giving up the fight against the unions. In the 1920s there was business aplenty and Hennessey Construction got its fair share of it. The unions, though, wanted to make all the rules and squeeze his margins and he fought them every step of the way. And with men like Paddy Riley, he'd stayed ahead of them. But that was then. In 1935, the Democrats had rammed through the Wagner Act and anyone with an open shop like his had to start paying attention.

Hennessey 's biggest current job was an extension on the Agriculture Department building on the south side of Independence Avenue. Next big deal coming up Hennessey had a shot at was the Hecht Department Store chain's new warehouse. It was going up on land in the Northeast quadrant of the city and it was to be huge. It would mean two years work and Jack Hennessey was out to get it. He'd met with Tim Riordan three weeks previous to explore submitting his bid with the unions already signed on. But this would mean work rules and if there was one thing in construction that Jack Hennessey truly hated, it was union work rules.

Work rules meant the unions got to tell you how many bricks a brick layer could lay in an hour or a day, or even how many his apprentice could carry up to him at a time. It made bureaucrats out of working men. It meant that everyone was somehow supposed to be the same, and if there was one thing that Jack Hennessey had learned in his 88 years of living it was that everyone was *not* the same. In fact, no one was the same. What the unions wanted was to stretch the work so the job would take longer and require more men. And this went against everything that made Jack Hennessey Jack Hennessey. His instincts were to get the job done under budget and sooner than contracted. This was how he had built his business.

He had prided himself on finding good people to work hard and he paid them well for it, and different. If one man could do the work of two, he got twice the pay. What could be simpler than that? Or fairer? Jack Hennessey didn't want some union boss coming between him and his men because his men were the most important asset he had. But if he could get this contract and make it work, he'd be better positioned for government work which was most of what was going to happen in Washington DC for as far as anyone could see.

One problem in all this was Paddy Riley, his Vice President of Operations. He had started with Hennessey in 1920 as a brick layer–a 6 foot 2 inch, 220 pound, 20 year old dynamo who earned his keep the first day on the job. Paddy Riley had what Jack Hennessey sought most in his company – an unfailing desire to get things done. Jack

Hennessey had put him over a crew when he was just 23 years old, and he just kept on growing from there. He drove his men hard, and they took it from him, taking pride beating a deadline, and the extra there'd be in their pay envelopes for doing it.

While their instincts were the same, there was a difference on unions between Paddy Riley and Jack Hennessey. Paddy took the whole thing personally. He would build a work gang, make them worth more than they were before he brought them on and together, and for this he expected loyalty. If a union organizer showed up, Paddy would run him off. If one of his crew started talking about organizing, Paddy would run him off, too. Paddy Riley had served in France in a construction battalion and had come under fire several times, even earned a battlefield promotion to sergeant in the Ardennes. Fact is, Paddy Riley liked a fight and taking on someone looking to break up a crew he'd built, well, that was just the sort of thing to make his day.

Michael Byrnes did a quick U-turn on Independence and pulled up to the curb on the south side of the Avenue, in behind the Hennessey Construction Co. trailer. Jack Hennessey let himself out, checking his watch as he closed the car door. Eleven fifteen on the nose. Looking about the site, he could see that the clean up was well under way. Final inspection was scheduled for two weeks but it looked like they'd be ready for it in a couple of days. Several men walked by, one nodding to him and the other touching his cap. Jack Hennessey nodded back, a smile on his face. He just loved being on a site with men and things moving about, things getting done.

Looking east down Independence at the extension, the sun was in his eyes. Raising his right hand for shade, he walked around and behind the Packard, to the edge of the Avenue, even into the first lane. Here he had a clear view of it. The lines were true and the sandstone facing matched the original building perfectly, color and cut. At five stories tall, 180 feet long and over 140 deep, it was the largest building Hennessey Construction had ever done and he loved the feeling of it. From the first house he built in Southeast more than 60 years ago, it was always the same.

"Jack! Get out of the street, for Chrissake! You trying to get killed two weeks before delivery?" Paddy Riley stood in the doorway of the trailer, filling it with his size and energy.

Jack Hennessey smiled and waved him off as he quick-stepped out of the street and started for the trailer, still working his mind about how exactly he was going to handle this. Paddy Riley ran operations. They had four projects going. Paddy had direct charge of this one and oversaw the other three. He got things done, and for the joy and pride of it as much as anything else, and a quick learner, too. When Jack Hennessey realized his potential, he paid for night school in accountancy and finance, and later draftsmanship. He didn't need Paddy to be an accountant or a draftsman, though. He needed him to know what they did so he could supervise them.

Paddy Riley was the future of Hennessey Construction and Jack Hennessey had been grooming him for the part for the last ten years. Moving him into the social part of it, the politics, had started several years ago. After making him a vice president, he had begun taking Paddy to Board of Trade meetings and having Paddy and his wife Mary use tickets for charity events. When a Broadway show was in town, he'd buy them tickets for that. And when a house nearby his own, at Fourth Street in Southwest, came up for sale in 1935, Jack Hennessey double bonused Paddy so he could buy it. Paddy and Mary were now on the west side of Fourth Street just around the corner from himself. And, truth be told, their children would be closer, too. He loved Paddy as he would have a son, and so his wife and their children, as well.

Paddy held the screen door of the trailer open. Jack Hennessey mounted the three steps and passed through, shaking Paddy's offered hand, comforted by the size and strength of it. He hiked himself up on a drafting stool by Paddy's work table. "So, Paddy, where do we stand?"

"Ahead. The clean-up will be done by Friday and then there's the odds and ends inside, but we could deliver it Tuesday."

"I like that. Good work, Paddy. We showed them who could do a job, didn't we?'

"That was the plan." Paddy sat on the other drafting stool and fixed on Jack Hennessey. "What's next, though."

Jack Hennessey cleared his throat, sat up a little straighter. "The Hecht Warehouse. Tom Gleason's finalizing the bid papers right now. I'm going to see him this afternoon."

"Cutting it a little close, isn't it?"

"Well, I've asked him to make some changes." Jack Hennessey looked north, across the National Mall to the Department of Commerce building on the north side of Constitution Avenue. Hollinger had got that contract, and he would be bidding on the Hecht deal as well, him and everyone else in the city with a shovel and a mule. "Paddy, I've been talking with Tim Riordan. In fact, I have a lunch with him today." He focused on Paddy, held his eyes to be sure he understood. "I'm bringing the trades in on the bid, Paddy. Tim Riordan's been working it for me..."

"Jesus Christ, Jack! The unions? Hell, it's a depression, that's all, just a depression. Happens all the time. It'll pass. It's not like it's the end of the goddam world, for Chrissake!"

Jack Hennessey stood off the stool and pushed it back under the work table. "Paddy, you got to know your luck, and that means knowing where things are going." He stood square and up. "I've been watching this union thing for more than forty years, since before there were cars or let alone factories to build them. Companies got bigger, that's all. Hell, everything got bigger, and labor's just the little guy's way of trying stay even, shouldering up with the bosses." He looked up at Paddy Riley, fixing hard on him. "Things change, Paddy. They never stay the same, and you got to be ready to change with them, or just get rolled over. What I know is this, with Wagner and prevailing wage and all the rest of it, labor's time has come. It's sure where these New Dealers are headed, and they're in charge, and likely to be for some time."

Jack Hennessey felt a twinge of pain and gripped the edge of Paddy Riley's work table, fixed on him. "And then there's being Irish. We still get hind teat, Paddy, every time. We're the last bid opened. Count on it. They just don't like us. We were lucky to get this job, still not sure how. But we got it and showed them we could do it. We're still Irish, though, and we still need every angle we can get. And that's another bit of luck—Tim Riordan. He trusts me, and I trust him." He paused, fixing on Paddy Riley. "We've got to go in with the trades, Paddy…"

Another twinge. Jack Hennessey gripped the table harder and moved to it, leaning against it slightly.

"Just like the big boys, Paddy…" He tightened the muscles in his stomach, fighting the pain as he avoided bringing his hands to his upper abdomen where it was the worst. "With labor so tight with the White House, Paddy, and FDR a shoo-in this November, we've just got to play ball if we ever hope to get another deal like this." He motioned outside to the building site. "And we've got this, what we've done here, on this job, to show'em we know what we're doing." He stood away from the table. "So, that's how we're going, with the unions in."

Paddy was silent, sitting back on his stool. "Well, it's your company, Jack, your call..."

"Like you said, Paddy, it's not the end of the world. It's still the beginning. It's always the beginning for the fella out in front." He fixed again on Paddy Riley, raised his head a measure. "The question is, Paddy, can you get out in front with me?"

Paddy Riley stood off his stool, took half a step back. "What do you, mean, Jack?"

"You have to be with me on this, Paddy, all the way. You're as much of Hennessey Construction as I am. We fought those fellas for years together, and now we're looking to bring them on board." He pointed in the direction of O'Donnell's Seafood House on the far side of the Mall. "I've got Tim Riordan for lunch at O'Donnell's now, right now, and I've got to deliver Hennessey Construction, and that means you, too...Paddy Riley, on board, okay with working with the unions. Can you do that, Paddy? Are you with me?"

Paddy Riley looked left across the Mall, and then back at Jack Hennessey. "I can do it for you, Jack. Hell, I can do anything for you." He put out his hand to shake and Jack Hennessey took it.

CHAPTER NINE
Lunch at O'Donnell's

L ooking ahead, the passenger window open, Jack Hennessey reached for the water flask inside his suit jacket as Michael Byrnes pointed the Packard north on 14th Street. There had been another quiver of pain as he had gotten in the car. It was never sharp, like a cut. But it could build to the point of doubling him over. Flipping the flask open, he reached into the change pocket of his jacket, took out three pills and swallowed them down with a long, full drink of water then put the flask away.

"Is it worse today, Mr. Hennessey?"

"No, Michael, not really. Actually, it's been a good day so far. Just don't want it coming up and have Tim Riordan thinking something's wrong." The pain had begun in February, off and on. And there had been some weight loss, as well. Jack Hennessey had enjoyed good health his entire life, something to which he credited moderation in living, paying attention in general and Tom Brady in particular. Tom Brady had introduced him to the *Merck Manual.* "If it ain't in there, Jack-O, you ain't got it." He'd thunked the book down on Jack Hennessey's desk, all 900 pages of it, a fortieth birthday present. "Every disease known to man, and cross referenced, if you please, with what pills to take and poisons to avoid. It's all there, laddy. Use it well, and you'll do another forty."

Jack Hennessey had introduced each of the squires to the "Merck" as he called it. Of them all, Michael Byrnes had taken the greatest interest. When the pain started in Jack Hennessey's upper chest, they looked through it, putting it down as most likely dyspepsia or another digestive disorder. Over the balance of the winter, the pain came and went, though rising with a purpose in

April. Seeing a pharmacist in mid-month, Jack Hennessey had got some pills for the pain. This had tided him over till the end of the month. By the first of May, though, it had gotten still worse and Michael Byrnes convinced him to see a doctor. Jack Hennessey had selected Terrence Lynch, MD, from among those identified by Michal Byrnes to choose from, more for him having his office by Folger Park than any other reason. And he had seen Dr. Lynch the previous Wednesday, with tests done and x-rays taken and the results to be learned tomorrow morning.

"Here we are..." Michael Byrnes pulled the car over the curb at 14th Street and F Street.

Jack Hennessey sat up, glad for the distraction from his appointment with Dr. Lynch, and let himself out of the car. He generally took a booth in the front bar of O'Donnell's. Jack Hennessey liked people and he liked being around them, and for this, O'Donnell's on F Street at noon on a business day was a great place to be. Today, though, he had arranged for a corner booth in the dining room. Tim Riordan was there first, a glass of iced tea at hand. He was *always* early. Half rising against the table as he offered his hand, Jack Hennessey took it for a good hard shake and slid left into the booth to be at Tim Riordan's right. They had discovered some years back that Tim Riordan's right ear was better than his left, and that Jack Hennessey's left ear was better than his right. Some things are just meant to be, Tim Riordan had said.

"Good morning to you, Jack. Hope all is well?"

"Well, indeed, well indeed. We're ten days ahead on the Ag extension." He smiled. "And your Esther? Well I hope?" He signaled to the waiter for a ginger ale.

"Esther remains lovely, thank you, Jack. I have been blessed, truly blessed." He raised his iced tea. "We will celebrate our fortieth wedding anniversary in July. Hope you'll be joining us. It's the 19th, a Sunday."

Jack Hennessey took out a pocket calendar from his suit jacket and a pen from his shirt pocket, noting the date. "I'll look forward to it with pleasure, Tim. Thank you for including me." He looked up. "And please give Esther my best." He put away the calendar and pen as the waiter arrived with his ginger ale and took their lunch orders. Crab cakes for Tim Riordan and rockfish for him, broiled through.

Jack Hennessey watched as the waiter disappeared behind the swinging door to the kitchen then picked up his glass, raised it toward Tim Riordan, took a sip, and sat back.

"So, Tim, how's all this coming? Where are we?"

"They like the idea of being in on the bid..."

"Now, Tim, they're not exactly *in* the bid..."

"Yes, they know that, Jack. Yes. I meant to say in this stage of the process. In at the beginning, so to speak."

"Yes, well, they are that. Certainly they are that. That's the whole idea, now, isn't it?"

"Exactly. What's key to them is a written commitment..."

"Yes. Absolutely, and they'll have it. Gleason's working the letter right now. I'm going to see him at three today. It's the language you specified."

"Good, good..."

"So, we're ready to go then?" Jack Hennessey raised his glass as if to toast.

Tim Riordan picked his glass up but did not offer it, fixing his eyes on Jack Hennessey .

"Couple things more, Jack. Couple things more."

Jack Hennessey brought his glass down and sipped it. "Such as..."

"Term of contract. They want three years on average, but staggered..."

"Staggered?"

"Yes. The electricians will come in for two years, the Bricklayers for two and half, the Carpenters and the steam fitters at three and the plumbers in three and half. After that, each contract renews, by mutual agreement, for three years."

"So I can expect a job action every six months, then?" Jack Hennessey took another sip of his ginger ale. "That's a new wrinkle, Tim. And not a pretty one, either. What else you got?"

Tim Riordan sat back, studied Jack Hennessey. "Paddy Riley. How's he with all this?"

"He's fine. Just spoke to him. Have his hand on it."

"He's a tough one, that Paddy of yours…"

Jack Hennessey took another sip of ginger ale and fixed on Tim Riordan. "This is a tough business, Tim. And tough times, too. Paddy Riley's never done anything that I haven't wanted him to."

Tim Riordan nodded. "He's a good soldier, Jack. I'll give him that." He looked at Jack Hennessey. "Mike Conley's going be elected president of the Bricklayers Local 332 next week…"

"The Mike Conley from Baltimore?"

"Now, yes. He grew up here, though." Jack Hennessey nodded that he understood. "Anyway, he's in line for District Rep to the AFL…the national level rep…"

"Christ…" Jack Hennessey turned the ginger ale on the table, raised it to his lips and took a swallow. He fixed at Tim Riordan. "You know, Tim, a guy's gotta know when to duck…"

Tim Riordan laughed. "This is true, Jack. This is true. But he didn't duck, and his nose is still crooked, shall we say."

"He had no business coming onto that site. It wasn't organized and he knew it. And he had even less business giving Paddy lip. And then the dumb son of a bitch, all five feet six of him, shoves Paddy Riley. Hands on his chest. Right in front of Paddy's crew. What's Paddy supposed to do with that? Conley got exactly what he was asking for, that's what, all five fingers and fist worth." He fixed on Tim Riordan who was quiet, staring at his iced tea. "I'd hate to see this deal go down on that, Tim…"

Tim Riordan was silent for a moment then reached for his drink, holding it above the surface of the table. "Well, if you can take the staggering, Jack, I think I can bring Conley along." He turned to Jack Hennessey and fixed on him as he sipped his drink.

Jack Hennessey sat back, looking at Tim Riordan, waiting for him to say more, but nothing came. Something's up. You don't put something like staggering labor contracts on the table, something that could change the whole deal, and then try to swap it off for a well deserved, ten-year-old punch in the nose.

"Gentlemen…" The waiter arrived with the food, reaching across the table to serve each. "Refresh on the drinks, gentlemen?"

"Thank you, Daniel." Jack Hennessey spread his napkin on his lap as he looked at Tim Riordan. "Getting pretty complicated, Tim. *Comp-li-ca-ted*." Tim Riordan had picked up his knife and fork and was cutting into one of the crab cakes. Jack Hennessey waited until he finished and had looked back over at him.

"We want to do this, Tim, but I got to tell you, this staggering thing bothers me." Jack Hennessey picked up his knife and fork, cut down the middle line of the fillet and split it in two, cutting one half into quarters and putting one piece in his mouth, chewing and swallowing it quickly before speaking. "The way you want it, any one of the five can shut down the whole site." Jack Hennessey put his knife and fork down and took a large swallow of ginger ale, waiting for Tim Riordan to sip his iced tea. "Here's what, Tim. You break them into two and three. I don't care which way. Then one group goes for two years and the other for three. How's that?"

Tim Riordan had returned to picking at his crab cakes. He lifted his napkin and wiped his lips before fixing on Jack Hennessey for a second or two, maybe three. "Jack, I'd put Hennessey Construction at fourth to get the Hecht job. Maybe third with the work you've done on the Ag extension job. That's certainly a mark in your favor. Not bad for a Mick outfit. But you're still third, Jack. That's the best you can do no matter how you look at it, you being an open shop contractor. Now, you show up with the unions signed on? Different story altogether, Jack. In fact, it's a done deal." He leaned closer, his eyes focused sharply. "Done, Jack."

Jack Hennessey sat back, felt a twinge in his gut. It was starting sooner than he had expected. At least he'd know tomorrow for sure. 'Know your luck'. Tom Brady's words rolled over in this mind. Tim Riordan was right. Hollinger is the odds on favorite to win this one. The Commerce Department building was huge, and he did it right and on time. Second? That'd be Collier. And third? Maybe Harrison. Yes, Harrison for sure, and he'd take this deal in a second. Hasn't had a big job in two years.

Truth be told, Jack Hennessey had wondered earlier why Tim Riordan hadn't gone to Harrison first. Harrison was the weakest of the large local firms, and didn't have the Irish thing around their neck. Well, now maybe Jack Hennessey had his answer. While no one in the industry wanted anything to do with the unions, Paddy Riley did more than talk about it. Mike Conley wasn't the only union organizer walking around with a broken nose, or some other part. They wanted Hennessey Construction in particular, by name. It was the last open shop of any size in the area.

"Done, you say, Tim?"

"Yes, Jack, DONE. Just for you, now, Jack, just for you." He winked.

"Like I said, Tim, it's getting complicated. I've got a meeting with Gleason at three this afternoon. I'd like to speak with him about it. You at the Board of Trade lunch tomorrow?"

"If you mean at the Mayflower, yes."

"I'll look for you in the Town and Country Room at noon."

"I'll be there, Jack. But that's all the time I can get you."

Jack Hennessey nodded that he understood and cut another piece of rockfish.

The waiter returned. "How's the food, gentlemen?"

Tim Riordan nodded that it was fine. Jack Hennessey looked at him, and then up to the waiter. "A little tough, Dennis. Overdone maybe." He looked back at Tim Riordan and winked, a twinge rising and holding a little longer.

CHAPTER TEN
Mary Riley

O f the changes in Mary Riley's life from the purchase of the house on Fourth Street, none was more telling than the getting of her groceries.

Now she had come to Southwest in 1925, the bride of Paddy Riley, raised though she was in Brookland, this being in the Northeast quadrant of the city, four miles distant and, by her reckoning, a better place to be altogether. Brookland, you see, was where the better Irish had settled and lived, miles off and well above the bogs by the Potomac. Sure it was better when the weather was its worst, that being summertime with mosquitoes out large enough to name and the high stench of St. James Creek, even filled-in these many years, rising up in a rain like a corpse from the grave.

Mary had come over at six years in 1908, daughter to Sean Coughlin, master stonemason, and Norah her mother, along with brothers Bryan at five years and Dennis at two. There being a great demand for stonemasons at the time, Sean Coughlin was quick to find work and with Norah managing their affairs, they'd done better in their new land than all their imagining before they come. It was Paddy's family that had settled in Southwest, this being before the turn of the century.

Now Southwest, like most places, had its parts to it. The parts to the West of Fourth Street, then, them running from there to the water, these were the better parts. Those parts to the east of Fourth Street, them running to South Capitol Street and including St. James Creek, later made a canal, and then filled in altogether, well, these were the lesser parts. And it was here that Sean Riley, father to Paddy, had made his home. Taking a wife in 1894, they'd settled in a rented house where his three sons were born, one dying young and the others, Patrick and Edward, getting on.

And the groceries? Well, living as she had east of Fourth Street, Mary, like others about, walked to the market each morning, trailing a shopping cart, planning her day and what's to be done for supper. And this was the part of her day that she'd come to treasure, a good stretch of the legs with folks to nod to and speak with, and then the learning in general as to what was going about. Well, having come, now, to the *west* of side Fourth Street, there were complications of an unanticipated nature.

The place they bought, you see, was a town house, and being built in 1796, among the first such to go up in the Capitol City all together. *Wheat Row* it was by name and the Rileys had the northern most of the four of it. In its 140 years, the property had been in only two families. Of these, the latter had come to it just before the civil war, the original family, being of Confederate sympathies, relocating accordingly. Paddy and Mary, now, had got the place in a tax sale. Always a bit of mess, this is, folks being turned out, now, and neighbors looking on, not knowing of who to think the less of, the people who couldn't pay their taxes, or those who'd stoop so low as to take so fine a house as this in a public auction.

So here's Mary, then, just moved in and thinking about the furniture to come, on her way to the market, crossing Fourth Street looking to see those she knew and treasured, planning her day and her meals as she's done now these ten years. But on her way, this first full day in her new home, the nods are coming fewer and chats are shorter and she's wondering what's it about, with only more to come.

Getting back to her new place, now, trailing her cart near bursting with cabbage and cans of this and of that, the neighbor's help are at the stoop asking her name and that of the new missus, and was she to home? 'Well,' says she, 'Mary Riley's the name, wife to Patrick, and *I* am the new missus, and I *am* to home!' They saying now, gaggling into their shawls, 'The missus of this fine house wouldn't be about with a cart and walking to the market, now would she?' 'Wouldn't she, now,' says Mary, 'and why not?' 'Because she wouldn't' says they, the shawls gone down now and their noses in the air, as off they are to sweeping the stoop and the brickwork to the street.

And in the telling of her day to Paddy that evening, now, there's not an ounce of sympathy to be had. 'You've been pining for a place like this since you left Brookland, Mary, and now you've got it. And if people in places like this don't take their carts to market, then that's just how it is. You can't have all sides of everything. Now we can rent this place out and go back to where we were, or you can get used to it. It's no difference to me. You just let me know what you've decided, and we'll do it. One thing, though, whatever you decide, get it done quick. The furniture's due Monday and I don't want to pay the cartage just to have it all taken back.'

Aye! The furniture! A mahogany breakfront with table to match, and the chairs, too. Then there's that for the sitting room, arm chairs and a tufted velvet couch and coffee table with marble inset. And the standing clock as well, and more and more all together. Aye, all sides, indeed! So it was on Fourth Street they stayed. Mary, now, though, wouldn't be doing without her walk. Each morning, then, she's off to market to pick her meats and breads and vegetables and whatever else is needed, having it all delivered, and to the service entrance, of course. And she'd pay cash, too, not being interested in the grocer's credit, or anyone else's, it being the devil's own invention and the first step to ruin.

There were other adjustments as well. As broad and grand as Fourth Street might be, sure it wasn't a place for stick ball and the running about of children and Mary missing the noise of such about. But sure there was no complaining to be heard from Norah Coughlin or Daddy Riley, what Sean had come to be called with the grand children coming, each now with their own room, and a toilet to share, all on the first floor, as well. And for Daddy Riley, there was the special pleasure of being three blocks closer to the water he loved and his scow for fishing and rowing.

For all the change of the first year at Fourth Street, though, it was really just more of the same since Paddy had been made vice president at Hennessey Construction five years previous. He was too young for it by most accounts, some on First Street working at Hennessey not liking him getting it in front of them, or others they knew. But not Mary, now, not one bit. Mary Riley knew her man and his place among men, too. It was more than his size and his swagger, you see. Paddy Riley of Southwest was just born to lead and that was all there was to it. Like Mary, he hated laggards, boot lickers and hangers-on of every sort and type. If you worked and pulled your weight, Paddy Riley was your man. If you pulled more than your weight, he was your brother. And the rest? Paddy Riley wasn't interested in helping or hurting them. He just wouldn't have them around – at all.

Running a job site, though, getting the right lads aboard and driving them, that was the first part of the business. The next part was getting the work to do, and this was a different game altogether. A building is worth no more than its use to someone, Jack Hennessey had told him, and that's where the other part starts. There's the fella who wants the thing built, for his own use or to let, and then there's the banker who'll be lending the money, too, wanting to know if you can get it built, and at what cost, and then there's all the lawyers and the agents and inspectors and the bonders and sure more parts and pieces to it than Paddy Riley had any sense of at all.

When Jack Hennessey made Paddy Riley a vice president, he took them–Paddy and Mary–to dinner at the Willard Hotel, high over Pennsylvania Avenue, the Capitol building now standing grand and tall and away in the evening sun. It was here that Jack Hennessey explained that the folks who decide what's to be built don't spend a lot of time with the folks who do the building. No. They spend a lot of time with each other, that's where they spend their time, with each other. And of the places they spend their time, there were two types, those with the ladies and those without. And for those with the ladies, Paddy and Mary were going to be getting about.

Of all the things Mary Riley had done in her life, now, nothing was to come with greater discomfort and worry than this. Of a sudden, you see, she's off to the theater and the opera and charity galas and dinners at the Shoreham and the Mayflower, aye, such that she couldn't keep all the diseases and poverties straight in her head, not to mention the names of matrons and ambassadors and the legions of monsignors attending the Arch Bishop himself!

The more they went to, the less she liked it. And the more Paddy bragged she was the prettiest girl in the house, the less she believed him with all the society ladies about, their hair done up and knowing what wines to chose and what color to wear. 'New ponds are never easy' Jack Hennessey would be telling her, but of no use at all. And it wasn't that she wasn't pretty, neither now . No, not at all. Stately is what some would say, at five feet eight and her being of full figure by fifteen years with amber hair worn full past her shoulders. Though plain in dress about the house, when she had the care and took the time, she was a stunner, she was, with brilliant green eyes and a smile that could melt the coldest heart.

And then there come a miracle of sorts. Right there in the *Evening Star* of a Monday afternoon, top center of the society page, a picture of her next to Paddy talking with some swell and his lady. There's Paddy, now, laughing and looking grand in his tuxedo and bow tie and her, too, in her new dress, with the swell and his lady looking at the two them like they'd just got back from Paris on their way to a White House ball! Sure there were jokes and jibes about it on both sides of Fourth Street, with Daddy Riley not letting it go for a full month or more, but it put Mary in a mind that she could do this thing. It wasn't that she'd ever come to like it, now, or ever *want* to do it, but by the picture she saw she was as good as any and that had made all the difference.

Mary Riley's only true happiness, you see, was her Paddy and her young ones, John, Mary Catherine and Michael. John, her first, was now ten and in the fourth grade at St. Dominic's school. Then there'd come Dennis, poor Dennis. Born weak he was and gone in two years, sure Mary's greatest sorrow. Mary Catherine, now four, come next, with Michael to follow, now at three. Mary Riley had built her life and theirs in St. Dominic's parish, the church being on 6th Street and E, not a full half mile from the Capitol itself.

And what could have made her life more complete than the coming of Joseph Hara as assistant pastor. Fr. Hara grew up in St. Dominic's, born as he was on March 19, 1900, two days after Paddy Riley himself. The two met in kindergarten and had been inseparable since. 'Stuck to one another' is what Daddy Riley had said. Joe Hara went into the seminary straight out of eighth grade. For his part, with Paddy was apprenticed to a brick layer, and for this Daddy Riley was glad. Paid well, he was, and in a trade, too, one that could use his size and energy. 'Nothing like ten hours on a scaffold laying bricks in the sun to keep a lad like that out of trouble,' he was thinking.

And for Paddy Riley, sure, there would be no priest to marry him to Mary but his best friend Joseph Hara. Now they'd waited two years past their betrothal for him to get his Holy Orders, with the both of them, Paddy and Mary, aching for each other the last year of it near past endurance. But they did it, and this bound the three all the closer. It was a good life Mary Riley had come to this May of 1936, it was, the only burden now being Norah Coughlin, her mother. Sean Coughlin, gone now these two years, and Norah coming to live with them for a year before the move to Fourth Street, and her being past 70, it all now starting to tell. In bed these three days she was with a cough of sorts and a touch of the fever. The doctor had stopped by that morning with nothing to report for his time. It was the wink he gave Mary as he wouldn't take her money, it saying 'she'll be fine, if she's not fine already.'

So it's Mary now in her kitchen and starting dinner when what does she see but Norah Coughlin up and about fixing her room.

"And what's all this, now? If it's poor enough you're feeling to trouble the doctor on his busy day, it's in bed you should be."

"Well, I can't be having Fr. Hara to a room like this, now, can I?"

"Fr. Hara? Here? *Today*? What are you talking about, now?"

"The arrangements…"

"Arrangements? And what arrangements would these be?"

"My passing, is all." She placed a folded towel at the foot of her bed and climbed back in. "And don't be bothering yourself, now. I've already called him on the telephone in the hall." She managed a slight cough. "He'll be here at four."

A check of the clock telling Mary Riley it was near that now, she set about her dinner, putting things straight, wiping the counter tops, when who should come bursting in the screen door but John Riley, running in from the porch and setting his school books on the on the table with a thud, his eyes searching about. "Is Daddy Riley home yet?"

"Is it a heathen I'm raising, now, or just a barbarian?" Mary Riley's eyes fixed on the books with her arm and thumb to the door he just come in. "Out with you, now, and come in like the Christian gentlemen we all hope you'll someday be…"

He looked up at her.

"Now!" says she.

Quick as a snap he's out the door and in, his books in the hall by the stair and back again. "Is Daddy Riley home yet, ma?"

"Not yet, son. Get yourself changed and he'll be here before you know it."

"Good afternoon, Mary." Fr. Joseph Hara stepped across the porch and let himself in the screen door, making the sign of the cross. "God bless this house and all in it."

Mary blessed herself quickly, her eye falling on John Riley to make sure he had done as well. "Welcome, Joe, welcome. Good of you to come." She turned to John Riley. "Now don't you see how a gentleman comes into a room, Sean Riley?"

"Yes, ma, but he didn't knock…"

She started at him but he was too quick, into the hall and laughing his way up the stairs before she could get a hand on him. She turned back at Joseph Hara, shaking her head.

"The boy's right, Mary. I didn't knock."

"Now don't you be taking his side…"

"Is that you, father?"

Mary turned toward the hall and the half opened door to Norah Coughlin's room. "It is, now. He'll be along." She turned to Joseph Hara and motioned him out to the porch.

The sun was full on them as she stepped past Joseph Hara to a picnic table set under a fixed awning. "Sit, now won't you, Joe." Taking her place opposite, she busied her hands in her apron. "It's good of you to come, Joe. But she's fine. The doctor was here this morning, good man that he is, and it's nothing."

He smiled, nodding. "Well nothing of the body, I'm sure." He reached for her hand. "She loved your father so, Mary, and with Bryan gone and Dennis away in Chicago, her world's getting smaller every day." He looked away, past her and the English garden behind the house and to the houses beyond to the water. "There may be something else, too, Mary." He fixed on her. "I've been watching her for a while, her memory and things like that. It could be more than just getting old…"

She sat back, pulling her hand away. "What are you saying now, Joe?"

"Just that there are diseases, of the brain, that we have to be watching for…"

"The *brain* is it, now?" She turned away.

"Well, you just never know, Mary." She had turned back to him. "We just have to keep a close eye on her." He leaned right to catch her eye. "Moving over to this side of Fourth Street, away from her friends who she just got to know there, and that after moving from Brookland. Not knowing the street as she did…"

Mary bent closer. "There're Jews here, Joe, you know that, now. And they're not friendly, not at all…"

"None of that, now, Mary. Jesus Christ was born a Jew and died one…"

"Aye, and who killed him? The Jews…"

"We won't be talking that way, Mary. I've told you before. It's wrong headed." He sat back. "Now, I've come to see Norah, and...

"And what?"

"And to tell you, to suggest, that you find a place for Norah in the house here. Make sure she's got something to do with it, and with her time. She's spent a life working and helping others, her last two years nursing Sean, and after he died she's gone from Brookland to here, struggling to find a place. Most of us are what we *do*, Mary, and she's trying to find out what that is with all the change in her life."

"So it's on me, then, is it?"

"In a way. You're so strong, you see, Mary, and getting stronger all the time. Norah's past 70 and she's getting weaker. Without knowing it, she's afraid of getting left behind and..."

"Is Fr. Hara still here?"

They both looked at the screen door to the kitchen. Mary stood up, straightened her apron down her front. "You'd best be getting to her, Joe."

He rose from the table. "We should talk about this again, Mary."

"Aye, Joe. Aye. We'll be talking about it, sure. Now off you go to her..."

CHAPTER ELEVEN
Daddy Riley

P addy Riley had framed out a utility shed beneath the back porch, one corner of which was set aside for Daddy Riley's fishing gear. Here were rods of different lengths, boxes of lures and hooks and spools of line. Nets hung from the rafters, some for boating a catch, others for the catching of bait. Five crab pots were stacked in the corner, each with a line and buoy, a long handled wire crab net resting against them.

Having changed from his school clothes into shorts, a tee shirt and canvass sneakers, John Riley stepped carefully among the things of the shed in the half light of the door left open, picking out Daddy Riley's short rod, along with his own. Carrying these out to the back yard, he leaned them against the fence gate that opened on the alley leading on the right to N Street. Two seat cushions were next, and then the fishing box. It contained the lures, lead sinkers, hooks, wire leaders, cleaning knives and such Daddy Riley had collected over the years in the pursuit and catching of fish. The only thing John Riley needed now was bait – and Daddy Riley.

Now Daddy Riley had come over in 1883, his mother having died and there being nothing then to hold him in Ireland but the damp and the want of the place. It was at Boston that he had landed and it was there that he learned to read and to write and to clean up a building. Of the weather, though, he was soon to discover he'd swapped the damp for the cold. And a hand numbing, lung stinging, arse freezing cold it was, one that lasted for months on end, from October some years near into May. God's truth, Sean Riley didn't think a man could be that cold and live! Coming to the knowledge of warmer weather to the south, he had struck out and, in time, settled in Washington, DC, this being 1891. And it was here that he found employment at the Bureau of Mines, coming to a situation in building maintenance that paid regular and with the promise of a pension. Aye, an agreeable situation altogether.

Like many sons of Erin, you see, Sean Riley had not come to America to get rich. No. He come to get on as best he might, and this he had. It was by Washington City's waterfront that he made his home. It ran from Georgetown south along the east side of the Potomac River to the Anacostia River which it joined at the southern most point of Southwest. Here he could fish at his leisure and row a boat on the river, and if the summers were a bit tropic, the winters weren't at all arctic, this being as fair a bargain with the weather as Sean Riley had ever hoped to strike.

Daddy Riley had never owned a car. He'd gotten a driver's license so he could drive the trucks at work, which he avoided doing whenever possible. His principal mode of transportation, other than walking, was his bicycle, painted black and kept simple, and suited perfectly to the flat of Southwest. And of the things Daddy Riley landed with in Boston these many years past, only three remained–his brogue, his Catholic faith, and his sense and need of place. He'd come from the west of Ireland, you see, where the people he would see in a week or a month, or even a year, were at places he could walk to. There was a village, but only barely, the general sense being of those in it that a careful man would never have need to travel beyond it. And it was in just this that Daddy Riley had found in Washington the life he had wanted to live in Ireland, happily free of the damp and the want.

And more than forty years in Southwest, he'd come to know every part of it, as well as those places north along the waterfront – Foggy Bottom and Georgetown and the falls just beyond. He'd come to his knowledge of these places by his fishing of them. And, as everywhere, the fish had their seasons and their tastes, their preferences on a tide and the phase of the moon and the runoff from a summer storm. And it was in joining himself to this cycle of life on the water that Daddy Riley took his comfort and found his place. And if you were to ask him how this was different from the cycle and seasons of his faith, he might not have the answer. In each, though, he knew there was a life force he drew on, and that drew him on further, as well.

Daddy Riley's not being in the shed told John Riley that he was at Buzzard Point, netting killies for bait. The water came to ground there and, depending on the tide and the season, a person could wade out and net 20 or 30 killies in a couple of passes. The water where N Street met the river was too deep for this with its bulkheads and pilings, and all manner of boat traffic and noise, as well. This was Sixth Street Wharf and it was here that boats landed for market with produce and fish and crabs from down river and across the Chesapeake. Passenger ferries landed here as well, the overnight packet to Norfolk the most notable among them.

If Daddy Riley had gone for bait, he'd soon be coming in the alley that ran behind the house to N Street, and so it was at this corner that John Riley waited, sitting on the curb. The killies would be in a small pail that Daddy Riley had rigged to fit behind the seat of his bike. At 76, though, he had become less skilled at slowing the bike down and getting it stopped, and himself off of it, without spilling the water and the bait, or falling down altogether. Increasingly, John Riley's help in this had become crucial to the success of the enterprise. Sitting on the curb, John Riley did not know the exact sound that alerted him to Daddy Riley's turning from Fourth Street onto N Street, but it caught his ear and he rose, readying himself for the arrival of his grandfather. He waved his hand. "Hey, Daddy Riley! Get the bait?"

"And what else would I be doing? Twenty plus is what we got. Sure all we'll be needing." Peddling at his ease, Daddy Riley guided his bike over the brick surface of N Street in the speckled shade of the poplar trees lining it. Bent forward over the handle bars, his head and eyes were fixed ahead, his wool cap shading his forehead. Slowing at the alley, he turned into it as John Riley squared up in the path of the bike, taking hold of the handle bars and steadying it as Daddy Riley dismounted, arching his right leg over the seat and finding the ground now with both feet.

"There's a good lad." He smiled at John Riley, rustling his auburn hair with his near hand before turning to the bait pail. He loosened it from its fixing and checked its contents before looking up through the shade trees at the sun. "The tide will be right in half an hour." He nodded in satisfaction at John Riley who nodded back and started down the alley with the bike, calling over his shoulder that he'd be right back with the rods and the gear.

Daddy Riley set the bait pail on the curb. Steadying himself against a tree, he removed the metal clip from his right ankle that he kept his pants leg from the bicycle chain and put it in the pocket of his jacket. Stepping back from the tree he turned toward Fourth Street as Jack Hennessey's Packard turned onto N Street and pulled up to a stop.

"And how are you today, Daddy Riley?" Jack Hennessey hailed him across the drivers seat, past Michael Byrnes who sat back in his seat.

"On such as day as this, now, Mr. Jack, what can any sane man be but grateful? And yourself?"

"Fine, as well. And yes, 'grateful' is the perfect word." Jack Hennessey nodded toward Michael Byrnes. "You know Michael Byrnes, here?'

"Sure don't I see him every day, now, driving down N Street and with you sitting beside him?" He fixed on Michael Byrnes. "About a year now, isn't it, lad?"

"Just that."

"Mr. Jack!" John Riley was fast stepping out the alley with the rods and fishing box. This brought Jack Hennessey out of his car. He waved Michael Byrnes on with a 'See you at the house' nod, stepping behind the car as it passed. He offered his hand to Daddy Riley, then John Riley.

"And how are you today, John Riley." He looked at the gear the boy was carrying and the bait pail. "Looks like you men are going fishing…"

"Sure am. Right now. Want to come?" He looked up at Daddy Riley who nodded.

Jack Hennessey looked down at the boy, his eyes bright and expectant, so full of life that he gave no sense or appreciation of it. "No, son, but it's kind of you to ask. You catch one for me, though, will you?"

"Sure will."

Jack Hennessey reached out and jostled the boy's hair, bringing him close for the briefest moment before standing back and holding him by the shoulders. "Tell you what, John Riley. How about you and me and your dad and Daddy Riley, here, going out to the Bay on Saturday. Rockfish season just opened. How about that?"

"Wow! The Bay! Rockfish! Sure…"

"Okay. You tell your daddy when he gets home tonight. You tell him that it's a special day. Tell him that, and that I need him to come. Can you do that?" He looked at Daddy Riley who nodded quietly.

"You bet…"

"Good afternoon all." Fr. Hara, stepped out from the alley. "Daddy Riley, John, Mr. Hennessey..."

Jack Hennessey turned, his head back on seeing it was Fr. Hara. He nodded. "Joe." A smile came to his face as he offered his hand. "Good to see you, Joe." He gave the priest's hand an extra pump. "And when are you going to start calling me 'Jack'?"

"As soon as Pastor Ryan does."

Jack Hennessey and Daddy Riley laughed softly as John Riley started for the water with Daddy Riley picking up the bait pail and taking his leave as he nodded to the others. Jack Hennessey called after John. "John, you remember, now, to tell your daddy about Saturday."

"Sure will!"

Jack Hennessey waited until they were both away and turned to Joe Hara. "Good to see you, Joe. And you saved me a nickel. I was going to call you tonight to see if you could come by for dinner on Thursday. I know it's short notice, but..."

"Don't worry about that. I'm free as far as I know. Let me check with the Monsignor when I get back to the rectory. Can I call you at the house then, to confirm?"

"Certainly."

"What time would you want me?"

"Is seven too late?"

"No, not at all. That'd be fine."

"Thank you father, I'll look for you then."

They shook hands, both turning west on N Street, toward the water, Joe Hara crossing the street to his car and Jack Hennessey taking the sidewalk to his house. Looking up, a steam ferry was landing, its whistle breaking the quiet of the afternoon. The day had remained warm and brilliant, and dry, as well, the rare gift of a Washington spring, all the graces of the season and not the slightest hint of the summer's crushing heat and humidity so certain to follow.

CHAPTER TWELVE
Christine McCarthy

J ack Hennessey had moved to Southwest in 1898. For several years after Christine had died, he had remained in their house on Folger Park in Southeast. But for reasons of which he was never quite certain, he had moved to a large apartment building in Northwest, several blocks north of the White House, off 16th Street.

For Washington, it was the Gilded Age, from the Civil War to the turn of the century, with society families from New York and Boston building grand homes and taking up residence for the winter months. As it turned out, though, this was more society than Jack Hennessey had needed, if he had ever needed any at all. He wasn't easy with the grandness of the place, *The Cairo*, and its ornate public rooms and what to wear, and then the doormen to nod to and thank for letting him into and out of his own place. The dead worst of it, though, was the small talk with people who he just couldn't find a way to care anything about.

In the warm months, he would go down to the Southwest waterfront where on a particular Saturday afternoon in June of 1898 he came upon a house for sale at the corner of N and 6th Street, facing west on the river. Three stories above a windowed half-basement and of red brick, it had a mansard roof and a full veranda in front, the southern portion of which was screened. The house sat on a large lot with a wide lawn running to the willow oaks along Sixth Street, beyond which was the water's edge. Its eleven rooms were more than he would ever use, but from the moment he mounted the steps of the veranda and turned west toward the river Jack Hennessey knew it was where he wanted to live.

He had had the kitchen moved from the basement to the first floor, and set up an office in a second floor bedroom. A cook had been hired when he first moved in, along with a cleaning woman, but they proved more than was needed. The pastor at St. Dominic's had introduced him to Mrs. Catherine Kennedy, recently widowed. She was to move in as the century turned with her two sons who she was to raise out of the basement apartment. And it was in a basement room that the squires were boarded, as well. A squire had full run of the basement and the first floor which, for Michael Byrnes, had come to mean the kitchen and the library where were kept the books of the "Squire's List." Also in the library were the books Jack Hennessey had read over his lifetime, or hoped to, as well as the *Encyclopedia Britannica*.

Jack Hennessey walked past the Packard parked on N Street, beside the house, and turned left onto the red brick path that led to the veranda. Climbing its nine steps, he was grateful for the wrought iron hand rail that eased his way. At the top, he turned back toward the water as he caught his breath. Looking down a small pier to his left, he could see the Rileys, grandfather and grandson, pushing off and settling in the scow. John Riley sat forward and Daddy Riley aft, the sound of their oars working coming across the lawn as they started south on the river. John Riley's eyes came back to him, the excitement and enthusiasm, an unconscious, infectious hope. His father's son, no doubt of that...

"Good evening, Mr. Hennessey."

Mrs. Kennedy stepped out onto the veranda, closing the screen door behind her. Jack Hennessey smiled at her and nodded. "It *is* a good evening, Mrs. Kennedy. Yes, indeed." He looked past her through the hall and to the kitchen. "Did Michael tell you we will have a guest for dinner?"

"Yes, sir. Mr. Molloy. A nice boy, like them all. I haven't seen him since he was a squire."

"I guess you wouldn't, now, would you…" He shook head with a smile. "They do come and go, don't they?"

"Yes, sir, they surely do."

"Well, I'm happy to say that Matt Molloy's done very well for himself. Worked his way through college and law school. With a big firm, now, downtown."

"A lawyer?" An air came up off the water and she turned to it. "Yes, I can see that." She cleared her throat and looked up at him. "I was planning crab cakes, if that's alright?"

"That'll be fine, Mrs. Kennedy, just fine." He rubbed his chest. The pain was rising. "I'll be up in my room, or the office. Maybe catch a nap."

"Yes, sir."

He turned toward the water, then back to her. "Would you mind setting dinner on the screen porch?"

She smiled and nodded as if she had expected him to say this.

"Thank you." He opened the screen door and held it for her, and then followed her in, she going to the kitchen and he upstairs.

The master bedroom had three tall windows, looking west over the river, and an adjoining bathroom. Jack Hennessey went into the bathroom. Pouring a glass of water, he took two pills from the change pocket of his jacket, put them in his mouth and then swallowed them down with the water. Pouring out the rest of the water, he caught his image in the mirror over the sink, fixing on his shirt collar. The weight loss was starting to show. He wondered if Tim Riordan had noticed. He didn't seem to have. There wasn't much light in the dining room at O'Donnell's. He slipped his index finger between the shirt collar and his neck. Too much room. He made a mental note to buy new shirts with tighter collars. There was time do that between breakfast and the doctor's.

He loosened his tie as he walked to the closet where he hung it up and changed into cotton pants and a pullover shirt and sweater. The early evening sun streamed into the room, bright on the varnished pine floor and the mahogany posts of his bed, a rich, deep amber against the white of the cotton coverlet. Going to the middle of the three windows, he looked for Daddy Riley's scow but there was no sign of it. To his left was a chaise lounge. It was his gift to Christine on their first anniversary. Of tufted green velvet, he settled in it, bringing his legs up and extended, warmed by the late afternoon sun. To his left was a reading table and on it Christine's engagement picture.

Picking it up, he held it before him with both hands. For it, she had worn her hair up, raven and full, showing the line of her neck and the graceful turn of her face from ear to chin. Though in black and white, he could see in it the blue of her eyes, feel their warmth and excitement. So clear, so alive...it was as if she was speaking to him and he could feel her breath. His mind went back to the day with her at Mt. Olivet, her gait as she moved over the grass and knolls, and then to before that, when they courted and first met, and of the stories she told him of her life before then...

Aye, the famine was done. But it'd done its job on Ireland, now, with all the dying and the leaving. It was a different place, says my ma. Changed everything, it did. The ones that lived through it, well, they were not the same coming out at all, at all. And as changed they were, they had their change on those that come after, much of the land about now gone to grazing, and the land that stayed for farming going to the oldest son, and him alone. Aye, there were few men with their own place, and so many fewer for marrying. And then come the goods from

England, the same as the girls would be making in their time, and cheaper, too. So there it is, and there it was – fewer men to marry, and less work to do.

My da's holding being bigger than most, he got me to school where I learned to clerk. Dublin is where, and for three years and more. Then he came ill and I moved back to help with him, and the place, too. Two years it took and he was gone, poor man. So there I am, now, sitting on my brother's place, and he younger than me, barely a village nearby and no work to do but milk the cows and mend the clothes. Sure the best part of any week was a letter from Dublin about those who'd gone to America, all going on about the good pay and the moving about, and all. Well, sure, in time I said to myself, says I, Why not? And so I did!

I had my money saved from Dublin, and what da left, as well, and got passage, I did, from Cork. Cheapest to go to was Baltimore, so there I went. Liked to break my poor ma's heart, it did, but she was with me all the way. 'A brother's farm is no place for a girl like you,' says she, the tears coming in buckets, and mine, too. And crying I was the whole way to Cork, and for the first day on the boat, and sick, from it, too.

But 'twas a warm May crossing, and as soon as morning it's up on deck, I am, meeting and talking with others and we all reading what we could about our new land and how we were going live! Aye! What we knew and what didn't! But wasn't that the fun of it, now! Sure most of the lads on the boat were Yanks, and what a lot of fun they were! Said anything that come to their mind, they would. And laugh? Aye, it seems that's all they ever did!

Well, I'd gotten a letter from my situation in Dublin, and the name of a service in Baltimore, too. So off we were the morning we landed. Work is what we needed, but there was no work to be had. 'Irish need not apply,' says he. Such a thing! 'Speaking as you do,' says he, 'your only chance would be at a school for the deaf, there being at present no such openings!' Kind man that he was, though, he gave us the name of a service in Washington. 'There's need for clerks there, and less Irish in general to give people pause.' He walks us back to the street, he does, and points us to the B&O Railroad.

Such a place, we're thinking! No jobs in one city, so off you go to the next! And who do we see on the train? Two of the lads from the boat to show us about! And as bright a day as any on the crossing, it is, with me and the others thinking Are there no clouds here at all, at all? And maybe no rain, neither? And the train, now, too. As long as a village and taller than my da's house, and sure it's hurtling fifty miles an hour, I don't know how fast, rattling down the track, and before we know it, here we are and off the train with our gear and looking for a place to stay. The lads helped us find a boarding house and we're all to dinner that night and gawking about, the Capitol as white in the sun as a snow topped mountain and sure more grand in the evening than anything ever I saw. And it's pinching ourselves, we are, with Ireland and its damp on the far side of the moon, if as near as that!

And as quick as you like I'm in a firm, I am, ten hours a day and till noon on Saturday. Clerk apprentice, is what they call it. Me, now, I call it a miracle! Here am I, not a full week off the boat and making near forty five a month in an office so clean with people who smile and mind their own business.

All too soon, though, come the first summer's heat, and it's wondering I am if it's to hell itself I've fallen, and without the pleasure of a sin to put me here! But then, at the dead worst of it, 101 degrees of an August noon, with folks frying eggs in pans on the pavement for their amusement, I turn a corner and bump into the handsomest man ever my eyes did behold, and he with a smile that sure melted my heart, and that quick.

Stunned, I am, stammering "Sorry, sir," my eyes locked on him now as he steps down Seventh Street. People moving all about and here's me, my legs frozen on the sidewalk, my heart off to heaven and my feet stuck in hell. Gone he is! Never to be seen again? 'Tis life so cruel that I find love this quick to lose it as fast?

Well, out I am the next day's noon and there he stands, at the same corner, at the same time, looking at all who pass, turning left and right, stepping here and there to catch a face going by. It's older, he seems, but nicely done, his rich auburn hair all wavy and back off a fine, square forehead. Scared to my soul, I am, but bold as well! "'Tis America," says I to me self, and it's to his side that I go. Taking a deep breath, 'tis his shoulder I touch, my hand aquivering in fear and excitement. "Can I help you, sir?" says I.

He turns and sure my heart's gone, heaven knows where for 'tis heaven I'm in, his eyes so blue and his smile so warm. "You have," says he, his hand out to me now and open it is. "My name is Jack Hennessey, and I've been waiting for you..."

CHAPTER THIRTEEN
Matt Malloy

"Mr. Hennessey..." Michael Byrnes touched Jack Hennessey's right hand as it lay across the back of Christine Hennessey's picture, standing close to catch it should it start to slip off his chest. "Mr. Hennessey..."

Jack Hennessey woke with a start, his head up and bringing the picture tightly to his chest. "Where am..? Chris..."

"It's me, Mr. Hennessey, Michael Byrnes."

Jack Hennessey's eyes blinked as he turned to the sound of Michael Byrnes voice, now fixing on him. "Where am..?"

"In your room, Mr. Hennessey. On your chaise." Michael Byrnes smiled at Jack Hennessey, nodding to say that he had the picture and Jack Hennessey could release it. Lifting it gently, he placed it on the table by the reading lamp and stood back.

Jack Hennessey sat forward. He looked from Michael Byrnes to his left, out the window, the evening sun on his face. "What time is it, Michael?"

"A little before seven."

"Good, good. Is Matt Malloy here?"

"Yes, sir. I just got back with him."

"Good, good." Jack Hennessey rose next to the chaise, using its arm to steady himself. Now standing, he smoothed his sweater and pants straight with his hands and started toward the bathroom, speaking over his shoulder. "I'll be down in a minute, Michael. You go ahead, keep Matt company." He turned. "Had you met him before?"

"No, sir. This was the first time."

"Okay, okay. Be right down...Oh, Michael." He fixed on Michael Byrnes. "When you picked him up, did you do as I asked?"

"You mean about opening the back door of the car for him?"

"Yes."

"What did he do?"

"He thanked me, then got in front with me."

Jack Hennessey nodded and waved Michael Byrnes downstairs as he started back to the bathroom.

———

Jack Hennessey stepped onto the veranda, turning left toward the door of the screened part of it. He offered at slight wave of the hand and nod to Matt Molloy who sat at the rectangular rattan table with Michael Byrnes. A white ceiling fan hung above, still. They both rose as he let himself in, reaching for Matt Molloy's hand and shaking it firmly.

"Good of you to come, Matt, and so good to see you again." Still holding his hand, he fixed on Matt Molloy's eyes, hazel and clear under reddish eyebrows and a hairline that appeared to be in a decided retreat. He seemed taller than when they last met, maybe a full inch taller than himself now. What ever the measure, thirty-something men don't grow, Jack Hennessey knew. It was the eighty-somethings that shrink. "Here, Matt, have a seat." He nodded to Michael Byrnes. "I guess you two have gotten to know one another?" Jack Hennessey sat down, facing the water and between the two squires.

"Indeed." Matt Molloy took his seat at Jack Hennessey's left. "We're related!"

"You're not serious?" Jack Hennessey sat back, amazed, looking at Michael Byrnes who nodded and then back at Matt Molloy.

"Yes, it's true." Matt Molloy nodded at Michael Byrnes. "Turns out, Michael here's grandmother was my grandfather's first cousin!"

"The hell you say?" Jack Hennessey looked at Michael Byrnes again for confirmation, still amazed, then back at Matt Molloy. "So what does that make you?"

"I wouldn't even want to guess…"

Jack Hennessey laughed. "And how is your lovely wife, Elizabeth?"

"She's fine, fine." Matt Malloy, sat back, fixing on Jack Hennessey, beaming. "She's due in October."

"Well, congratulations!" Jack Hennessey rocked back in his chair, bracing himself off the edge of the table, his arms extended, beaming himself, a fullness coming to his entire body. He nodded at Michael Byrnes, then turned back to Matt Molloy, reaching for his hand. "A fine day, indeed, Matt. I couldn't be happier for you. Please be certain to give Elizabeth my very best wishes."

"Be assured. And I'll be by with a cigar the day it comes."

Michael Byrnes' eyes shifted quickly to Jack Hennessey who paused for only an instant. "Thank you, Matt. That would be very kind of you." He looked away, out on the water, holding a smile. "I'll look forward to it…"

Mrs. Kennedy had a reputation for her crab cakes. There was no secret to them, though, not really. Bay seasoning, a touch of mustard and some mayonnaise, and large, 'make them large and thick,' she'd say, 'being careful in the handling not to crumple the chunks of backfin.' Being so thick meant their broiling would singe the outside to a crust to get the center cooked. This was key. Taking so much backfin to do it right made them dear, and they took a lot of time and patience, too. But with Jack Hennessey paying the bills and giving her all the time she needed to get them done right, there wasn't so much for Mrs. Kennedy to get too proud about.

There was, though, about her Maryland She Crab soup, and in this she took a just pride. Prepared from her own recipe, timing was important here, too, letting it simmer for a full day to give the spices their own time to get into the crab meat and the vegetables. Backing out through the screen door to the veranda, she carried a large tray on which were three bowls of soup along with fresh baked corn muffins and a quarter pound stick of butter. Michael Byrnes rose quickly to open the door to the screen porch. Entering, she reached over Michael Byrnes' chair and placed the tray in the middle of the table. "Gentlemen, the soup is served."

"Thank you, Mrs. Kennedy." Jack Hennessey lifted one of the bowls and rested it on the place mat in front of him, breathing in its vapors. "Yes, indeed, Mrs. Kennedy, what can we say but 'thank you'." He smiled at her. "It can never get better, Mrs. Kennedy, we all appreciate that. Your particular gift, now, is in doing it so perfectly every time."

"That's very kind of you to say, Mr. Hennessey." She worked her hands in her apron. "There's more muffins if you want them. The crab cakes will be out directly."

"Thank you." Jack Hennessey smiled at Mrs. Kennedy as she left through the screen door, Michael Byrnes holding it open for her, he and Matt Molloy thanking her as well.

Jack Hennessey waited for Michael Byrnes to retake his seat before picking up his spoon and tasting his soup, sitting back with his napkin to his lips, savoring it. "Gentlemen, I have misspoken. This is better than any other she's ever done." Spooning their soup, they both nodded as he reached for a corn muffin and, having it in hand, separated the top from the bottom. Cutting a slice of butter, he spread it over the underside of the top portion of the muffin as he cradled it the palm of his left hand. Waiting until the butter had begun to melt, he bit into it, tasting the full, joined sweetness of the hot muffin and the melting butter. He nodded at the muffins. "Gentlemen, it does get better. You must try the muffins while they are still oven warm."

Michael Byrnes and Matt Molloy each reached for a muffin as Jack Hennessey returned to his soup, savoring it still, thinking of the years Mrs. Kennedy had been with him, and the times he had spent on this porch in the near forty years he had lived on the river. A sadness began to build in him as he finished his soup and sat back. His eyes now closed, he breathed in deeply, the bouquet of wisteria at the side of the house and river water bringing memories of times passed and friends gone…

"Mr. Jack! Mr. Jack!"

He opened his eyes, looking up beyond the rail of the veranda to the lawn, and across it came John Riley at a full run, his eyes beaming and his right hand cupped under the gills of the largest rockfish Jack Hennessey had seen this season.

"Mr. Jack! Mr. Jack!" John Riley took the porch steps two at a time and burst through the screen porch door. "Here, Mr. Jack! Here's the one I caught for you!"

Jack Hennessey stood up sharply, his eyes fixed on the rockfish, reaching to take it from John Riley to feel its weight. "By God, John Riley, that's quite a fish. A whole week's fishing done in an afternoon." He looked at Matt Molloy and Michael Byrnes, pointing to the fish. "Have you ever seen such a rockfish around here? Ever?" He turned to John Riley. "How long did it take you to boat him?"

"Fifty yards…" Daddy Riley stepped across the veranda, nodding to Matt Molloy and Michael Byrnes, smiling at Jack Hennessey.

"What do you mean, 'fifty yards'?'

"Well, we was drifting down by the point, you know, just inside the wreck. That's when he struck the bait. By the time we landed him, now, we were outside the wreck, maybe twenty five yards. Sure it dragged us fifty yards or more."

"It pulled your scow? Never heard of such a thing."

"And myself, now, too, Mr. Jack. And it's alright your not believing us, now, too. Sure, if I hadn't seen with my own eyes, I'd never believe it myself, neither."

Michael Byrnes and Matt Molloy were standing now, each having held the fish to test its weight, nodding their amazement all around. Jack Hennessey took it next, holding it out again at arm's length. "There's a problem here, though." They all turned to him, waiting. "Don't see much sense in going to the Bay Saturday for rockfish. There's sure nothing out there that'll top this."

John Riley reached for the fish and then held it behind him, hiding it. "It's not as big as that, Mr. Jack." He looked at Daddy Riley and then back at Jack Hennessey. "Dad caught a rockfish three times as big as this last year. You remember, Daddy Riley. Right?" He looked up at Jack Hennessey. "Three times!"

"Aye. That was a big one, now, and no mistake. Sure, it would have dragged us all the way to Georgetown..."

"Crab cakes coming through, gentleman..." Mrs. Kennedy backed out the front screen door, her tray loaded down with crab cakes, corn on the cob, greens, butter and more muffins. They each stood away, Matt Molloy opening the screen door to the table and holding it for her, then passing her to make room on the table for the corn and the butter dish.

Jack Hennessey turned to Daddy Riley. "I'm afraid you'll have to excuse us for dinner, Mr. Riley." He looked at John Riley and shook his hand. "That's quite a trophy, young man. Get on home now and show it to your mother, and your dad, too. And be sure to tell him about fishing on Saturday."

"Yes, sir. Mr. Jack, sure will." He moved quickly down the steps, the rockfish firmly in hand, turning right for N Street, slowing near the corner for Daddy Riley to catch up.

———————

It was dark by the time Mrs. Kennedy had cleared the table and served the coffee. Michael Byrnes had excused himself for the evening. Ferry landings on the wharf had done for the night with the occasional cabin cruiser making its way up or down the river, broken sounds of talk and music coming across the lawn. They had talked at dinner of many things, of baseball and Gonzaga and the election coming up and Roosevelt, and maybe war in Europe again. While Jack Hennessey had come to treasure Michael Byrnes' company, Matt Malloy this night was a wonder, so grown and on in his life. Though respectful throughout the evening, Jack Hennessey saw in him an independence, a founding on which he was building his life.

Sitting to Jack Hennessey's left, Matt Malloy had just lit a cigarette, now exhaling and watching the smoke waft toward the screen. The lawn and the trees on Sixth Street were bathed in the light of a brilliantly full moon with the temperature and the still of the evening such that Jack Hennessey had no sense of the air about him, of his body as separate from those things about him. 'Is this what it is to be a spirit,' he wondered. No sense of needing a body at all..? Jack Hennessey closed his eyes, his hands resting on his thighs, completely still...A car starting on N Street stirred him. He sat up, looking at Matt Malloy who had just then turned to him, smiling. He reached for Matt

Malloy's arm, gripping it softly. "I'm sick, Matt. Real sick..."

Matt Malloy sat up, away at first then leaning forward, his hand covering Jack Hennessey's. "I...What is it? How sick are..."

Jack Hennessey looked away. "A lot of pain...in the upper chest..."

"Your heart?"

"No, not that." He turned to Matt Malloy. "They took a bunch of tests last week – blood, urine, x-rays. You can imagine. Anyway, we're going back tomorrow morning to get the results." He looked toward the river for a moment and then back. "We're not optimistic, Matt. Michael Byrnes and I have been looking through the Merck. From the tests they took, and the symptoms – chest and back pain, weight loss, skin color – it looks to be pancreatic cancer..."

Matt Malloy drew a quick breath, his shoulders up. "Cancer? God..."

"Yes, His name does come to mind whenever I think about it as well." Jack Hennessey smiled at Matt Malloy. "If it is pancreatic cancer, and some how I know that it is, I've got about three months..."

Matt Molloy's eyes fixed on Jack Hennessey. "Is there anything I can do, Jack?"

Jack Hennessey turned now, a wonderment upon him, a fulfillment of an unexpected dimension. A squire had never addressed him by his first name before and there was a closeness to it that surprised him, and warmed him deeply. He looked at Matt Molloy and could see the compassion in his eyes, the love. "Yes, there is... It's why I've asked you here tonight. There's so much to do, and not much time." He released Matt Molloy's arm and sat back, looking out across the lawn and then back, focused and clear.

"As you know, Eddie Gleason is Hennessey's counsel. He's okay. Knows the law. Gets the *i*'s dotted and the *t*'s crossed, alright. But he's down to one partner now and they're both old. My bet is that he's only got one girl left. It's that slow for him. We can keep him on for contract work, but Hennessey Construction is going to need more than that." He sat forward. "Matt, Paddy Riley could be the best all around construction manager in this city. He's certainly the best I've ever met, bar none, even me. But he's going to have to be more than that if he's going to run Hennessey Construction, and that's coming up now sooner than I was expecting."

Jack Hennessey's eyes fixed hard on Matt Molloy. "We're going all out for the Hecht Warehouse contract." Matt Molloy sat up, nodding. "I've been meeting with Tim Riordan about it. You know Tim?"

"Yes. You introduced me to him when I was a squire. I've seen him around since."

"Good." Jack Hennessey looked away, then quickly back to Matt Molloy. "I should ask, Matt, if any of your clients are looking at the Hecht job…?"

"No." Matt Molloy smiled and nodded. "I would have told you, but thanks for asking, anyway."

Jack Hennessey nodded back, looked out to the river. "Well, Tim's been talking to the boys at the AFL." He turned back. "We're going in on the bid with a commitment to make Hennessey a union shop. With Wagner and the rest of it, unions are on the rise…Hell, what am I talking about. They're on top, now, and there's just no sense in losing good work trying to fight them." Matt Molloy was nodding in a way that said he understood and agreed.

"Paddy Riley, now, well, he's none too happy about all this, as you might imagine." Matt Malloy nodded, smiling. He was the squire the year Paddy Riley punched out Conley on a job site. "I got his word today, though, that he's okay with it. But his heart's not there yet, and he's going to need help get it all down and stick with it. He's amazing, Matt, what he's learned since I made him Vice President. Answered the bell every time I've put something to him. But this is an entirely different world he'll be in and I'm not going to be there to clear the way and show him the ropes, tell him when to duck and when to stand. There's just so much a man can learn about the politics of a thing while he's putting up buildings on time and under budget." He fixed on Matt Molloy, gripped on his forearm again.

"I need you, Matt. I need you to help Paddy think, to be his counsel, to help him through the soft parts of this business, the *NU-ance* of it. What to listen for, how to deal with some of the lying sons a bitches we have in this line of work." He gripped Matt Malloy's forearm more firmly. "I've spent my life building Hennessey Construction and I want to go out knowing that it will continue to thrive. It's how I'm related to so many of my friends and...others. It's more than a company to me, Matt, a business...far more. It's my ground, and I want it kept safe and whole."

Matt Molloy was about to speak but Jack Hennessey raised his hand to stop him. "I don't want an answer now, Matt, no matter what it is. Like I taught, you...Sleep on the big ones. Talk to Elizabeth. Think it through." Matt Molloy nodded, his eyes locked on Jack Hennessey's.

"Another thing. Rather than bringing you on as an employee, it might be better if you set up your own firm with Hennessey Construction as your sole client, on retainer for an amount that would make it work for you. Paddy's going to need you full time for two, maybe three years. After that, well, then you could trail off, build a practice beyond Hennessey." He nodded his head, a short quick one to reassure Matt Malloy that is was good deal for him, that there was nothing to worry about. He sat back.

"And there's something else, too, Matt. I'm going to need a lawyer to take care of some personal affairs. I've let a lot of things slide. Not like me, but, you know, always figured I'd live forever." He smiled at Matt Malloy who smiled back, leaning forward to speak. Jack Hennessey raised his hand to stop him.

"Not tonight, Matt. Think about it. Call me in the morning. You know the number." Jack Hennessey sat back and took a deep breath, exhaling as he turned to Matt Molloy. "It's so good to see you, Matt. So good." He rose from his chair. Matt Molloy rose as well, stepping to the screen door to open it. "Now, let's find Michael and get you home to Elizabeth…"

CHAPTER FOURTEEN
The Wedding Night

"**M**r. Hennessey? Are you alright?" Mrs. Kennedy called from the hall. By her voice, she did not know where he was.

"Yes, Mrs. Kennedy, I'm fine." Jack Hennessey came in from the front porch, closing the screen door behind him, hooking it shut. She could see him now. He nodded to her. "Just fine. And thank you for a wonderful dinner." He stifled a yawn. "Now you get to bed, Mrs. Kennedy. It was a full night."

"Yes, sir, and I will. Good night."

"Good night." He stood in the hall as Mrs. Kennedy turned out the kitchen light and went down to her basement apartment. He waited as his eyes adjusted to the dark, the moonlight now showing on the floor at his feet. To his right was the sitting room. In it was the furniture he and Christine had had in their house on Folger Park, his wedding present to her. He'd had it set in the sitting room on Sixth Street just as it was there, the forms of its chairs and tables and lamps emerging in silhouette against the moonlit windows.

This and all the furniture from their Folger Park house had been put in storage when he moved to *The Cairo*. Friends had been urging him to move from the house. He had resisted. Though he missed Christine deeply, the house had not made him sad. Just the opposite. He felt closer to her in it. She was gone, but part of her was still there in the house, and among their things in it. In time, though, this had lessened. Then, on visiting a friend who lived at *The Cairo*, he looked at a vacant apartment there and, sensing the time had come, he took it. And for the two weeks before the move, he found himself excited about it. As soon as he and the movers had placed the furniture in the sitting room of the apartment, though, he realized his mistake. This was a place where Christine McCarthy Hennessey would never have lived. He had the furniture removed that day to storage. The idea of her things being on the eighth floor of anything was just wrong, stuck above and away from the ground and not part of the greens of a place. No, Christine would never have had it.

Being Irish, now, Jack Hennessey had stuck it out for several years. As it would never have been for her, though, it would never be for him. When he looked at the house on Sixth Street, the first thing he made certain was that the furniture would fit in the sitting room. He wanted that house, but he needed her room in it, as well. As it happened, it did fit, and perfectly so, only the drapes needing alterations and wall paper redone to match.

As in the sitting room on Folger Park, there were no electric lights, only whale oil lamps which had been placed throughout the room. Stepping in from the hall, he struck a match, lifting the globe of the lamp on the table next to his chair and lighting it, as well as three others– one by the settee and two others bracketing the mantle. These last were set before a large mirror extending the full width of the fireplace which had the effect of doubling the illumination of each lamp, bringing the room to a brilliant glow against the dark of the hall and the veranda. He looked about, the coffee table in front of the settee, her silver service centered on it, the portraits on the wall opposite, odd pieces on the tables and the walls, figurines of children and young couples all set against broad striped wallpaper running to a heavy crown molding, matched in style and flourish to the plaster medallion at the center of the ceiling.

Fixing on his chair, his eyes moved from it to the lamp on the table beside it, and then to Christine's chair. Turned slightly toward each other, the chairs were of tufted velvet, burgundy in color, with dark mahogany frames and upholstered arms. It was in these chairs that they would spend their evenings after dinner, reading or talking of the day's happenings. She loved to share what pleased her, and among his dearest memories were those of her reading aloud. It might be from a magazine, or a book of poems, or just the newspaper. The subject or source were of little matter. It was her voice that he treasured, her clear, sharp brogue, more song to him than speech. It brought to everything a new life and value, transporting him to a world he had never seen but somehow had never left. What Christine had done was to make him Irish in a way he had never known before.

And he was never to tire of her favorite limerick, the light it brought her eyes and the sound of her laugh as she finished it, always fresh, always new.

There once were two cats from Kilkenny
Each thought that was one cat too many
So they fought and they fit, and the scratched and they bit
'Til excepting their nails and the tips of their tails
Instead of two cats, there weren't any

He felt himself smile, the sound of her voice and the brightness of her eyes now in the room. Then a thought. There was a mahogany secretary to his left, set against the wall between two tall windows, its desk surface folded up. He fixed on it for a moment then started toward it, slowly and deliberately as if it were alive and he not wanting to startle it. Reaching for the desk surface, he pulled it toward him, lowering it with its braces beneath coming out and meeting it as he rested it upon them. Inside the desk, set square to its front edge, was her picture album. How long it had been since he had last looked at it, he did not know. And it was of no matter. Time seemed gone, as had his body for that moment after dinner with Matt Malloy. There was only now, and the album. He picked it up and went to his chair, sitting down and leaning toward the lamp to capture its full light.

Christine McCarthy was the most organized person Jack Hennessey had ever known. Ever. And she was more neat than she was organized. She had kept the house on Folger Park absolutely spotless. From the day they returned from their honeymoon forward, the only time he ever used the front door was to go out by it, with her, for Sunday mass at St. Peter's, three blocks north on C Street. Even after mass on the same Sunday, on the same sun filled morning, they would return by the alley at the back and the five steps to the porch and kitchen. "Mind your feet, now, Jack," she'd say, no matter the weather or the season.

And as with her house, so with her album. Bound in forest green lambskin, it opened to heavy stock black pages with four photographs each, each centered in its own quarter page. Held by paper brackets at its corners, each photograph had an entry beneath, centered and straight, in white ink and a clear script with the date given. The opening page held four pictures of Christine with the two friends she made on her crossing, Maureen Ryan and Kathleen Shaughnessey. Their broad hats held against the wind at sea, they smiled the bright, expectant smile of the adventurer, beaming at the camera with life boats behind and deck chairs about them, all under a brilliant ocean sun.

They had remained friends in Washington, with both being in the wedding. Serving as Maid of Honor, Maureen was to marry the next year, a dry goods salesman from Michigan to where they soon moved. Kathleen married the year following, an Irish carpenter from Baltimore. He was an average sort of a man with little humor. His life's struggle had been to find work in a city where there were more carpenters than needed, and more Irish than wanted. Jack Hennessey had offered him work in Washington, but he'd have none of it. He had settled in West Baltimore with others from County Mayo and couldn't bring himself to leave it... Some people you can help, some you can't...

Jack Hennessey turned the pages of Christine's first months in Washington, here with friends in front of monuments, now showing off a new hat, at a picnic, the church where she went to mass. Then there came pictures of Christine and him together, at the zoo, on the waterfront, on a day steamer to Mt. Vernon, and always with Maureen and Kathleen. It was to be an Irish courting with never the two of them alone, always with others, and she'd have it no other way.

This was all fine and good until he came to understand the time it would take. The bride's family was to host the wedding and Christine McCarthy was to be wedded and celebrated in a manner befitting her new land. And there was the rub. There being no family nearby, and no father at all, she would pay for it herself, out of what she arrived with and what she could save from her $45 a month. For Jack Hennessey, it was a dilemma from which there was no escape save her thrift and the passage of time.

There were words exchanged, and frustrations vented, but it all came back to the same she had said when it first started. *'Tis bad enough me having no dowry to bring you, Jack Hennessey. But to take your money for my wedding? Well, now, what's to be said of me? And what am I to be thinking of me self? The shame of it! No, Jack Hennessey, it'll be a fine wedding, and I'll be paying for it all, and that's just the way of it.*

Another page turned and there was Tom Brady in his best white suit wearing a straw boater set at an angle on his large head. Christine stood at his right arm and Maureen on his left, his wife beside. It was at the pier at Chesapeake Beach, on the Bay, southeast of Washington by some fifty miles. An early train would get them there by ten in the morning and the late train would have them home by nine that night. Tom had become a good friend over the years, a mentor of sorts and an early investor in Hennessey Construction. Jack Hennessey smiled at the picture of the two them, the same eyes and smile he'd seen in a life time of pictures of those who'd come over, adventurers every one, born in Ireland and come home to America.

Jack Hennessey kept his own counsel on personal things. His yearning for Christine, though, and the pain of the time together lost while she saved to pay for the wedding, well, this was more than he wanted to bear alone. And what's a friend for, especially one of Tom Brady's years and times? "Now, Jack lad, you just don't get to pick and choose all the parts and pieces of a person, certainly not a woman, and sure as stone not an *Irish* woman. They come all bundled together, now, and sure with the Irish there's not much about them likely to be changing, any one of them. She's a strong willed girleen, your Christine, and isn't that why we love them all? It's the Irish in her, Jack, and you can't get that and expect her not to be paying her own way, now, can you? So, know your luck, lad, just get yourself under a good cold shower and make the best of it."

On the next page there was a face he barely recognized, bringing the book close and then at arms length. It was Tim Riordan, here at a St. Peter's picnic on Buzzard Point. He had spoken to Tim, as well.

"You think you got problems," he started. "Try this on for size. I'm an Irish Catholic orphan from *New York, N.Y.,* picked off a train platform by a Jew in Richmond, the capital of the *Confederacy!* Yeah, you remember. Richmond, where there's still a market in Confederate war bonds, for Chrissakes! And that's for just starters. Next, I fall in love with his favorite niece, Esther. She's daughter to an Orthodox Rabbi, you know, the black hat and the curls, maybe singing *Havana Gela* before and after every crap, for all I know. Anyway, the dead worst he's thinking can ever happen to him, his darkest *nightmare*, is that his princess marries a non-orthodox *Jew*, on whom he would spit in a dark room. Yeah, you know. And so what does Esther show up with? An Irish Catholic cripple! Christ, Jack, all you got to do is hang on till Christine saves up a few bucks for a party. Hell, I got to wait until the old man dies or goes blind!"

Jack Hennessey had never laughed as hard in his life. More than anything, though, it cleared his head of the confusion and wants of a marriage. Since the moment their eyes first met, he wanted and needed to be with Christine McCarthy and understood from some deep, primordial part of him that they must be together, and would be. This was not an either or thing. It was an *only* thing. And the time waiting only came to build on this, not only in what he learned of himself, but of her as well. And while he knew Christine would never go back to Ireland, he came to understand as well that she yearned deeply for those she loved there, even though she hardly spoke of them.

What the wait did do was give him time to get done the one thing that would make her life here complete–her mother and her brother at her wedding. But it had to be a surprise. If Jack Hennessey offered it, she'd never take it. If he even broached the idea, she'd have to pay for it and then they would *never* get married. He had gotten the address of Christine's mother in Ireland from Maureen Ryan, and wrote to her directly, stressing the need for complete secrecy. In her first letter back to him, Mrs. McCarthy had balked. She had never left the county of her birth much less Ireland, and had an abiding fear of the water, most especially oceans, certainly what she'd heard and read about them.

Jack Hennessey had reassured her as best he could, writing her brother Liam as well, with a note in each letter from Monsignor Power, pastor at St. Peter's, and on his stationery. He was to be the celebrant. The only thing this got him was the name and address of the pastor of Mrs. McCarthy's parish, that being Tullaroan, west of Kilkenny City. Jack Hennessey 's luck held, though. Monsignor Power had made a practice of returning to Ireland every five years to visit his own family and he would be leaving the following month. As it happened, they lived not two counties from Kilkenny and a tea was arranged with the pastor and Mrs. McCarthy, with Liam attending. This did it for good, and not a word of it to Christine.

He turned another page, here the pictures of the rehearsal dinner. Now this he got to pay for, but even here had to be careful not to out do Christine's reception. The dinner was done at the Congressional Hotel where the reception would be held as well, New Jersey Avenue at Independence, a block west and north of St. Peter's.

Another page turned, scenes now coming to him, the perfect June weather, cool in the long evening, with the rehearsal set for seven and the dinner set at eight. Here a picture of the wedding party outside the church before the rehearsal, faces saved against time and memory, Christine and Maureen speaking, Monsignor Power in his cassock, seeming to beckon them in.

Jack Hennessey had gone ahead, to be at the groom's station by the altar, on the right side of the aisle. The evening sun shone through the stained glass windows behind the altar, bathing the church's pews and columns golden in reds and blues and greens, and yellows, too, soft in the quiet of the near empty church. Those in the wedding party arranged themselves in silence, motioning one to the other to get in line. The bridesmaids were to start, Kathleen Shaughnessy first, then Tom Brady's wife

Helen, now Maureen Ryan as Maid of Honor, and then Tom Brady with Christine at his side, he to give her away.

Squared up like a sergeant major on parade, he'd packed all six foot of himself into his best dark suit, walking Christine up the aisle, her arm in his and her smiling ahead at Jack, glowing, the lights and hues of the sun catching her eyes and hair as she stepped, an easy gait that somehow betrayed an internal excitement. All Jack Hennessey could think of was the waste of another day before they would be together. A whole day more...

As they approached the altar, Monsignor Power stepped forward, making the sign of the cross to bless them, motioning with his arm to Tom where he should stand, taking Christine's arm and moving her to his side, turning her away from the back of the church. He smiled at her, nodding to reassure, then looked up, passed them. "And who gives this woman in marriage?"

Christine looked up at Tom Brady, a hesitant smile from him, and just as he was about to speak a voice boomed from behind her, clear and true.

"I do," it said. "The brother!"

Christine caught her breath, her eyes as wide as Jack Hennessey had ever seen them, fixed straight ahead. Blessing herself in a flash, she turned, and up the aisle came Liam McCarthy, a face on him to light a cathedral, with Mrs. McCarthy at his arm, now breaking from him to Christine.

"Aye!" Christine started toward them. "Aye! You're here! You're here! Jesus, Mary and Joseph, you're here! Sure, 'tis a miracle!" She ran as well and the three closed, one on the other, her voice above theirs, sobs of joy among squeals of delirium, and not a dry eye in the church, Tom Brady near bawling...

Jack Hennessey was crying now, wiping his eyes with his hand, and his hand on his sweater. He breathed in deeply, trying to focus on the pictures, searching through his tears for his favorite among them, finding it two pages ahead. It was of him and Christine, just as the dinner party was breaking up. She had pulled him aside, their last night as only friends. Taken from across the room, she was speaking to him, looking up, the light on her hair, her words coming to him now. 'Tis this how it's to be, then, Jack Hennessey? I love you more than I can love each day, and then each day I love you more again? Is this how it's to be?' She kissed him then, more fully than ever before, her body moving to him, forming perfectly against his, and there was no time, no sound, no light, only each other, and more than that...

An evening air came up, the sheer curtains inside the drapes moving with it, then falling still. The tears had passed. Jack Hennessey closed the album, letting it rest on his lap for a moment before rising. Gripping the arm of the chair for support, he stood up, standing for a moment to get his balance, the album under his right arm. He looked about the room, touching the table next to his chair. He could feel the heat of oil lamp on his hand. "Real," he whispered, "all too real..."

It was all too real. He was back in the sitting room in his house on Sixth Street. The Congressional Hotel was gone, and so was the wedding party, gone in time and place, all but to him, drifting in the memories of his mind.

Jack Hennessey turned to the secretary, stepping carefully to it, returning the album. He set it square against the front edge of the desk, as it had been, then raising the surface of the desk, closing it over. Making his way to the mantle, he lifted on his toes to bring the lamps low enough to blow out the wicks, and so with the lamp by the settee and the one by his chair. Darkness now, all about him. Again he wondered how a spirit felt, if a spirit could feel at all. Reaching out in the darkness, he found the back of his chair, gripping it and moving behind it, more for a place to be than support. He waited as his eyes came to see in the dark, distant lights on the river beyond, the moonlight on the columns of the veranda. Turning to his right, the hall came into focus now and he stepped carefully to it and the stairs, his arms out in front of him.

He gripped the banister and looked up. The hall window at the top of the stairs lighted his way and he began pulling and stepping himself up, visions and scenes of the wedding and Christine rising and falling in his mind. They had spent their wedding night at the hotel. He remembered now…Christine standing on the stairs and throwing her bouquet to the cheers of those below, they kissing to even more cheers and still more as they waved good night and started up the stairs, the men shouting encouragement and the women all giggles and laughing…

Jack Hennessey was at the head of the stairs, now, and turned left toward his room. A light shone from it…as on that night a light had shone from their suite in the darkened corridor of the hotel, lighting an arrangement of flowers on a pedestal marking the room… He started down his hall to his room, his right hand sliding along the plaster wall to guide him…more visions, more memories, her laughing, now, skipping at his side down the hotel corridor like a school girl, holding his hand, then breaking ahead, shouting not to come in until she said so…And now in the hall, again, his hand missing the wall and him reaching toward it to get his bearings. Only a few steps more now to his room…then the sound of her closing the door of the bedroom in the suite, him getting nervous, wondering what was to come, how this was all to happen…

He froze. "Where am I?" Jack Hennessey turned back down the hall, fixed on the window at the head of his stairs. "Here, I'm here," this to himself, shaking his head, reaching back for the wall, his hand on it, the light from his room ahead, only a few steps more… 'Jack Hennessey! Where are you, now, lad?'…His heart now racing, pounding as he stepped toward the doorway to his room…and into the suite, the bedroom door of it closed and him walking to it. 'Are you there, now, Jack? Cat got your tongue, has it' He gripped the knob and turned it slowly, opening the door, and there she was, in the full light of the room, beneath the sheets, her head on the pillow, her hair raven and full against it, framing her face, her eyes glowing, bursting with life.

He stepped into the room, toward the bed, floating maybe, the world gone to wonder. She smiled, her chin up a measure, her eyes sure. 'So, now, Jack Hennessey, you've got your plot on Mt. Olivet, do you? Room for twelve, you say? Well, then, we'd best be getting to it!' She flung back the sheet and before Jack Hennessey lay a vision beyond all expectation and wonder, Christine entire, radiant, beckoning him to her side, her arms out and open, all his life till this moment but a passing second against the stunning brilliance of her presence…

CHAPTER FIFTEEN
Skeets Skilleen

J ack Hennessey began each day with the 6:45 mass at
St. Peter's, and so this Wednesday as well. The
celebrant was new to him but not the liturgy, recited in a
quiet, rhythmic Latin that floated off the altar over the
two dozen worshippers spread among the pews and pillars
of the church. Jack Hennessey sat off the main aisle to the
right, toward the front, with Michael Byrnes in the back.
Each to his own prayers, this morning Jack Hennessey's
being of hope.

There was the ten o'clock appointment with Dr.
Terrance Lynch. And it was here that he would learn his
fate, all but certainly that he had pancreatic cancer, that
eighty-eight years was to be his allotted time. He had
started a rosary, his fingers running across the beads, the
Glory Be's and the Hail Mary's and the Our Father's, but
hadn't finished. It all seemed so flat, a silent chant against
the winds of time and passing. The pain rose briefly, then
fell back, all the more there, though, and not for the
discomfort of it, but the fact of it, the reality that the
cancer was still there, alive and well, and that it would kill
him.

The mass was over with communion done and the
priest gone back to the sacristy. Jack Hennessey sat
motionless, blind to the splendor of the morning light
shining through the rose window facing east on Second
Street at the front of the church. His mind wandered in the
stillness of the place. What would I do with another five
years of life, he wondered, or even ten? More of what he
had already done, that's what he'd do. Sure, more of a
good life would be better, but a life lived free and full for
nearly ninety years, well, that should be enough for any
man. He gripped the back of the pew in front of him with

both hands and felt himself straighten up, his eyes now focused on the altar and frescos before him, brilliant in the sun-driven reds and yellows and greens of the rose window. Never mind five years more or ten. It was the time left that he did have, that's what counted now, and that meant *right now*...

Blessing himself, he rose and stepped into the aisle, genuflecting more carefully than in years past, steadying himself on the end of the pew as he rose. A slight bow toward the altar and a step or two back, he turned and started for the front of the church. He took a deep breath and began to run his day in his mind. There was breakfast at The Rose. This had become a tradition with each squire, a final exam of sorts. It was here that he would ask what the squire had learned in the time spent with him. Then the doctor's appointment. Enough on that already. And then the center of the day, the Mayflower. Yes, the Mayflower. This was where it was to be done. Another deep breath. How would Paddy manage it? Would he rise to this challenge as he had each time in the past?

Looking ahead, Michael Byrnes was at the front door, holding it for him as he spoke to someone just outside. Approaching the door, Jack Hennessey nodded to Michael Byrnes and, raising his hand to shield his eyes in the sunlight, saw Matt Malloy and his wife Elizabeth. "Well, Elizabeth! What a pleasant surprise! And congratulations!" Jack Hennessey took her hand and kissed her on the cheek. "I was so happy to hear of your wonderful news last night. So very happy."

She smiled a thank you, a slight bow of respect.

Jack Hennessey turned to Matt Molloy. "And good morning to you, too, Matt. Glad to see you at mass, and on such a day!" He motioned with his arm at the sky and the risen sun, breathing deeply, his eyes closing for a moment then fixing on Matt Molloy. "So, Matt, you're here...and...?

"...And 'Yes.' He's here to say 'Yes'." Elizabeth spoke quickly, rising a measure and leaning slightly in front of her husband.

Matt Molloy stepped back, catching himself from falling down the front steps of the church. His balance regained, he smiled and held out his hand, taking Jack Hennessey's. "I guess that says it all, Mr. Hennessey." He nodded at his wife. "When I told Elizabeth about it last night, she couldn't believe I didn't take it right away. So I told her about your rule, about sleeping on the big ones before making a decision? Well, she had me up at dawn saying that was all the sleep either one of us needed to say 'yes,' so here we are. And it's YES."

Jack Hennessey turned back to Elizabeth Molloy. "Thank you Elizabeth. You've made me very happy. And I'm so happy about your..." He paused, looking at Matt Molloy and Michael Byrnes for help, but none came. Neither was certain what he wanted to say. She moved to him, up on her toes, and kissed him on the cheek. "God bless you, Jack Hennessey," then turned down the steps, moving quickly to the sidewalk below before turning left toward the Capitol building.

The eyes of all three followed her down and away. Jack Hennessey cleared his throat, looked at Matt Molloy. "Okay. Okay, Matt. You start this morning. Be at the Mayflower Hotel, Town and Country room, 11:30 sharp. I've got Paddy Riley there then, and Tim Riordan at 11:45. It shouldn't take too long, but I want you there. It's important for both of them to know that there'll be no turning back. You being there will reinforce that message." He nodded at Matt Malloy to be certain he understood. "Okay. See you then." He started down the steps, then stopped half way and turned back. "And Matt, from now on, it's 'Jack.' 'Mr. Hennessey' won't work with what I need from you. Do you understand" He waved Michael Byrnes ahead for the car.

"Yes... Jack. I do"

"Good. See you then."

Brady's Irish Rose was on the corner of K Street and First, Northeast. It had been built into the office building Tom Brady had developed in 1896, with the same floor plan as his saloon, facing east on First Street. It had an ornate exterior of cast iron molding about the door and windows, all done in black and forest green with gilt lettering on the windows and signs. Around and above was a commercial building of six stories, finished by Hennessey Construction when the original firm had failed. Both a restaurant and a bar, it was open from breakfast through dinner on weekdays and closed for weekends. The Swampoodle of Tom Brady's early years – the prize fighting and gambling and other entertainments – was long gone. It was a business district now, with lawyers and accountants and lobbyists and bureaucrats filling the offices about, the largest being the Government Printing Office at North Capitol and H Street.

Jack Hennessey had asked Michael Byrnes to make a reservation for two at *The Rose*, the names being Jack Hennessey and Martin O'Connor. It was to be an 8 a.m. breakfast, specifying Table 14. Pulling up on First Street, Michael Byrnes parked the car, waiting for Jack Hennessey to get out before turning off the engine. After Jack Hennessey had stepped out, he turned back. "Why don't you lock this thing up, Michael, and come on in? Have yourself some breakfast."

Michael Byrnes nodded as he leaned over to the passenger side and cranked up the passenger window and locked the door, then doing the same on the driver's side. Getting out, he checked his appearance in his refection on the driver's side window, straightening his tie and brushing his hair back with both hands. Looking up and down the street, he stepped around the car and across the sidewalk into the restaurant, going to Jack Hennessey's side at the *maitre d'* stand. Jack Hennessey turned as the *maitre d'* arrived. "Michael, I'd like you to meet Martin O'Connor." He turned back. "Marty, this is Michael Byrnes."

"Pleased to meet you, Mr. Byrnes." Smiling, he offered his hand and, in a smooth, practiced motion, picked up two menus, wheeled around toward the tables, speaking over his shoulder. "Gentlemen, if you would follow me."

Jack Hennessey stepped aside and let Michael Byrnes go in front. It was a petty thing, but he enjoyed the bewilderment on the face of a squire as he tried to figure out who was having breakfast with whom – a reservation for two, the name of Jack Hennessey's guest being the same as the *maitre d'*, the three of them going to the table…

Having led them to a corner booth, Martin O'Connor laid the menus at each place setting, stepping aside with a slight bow and motioning them in with his arm. "Gentlemen." A brief smile and nod, and he was gone with Michael Byrnes still in front and still trying to figure what was going on. Hesitating only briefly, he moved left and slid into the booth. Jack Hennessey stepped to the right and sat down, fixing on him, smiling. "Well done, Michael. When things look to be going your way, go with them. 'Knowing your luck', that's what Tom Brady called it. 'Knowing your luck'."

The waiter arrived as they checked their menus, Michael Byrnes ordering eggs over with bacon and orange juice, Jack Hennessey having the same. He fixed on Michael Byrnes. "So Michael Byrnes, you're pretty close to the end of this now. Tell me, what have you learned from your 'year before the mast' at Hennessey Construction? Think on it, now. We've got all sorts of time."

The waiter brought two large glasses of orange juice. Michael Byrnes sipped his, carefully returning the glass to the table. "Well, Mr. Hennessey, I've learned a lot. It's been great. I'm just sorry it has to end." He took another sip. "Have you selected this year's squire yet?"

"No, and you haven't answered my question, Michael. So I'll make it harder this time. What is the *single* most important thing you've learned?"

Michael Byrnes sat back in the booth, his hands on the table's edge, staring at them for a minute and then looking up at Jack Hennessey. He sat forward, his head square and up. "I'm going to be a doctor. That's what I've learned."

Jack Hennessey sat back. "Really?"

"Yes, sir."

"That's pretty ambitious." He fixed on Michael Byrnes and sat forward. "And how's all this supposed to happen?"

"I'm not sure yet." Michael Byrnes pressed against the table. "Gonzaga graduates with a "B" average or better can get a half scholarship to Georgetown. I've spoken to Fr. Murphy and he said he could still get that for me. My father's been back at work since January now so I've been able to save most of the money I've earned with you since then. That's a start."

"Well, I know from Mrs. Kennedy how careful you are with your money." Jack Hennessey winked across the table. "She tells me you haven't missed a meal at Sixth Street yet. Moved her budget up a bit." He smiled. "Looks like you knew your luck there." The food arrived and Jack Hennessey picked up his knife and fork. "I'm very happy to hear that your father's back at work, Michael."

"Yes, sir, thank you. It's made all the difference at home, I can tell you that."

Jack Hennessey cut into his eggs and used his knife to break his bacon strips into pieces, scooping up some of egg and bacon on his fork and looking across at Michael Byrnes. "What else did you learn, Michael?" He put the egg and bacon in his mouth, savoring their flavor as he chewed and swallowed.

Michael Byrnes was chewing on a forkful of eggs and bacon. Swallowing, he wiped his mouth with his napkin, studying Jack Hennessey's face for a moment. "Well, it's complicated, but at the same time, it's really pretty simple." He used his knife as a backstop as he maneuvered more egg and bacon on to his fork and looked at Jack Hennessey. "Listening's important, but *who* we each are to be is on each one of us." He put the egg and bacon in his mouth.

Jack Hennessey let the words roll about in his mind for a moment, scooping up another forkful of egg and bacon. "Then we are, what? Separate and alone, each of us?

"No, not at all." Michael Byrnes put the last bit of egg in his mouth followed by half a stick of bacon, washing both down with a final large swallow of orange juice. "That's where it gets complicated. We form ourselves *from* the people we meet and share our lives with." He tapped the surface of the table for emphasis. "It comes down to this: Learning from others to become one's self, one's *own* self. Other people are part of you, you see, but they are *not* you. A person *creates* himself from what he's born with and what he learns from others, and keeps on learning. That's what I learned from you."

Jack Hennessey went still. After a moment, he rested his knife and fork on his plate, his hands finding the edge of the table. "Well, thank you, Michael." He studied Michael Byrnes' face, holding his eyes. "Never thought of it myself, Michael, in just so many words...Never did. But I guess that's what I've been doing all along..."

The waiter approached the table. "Coffee, gentlemen?"

Michael Byrnes looked up and shook his head no. Jack Hennessey turned the cup in front of him up and placed it on its saucer. The waiter filled it and left. Jack Hennessey stirred his coffee for a moment, though he had put neither sugar nor cream in it. He lifted it from the saucer, savoring its aroma, then took a sip. "Well, Michael Byrnes, I'd say you had a pretty good year." Another sip. "Yes, a pretty good year indeed. You know what you want to do with your life, and you've learned how it all works in the bargain. Yes, sir, Mr. Byrnes, I'd say that's quite a year." He smiled at Michael Byrnes and winked. "You know, Michael, a great number of people never, ever get the second part right. Never, not once." Jack Hennessey gave him a wink and a nod. "Good on you, lad." He raised his cup in toast, took a gulp and rose.

Standing next to the table, Jack Hennessey left a tip as Michael Byrnes slid out from the booth. "Thank you for breakfast, Mr. Hennessey."

"Don't mention it, son."

They started for the door, Jack Hennessey slowing to pay the check and Michael Byrnes passing to go to the car. "Wait a minute, Michael. I want to show you something." He took his change and a tooth pick and walked across the waiting area to the bar. *Brady's Irish Rose* was emblazoned in gold leaf on the glass windows in each of the interior swinging doors. He pushed through, motioning Michael Byrnes to follow. The chairs were upside down on their tables to sweep and mop. The bar ran along the wall on their left, the first half of its length bedecked with upside down barstools. The odor of beer and tobacco were heavy in the air–stale and flat.

Jack Hennessey stopped, looking down along the bar to its far end where a door opened out on to K Street. The sunlit brilliance outside put the upturned chairs and barstools in silhouette, a silent chaos of form against the square angles of the windows and doors and sun light beyond. Stepping to his left, Jack Hennessey went behind the bar, walking most of its length, beyond the upturned bar stools. Michael Byrnes kept pace along the bar, on the customer side. Jack Hennessey turned to him, placing both hands on his side of the bar, like a barman might to ask what a customer wanted.

"This is where I started in Washington, Michael." He motioned with his thumb over his right shoulder. "Back there, actually. I was a barback. Worked for leftover food, a cot to sleep on and any loose change I found sweeping up." He shook his head easily. "It was 1864. The Civil War was still on." For the briefest moment his mind flashed back the Monacacy River, bolting across the railroad bridge… "I was sixteen. Just down from Baltimore." He looked around the room, memories of the place racing through his mind – Tom Brady running the book on a prize fight, men pushing and shoving at the bar, shouting and laughing, and all in a darkness that seemed impossible in the light of a day such as this. Impossible.

"It was a Saturday night, late. Maybe two a.m., and jammed. Working men, almost all single, fellas with no place to go but a grate or maybe an alley shanty, or a boarding room for the well to do among them. Then of course the prossies and stupes…"

Michael Byrnes seemed puzzled. Jack Hennessey smiled. "Think about it…"

"Prostitutes…and *stupes*..?"

"That's it, *stupes*, short for 'stupids.' That's what Tom Brady called them. Them too stupid to know they could sell it, or were just too goddam lazy to try."

"Oh…"

"Anyway, Skeets was standing here." Jack Hennessey stepped back, his arms out indicating the space about him. "This was his end of the bar and he'd been at it for more than twenty years." He stepped forward to the bar, his hands returned to its edge. "Sean Skilleen was his real name, over from County Sligo. 'Skeets' came from everything about him – his name, his high pitched voice, his frame...He was so thin, thin as a rail, and a little jumpy, too. But he was all fight when it came to it, all fight and angles. When he punched someone, it was more a stabbing than anything else. One guy said he got splinters from a right jab." Jack Hennessey chuckled, shrugging his shoulders then looking up again. "Skeets had a narrow face and a pointed nose and he was the only person in Washington who treated me above dog for the first year I was here."

Jack Hennessey could see Skeets' face now, teeth yellow and broken, all jammed against one another, squeezing out in front, crossing. His work dress was a black bow tie, tied tight and square against his white collar, and a striped shirt. He wore red suspenders over his shoulders and an apron fixed just above his waist. And bright. In the dark of the bar, his face was always bright. In the chaos of any Saturday night, the room filled with cigar smoke and human vapors, Skeets' smile brought a light to it all. And he loved it. There was something about a busy night that excited him. Though he never drank himself, being the bartender made him part of it all, at the center even, that's where Skeets was. At the center. He knew it didn't work without him. Couldn't. Without the barman, a saloon was a back room full of booze and no way to get to it.

"So, Skeets was here." Jack Hennessey flexed his arms and legs, ready for action. "I was in the back, washing glasses or mugs or getting a case of liquor– whatever. 'BLAM!'" Jack Hennessey slammed his hand on the surface of the bar. "Never in my life had I heard such a sound. Maybe a ten gauge shotgun. Anyway, going off inside a bar, well, it sounded like a cannon. They wanted our attention, Michael, and sure as hell they had it!" Jack Hennessey laughed, took a deep breath. "I could see them from the back as they walked along the bar, from my right to left, back-to-back and large, big fellas, full out with bandannas over their faces, each with a sawed off shot gun. They were cleaning the cash off the bar, motioning with their guns to those at the bar to empty their pockets into a sack the lead man carried.

"Skeets had his hands up. I could see he was looking to do something. When they got to him along the bar, they motioned to the cash drawer. He put his hands down, picked it up off the backbar and emptied it into the sack, then stood back, his hands up again, his eyes fixing on the row of whiskey bottles just beneath the bar's edge. He started to move along with them, his hands up, in small side steps, keeping pace. Neither of them seemed to notice. There was total quiet now, except the girls whimpering and crying against the far wall.

"As the lead man approached the door, out to K Street, he leaned forward, moving faster, opening the distance from the man trailing. Remember, now, the trailer was walking backwards in a room full of hard men with a long night's drinking in them, and they're *stealing their money*. So he's real scared, breathing heavy, twisting and jerking his head around to see where the lead man was, how close. I'll never forget the whites of his eyes in the dark of the place. Never saw a man so scared...

"And now he's reaching back behind him with his free hand to find the lead, but he can't, the distance's opened too far. So, he starts to back up faster, and still can't make contact and this is when he panics, turning away from the bar, toward the door. Skeets sees his chance. In a flash he's up on a quarter keg behind the bar, a full bottle of whiskey in hand, swinging it hard and shattering it across the back of the man's head. Whiskey and blood's everywhere, the man collapsing, then 'BLAM', Skeets flying off the keg and tumbling along behind the bar."

Jack Hennessey closed his eyes, the sounds and scenes of the night racing through his mind. Opening his eyes, he focused on Michael Byrnes. "There was a third man, you see, Michael, covering for the trailer. I'd seen the flash of his gun and vaulted the bar, coming down on him with a hard right just behind his left ear. He went down like a stone, the men about closing quickly on him, kicking and stomping." The sounds of it came back to Jack Hennessey, a hundred men marching out of step, swearing at the downed man, shoving and pushing to get a piece of him, the crushing and glancing sounds of their work boots on the man's head and the floor. "The lead man had made it out the front door. Without a trailer for cover, though, he never had a chance. Three or four shots and that was the end of him, all three dead in not as many minutes. That quick"

Jack Hennessey looked down at the floor boards to his left. "I jumped back over the bar, just here. Skeets was down, not moving. Some of the buckshot went clear through him, dead center of his chest. I got my arms under his shoulders. He was limp, wet all over of his own blood, still warm on my hands as I tried to rouse him. Tom Brady came over, standing close. 'Now don't be bothering poor Skeets, there, Jack lad. He's gone for sure...holes like that in him.'

"I looked up. 'Why? Why'd he do it? Why'd he do it? It wasn't *his* money! It wasn't *his* place! Why'd he do it?' I was shouting, now, lurching up, half standing, half kneeling, holding Skeets.

"Tom Brady leaned over, his hand on my shoulder to settle me down. 'Easy lad, now, easy. Take a blow. Get some air in ya, now.' I closed my eyes, still in shock. It all happened so fast, so fast maybe it didn't happen at all. I opened my eyes, but Skeets' body, broken and bloody, was still there, still warm. I looked up at Tom Brady. "Why...

"He held my shoulder tighter. 'Listen to me, son,' he said, 'you don't got to own something to *own* it, to have a part of it.' He nodded at Skeets' body. 'This was his place, now, Jack, his end of the bar. For twenty and more years he worked it, near every night. Them fellas come in here, putting a gun in his face and stealing his people's money and Skeets, now, well, he wasn't having any of it. So he struck back, he did, killed the one of them, and then the last of them killed him, and that's the end of it. But Skeets died in his own place, Jack, and no mistaking that. This was Skeets' end of the bar. *His place.*' There was a murmuring of *aye's* from those standing about. 'And no man was going to be taking it from him, neither. That's more than can be said for most.' More *ayes*, louder now and longer. 'So, come on, now, Jack lad, give us a hand. Let's get Skeets over to Murphy's parlor where he can rest, poor man..."

Jack Hennessey took a deep breath that stood him full up, his eyes clearing themselves and then focusing on Michael Byrnes. "That's where *I* learned it, Michael, right there." Jack Hennessey pointed at the floor boards at his feet, behind the bar. "That's where *I* learned how it all works. That every man makes his own place, that it's on him to do it, that no one else can do it for him..." He looked down by his feet again, the exact spot where Skeets Skilleen had died now seventy years past. Jack Hennessey raised his head, turning toward the restaurant, starting slowly ahead, his right hand sliding over the surface of the backbar as he walked. "Come along, Michael, we've a doctor to see."

CHAPTER SIXTEEN
At the Mayflower

O f Washington's hotels, none was more grand than *The Mayflower,* filling half a city block on Connecticut Avenue and barely a ten minute walk to the White House. Certainly no other hotel could match its grand promenade, running the full depth of the place from Connecticut Avenue to Seventeenth Street, with ball rooms and restaurants lining its mirrored walls, and an afternoon tea in the reception area. And at the northwest corner of it all was the Town and Country Room, paneled in light stained oak with an outside entrance from the corner of Connecticut and DeSales Street.

Normally, Jack Hennessey would have entered through the main lobby at the head of the promenade, taking the opportunity to enjoy the grandness of the place and the mid-day comings and goings of Washington at work. But not today. The lobby and promenade would be filled with the building trades – contractors large and small, lawyers, labor bosses and those who would be, government officials and developers. It was the spring meeting of the Washington Building Trades Forum with all in attendance hoping to hear of better prospects from the Assistant Secretary of Commerce for Transportation and Construction.

Jack Hennessey had waited just inside the door at Connecticut and DeSales for Michael Byrnes to park the Packard and to join him before taking a table. Laid out in an L shape around the bar, a buffet lunch ran down the middle of the long part of the room, with tables and booths along each side and beyond it. The short part of the room faced on Connecticut Avenue. Michael Byrnes stepped in and Jack Hennessey motioned him to the right, the short part, and followed him over. They arranged five chairs in a tight circle around a coffee table, in the corner away from the Avenue and sat down, Jack Hennessey closest to the corner. Michael Byrnes moved to sit opposite. Jack Hennessey motioned him to the chair at his left. "Here, Michael. Sit here."

Jack Hennessey rested his head on the back of the red leather chair, his mind going back to the morning appointment with Dr. Lynch. It may have been the only time in his life that Jack Hennessey did not have to wait to see a doctor. The appointment was for 10 a.m. and at 10 a.m. they were ushered into the doctor's office. In the circumstances, though, such attention was not reassuring. The knock at the door had startled him, some primordial instinct signaling that a doctor knocking before entering his own office is not likely to have good news. Dr. Lynch stepped in with a file under this arm. His smile seemed practiced and stiff. He nodded a "Gentlemen" as he shook Jack Hennessey's hand and then Michael Byrnes', motioning them to return to their seats in front of his desk.

"Good to see you, Jack." He fixed on Michael Byrnes. "I'm glad you're here, as well. Michael." He stepped behind his desk and laid the file open on its surface as he sat down. Clearing his throat, he picked up the top paper from the file, holding it in both hands at its upper corners. He fixed on it for moment and then up, directly at Jack Hennessey. "Jack, I'm afraid..."

Jack Hennessey was unclear as to much of what followed. What he heard for certain, though, was a door slamming shut. Whether it had shut him out or shut him in was of no consequence. What mattered was that in the snap of a word, *'afraid'*, Jack Hennessey had become alone–completely and utterly alone. A lifetime of others now gone had flashed through his mind and in an instant of time these had all compressed into one thought and one thought only – *not being*. Dr. Lynch's words of controlling pain and providing comfort seeped in and out, but these were of little consequence.

Jack Hennessey was not afraid of pain and he had no expectation of comfort. Nor had he any fear of hell, or any desire to rank among the heavenly minions, the Seraphim and Cherubim, arrayed across an infinite, brilliant horizon in adorational psalm and hymn. No. None of this. What Jack Hennessey struggled with was no longer being – *anywhere*. No longer being *at all*. This was to him incomprehensible, impossible, yet in the same instant overpowering, crushing.

He closed his eyes, now, resting his arms on the arms of the chair of the Town and Country Room, the cool stillness of the place and the bouquet of its potted plants and oak paneling calming him. As his breathing eased, his eyes relaxed, now open and comforted by the brightness of the spring day beyond the curtained windows. The tightness in his chest was gone as well and he could feel that the blood had returned to his hands. He turned to his left. Michael Byrnes was there, looking at him, now smiling. Jack Hennessey reached over and laid his hand on Michael Byrnes' forearm and smiled. "So, Michael, no miracles today, it would seem…"

Michael Byrnes head shook 'no' ever so slightly as his eyes stayed fixed and bright in the dark of the corner.

"I'm glad you're here, son. Glad not to be alone." Looking forward, he rested his head on the back of the chair. "I have to confess to something, though, Michael. I don't remember much of what Dr. Lynch said after 'I'm afraid…'" He turned to Michael Byrnes. "So, Michael, what did I miss?"

"Do you remember how long he said you have?"

"I'm not sure." Jack Hennessey fixed on Michael Byrnes and laughed. "How could I miss *that*, for Chrissake?" He sat back. "So, what does he give me?"

Michael Byrnes cleared his throat and looked down at his hands. "On the outside, six months…but he stressed that wasn't very likely."

"What, then? What can I expect?"

"Two to four months. Anywhere in between."

Jack Hennessey was still, then nodded his head to show he understood. "Anything else?"

Michael Byrnes cleared his throat and sat up. "Sepsis."

Jack Hennessey turned to Michael Byrnes. "Don't like the sound of that…"

"Yes…" Michael Byrnes sat up straighter with his hands in front of him, motioning as he spoke. "It's what some people call *blood poisoning*. What it is, though, is a systemic infection that can come from the organ the cancer attacks. The infection then spreads throughout the whole body by way of the immune system…"

Jack Hennessey looked ahead, nodding.

Michael Byrnes took a deep breath. "If it gets ahead of the body's ability to fight it off it, it causes multiple organ failure. There's a fever with it, sometimes very high, and swelling and redness…" Michael Byrnes lowered his eyes. "Once it gets to that, there's nothing that can be done. The body just shuts down, one organ at a time."

Jack Hennessey turned to Michael Byrnes, fixing hard on him. "You have my complete attention, Michael." He sat up. "How often does this happen? How common is this 'sepsis?'"

"There's no way of predicting who's going to get it. But it's common enough, and…"

"And…?"

"And the older the patient, the greater the risk…"

"I see." Jack Hennessey sat back in his chair. His eyes forward. "Then it could be less than two months…"

"Yes. Once this sets in, and the fever's on, it could be a matter of days."

"Then I wouldn't have died of pancreatic cancer?"

Michael Byrnes sat back a measure. "Yes...I guess you could say that..."

"Well, that's something, anyway." He shrugged. "One hell of a way to beat a cancer, though." He looked at Michael Byrnes and smiled before rocking forward in his chair and rising. "Here's Matt Malloy. Our work begins." He waved Matt Malloy over. "Welcome Matt, have a seat. We're just about to start."

Matt Malloy stepped in briskly, going to the table and taking Jack Hennessey 's hand and then Michael Byrnes', sitting to his left, opposite Jack Hennessey. His arrival brought the attention of the barman who came around and took an order of drinks. Jack Hennessey breathed in deeply and fixed on Matt Malloy, now grown up and a lawyer, one of his first squires–and one of the best. "So, Matt, you ready to go to work?"

"Yes, sir."

"It's 'Jack', now, Matt. You have to get that straight, especially with Tim Riordan around." He motioned at Michael Byrnes who took out a legal size envelope and handed it to Matt Malloy. "This is a letter of understanding between Hennessey Construction and the local president of the AFL. By it, we commit to becoming a union shop if we get the Hecht contract. Take a minute to look it over..." He looked up. "Here's Paddy, now." He checked his pocket watch. "Right on time, every time. That's Paddy." They all rose. "Paddy, over here." He waved Paddy Riley to the corner, stepping away from his chair. "You know Michael Byrnes. Do you remember Matt Malloy."

"Of course." Paddy Riley took Matt Malloy's hand and shook it hard with deep, full pumps. "Good to see you, Matt."

Jack Hennessey motioned them down as the waiter returned with their drinks. "Paddy?"

Paddy Riley looked at the three iced teas and ordered the same as he sat at Jack Hennessey's right hand.

"So, gentleman, here we are." He checked around and spoke in a low voice. "Tim Riordan's due in ten minutes, and he's usually early. So, let's get to it." He looked at Matt Malloy. "What about that letter, Matt. Any issues?"

"No. It's pretty simple. Looks fine"

"Good. Let Paddy have a look at it." The letter was passed and Paddy Riley who began to read it. "I want Tim Riordan to sit between Matt and Paddy. Paddy?"

"Give me a minute." Paddy Riley rose and went to the windows on Connecticut Avenue to read the letter more carefully, then folded it over and gave it back to Matt Malloy and sat down.

Jack Hennessey reached for the letter and put it back in the envelope that Matt Malloy had just handed him. "Any problems with this, Paddy?"

"No." He nodded toward Matt Malloy. "It's pretty simple." He motioned to the letter. "Should you sign it, though, before he gets here?"

Jack Hennessey put the letter in his inside jacket pocket. "I'll do that in front of him. Be more effective that way." He sat forward with his elbows on his knees. "I want this over quick. Tim Riordan's been their point man on this all the way through. But the deal's basically done. All there's left to do is for him to pick up the letter and get it to them." He fixed on Paddy Riley, then Matt. "Tim Riordan and me, well, we go back years, centuries. The boys at the AFL picked him to speak with us because they know I'd never break my word with him. What we have to do today is get him comfortable with my word going beyond me, that this is a deal between them and Hennessey Construction."

He sat back, looking at Paddy Riley as he motioned to Matt Malloy. "Paddy, Hennessey Construction has just changed lawyers. Matt Malloy is our new law firm. We'll give Gleason some technical work and keep him as busy as good sense allows. But Matt Malloy is our lawyer. And he'll be more than just a lawyer, too. He's to be my counsel on legal and related matters. Throwing in with the AFL is going to open a pail of worms of which, I am certain, we have no real appreciation. I want to have as much of the law on our side as possible, and fair warning when it's not." He looked at Paddy Riley who was sitting back in his chair now, his eyes fixed on Jack Hennessey, nodding .

"So, Tim Riordan will sit between Paddy and Matt. I've got the letter here. We'll shake hands around, order him a drink of something then…" Jack Hennessey looked up, and for the first time in this whole enterprise got nervous. Tim Riordan had just entered from DeSales Street and was walking to the table. "Tim, Tim, good to see you." Jack Hennessey rose, with the others following, offering his hand and motioning to the others. "You know Paddy, of course." Paddy Riley smiled and shook hands. "You remember Michael Byrnes, this year's squire." They shook hands, "And this is Matt Malloy." They shook hands. "Matt's our lawyer on labor and related issues…"

Tim Riordan held Matt Malloy's hand more firmly, fixing on Jack Hennessey. "And Gleason…?"

"He'll be getting some contract and transactional work. The usual. But Hennessey and the trade unions? That's not 'usual,' and we want to be certain we get it all right and straight from the start. No surprises, if you take my meaning."

Tim Riordan nodded, fixing back on Matt Malloy for a moment longer before releasing his hand and turning to Jack Hennessey. "Yes. That works with me Jack." He looked back at Matt Malloy and gave his hand another quick shake. "Good to have you on board, Matt. Look forward to working with you."

Jack Hennessey sat down and they each followed his lead. The waiter arrived with Paddy's iced tea and Tim Riordan ordering one for himself.

"So, Tim," Jack Hennessey began. "Here we are." He smiled comfortably and took the envelope from his suit pocket, opening it and taking out the letter. "I think you'll find everything you were looking for…"

Tim Riordan took the letter and rested it on his lap as he put on his reading glasses. Raising the letter to the light, he read over its four paragraphs. Jack Hennessey could see his lips moving as he got to the meat of it, the third paragraph. This was where Hennessey Construction committed to becoming a union shop in the event it is awarded the Hecht Warehouse contract. Tim Riordan needed the language they agreed to word-for-word, no deviations. He took off his reading glasses and returned them to his pocket as he made room for the letter on table, wiping the table surface clean with a paper napkin. "Looks fine to me, Jack. Just two things."

Jack Hennessey had his pen open and ready sign. "*Two* things…?"

"Yeah, your signature, and Paddy's here." He motioned to Paddy Riley, then winked at him. "That a problem for you, Paddy?"

Paddy sat forward, a smile on face. "Not for me." He waited as Jack Hennessey signed the letter then took his pen and signed his name beneath it and looked up. "Did you want Matt, here, down as a witness?"

Tim Riordan held Paddy Riley's eyes for a moment. "Sure. Why not. The more the merrier…"

Paddy Riley handed the pen to Matt Malloy who signed as witness on the lower left corner of the letter and dated it before returning the pen to Jack Hennessey and handing the letter to Tim Riordan.

Jack Hennessey was looking at Paddy Riley in wonderment. Somehow Paddy Riley had managed the exact balance between accommodation and push. Looking to Tim Riordan, he handed over the envelope for the letter. "Well, Tim. Anything else?"

"No, Jack. We're done. It's done." He reached over as he rose, offering his hand. "Congratulations, Jack. You made a good deal here today, for everyone..." He looked at Paddy Riley. "Look forward to working with you, Paddy." He shook Paddy Riley's hand and then the others as he put the envelope in his suit jacket pocket, nodding to them all, a full smile across his face. "Gentlemen, a very good day to you."

They all watched as Tim Riordan left by the DeSales Street door. As the door closed behind him, they looked at each other, smiles around and handshakes too, though with Jack Hennessey's eyes fixed on Paddy Riley alone. He'd answered again, come through. How much more could a man expect or want? Could having a son of his own mean more than this? He couldn't see how.

CHAPTER SEVENTEEN
A New Day

P addy Riley had started this day early with his son John, the two of them to help Daddy Riley haul his scow out at Buzzard Point for its annual caulking and painting. Daddy Riley and John Riley had left Sixth Street Wharf at first light and by 6:30 were pulling up the Anacostia River. Paddy Riley was waiting for them at the launching ramp, ankle deep in the water, his pants legs tucked into his hunting boots. Mud banks at the water's edge stretched to his left and right, coal black and sprouting saw-grass in and off the water, flat and still in the morning calm.

He could hear them now, the sound of their oars working in their locks coming across the water as they turned toward the ramp, the wake of the scow spreading ripples across the river's surface as it approached. Stepping further into the water, he caught the bow of the boat as it glided in, holding it firm. He helped John out by his upper arm, lowering him bare foot to the ramp. They both then steadied the boat for Daddy Riley, hands out to him as he climbed over the side of the scow and found his footing in the shallow water of the ramp.

They had all done this before, Daddy Riley and Paddy Riley since Paddy had known there was a river, and now the three of them since John Riley had turned six. Hardly a word was spoken, each knowing what had to be done and his role in it. Daddy Riley held the bow line as Paddy and John brought the rollers to hand, John placing one under the bow at water's edge. Stepping back, he picked up the second roller as Daddy Riley and Paddy stood each on opposite sides of the boat and began to heave it forward out of the water. The first roller took the weight of the bow with John laying down the second roller as it rode up out of the river, standing ready to place the third roller which he positioned at the bow as the stern came out of the water. Quick stepping aft, he got to the first roller and ran it up to and under the bow, and again, and again until the boat was to the top of the ramp and onto the flat of the landing.

Paddy Riley was breathing heavy, happy for the sweat and work of it as he went to the bow of the boat and, with a grunt and heave, lifted it and the length of the scow from its stern forward, above and clear of the three rollers which John quickly pulled away. Letting the boat down and moving to his left, Paddy Riley positioned himself at the mid-length of the boat with Daddy Riley and John together on the other side of it and away.

Nodding to them, he heaved again, pushing the boat up and onto its side, careful to steady it so that his father and son could catch it safely and lower it to the ground, which they did. The boat was now bottom side up, flat down on the surface of the landing area. Paddy Riley went to the stern, lifting it off the ground as John put one of the rollers under it, and repeated the process at the bow. Standing back, Paddy Riley clapped his hands clean of sand and flecks of paint from the boat, wiping them on the seat of his pants. "Well, Daddy Riley, there she is– high and dry."

"Thank you, son." Daddy Riley looked at John Riley. "And we'll be letting her dry out, now, for a day or three, and back we'll be to check the caulking and whatever else needs tending to…"

Paddy Riley looked over the boat and out onto the river and the rising hills of Capital Heights on the far side of it. Breathing deep, his body seemed to feed on the air of the place, what came out of the living things about him, the saw-grass and the water. He could feel the warmth of the sun on his head and face as he exhaled, the day before him now rising in his mind. There was the final clean up of the Ag site on Independence Avenue to start, then getting home for a shower and change of clothes before meeting Jack Hennessey and Tim Riordan at the Mayflower.

Paddy Riley had been going to the spring Building Trades Forum lunch with Jack Hennessey since he'd been made vice president at Hennessey Construction. Today, though, was different. More than signing the letter for Tim Riordan, there was something about how Jack Hennessey treated him, stood less out in front of him when they stepped down the Promenade, even holding him at the elbow as they walked abreast.

Hennessey Construction had its normal table, front row just off center to the dais. Paddy Riley was normally seated with his back to the dais and facing Jack Hennessey with their guests around. Today, he had been seated next to Jack Hennessey, facing the speakers' podium. And during the 15 minutes before they were all to be seated, the time when much of the meeting and greeting and pointing at each other that happens at such events, Jack Hennessey had excused himself, leaving the Hennessey Construction table and its guests to Paddy Riley's care and keeping.

But more than all this, there was something in him, in Paddy Riley, that had changed, and it wasn't until driving home after the lunch to change clothes that he came to understand it. He remembered Tim Riordan's eyes as he turned from Jack Hennessey and prodded Paddy to sign the letter as well. Paddy Riley had brayed at this inside but kept it there, signing the letter and pushing back by going Tim Riordan one better. By suggesting Matt Malloy sign it as well, he had taken control, and in a way that he had not actually intended. And as these thoughts developed in his mind, he came to realize that Tim Riordan had made Paddy Riley a partner in Hennessey Construction. Yes, a *partner*. Tim Riordan had told the others at the table, Jack Hennessey included, that if Paddy Riley's signature was not on the letter, there was no deal. Jack Hennessey's signature wasn't enough. If Paddy Riley wasn't down and good for it, the deal was off.

Paddy Riley had been at a red light when this came to him and he might have spent the afternoon there had he not been honked ahead by the car behind when the light turned green. And in all this there came a great tumbling in his mind of names and places and organizations, moving in and among one another and at great speed, forces finding new places and taking new shapes and in a flash there came to him an awareness, an appreciation and understanding of the difference between *strength* and *power*. This so affected him that he pulled his car to curb and let it play and settle in his mind.

He had been fighting the unions for as long as he knew what they were. There was something in him that resisted the structure and conformity that a union required.

And Jack Hennessey, too. He had built his company from nothing, from the backroom of a saloon in Swampoodle, and had done it on fair dealing and hard work, his own and that of those who worked for him. He treated others square and up and expected as much from them – his customers and his hands. It had made him successful and the company profitable. Jack Hennessey had fought the unions because he didn't like being told what he should pay his men or how to run his company. And he couldn't have succeeded in this if, at the end of the day, his men weren't with him.

But a new world was coming at Hennessey Construction. Paddy Riley had all the strength a man could have, and of every sort. And so did Jack Hennessey.

The world coming at them, though, the world of the New Deal and the rising of the unions, they were powerless to stop. What Paddy Riley had learned this day was the difference between the strength of an individual and the power of structure and circumstance, the things that determined the destinies of each and all. Strength was one thing. The key to running a company, though, was using and directing the power at play in the game, whose ever it was, to your advantage.

Jack Hennessey was using the power of the union movement to beat his competitors to the Hecht deal. By bringing Hennessey Construction–with its reputation as the most anti-union shop in Washington–on as a union shop, Tim Riordan would force the remaining non-union shops to think about it. And Paddy Riley–who stood second to no man in Washington against the unions – was key in this. His strength as a force against the unions was a *power* that Tim Riordan was using to strengthen the very unions that Paddy Riley had so long opposed. "So, this is how it works…" Paddy Riley spoke these words as he eased back into the traffic on M Street, turning right on Fourth Street. "So, this is the *soft part* Jack's been talking about." He pulled in front of his house and turned off the engine, setting the emergency brake and getting out of the car. "And it looks like I just got my first hit, maybe a double…"

Being in his business suit and wingtips with no mud to track into the house, Paddy Riley entered through the front door, stepping through the hall to the kitchen. Mary Riley was at the sink, cleaning greens for the night's meal. She'd turned at the sound of him coming, a smile coming to her face. "You're home early, in your business suit and tie."

She dried her hands on a dish towel as she stepped to kiss him, he giving a light smack with his right hand to the top of her rump, pulling her close and then letting her go. Standing back, she looked at him. "It's a queer look you have about you, Paddy Riley, with your hands so bold in the afternoon, and maybe the children about. Anything you should be telling me, now?"

Paddy Riley took off his jacket and fitted it over the back of his chair at the kitchen table, fixing on its surface. "You could say that, yes." He looked at her. "Something's up, Mary. Not sure what it is. But it's good, I think."

"You think, now, do you? Well, if it's affected you so, let's all say a prayer that it is..."

He smiled, shrugged his shoulders as he went to the refrigerator and took out the pitcher of lemonade and a tumbler from a cabinet, pouring himself a full glass. Looking at Mary, he raised it in a toast, a smile on his face, and drank the glass empty before filling it again.

"What's this about, now, Paddy? Toasting me with lemonade and all on a Wednesday afternoon?"

He got her a tumbler and sat down, motioning her to her chair as he poured her a glass full. Passing it to her, he nodded, raising his glass and urging her to as well. They clinked their glasses. "To Jack Hennessey!" They clinked their glasses again and each took a drink.

She put her glass down and leaned forward on the table. "Jesus, Mary and Joseph, and all the saints in heaven besides will you be telling me, now, Paddy Riley, what's to come?"

"Well, Mary, unless there's another World War, or Franklin Roosevelt is impeached and run out of town before next Wednesday, we've got the Hecht job..."

"You don't! You don't! You mean you do?" She gave his shoulder a mighty shove. "And why wouldn't you be saying as much when you come in, you big Mick!" They were up and hugging and she doing a quick jig and then a big kiss on the lips for him, but now looking at him again, his smile saying there's more.

"Sit down, Mary. Go on, sit." He sat back down as well, taking her hands. "I told you about the meeting at The Mayflower today…"

"The Forum, yes…"

"No, it was before that. Just before that. With Tim Riordan."

"Jack's mate?"

"The same." Paddy Riley sat back, took a breath. "Jack's been working with Tim and the unions, the AFL…"

"The unions? And what's that about, now?"

"That's how we're getting the Hecht deal. We're going in with them…"

Mary had sat back, her arms stiff out against the table, her green eyes fixed hard at him.

"And what's wrong with that?"

"Nothing, I suppose…" Mary Riley's head was back, her eyes sharp on him. "Maybe it's just that you've been fighting the buggers since you joined Hennessey, and now you're with them. Nothing, I guess, just that my da had to fight their goons off just to get to work! And to keep his pay, all of it…" She stood up, walked to the screen door and back. "Jesus, Mary and Joseph, now, Paddy what's going on?"

Paddy Riley was up now, as well, his hands on the back of his chair, waiting to be sure she'd done. "What's 'going on' is two year's or more work for Hennessey and a step up against every other outfit in the city. That's what's going on." He stood square up, his arms across his chest. "And what's it to you, now, Mary Riley but the work it gets Hennessey and the money in my envelope?"

"What's it to me, is it, now, with your mighty shoulders all gone square and your big arms across your chest? I'll tell you what it's to me–they're *Communists*, that's what! The union people are Communists, every one! Godless is what they are and taking their lead from

Moscow and worse, sure the devil himself! And run by
the Jews, too. They're all in it together, don't you know?
Aye, they are."

"The *Jews*? Jesus Christ, Mary Riley, how'd you
come up that? They're all Micks, for Chrissake! There's
not a Jew in the crowd. Hell, I grew up with most of them,
and a lot of them from St. Dominic's. The list of them
sounds like an Irish wake–O'Halloran and Cassidy, and
that little shit Conley. He's going to be running the outfit
in July! He's from St. Peter's. I played basketball against
him in eighth grade!" He leaned forward on the table,
pumping his thumb at his chest. "'Traitor'. That's what
they call me. 'Paddy Riley, class traitor! Born in
Southwest and too good to be a union man!'"

"And there you go, don't you see. Your own words
saying it…'Class traitor' you said, you did. And who's on
about the classes? The Communists, that's who. Atheists
every one! That's them…"

"So Tim Riordan's a Communist? You're sure about
that are you?"

"Sure, now, he's married to a Jew…"

Paddy's eyes locked on Mary Riley as he rose to his
full height, a step back…

"Mary?" Norah Coughlin came in from the hall, her
hair awry and her eyes avoiding the afternoon sun in from
the porch. Clutching her night clothes at her waist and
chest, she leaned against the refrigerator. "My throat's
gone dry, Mary, dear. Near closed, it is. Can you be
getting me a glass of water?"

Paddy Riley turned to Norah Coughlin as he took his
suit jacket off the chair back, swinging it over his
shoulder. "I'm going upstairs to change, then back on
down to the site." He stepped into the hall, speaking to
Mary Riley over his shoulder. "Go on, now. Fetch your
mother some water…"

CHAPTER EIGHTEEN
Folger Park

J ack Hennessey had held the house on Folger Park. To his thinking, property free of debt was always safer than cash or another man's paper. In time, though, others living in the house he and Christine had shared began to wear on him. In renting it, a house once cherished had become just another thing he owned, another asset, and this had diminished his memories of the place. The sale was all done through agents and lawyers, and had proved a more trying enterprise than he had anticipated. Once done and over, though, it was over and done, and in a month's time forgotten.

Sitting in the front seat of the Packard, on the north side of Folger Park, just east of Second Street, Jack Hennessey looked ahead to the left. One of six homes on Second Street facing east toward the park, the red brick front of the house had been painted yellow with white trim and a bird shell blue door, the colors muted in the shadows of the evening's fading light. Cast iron steps rose from the street above the basement windows and glistened in the lights bracketing the front door. The front sitting room was lit, its windows open. It was done in a deep wine red that set off the gilted frame of a landscape hung over the mantle piece. A woman had just stepped into the room with a tray, speaking to someone out of sight.

"Wait here, please, Michael." Jack Hennessey let himself out of the car and walked around behind it, crossing D Street. Entering the park, he followed a large interior oval path to its west end. Coming to an iron and wooden bench on the oval facing west, he paused, his eyes fixed on the house. He could see a man now, sitting down, the woman nearby. He was reading as she fixed tea or coffee, speaking as she placed a cup on a table at his side. Jack Hennessey's eyes now rose to the bedroom above the sitting room, a hall light giving the open windows definition and showing sheer curtains that hung straight in the still evening air. Reaching for the back of the bench to steady himself, he sat down, his eyes away, staring blankly into the fading light.

It had been an evening like this, in July, though, a full summer's heat on the city. The labor had begun early that afternoon. A midwife, Maura Haggerty, had been engaged and was living in the basement apartment. Over from Kilkenny, she was down from Baltimore where she'd landed some years back. Taking fast to her, Christine had little interest in seeing a doctor. He had pressed her to see Harry Crawford, a third generation Washingtonian on the staff of Providence Hospital, facing on the south side of Folger Park. To ease Jack Hennessey's mind, Christine had met with him at the hospital several times. Being Irish, though, her trust was with Maura and it was Maura who helped her through the start of it.

The baby was to be born in their bedroom and it was to there that Maura had taken Christine as the pains grew harder and closer. Jack Hennessey was with her, holding her hand, wiping her brow, shaking in fear and excitement, her smiles coming through even in the worst of it. "Let me get Harry Crawford, Christine. He's just across the way. I've asked him to be ready. I spoke to him this morning. He's there right now. He can be here in a minute. Please let me get him…"

"Now, Jack, don't' be worrying like you do. 'Tis fine. A good stretch of the legs, so to speak. And I've got my Maura with me." She smiled like a mother might at a child. "'Tis how it's done, now, Jack. Sure, I've seen it a dozen…" She gripped his hand to near breaking it as Maura Haggerty placed a stick of wood across her mouth to bite. Christine arched up in pain, holding it for a moment then down, her eyes away, dazed. Jack

Hennessey cupped her forehead in his hand and looked at Maura Haggerty. She managed a nervous smile as she motioned him to the door and followed him out.

"It's a tough one, now, Mr. Hennessey, that's sure." She spoke in a hushed tone, her hand on his forearm. "But I've seen a lot worse. And she's late to be having her first, now, too, you know. But she's a tough one, your Christine. Why don't you step outside, take a blow. The windows are open. I'll call if you're needed..."

Jack Hennessey's eyes now fixed on the cast iron steps. He remembered having sat there that night, in the evening heat, then standing, then pacing, then looking up and down Second Street, then over to the hospital, but never more than a quick bolt to the stairs if called. Through the open windows above he had heard Christine grit as a pain would come, a deep, guttural moan as it would rise and rise, then fall and the heavy breathing after, Maura speaking to her in Irish, at turns humming or whispering a lullaby. Sitting on the bench, he remembered that his hand had been on the railing and his right foot on the first step, looking up at the room and then over toward Providence Hospital thinking "Jesus Christ in heaven, what am I doing here? Harry Crawford is there, *waiting for me to get him!*" He had just started for the hospital when Christine let out a scream like none before. Bracing himself against a lamppost to break his run, he turned back, his eyes on the bedroom window, Maura now at it. "Mr. Hennessey! Mr. Hennessey! Get your doctor here *now*! As soon as you can!"

He had no memory of running to the hospital, or even finding Harry Crawford. What he did remember was having Harry Crawford's upper arm in his grip as he ran him up Second Street to the house, pushing him up the stairs to the bedroom and inside with his bag. Christine's face was pale against the pillows, her eyes glazed and away. Maura was kneeling at her side, trembling, mumbling in Irish. And then the blood at Christine's middle, bright and red and shocking against the white of the sheets...

Harry Crawford moved quickly between him and the bed, breaking his eyes from the blood and moving him out of the room. "Okay, Jack. Leave it to me, now." He shook him at the shoulder to get his eyes on him. "Jack, listen to me. Get down stairs. I'll be along..."

He had made it down to the hall, his hands trembling on the banister as he went, turning and sitting on a hall bench. He was nauseous, dizzy, a poison seeming to course though his veins, making his skin itch. It was impossible to sit. He stood, looked up the stairs. There were no sounds, nothing to be heard. He paced to the front door and then back to the bench, sitting again, his elbows on his knees, his head bowed, now speaking Hail Marys over and over and over and over...and a hand now at his shoulder, his name spoken.

"Jack..."

He looked up, rising slowly. Harry Crawford's hands reached for Jack Hennessey's shoulders, his eyes telling all.

"I'm sorry, Jack. I'm sorry. The child's lost and...and I'm afraid Christine's slipping by. You'd best go up."

He took the steps two at a time and turned right at the head of the stairs to the bedroom, freezing in mid-step at the door. A comforter covered Christine from chest to the foot of the bed. Maura Haggerty knelt at her side, holding her hand, crying. Christine's eyes were closed. He stepped to her side and reached for her shoulder. "Christine..."

Her eyes opened slowly, searching for him. "Jack? Is that you, now, Jack...?

"I'm here..."

"Aye, Jack." Her voice was weak, a breath taken at near every word. "I'm sorry Jack, I'm so sorry..." She tried to raise her head, turning to him. "I love you, Jack Hennessey, I love...Are you there, Jack? Kiss me, Jack..."

Jack Hennessey bent over and kissed her on the lips. He could feel their warmth and life, her breath on him as her chest fell...she was gone...

"Christine..." Jack Hennessey spoke her name as he sat on the bench in the quiet of Folger Park. He remembered now a loud, roaring sound coming from his chest, from his entire being, as if his very soul was bursting long and full from his body. It was a roar against time and death, against all that there is to hate and fear in the living of a life. For all the fury and the sound of it, though, his most vivid memory was the overpowering awareness of its utter futility. He remembered now the complete emptiness of his being – that he hadn't lost half of him, that he had lost *all* of him. All that he had become was Christine, and she was gone, and in the pain and agony of birthing *life*. There was no reason or sense in any or all of it, just an emptiness without limit or boundary, an infinity of nothingness. All he had become was love, and it had died, and him with it...

Jack Hennessey looked up from the bench. The lights bracketing the front door of the house went out, and those in the sitting room soon after. The light in the bedroom above now went on and the curtains drawn. Jack Hennessey could feel himself breathing as if he had just finished a long walk. He sat back, calmed himself, looking again at the house and the steps where he had waited that night. He remembered now his life in the weeks and months after Christine had died – his life as a walking dead person among the living. There was sensation – taste and smell and touch – but in the complete absence of any sense of being or purpose.

And in time it had come to be more than a nothingness. It had become a physical pain, a place in his mind or brain that had broken or collapsed. "How long did it go on?" He listened to the words he had just spoken in the dark of the evening on Folger Park, wondering how he had he survived it, gotten through. And then he thought of his life since that night, the fullness of it, the friends kept and made, the buildings built and the fish caught and the times he had had. The wonder of it all. "How did that happen? How?" And soon his memories of Ireland came back to him, his journey to Kilkenny, seeing Christine's mother...and the west...

"Mr. Hennessey?" Michael Byrnes was approaching from his right, a silhouette against the street light in the dark of Folger Park. "Are you alright? It's getting pretty late, now..."

Jack Hennessey nodded and motioned with his hand, reaching behind and steadying himself on the back of the bench as he rose. Standing, he looked around the park, then at Providence Hospital, rebuilt and grown, hulking large in shadows and bright lights, an ambulance just pulling in. He surveyed the oval of the park, memories coming now of walking it with Christine in the months before the end, the music of her voice, her hopes of a family of her own, visions of children running and laughing in the sun. He searched his memory for something she might have said, a smile maybe, or the flash of her eyes as she laughed. Turning, he fixed on Michael Byrnes. "Will you walk with me, Michael?"

Michael Byrnes nodded and they started around the oval. Jack Hennessey could hear the pebbles of the path beneath their feet as they walked, the night Christine died coming back. Others living on the park had come out. Their windows had been open and they had heard her cries of pain and then the scream and then silence. Standing in huddled groups of three or four, they murmured in quiet voices, heads bowed and leaning closely to each other. Tom Brady had come by with

Helen. Stunned and crushed to hear of Christine's passing, and the loss of the child, they took Jack Hennessey back to their house for the night. He stayed there through the waking and burying, with Tom staying with him on Folger Park the first night back.

They had come near full circle now. Jack Hennessey took a final look at the house. All the lights were off and in the darkness of the night it stood in the shadows as only one of six in a row on a park in Southeast. He closed his eyes for a moment and thought of Christine asleep in bed, on her side, the softness of her skin, the ease and quiet of her breathing, the perfume of her hair and in this vision understood as never before why he had not married again. Christine McCarthy was to him all beauty and love, complete, his full measure for a lifetime. And if their time was cut short, it was of no matter over his life as it now closed. His time with her had marked the center of his life, living to it before they had met, and from it in the times after she was gone. To have had these years with her, to have loved so deeply and so dearly, had proved enough for a lifetime.

Jack Hennessey's eyes came open and he turned to Michael Byrnes, happy to see his young face in the dark of the night. It brought a comfort to him, and hope. Jack Hennessey started back around the oval toward the car, Michael Byrnes coming along, now beside him. Looking ahead, Jack Hennessey found a lightness to his step and delighted in it as he took Michael Byrnes' arm at the elbow. "Michael, did I ever tell you about the day I met Christine? It was an August noon and hot…"

CHAPTER NINETEEN
Home Coming

I t was raining. The sky had been overcast when they went into the 6:45 at St. Peter's and it was showering as they quick-stepped to the Packard afterwards. By the time they had picked up Matt Malloy at his apartment off North Capitol Street, it was a steady rain with a northeast wind coming up. Jack Hennessey had placed a thick legal file in the back seat of the Packard. He spoke over this shoulder as Michael Byrnes turned right and north on Rhode Island Avenue heading for Route 1 and Baltimore. "Matt, get a look at that file, if you could. We should have time for breakfast in Baltimore and I can give you some background on it then."

Jack Hennessey settled in the front seat, his mind on the day ahead. They were on their way to the law office of Harold K. Larkin, Attorney at Law, partner in *Larkin and Gallagher*, 12 Charles Street, Baltimore, Maryland. Charles Larkin, Esq., the Larkin who had met Mary Mulholland at the dock in 1848 and been her lawyer until her passing, was long gone. Since the early 1900s, Harold Larkin, grandson to Charles, had managed the trust she'd had set up. Looking ahead, the windshield wipers beating time with the Packard as it rolled north on Route 1, Jack Hennessey's mind drifted back to his years in Baltimore and Mary Mulholland, and then his going to Ireland more than forty years ago.

Of all the burdens of Christine's passing, none had been more agonizing than the writing of it to her mother. Rose McCarthy would be opening a letter expecting to read of the birth of a grandchild only to learn that her own daughter had died, and her child with her. Jack Hennessey had thought of going to Ireland then, to tell her in person. But being away from his own at that time, for the weeks it would have taken, was more than he wanted to attempt. So they had exchanged letters and, in each of hers, Rose McCarthy had asked him to come, to speak to her about Christine.

To save his mind after Christine's passing, Jack Hennessey had thrown himself into his work as never before, exhaustion his only remedy against the loneliness and heartache. Working with his crews by day and the accountants and lawyers and agents by night, in ten months he had delivered his entire book of houses to be built. And for all the tragedy of his life at that time, he was free of debt and of land to hold when the Panic of 1893 struck. With time on his hands and no business to get–and his life approaching some new sense of normal– there was no longer a reason not to go, so he had.

———

There had been no real dawn on the day he landed, only a gradual turn from the dark of night to the dark of day. Heavy, low clouds marked the horizon and a misting rain fell as the White Star Line's *Umbria* passed over and through the rolling calm of the Irish Sea. The rain had ended as they approached Cork, with the overcast breaking up as the ship slowed to take on a pilot to guide it north across the harbor near to Lough Mahon and the River Lee. By late afternoon, the sky had cleared bright with sun on the hills beyond and above Cork, all amid a symphony of ship whistles and horns, a band playing a welcome as the ship landed, its passengers at her rails looking and shouting for those come to meet them. For Jack Hennessey, though, there was only the finding of his way to the gangway and his luggage through and around a profusion of welcomers and stevedores, all moving about and among horse drawn carriages making their way on to and off the pier.

It was 8 pm by the time he had registered at Windsor Inn on Front Street, his steamer trunk now secure in his room. Dinner was next, a shepherd's pie good enough to have another of and a beer or two more as well. He felt a comfort to the hotel dining room, the others nodding and smiling at him, the waiter asking if he was 'over from America', seemingly already certain that he was. For someone who had lived his entire life from just north of Baltimore to just south of Washington, he found himself strangely at ease in this foreign land. And it was then that it struck him that it was here, in *this* foreign land, that he had been *born!* This was the place Mary Mulholland had spoke of, of what it was like before the Hunger. He sat back, looked about. These are the people, not here in Cork, but these same by birth, and those in Galway, too.

He paid the bill and stepped outside on Front Street, a purpose now to his stride. All the talk from Lemmon Street as he grew up in Baltimore, and later in Swampoodle, and after that in all his years among Irish, *this* is what they were talking about! This was home, this was *Ireland!* Walking the length of Patrick Street, he came under the hills he'd seen from the ship, closer now, a darker green in the shadows of the evening. He checked his pocket watch, 9:15. Still sunlight in the July of an Irish summer. An excitement rose in him. He had come to see Christine's mother, but there was more now. In all his years of being Irish-American, and all the talk and times of sorrow and yearning, the longing for home, he was here now, in Ireland, *on* it.

He walked the streets and shops and restaurants of the city, the island of Cork in the River Lee and beyond, all till after midnight. The smell of the sea and the ground were full in him, resonating in some way unknown, deep inside. He caught the eyes of others about, they answering with a nod or smile, even the touch of a hat by some. It was by chance a Saturday night and there were people about, after dinner or a play, coming and going, pubs open and singing to be heard. There was a life in Jack Hennessey now, an energy, one he never quite felt before. He sensed it in his step and on his face. Getting back to the hotel, he went to the bar, those there welcoming him, all seeming to know he was 'over from America' which, by their smiles, seemed to be something special to them.

He woke at 6 a.m., the sun already full up. Having brought a travelling case, he now packed it from his steamer trunk for a five day trip. The train ride to Kilkenny was to be the better part of the day, traveling by way of Mallow and Waterford on the sea. The excitement of the night before built stronger in him now, a need growing in him to see more of all of it as he carried his bag to the lobby. Arranging for a carriage to the railroad station, he had breakfast in the hotel dining room. And it was more of the same – warm, quiet faces welcoming him and now a comfort in being with and among them that he found himself already expecting.

There would be train connections to make for Kilkenny, in Mallow and Waterford, but no matter. He had the time for there was none really to mark or to lose, only wonders unrolling before him at every turn. Jack Hennessey was like a child at a three ring circus, every ring of it filled with things new and moving, and somehow not so new at all. Why did the sunlight seem so right to him? What was it about the air? And always the smiles. In his compartment on the trains, at the pub in Waterford where he had lunch, why was it so natural to him? And every where it was the same, from Waterford north to Kilkenny, along the calm and easy valley of the River Nore, the fields stretching west and east up the inclines and slopes of Blackstairs Mountains, worn round by wind and rain, now in differing shades of green as the sun worked around and through high billowing clouds, brilliantly white across a crystal sky.

Hedgerows and cottages marked the fields, and villages, too, some little more than clusters of white cottages with thatched roofs of a gray brown. No people were to be seen, all gone on a July Sunday to the shade of summer glens, aye, nearby a stream with pipers to play for the dancing. The windows of the rail carriages he rode were open, the clacking of steel wheels marking their way through the airs of the ground and that which grew in and on it, and he knew, Jack Hennessey now knew what all the talk back home was about. This was summer in Ireland, under a warming sun and God's own sky, and sure wasn't it grand!

He had booked a room at the Kilford Arms in Kilkinney. With a red-brick and cut limestone façade, it seemed a fitting end to his journey. On his arrival, he sent a message to the McCarthy farm in Tullaroan Parish, alerting them that he had arrived and when to expect him the day following. As he set about unpacking, the purpose of his coming rose in his mind–to comfort Rose McCarthy, to be with her in her mourning and grief, it just now being a full year since Christine had died. The wonders of Ireland, the excitement he had come to since landing in Cork, all this began to fade as he considered what he might say when they met. His clothes put away, Jack Hennessey stood square to the dresser, his eyes fixed on his image in a mirror hung over it, his face frozen and stiff in the shadows of the room, now suddenly shaken by a knock on the door. "Mr. Hennessey, sir. A message for you." Jack Hennessey went to the door and pulled it open.

"Welcome, now, Jack! Welcome to Ireland!"

Before him in the dark of the hallway was the bright smile and brilliant blue of the eyes of Liam McCarthy. Stunned for the briefest instant, seeing only the eyes, the same as Christine's, he steadied himself against the door frame then stepped forward, into Liam McCarthy's open arms, holding him dear. Feelings resisted and held back now these twelve months burst from within and he began to cry, more fully and freely than at any time since Christine had died. Holding Liam McCarthy until the crying had stopped, Jack Hennessey caught his breath, slowly stepping back. Gripping Liam McCarthy at the shoulders, feeling the warmth and comfort of his smile, Jack Hennessey was once again whole, complete, Liam McCarthy's eyes telling him that it was alright, that everything was alright, that, in some unknown way, he had come home.

CHAPTER TWENTY
Breakfast on Charles Street

J ack Hennessey was roused by the stopping and tight turns of the Packard as it entered Baltimore proper and made its way to 12 Charles Street. "Here, on the right...Just there."

Michael Byrnes eased into a parking space across from a corner restaurant, backing it tight against the car behind and then giving a couple of feet back, setting the hand brake and turning off the engine. Jack Hennessey was the first out, stepping around in front of the car and crossing Charles Street, a slight drizzle quickening his step but keeping him sharp as well for anything on the pavement that might be slippery. Holding the door for Michael Byrnes and Matt Malloy, he followed them in, motioning to an open section to the right, taking a corner booth.

"Did you bring that file, Matt."

"Right here." Matt Malloy opened his rain coat and produced the file, laying it on the table before hanging up his rain coat and reaching for Jack Hennessey's to hang up as well. Michael Byrnes had gone in first with Jack Hennessey sliding in opposite Matt Malloy.

"Good morning, gentlemen, and welcome."

There's a way of knowing when a man owns a place, no matter what he might happen to be doing in it at any particular time. And this was the owner, no doubt of it. "Arlene will be your waitress, gentlemen. I'd be happy to take your orders now, though, to get things moving." Jack Hennessey nodded his appreciation for the attention and ordered a cup of coffee with a large orange juice and two eggs over with bacon and potatoes. Michael Byrnes and Matt Malloy nodded the same. "Thank you, gentlemen, and, again, welcome."

Jack Hennessey smiled and turned to Matt Malloy, nodding to the file. "So, Matt, what'd you think about all that?"

Matt Malloy set the file straight in front of him. "Well, on a quick read, there's not really all that much to it."

Jack Hennessey nodded for him to go on.

"Well, there's a house on Lemmon Street. It's been rented to the same family for 18 years and brings in $35 a month and looks to cost about $20 a month, full cost, to keep. Next, there's the orphanage, the Mary Mulholland Home for Boys." Matt Malloy looked up as if to ask who Mary Mulholland was, but Jack Hennessey motioned him on. "It's fully owned by the trust, free of debt, and leased to St. Peter the Apostle Catholic Church for $1 a year. Then there's the account with *Alex Brown*. As of March 31, the balance was $138,000, give or take, in cash and securities. That's about it."

Jack Hennessey nodded. "Is there an appraisal of the orphanage building there?"

"Yes. Done in February. They have it at $73,500, building and property."

"And the house on Lemmon Street? Is there an appraisal for that?"

Matt Malloy opened the file and thumbed through its contents, stopping about a third of the way through. "Here." He passed the paper to Jack Hennessey. "They have it down at $2,400."

Jack Hennessey examined the appraisal, checking the address, noting the particulars – two floors plus a basement, two rooms on the main floor, two on the second, a back garden, water but no indoor toilet. He thought of the inside of the house, the kitchen made into Mary Mulholland's room for her last days, the wake and then leaving it.

The coffee and juice arrived, they each sipping and sweetening to their likes.

Jack Hennessey reached over for the file and opened it in front of him. The papers of the original trust were there, frayed at the edges, all gone yellow. Then the deeds and accounts from Alex Brown, year upon year of them, up and down over time, but always well managed and growing. He looked up at Matt Malloy. "Okay, Matt, here's what I need."

Matt Malloy opened his portfolio and readied to write.

"As you saw, the trust expires on my passing." He could see that Matt Malloy fought the urge to look up, his pen more tightly gripped, Michael Byrnes freezing in mid-sip of his coffee. "I have the power of designation." He looked at Michael Byrnes. "That means that I can direct the assets of the trust in any way I like, provided I do it before I die. Right Matt?"

"That's the law."

"So, here's what. I want the house of Lemmon Street sold. See if there's some way to sell it to the people in it. Make it easy for them. Maybe move the monthly up another ten dollars and roll it into a ten year mortgage. Make it work, if you can." Matt Malloy nodded as he wrote.

"Next, I want the orphanage building deeded over to St. Peter's parish. Next..." Jack Hennessey sat back and turned to Michael Byrnes. "Christ, Michael, I'm sorry. I'm going to have to ask you to excuse us for a minute. It'll be only be that, but I need to speak with Matt in private. I should have thought of this before we all sat down. I apologize..."

Matt Malloy was already making way for Michael Byrnes. "No problem, Mr. Hennessey. I'll just eat at the counter..."

"No, Michael, no. I want you near, to eat with us. This'll just take a minute…"

Jack Hennessey watched Michael Byrnes go to the lunch counter, then turned to Matt Malloy. "I want you to move $50,000 from that *Alex Brown* account into a new trust you'll be setting up in Washington, *The Gonzaga Squires Trust.* I want you to get started on that this afternoon when we get back. There's no time to lose on that. That's your first priority. Understood?"

Matt Malloy nodded, again, his head down and his right hand writing across the legal pad.

"I want Fr. Murphy at Gonzaga and you to be the Trustees. Be sure to tell Harold Larkin about it today. There can be no delays. He's one of the trustees on the Jack Mulholland Trust. The other is Fr. Father Seaton Fitzhugh. He's new to the parish. I've spoken to him several times on the phone. Haven't met him in person yet. We can assume, of course, that he's not going to like $50,000 coming out of the trust. They use its income to keep the orphanage going." Jack Hennessey paused, a smile coming to his face. "Looks like he's just going to have to raise more money…a specialty of his, I'm told. So, let's play it safe. Let's get him down on the $50,000 to the Squires before you deed over the orphanage." Jack Hennessey tapped the surface of the table for emphasis with Matt Malloy nodding his head to reassure. "Alright? Any questions on that part of it?

"No, Jack. Like I said, it's not too complicated."

"Okay, now for the remainder of Jack Mulholland Trust. That's to go into a new trust for the sole benefit of the orphanage, not the parish. I want to be clear on that. They're separate." Matt Malloy nodded. "Put the proceeds of the house on Lemmon Street in that, as well. That money's to be used to support the orphanage in any way the trustees deem proper. And on that, I want you made a trustee, so there'll be three of you – you, Harold

Larkin and Fitzmaurice, or whatever his name is. The pastor." He looked down at Matt Malloy's notes. "You got all that?"

"Yup." Matt Malloy looked up, screwing the top back on his pen. "Monday, close of business. Very doable."

Jack Hennessey reached over and patted his forearm as he waved to Michael Byrnes back to the table, the waiter coming with the food at the same time.

Settling back around the table, they began to eat, the cutting of bacon and eggs marking the silence of the booth as they drank their orange juice and chewed their food, passing butter and jam among themselves. Jack Hennessey finished first, removing his napkin from his collar. Looking over, he signaled to the waiter for more coffee and sat back, fixing on Michael Byrnes. "Sorry, Michael, about having to ask you to leave the table. I generally plan ahead better than that."

Michael Byrnes nodded, managing a smile as he chewed the last of his toasted bread and jam.

Jack Hennessey now fixed on Matt Malloy. "So, Matt, who's Mary Mulholland, I'm sure you're wondering?" He sat forward sipped his coffee, looked at Michael Byrnes and then at his coffee. "Well, first off, she saved my life. Got me out of Ireland in '48 when most everyone in the west who didn't get out got dead. Then she made me an American, legally, that is." A sip of coffee and a smile, fixing on Matt Malloy. "I was less than week old when she took me out of Ireland, so when she landed here, it wasn't too much of a stretch to tell to the priest that baptized me that I was born on the boat coming over. When a person's born at sea, that person is natural born to the first landfall after birth. He did the Certificate of Baptism that way, and that's all there was to it."

Matt Malloy was staring at him. Closing his portfolio, he sat back, his coffee cup in hand, now sipping at it.

"So who, then, is Jack Mulholland in all this?" Jack Hennessey motioned to the file as he looked over at Michael Byrnes. "This file is all about a trust Mary Mulholland set up for her 'son,' Jack Mulholland." Now at both of them. "Well, of course, that's me. I wasn't her blood son, you'll understand, but she raised me as if I were and I used that name until I was 16 years old. When she died, she left what she had to me, in a trust." He nodded to files. "The Jack Mulholland Trust." He shifted in his seat and out of the booth, standing beside it. "For reasons we needn't go into here, I left Baltimore just after she died and took the name of my birth mother, Hennessey, and have used it ever since."

Jack Hennessey checked his watch. "Matt, you and I have to get up to Lawyer Larkin's office right now. Michael, you stand by the car. I'm just going to introduce Matt here to Harold Larkin, sign a power of attorney, and come back on down. You and I are going to West Baltimore to see a priest."

CHAPTER TWENTY ONE
The House on Lemmon Street

I t had stopped raining by the time Michael Byrnes had the Packard heading west on Pratt Street. Turning right on Parkin Street for several blocks to a left on Hollins, Jack Hennessey had him pull over on the right at the Rectory of St. Peter the Apostle Church. Getting out of the car, Jack Hennessey had just started for the steps of the Rectory when the door opened. Stepping out, his head back to welcome the day, his arms extended, Fr. Seton Fitzhugh presented himself, all six foot two and three hundred pounds of him, his Franciscan habit flowing gracefully with each step as he came down to the sidewalk.

"Good morning, Mr. Hennessey." A smile and pause. "May I call you Jack? All whom we know in common do?"

Jack Hennessey nodded. "By all means, father…"

"Yes, thank you. A pleasant journey, I trust?" He offered his hand.

Jack Hennessey shook the priest's hand, a bit too fleshy for his liking. Smiling, he opened the back door of the Packard, motioning the priest in, noting the dip in the car as it received the bulk of him as he settled his weight in the rear seat. Stepping around behind the car and getting in on the street side, Jack Hennessey tapped Michael Byrnes on the shoulder. "Take a left at the corner, Michael, then three blocks to a right on Lemmon Street. You can pull over near the corner." Jack Hennessey sat back, looked at Fr. Fitzhugh. "So, father, how's the church business?"

"Well, enough, Jack well, enough." He looked across at Jack Hennessey, a broad, practiced smile, then ahead. "We all suffer the times, as you know, as we must. But we manage, we manage. I must say, though, I don't know what we would do without your orphanage. As over crowded as it is, Jack, we would be desperate without it. Desperate..."

Jack Hennessey wondered if he had yet heard three sentences in a row from Fr. Seton Fitzhugh that did not include some sense of need, and Jack Hennessey's obligation to meet it, to *give*. This seemed especially to occur when Fr. Fitzhugh was speaking of what Jack Hennessey had already given. The operative word clearly, the command from on high, was *to give*. "Yes, well it's nice to be able help, father, as we can." Jack Hennessey fixed ahead.

Poppleton Street unfolded before them, freshly paved in asphalt. Jack Hennessey remembered it with a macadam surface, the residue of burnt coal from B&O steam engines, crushed to pebble size and spread thick over a hard packed dirt surface. He looked at the houses, brick fronts some of them, the rest wood, all needing paint at the trim or their clapboard sides. He tried to remember who lived where, and when he had last seen them. He had left Baltimore the night after the day of his mother's funeral, and had not returned until 1893, almost 30 years later. In this time, most of those he knew had left – east or west, north or south, heaven or hell, who's to know? Michael Byrnes turned right on Lemmon and pulled to a stop, looking in the rearview mirror for instructions. "That's fine, Michael. Give us a minute, will you?"

Michael Byrnes turned the engine off and set the hand brake before letting himself out of the car. Jack Hennessey watched as he stepped around the front of the car to the sidewalk, sitting back against the right front fender. He turned to Fr. Fitzhugh. "I have bad news, father." He paused to give Fr. Fitzhugh's mind time run the possibilities, and the perspectives, such as for whom was the news bad. "I'm dying, father. Pancreatic cancer."

Fr. Fitzhugh blanched, drew back, his hand to his mouth. "This is impossible...What's to be done, dear Jack? Is there no hope?"

"None, I'm afraid." Jack Hennessey looked front, in the direction of 934 Lemmon Street. "You've called ahead on this? It's alright? You're sure?"

"Yes, yes. Certainly alright. They wanted to meet you, as well. I'm afraid, though, Mr. Curley is not available. At work, you'll understand. But, Jack, dear Jack..."

"And how are they, the Curleys? Good people?"

Fr. Fitzhugh turned from Jack Hennessey in the direction of 934 Lemmon Street. "Oh, the best, the best. Salt of the earth. He's with the railroad, you'll understand. Thirty years and more." Fr. Seton Fitzhugh looked at Jack Hennessey. "Very loyal. Temperate of thirst and word. A model parishioner. And she, as well. Raised their four children, three boys and girl, all gone now to good lives about the city. Good working stock, Jack, the lot of them." He put his hand on Jack Hennessey's knee. "But is there anything I can do for you, Jack."

"Yes, there is." Jack Hennessey's eyes fixed ahead. "You can pray for me."

"Be assured, Jack..."

Jack Hennessey opened the door. This alerted Michael Byrnes who stepped back quickly to open the door for Fr. Fitzhugh. Jack Hennessey walked down the middle of the empty street, its cobblestones familiar under his feet. The names of those in these houses he knew. McGann. O'Brien. Dowd. And then the McAllisters, a bad bunch they were. Nothing but noise and trouble. Coming to 934, he turned to the house, looking up, the brick front, the steps, remembering Mary Mulholland's telling the story of when she first saw it, the day off the boat with Charles Larkin at her side.

It was the face of Mrs. O'Connell she spoke of with a particular bite. "Narrow, now it was, with squinty eyes and a pinched mouth, her nose in the air at us. 'Fresh off the boat and smelling for all of it.' I could see those words in her face, shrill that she was. Well," Mary Mulholland would say, "she died in Ohio, poor and alone, her husband no doubt happy for the grace of an early grave, a three year head start on her in paradise!" Mary Mulholland laughed every time she told of it, the laugh now ringing in Jack Hennessey's ears.

Waiting for Fr. Fitzhugh to get out of the car and to the front of the house, Jack Hennessey motioned to him to knock on the front door.

Raising up to his full height on the first step of the stoop, Fr. Fitzhugh knocked sharply on the door, which opened, it seemed, just as the last knock landed, a crack only at first, then wide. Mrs. Patrick Curley stepped forward, short, not much above five feet, wearing a house dress and apron, her hands working it, a nervous smile on her face.

"Good morning to you, Mrs. Curley, and so good it is of you to be in." Fr. Fitzhugh turned toward Jack Hennessey, his arm out as to present him, then his eyes back on her. "May I present Mr. Jack Hennessey, of Washington. Your landlord. As we discussed last week, Mrs. Curley, Mr. Hennessey wishes to inspect his property."

Jack Hennessey stepped forward. "Visit,' Mrs. Curley. I wish to visit your home." He shook her hand. "And it's kind of you to have us." He stood back and looked at the front of the house then its doorway and inside. "I lived here some years ago. Just wanted to get a look at it, to refresh some old memories."

Mrs. Curley curtsied as she shook his offered hand then backed away for him to pass.

Small. That was what came first to Jack Hennessey's mind. How *small* it was. He had not been inside since the night he left, more than seventy years ago. The front room had a short sofa and two chairs separated by a *Philco* radio, its speaker in a wooden veneer cabinet beneath the tuning dial. The kitchen had a square table with a sink across the back, all beneath a window. A door to the left led to the back garden. He stepped to the door. It was held open by a hook, the morning air passing through the house. Beyond the door was a patch of grass, fenced in and leading to the alley, the outhouse on the left of the path, a flat, dark green with white trim.

Turning inside, he looked at the stairs, then at Mrs. Curley. "Yes, Mr. Hennessey, please, go up if you like." He nodded, turning to the stairs and mounting them, carefully in the dark of the place, the narrow steps not deep enough for the full length of his foot. Half way up, there was a landing with a shelf on the wall holding a statute of the Blessed Virgin and a votive candle before it. Mary Mulholland had kept a vase there for flowers that she kept fresh according to the growing season. He turned up toward the second floor, taking the seven steps to reach it. Mary Mulholland's room was on this right, his own room to the left.

Stepping to the doorway on his right, he entered the room, remembering the letter he had found, learning the name of the parish Mary Mulholland had left from for America, and what had become of Bridget Hennessey and her other children. The windows were open, street sounds outside, children talking. He closed his eyes and searched for Mary Mulholland in his mind, their last good-bye, she in her bed and him off Monacacy Junction, now listening in his mind and memory for her laugh…

As the bright of her eyes flashed before him he felt faint, his heart racing, his breath short. Reaching for the post at the foot of Mrs. Curley's bed, he steadied himself, stepping to it to hold his weight and balance, his hands going cold. Standing erect, he fought for a deep breath and found one and then another, his heart calming now.

Recovered, he looked at the bed, considered sitting down but he found the closeness of the room increasingly uncomfortable. He wanted to be outside, needed to be outside. In small, measured steps, he started for the door, reaching for the frame of it as he turned toward the stairs, starting down in careful steps, each foot secure before the next step taken. At the landing, he held his arms out, steadying himself against each wall, easing himself through the turn, his eyes coming to fix on the far corner of the kitchen. He stopped. It was here where they had bedded Mary Mulholland when she was dying. His mind went back to it now, her cuddled in the corner of it, away from him, telling of taking him from Bridget Hennessey and coming to America...

Bracing himself against the narrow walls of the stairway, he got to the bottom of the stairs and then back out the front door and down the steps. On the sidewalk, he gripped the handrail and breathed deeply several times more, finding his balance.

"Are you alright, Mr. Hennessey?" It was Mrs. Curley, anxious for his answer and, by her look, afraid for his health. He reached for her hand, taking it firmly to show her he was alright. "I'm fine Mrs. Curley, just fine, and all the better for your kindness in letting me visit your home."

She curtsied again as the Packard drew up. Michael Byrnes had sensed he was struggling and brought the car up closer, jumping out. Reaching for Jack Hennessey's upper arm, he opened the front door and helped him in. "Are you aright, Mr. Hennessey?"

"I'm fine, Michael, fine." Jack Hennessey sat in the front seat, his head resting back, his eyes closed. "Let's get back to Charles Street for Matt, then home..."

Michael Byrnes quick-stepped around the front of the car and got in, shifting into first gear. Looking left down Lemmon Street to check for traffic, he spoke under his breath. "What about Fr. Fitzhugh, Mr. Hennessey? Do we want to just leave him here?"

"Sure, why not? He could use a good walk by the look of him..."

CHAPTER TWENTY TWO
The Hunger

M ichael Byrnes wheeled the Packard through West Baltimore to Route 1 and south on it to Washington. Exhausted, Jack Hennessey had moved to the back, alone, hoping to get a nap, but it was not to be. His mind ran from point to point, year to year, place to place – the Trust, Mary Mulholland's room, the letter, now Swampoodle and Monacacy Junction, Fr. McColgan, Tom Brady, Skeets Skilleen... He closed his eyes, worked to focus, to slow things down. What was it this morning, on the way north? What was he thinking of? *Kilkenny.* Yes, the *Kilford Arms* and Liam McCarthy...his eyes...

He and Liam McCarthy had had dinner that night, talking of the wedding and the month that Liam McCarthy and his mother Rose had spent in Washington after it, memories of the heat of the place, the wonder to Christine of her two worlds at one. The ride out to Tullaroan began at six the next morning, Liam McCarthy guiding his pony and trap west. Its large wheels moved easily across the dry roads, farms closer now, the smell of them heavy in the morning air, the sounds of roosters, and of horses braying with birds above and about. And the weather, moving quickly, a brilliant sun now to a fleeting rain then overcast and back to a clear sky broken wide by bright white clouds.

"'Tis here, now, Jack." Liam McCarthy turned the trap off the road, onto a path dipping down through a grove of trees and out across open fields, rising and falling before them, grain growing yellow under the sun to hills rising on either side. "It's been a good grow, Jack, this year. Grain and oats. If the weather holds true, 'tis another good year we'll be having..."

Jack Hennessey struggled to remember the particulars of the day, so long ago. Rose McCarthy and her sister Naola were in front of the cottage as they pulled up in the trap, two farm hands stopping their work, smiling, coming by. Rose embraced him, holding him close, her head resting against his front, patting his chest, saying softly Christine's name, then her smile and the welcome...

What then? Lunch? What time was it? Forty years and more gone it was...a walk-about the farm, Christine's room, kept as it was the day she'd left, her things on the dresser, not moved the aunt said, not touched, the window open and the air in. And then the 'sit'. By a tree off the house, a place alone, Liam now gone to his work and the others to theirs. It was afternoon. Yes, Rose McCarthy looking at him, now, smiling as a mother at her child. "She's in you, now, you know, Jack Hennessey. Aye, my Christine is. She's in you and you've brought her home, you have. Home to her ma."

He could see the sadness in her eyes, the longing. "I'm so sorry, Rose. I should've..."

"Ach!" Her hand waved him silent. "Not a word of it, now, Jack Hennessey, not a word." Her head came up, turning to some sound unheard by him in the fields beyond, then back at him. "She's gone and that's done. And what a life she had, now, Jack! From here to Dublin and back. Come home to be with her da as he passed, she did." Rose McCarthy looked at him, then away again, the softest of smiles now to her face.

"As much as I loved that girl, and God's word I did, there was something, now, between her and her da that was well past it...so special it was. To see his eyes when they fell on her...Aye, a joy to me I'll be holding dear, never to lose. And when he passed, sure it was that she'd be moving on. A farm's no place for such as she." Rose McCarthy looked at him, her eyes sharp and clear, alive.

"And to America! Aye, to see her there Jack, to see her with you and your fine friends and the good father and your house so grand. Well, there's a special joy in a mother's heart to see one of her own come to the place she's meant to be." Her eyes closed now, her breathing soft, like in a prayer, then at him.

"And you brought her back today, Jack, you did. So they're both here, don't you see? Christine and her da? Aye, it's been so long, so long." She was quiet now. He knew not to speak, that he wasn't even really there to her. By-and-by the air came up and Rose McCarthy's head lifted to it, breathing in deeply, drawing her head toward the fields, then back at him. "Thank you, Jack Hennessey, for coming. For being with us for a bit."

Rose McCarthy stood from her stool and, as she turned to the cottage, he caught the line of Christine in her shoulders and back, a grace to her step. She smiled. "Would you be liking a drink of water, now, Jack, with the sun coming full on us, now?"

It was Christine's smile that he now saw in her, bright and open. He nodded a 'yes' as she went to the well. Breathing deep, it was as the day before at breakfast, on the train, in the stations, a foreign land so natural to him. Even the sound of the pulley Rose McCarthy worked to draw the water from the well, even this he seemed to have heard before. He watched her come back, her hair up and a full dress with a dark apron across the front, bits of leaves and twigs on it from the work she'd been doing when they'd come. She smiled as she sat down next to him at the table, handing him a metal cup filled with water.

He smiled a thank you and sipped, struck by the cool of it, and a sweetness in its taste, too, looking at her. " Rose, that's wonderful. Delicious!" He looked at the cup. "What's in it?"

"Well, you saw for yourself, now, didn't you? It come out of the well and to the table. Not a thing added! 'Kilkenny water's what we call it, and glad we are for the taste of it!" She looked over the table and across the fields. "If it's all the same to you, now, Jack, you'll be staying here, with us in Tullaroan. You will, now, won't you?" She looked at him. "We've plenty of room. You can stay in Christine's room if you like...I wish you would." She turned to him, her eyes offering and asking at he same time.

"Well, that's kind of you Rose, but..."

"Now don't you be worrying about the *Kilford Arms*. Liam's already paid them off the week you've signed with them. You'll stay with us, now, Jack?"

And stay he did, for a week or more. It all coming so clear to him now as the Packard rolled south toward Washington. He'd slept in the first day, a man at his leisure. But as he watched the men work about the farm and Liam doing this and doing that, he came to join them, working the fields and the animals, breaking a sweat, ducking under a tree against a passing shower, breathing in what come up from the ground, even so that it was part of him. The wonder of it all! High summer in the fields and glens and greens of Ireland. But there was more to see in Ireland than Tullaroan and Rose McCarthy, and her son Liam. There was Athenry.

When he had told Fr. Power at St. Peters that he was going to Ireland to see the McCarthys, there was great joy in the priest's face. 'Tis time,' he'd said. 'Time to see Rose and be with her for a bit. And you'll be going to your own place, then, too, Jack? Galway, was it?' 'No,' he'd said, he hadn't thought of it. 'Well, you have to now, don't you? To go all that way and never see where you're from, now, what's the sense in that?'

It was at dinner that they had spoken. Fr. Power knew from the paper work and licensing for the wedding that

Jack Hennessey had come over as Jack Mulholland. The baptism certificate had him as Mulholland and everything he was in Washington was Hennessey. It had taken some doing, but his name was changed proper in all the places the law and the church required. In the process, though, he'd told the priest of his years in Baltimore and the reasons for leaving it. 'Tend to that' the priest had said. 'There's a part of you, Jack, that's not right, not right at all. The woman who raised you, now, Jack, the one you took for mother for 16 years? Ach! A tear in yourself, that's what it is, Jack, and only you can mend it. Won't do, now, Jack, to let that lay…'

The letter in Mary Mulholland's room had the parish she had come from, *Athenry*, County Galway. It was large enough, Fr. Power guessed, to have records back, baptisms and weddings and the passing of those in the parish. And it was at dinner that Jack Hennessey had told Rose and Liam McCarthy of his plans to find where he'd come from. The table had gone quiet. Liam McCarthy rising and out, speaking of things needing tending in the barn.

"Aye. The west, and you should be seeing it, now." Rose McCarthy spoke as she busied herself with the table, clearing it. Jack Hennessey stood to help, but she sat him down. "Leave it to me, now, Jack. 'Tis what I do…" Her back to him now, she spoke above the dipping and racking of the dishes at the sink. "Sure, now, Jack, Christine told me of you being raised Jack Mulholland in Baltimore, leaving for Washington after Mary Mulholland had passed, taking your blood mother's name, 'Hennessey.' She told me about Mary Mulholland and getting passage to America, and all of that, she did.' While Jack Hennessey had spoken of this to others – Christine McCarthy and Fr. Power – hearing it said by another made him uneasy, his mind back to the kitchen at the house on Lemmon Street…

"Aye, 'tis to Athenry you need going, Jack Hennessey, though there's little there to see, I'm told." She looked at him. "But maybe just the being there will help. Crossing the land, walking the fields..." Rose McCarthy pumped the sink full of water and laid in the roasting pan and cover, leaning back against the counter as she dried her hands on the apron at her front, fixing on him. "Don't be judging Mary Mulholland, now, Jack Hennessey. Don't you be doing that. Worse things were done by better people than she, swapping off a dead one, and such."

Rose McCarthy came back to the table, sitting across from him. "We don't talk about it now, Jack, we don't. Not even after all the years. And it's not because of the pain of it all, the suffering or those lost. No, Jack. It's the fear of it is what, and what we learned about ourselves, each one of us that got through it...When you get that hungry, son, you go away, now, you do...All the things that make you, make you who you are, all that makes you a Christian, well, they're stripped from you, now, torn from your chest." She fixed on her hands spread flat on the surface of the table.

"There's no God in that place, Jack Hennessey, and no family neither..." She looked up at him. "The only thing in that place is the ache and pain of the hunger, driving you like a beast in the wood. I can tell you Jack Hennessey, husband to my Christine, that anyone who has never been that hungry can say anything about those that have. You have to get that hungry to know the dark side of what's in us." Her head rose sharply at him, her eyes piercing his in the silence of the room. "And you be taking this from someone who's been to that place, Jack Hennessey – Don't be judging us. Be thankful for not knowing." She looked away, her eyes closed for a moment, then back at him, open.

"Take your luck and be on with your life, Jack Hennessey. You didn't starve under that tree next to Bridget Hennessey and her other young ones. You didn't rot in the rain and mud with starving birds picking at your eyes and tearing at the rest of you..." Her eyes went blank for a moment, empty, off, then back at him again, now bright.

"She got you got to America, Jack, Mary Mulholland did. She got you to where you made a life for yourself, where you met my Christine and had four years of wonder and love with her." Rose McCarthy reached for his hands, held them in hers. "Cherish these years with Christine, Jack Hennessey, and pray God you'll find another such." Her voice rose a measure. "And be thanking Mary Mulholland for those times and these, and the time you got left here on God's good earth, and in His favor." She pressed forward, against the table, her grip on his hands firmer still. "She loved you, lad, rely on it. Don't be worrying yourself about the particulars of it, now. She raised you as her own, and that's what you come to be to her...her own, and sure as close as blood..."

"As close as blood..." Jack Hennessey spoke these words softly in the back of the car, sitting up, looking left and right for his bearings. They were just leaving Rhode Island Avenue and turning on Vermont, heading south, Fourteenth Street just ahead. "What's the time, Michael?"

"Just past noon..."

"Okay, okay." He shook his head to clear it, looked at his hands, flexed them, felt the blood coming through. He sat up straighter, away from the window as he took a deep breath, looking forward as he let it out. "Where can we drop you, Matt? Home?"

"No. Fifteenth and K. That's where we're headed."

"Burlington and White? Have you told them?"

"Yes, sir. First thing yesterday morning. When I told them it was with Hennessey Construction, they offered to rent my office to me until I got set up." He turned around, facing Jack Hennessey. "Might even make sense to stay there, if that's alright with you."

"It's all no never mind to me Matt. Whatever suits you. I don't care where you hang your shingle, so long as Hennessey Construction has you 24 hours a day," He turned to Michael Byrnes. "What do we have this afternoon, Michael?"

"Not much. You said something after mass about seeing if Fr. Murphy had any time this afternoon." He pulled into a parking place on 15th Street and looked back over his shoulder. "There's a phone here in *People's*. I can call and see if he's free..."

"Do that. Tell Mrs. Rourke that it's important. And see if she can have the boys he's lined up for squires this year standing by."

Michael Byrnes nodded and started for *Peoples*. Jack Hennessey stepped out of the car as Matt Malloy opened his door and got out as well, his brief case heavy with the trust papers. Jack Hennessey walked him a few feet from the car. "Okay, Matt, get going on all this. As fast as you can."

"Right. Monday close of business."

"Okay, okay." Jack Hennessey looked away, his dizziness in Mary Mulholland's room coming to mind. "Can we do the designation part of it separate from the new trusts?"

"Sure, you can that any time before..."

"Okay, do that first. How long will it take?"

"It's simple. Has to be notarized. Maybe an hour."

"Okay. We'll be back in one hour." He offered his hand and Matt Malloy took it, turning to leave, Jack Hennessey now gripping his hand firmer and pulling him back. "One thing, Matt."

"Yes?"

"I want that house on Lemmon Street deeded over to the Curley's on the expiration of the trust. Free and clear to them. Theirs. No cost. I want them to have it." He fixed on Matt Malloy, a determined smile coming to face. "Getting them out from under that pompous son of a bitch Fitzhugh almost makes dying worthwhile."

Matt Malloy laughed out loud. "Yes, sir, yes, sir… You got it."

CHAPTER TWENTY THREE
Indulgences

J ack Hennessey sat in the visitors reception room on the first floor of Gonzaga College High School. An afternoon sun streamed through the tall windows facing I Street, open at bottom and top, a diesel truck idling in front of the school, traces of its exhaust drifting in the air. Sitting at a small, rectangular table, Jack Hennessey thumbed through the transcripts of Tim Reagan and Martin Barry, his interview with each running through his mind. They were so young, barely his age when he had first come to Washington. He wondered about the world they would live in, and then the changes he'd seen since he was 16 years old. Yes, the lives they will live... Maybe see the twenty-first century, the both of them, the year *2000*. Amazing... To have that time, just a tenth of it, to be that young...

A knock at the door turned his head. Bill Murphy's face quickly appeared as he stepped in, his hand out, motioning to Jack Hennessey to remain seated. "Good afternoon, Jack. Didn't mean to startle you." Jack Hennessey took the offered hand, not rising, smiling hello. He was tired, and wondering why.

Bill Murphy sat opposite, settling in the hardwood chair, the room's bare walls marked only by a crucifix behind Jack Hennessey and a portrait of a praying St. Ignatius Loyola on the wall opposite. Bill Murphy began to speak, his arms and hands resting easily on the surface of he table. "So, Jack, Mrs. Rourke tells me you've met with Marty and Tim." His hands opened as his head leaned forward. "What do you think? Who's it to be?"

Jack Hennessey forced a smile, pulling the transcripts closer, his eyes fixing on them, though more away from Bill Murphy than anything else. This was going to be more difficult that he had anticipated. He looked up, then quickly away, out the window on I Street. He lowered his head and reached across the table for Fr. Murphy's hand. "I'm sorry, Bill, but there'll be no..." He looked across the table, his head shaking in sorrow and regret, a sense of failure rising in him. "I'm dying, Bill..."

Bill Murphy caught his breath, reaching to cover Jack Hennessey's hand with his own, holding it, stunned, now making the sign of the cross. "Dear God, Jack..."

They sat in silence, each of their own making. After a moment, Jack Hennessey raised his eyes, working to smile, to not tear. The warmth of Bill Murphy's hands on his own had strengthened him, eased his breathing. He was so glad to have such a good friend nearby. He looked away, then back again, fixing closely on him. "Don't know, Bill... So many of my friends gone, and now it's my time..."

"Is there anything I can do, Jack?"

Jack Hennessey studied Bill Murphy's face, felt the empathy in his eyes, could see the sadness and hurt, the shock it must have been to hear this out of the blue, no warning at all. The better the friend, the closer the friend, the deeper is the hurt. He looked away. "Well, Bill, there is one thing...maybe...I don't know..."

"Name it, Jack."

Jack Hennessey turned to Bill Murphy. "On the way over, I was thinking about all these 300 Days Indulgences I've been racking up all these years. You know, First Fridays, the odd novena, stations of the cross, that sort of thing. Must be years of them by now." He fixed closer now. "Any chance I can get paid forward on any of this? On this side, here, rather than, you know, after?" He pressed against the table. "An extra 300 days is looking pretty good to me right now, Bill..."

Bill Murphy's eyes locked on him, not understanding at first, then flashed open, wide and bright as he started to laugh. Jack Hennessey laughed, too, out loud, the both of them, now, catching their breath, heads nodding with Bill Murphy taking out his handkerchief to wipe his eyes. "Jesus, Jack, I'm going to miss you..." His eyes now slowed, teared again as he reached for Jack Hennessey 's hand, gripping it, pulling it to him, all brightness now gone to sorrow and hurt.

"Steady, Bill, Steady."

Bill Murphy nodded briefly, his eyes looking away, finding the transcripts, fixing on them. Jack Hennessey followed his lead, drawing the transcripts closer to him, scanning each for a minute then looking up. "So, Bill, what do we do with these boys?"

Bill Murphy sat back, wiped his eyes quickly, blew his nose and returned his handkerchief to his jacket pocket. "Well, I'll have to think about it, Jack." He looked across to Jack Hennessey, seeming to search for a lead as to where to go. "Doesn't look like either one of them will make squire, now, does it? No chance at all, then, Jack..?"

Jack Hennessey held Bill Murphy's eyes, studied them. He did not look away, the briefest sigh now coming. "No, Bill, 'fraid not. Not this year...Not..."

"Yes, well..." Bill Murphy looked away, then back. "Well...well, Jack, they'd each have some reason to expect at $100, I guess..." He fixed on Jack Hennessey, his eyes tearing. "Jack, I'm sorry, I just can't think, can't concentrate right now..."

"I know... It's alright." Jack Hennessey squeezed Bill Murphy's hand. "It's a one-day-at-a-time thing for me now, and some things have to get done, settled before it's done...And that could be soon." He cleared his throat as he picked up the transcripts. "So, what do we do about Tim and Martin? In a normal year, which of the two would you recommend?"

"In a normal year, I never made a recommendation. I picked two candidates, you met them, then you made the decision, and always the right one. Every time. But what's the point, now, Jack? If there's no..."

"Well, that's one of the things I wanted to see you about today." Jack Hennessey sat back, "You remember Matt Malloy?"

"Of course. Burlington and White, now, isn't it?"

"Well, it was. Now he's on his own. Hennessey Construction is his principal client, and me, for my personal affairs." Jack Hennessey sat forward. "Matt's going to be setting up a trust. We haven't named it yet, but there'll be $50,000 in it. Matt will be one of the trustees, and I'd like you to be the other."

"Of, course, Jack. that I *can* do..."

Jack Hennessey smiled. "The trust is going to be a bank of sorts. It's to be available to Squires past and squires future. It'll lend money out at commercial rates, but on extended terms. Any squire past will have access to it. Its resources are for education only, with loans to be repaid within time periods that make sense to each situation. I'd like it to work pretty much how this program's worked. The best, smartest kid who wouldn't be able to get to college without it. Instead of being my squire for a year, though, they go on to college, maybe law or medical school. I'll leave that to you and Matt."

Fr. Murphy's head nodded, his eyes misting. "Yes, Jack. A wonderful idea, wonderful..."

"They got to pay it back, now, Bill. It doesn't work if they don't pay it back. Doesn't work in any way..."

"I understand." Bill Murphy looked at the transcripts on the table, motioned to them with his hand. "So, what do we do with Marty and Tim?"

"Well, I met them both." Jack Hennessey tapped his fingers on the transcripts. "And I liked them, both of them, which seems always to have been the case. And, as usual, I did like one over the other...But let's leave it up to them."

Fr. Murphy looked across the table, by his face uncertain where this was heading.

"Do they each qualify for the half scholarship at Georgetown?"

"Yes. That's been something of a rule for anyone you've met..."

"Well, then, tell them both this. Tell that you can arrange a loan for the other half. Enough to cover tuition and $50 a month for incidentals, all to be paid back, in full, by what? Seven years from graduation? That reasonable, Bill?"

"Very, but I..."

Jack Hennessey raised his hand, nodding the nod of a man who knows. "My bet, Bill, is that one of them will turn it down. If they both say yes, then all the better...The more the merrier. But one of them will turn it down. Let's just see what develops."

Bill Murphy smiled across the table, his head shaking slightly from side to side.

"What?" Jack Hennessey leaned forward, showing his teeth. "What's that all about, you shaking your head? Like you think you know something?"

"I know which one you like, Jack Hennessey , and he's the one you think will be taking it, right?"

Jack Hennessey pushed back from the table and rose, his hand finding the back of the chair to steady himself, rising to his full height. "Well, like I said, let's just see what develops." He stood behind the chair, studying Bill Murphy, still seated. "You've done one hell of a job here, Bill. You've made a good school a great school. I see the fruit of your labors every day, all over the city. Lawyers, engineers, teachers, doctors, businessmen, you name it. Hell, you can pick them out of a crowd, most of them.

Just something about them. Yes, sir, one hell of a job. What a great way to spend a life…"

Bill Murphy nodded, smiling a thank you, his hand waving it all away. He rose and they started for the door, Bill Murphy opening it for Jack Hennessey as he offered his hand.

Jack Hennessey took it. "Oh, Bill, one thing in particular. Michael Byrnes tells me he's spoken to you about the half scholarship at Georgetown."

"Yes, a couple of weeks ago. It's all set. Just got word."

"Good. He gets the first loan from the 'bank,' the trust. Matt will set it all up. But Michael Byrnes gets the first one. And for medical school, too, if he wants it. He's a great kid, you know. His first thought is always of others. Seems instinctive to it…" He gripped Bill Murphy's hand firmer. "But he's got to pay it back, now, Bill. Every dime, every cent. It's to be loans, not gifts. No exceptions. That's the only way it works."

"I understand, Jack. Completely."

As he stepped and turned into the corridor, Jack Hennessey felt weak. He leaned toward Bill Murphy who took his arm.

"Are you alright, Jack? Let me get a chair…"

"No, nothing serious. Just tired. Getting tired now when I didn't used to, Bill. Michael Byrnes should be just outside. He'll get me home and I'll lay down for a bit…I'll be fine." He fixed on Bill Murphy, smiling him a nod to reassure him.

Fr. Bill Murphy nodded back and walked him to the front door and down the steps to the Packard.

CHAPTER TWENTY FOUR
Catherine Hughes Kennedy

M rs. Kennedy made ready her kitchen. Tonight was special. Fr. Hara, her favorite among the priests at St. Dominic's, was coming for dinner, and on the porch, too. When she opened the refrigerator door, though, first to catch her eye was the remains of Jack Hennessey 's dinner from the night previous–the thigh and part of the breast of a roasted half chicken, all wrapped in wax paper. And Monday night's left over–half of a steak, and not a large one, was in the meat compartment below.

She had first noticed it in March, his eating lighter. And his color was off, as well. She would see him upstairs on occasion, his bare arms gone yellowish. And then his shirts. These had become too large for him at the neck. Jack Hennessey was ill, of that she was certain. Of what, though, she did not know. For as little time as they actually spent together on any given day or week, he was the center of her life and she was concerned, scared. What would her life be without him?

The sun had broken through that afternoon at about two-thirty, just as Jack Hennessey returned from Baltimore. The worry on Michael Byrnes' face when they drove up was clear. Something was wrong. Michael Byrnes had quick-stepped around the front of the car, helping Jack Hennessey out of it and along the front, then up the steps to the veranda. Jack Hennessey had rested there, on the cast iron bench, then came in, going directly upstairs, Michael Byrnes at his arm. She had watched and listened from the kitchen, thinking he might not want her to see him such, and frightened by her own saying of a Hail Mary for him.

It would be pork tonight, gotten that morning from Magruder's on Fourth Street. Jack Hennessey liked his chops thick, with corn off the cob, mashed potatoes, and applesauce on the side. And corn muffins, always corn muffins. She'd baked them the first meal she'd done for him. That was 1899. She had come with her two boys, then five and three. Born Catherine Hughes and raised in Foggy Bottom, she was the daughter of a shipwright, or so her mother told her. She, her mother, had left when Catherine Hughes was eight, leaving her and two younger brothers to the care of the parish orphanage, never to be seen again.

Of the things in her work, cooking was Catherine Kennedy's pleasure. She loved handling food, the meat and vegetables, knowing by feel and sight the freshest and the most tender. Running the potatoes under the faucet, she wiped them clean with her hands then began the peeling, working left hand and right as she shaved the skin clean, it all falling in a single piece in the sink, and then to the next.

She had met the husband, Harry Kennedy, at a church picnic. He was a journeyman plumber with good prospects, good friends and a manner about him that both calmed and excited her. But none of these were to keep him safe from the consumption. He had died of it on a winter's night, their savings gone in the months it took him to go. A domestic before she'd married him, Fr. Hanrahan, pastor at St. Dominic's at the time, recommended her to Jack Hennessey , and she'd been there since.

Reaching above the sink, off to the right, she took down a cooking pot and filled it with water, setting it on the stove to boil. Drying her hands on her apron, she caught her image in the glass pane of the kitchen window. Homely was what her mother had said, and homely she was. Turning at an angle, her eyes fixed on her image. There were traces of red yet in her hair, now pulled back in a bun, the curse gone these several years and her figure gone plump, even to full. It's a small place, Southwest, and it was maybe her plain looks and ways that kept those about from thinking ill of a 24 year widow moving in, alone but for her boys, with a 52 year old man, him still working with his crews some days, and handsome, too.

Catherine Hughes Kennedy had had the love of a good man, and her sons by him to raise, and this was all of a life she wanted. And running Jack Hennessey's house and cooking his meals had become more than a job to her, it was a place to be, her place. When she shopped at Magruder's or Lipinski the baker, or called in the plumber, she spoke for Jack Hennessey and was treated with the respect others had for him. When her oldest, Brian, had bought a house in Brookland, he'd found one with a large room and its own bath for her to move in. It was the proudest moment of her life, she'd remembered, when he opened the door to the room and said 'Welcome home, ma.' Her heart near burst with joy. But she had a home, she had to tell him, and her place, as well.

Michael Byrnes came into the kitchen from the library and opened the refrigerator. He looked at the wax paper wrapped chicken from the night before and then at her.

"Take it. It'll go to waste if you don't." She nodded at the meat compartment. "There's steak in there, too, beneath. That's from Monday night..." She tried to hold his eyes but he turned away.

"Thanks, Mrs. Kennedy. Didn't get a chance for lunch today."

She raised her head to speak, but he spoke before she could.

"Fr. Hara tonight?" His eyes fixed on her, his face blank, closed. He was taking no questions.

"Yes, seven o'clock..." She turned her head at an angle, hoping he's say something about Jack Hennessey. She would never ask.

"Anything you need at McGruder's? Butter? Tea..?"

"No, Michael, thank you for asking, but we're fine..."

He nodded and turned to the basement and down to his room.

Catherine Hughes Kennedy turned to the window over the sink and blessed herself, whispering a Hail Mary, thinking it's not for her to ask.

CHAPTER TWENTY FIVE
Dinner with Joe Hara

J ack Hennessey sat in the screen porch overlooking Sixth Street, refreshed and strengthened by a three hour nap. So deep was his sleep that he had no remembrance of it other than waking from it. Had he known he would feel as well and as strong, he would not have had Michael Byrnes take the Packard for an overnight service at the dealership, or given him Friday off. Taking a deep breath, he held it, his lungs at full expanse and capacity, now exhaling slowly. Gripping the arms of the chair, he sat up straight, felt his neck extend to its full length and gloried in the shards of an early evening sun streaming through the trees on Sixth Street. In the channel beyond, it was the close of a work day on the wharf, trucks and boats and hoists going quiet and off.

"Good evening, Mr. Hennessey." Fr. Joe Hara mounted the steps of the veranda.

Jack Hennessey felt himself nearly spring from his chair and out the screen door. "Joseph Hara! Welcome. Didn't hear you drive up."

"I walked. It's such a beautiful evening. Thought I'd take the full measure of it."

"Yes, such evenings are to be treasured, each one that we have." A ship's whistle sounded and they both turned to the channel. The Overnight packet for Norfolk had just cleared its pier and was turning down channel, its port paddle wheel working in the water at such speed and force that they could hear the rush of water it produced. One more quick blast from its whistle and the boat was turned, headed south, down river, the music of the Dixieland band on its fantail now clear and true over the water.

"Come on in, Joe. Please." Mrs. Kennedy appeared at the front door. "Ah, Mrs. Kennedy." Jack Hennessey turned to Joe Hara. "What will it be father?"

"Iced tea, for me, if you have it…"

"And for me, as well." Mrs. Kennedy turned as Jack Hennessey opened the door to the screen porch for Fr. Hara and followed him in, motioning him to a chair, retaking his own. "So, father, now how are the things of the heavens?"

Joe Hara took out a pack of cigarettes, shook a cigarette up from it that he took in his lips and lit it, the ceiling fan washing the smoke from the match and the cigarette away from the table. "The things of the heavens are pretty much in their place, as far as we aware, anyway. It's down here where the work remains."

Jack Hennessey smiled as Mrs. Kennedy returned and placed a tray with two glasses and a pitcher of iced tea on the table. Jack Hennessey looked at her. "Thank you." He turned to Fr. Hara. "We're having pork chops tonight, with mashed potatoes and corn muffins, and whatever vegetable Mrs. Kennedy may have chosen."

"Sounds wonderful." Fr. Hara smiled and nodded at Mrs. Kennedy, she taking the opportunity to stare at his cigarette, then back at him, before nodding and returning to her kitchen.

Jack Hennessey watched her leave, turning to Fr. Hara. "So, Joe, how long has it been for you at St. Dominic's, now? Three years?"

"No, sir." Fr. Hara smiled. "Five and counting, actually."

"Really?" Jack Hennessey was taken aback by the answer. It simply didn't seem possible. Time passes more quickly as you age, they say, but *five* years? "I have to tell you, Joe, that I'm shocked to hear that. Five years…Lord, where does the time go?" He fixed on him now, sitting up. "So, then, how much longer would you expect to be here?'

Fr. Hara took a drag of his cigarette, exhaling as he spoke. "Well, it's hard to say. There are so many priests right now for the number of parishes in the archdiocese...Almost too many. Some even have been lent out to other dioceses to get their first pastorate. A friend from the seminary just left for Michigan. Making pastor before 40 here is tough, and I'm only 36. So, if I stay in the Archdiocese of Baltimore, it's likely to be another five years here, maybe more."

"Here at St. Dominic's then?"

"Yes, that's what it looks like."

Mrs. Kennedy pushed through the front screen door with a tray of soup and corn muffins, taking Fr. Hara by surprise. Crushing his cigarette out in the ash tray, he rose quickly and opened the screen door of the porch for her.

"There was she crab soup from the other night. Thought I'd bring it out. And here are your muffins, as well." She laid the tray on the table.

"Why thank you, Mrs. Kennedy. That was very thoughtful." Jack Hennessey turned to Fr. Hara. "Have you ever had Mrs. Kennedy's she crab soup?"

"No." Joe Hara turned to Mrs. Kennedy, forcing a smile as the smoke from his just crushed cigarette swirled in the wash of the fan.

"Then you are in for a rare treat." He smiled and nodded at Mrs. Kennedy, then back at Joe Hara. "Please begin."

Turning to leave, Mrs. Kennedy reached over Fr. Hara's arm for the ash tray. "It seems you're done with this for the evening, then, father?"

Fr. Hara sat back. "Yes, yes. Done." He looked up at her. "And thank you, Mrs. Kennedy."

Jack Hennessey watched as Mrs. Kennedy left the veranda then turned to Fr. Hara, speaking under his breath. "You'll excuse Mrs. Kennedy, I am sure, father. Her late husband died of consumption which she believes he contracted from the smoking of cigarettes. She sees them as a waste of good money and injurious to health."

Fr. Hara stirred his soup with a spoon. "I understand, and I agree with her." He looked at Jack Hennessey. "As I said, much remains here below to be done. I shall quit one of these days."

"Yes." Jack Hennessey sipped his soup, the last two days having only enhanced its richness. He looked aside at Fr. Hara for his reaction.

Placing the spoon in his mouth, Joe Hara's face went still for an instant as the soup suffused his taste buds, his eyes then closing. Sitting back, he swallowed the soup and turned to Jack Hennessey. "By God, Mr. Hennessey, this is the best soup I have ever tasted, of any sort, ever. It is extraordinary!"

"Yes, I agree. That is the word. Extraordinary."

They were each silent as they continued with their soup, Jack Hennessey offering the corn muffins, breaking and buttering one for himself, eating it with soup, marveling silently at the sensations of taste and flavor as he swallowed. Such was the richness of the experience that neither was aware that Mrs. Kennedy was at the screen door of the porch and needing assistance to bring in the dinner. On hearing her clear her throat for their attention, Fr. Hara sprang from his seat and let her in, giving her a wide berth as he spoke. "Mrs. Kennedy, that is the most extraordinary soup I have ever tasted in my life. Really, it's delicious..."

"Well, thank you, father. That's kind of you to say." She reached over the table and placed the dinner tray down, a platter of pork chops with a full bowl of mashed potatoes and another of fresh cut corn. Nodding to each, she left by the door still held by Fr. Hara who retook his seat.

Jack Hennessey motioned to the food for Fr. Hara to help himself. "Please, go ahead, father." Each then put their portions on their plate. Jack Hennessey looked at Fr. Hara. "Would you lead us in grace, father?"

"Yes, of course." He bowed his head and began. "Bless us, O Lord, and these thy gifts which we are about to receive through thy bounty through Christ, our Lord. Amen."

———

There was a quiet after Mrs. Kennedy left with the dishes, having poured the coffee and leaving the pot on the side table. Jack Hennessey stirred his cup, looking out across the lawn, the fullness of the mid-spring evening before him–couples walking beneath the willow oaks on Sixth Street, the bouquet of wisteria wafting in and out of the screen porch. He considered for a moment letting the evening end now, a cup of coffee and then good night. There were not to be many more such evenings for Jack Hennessey. Why not just enjoy this one? There was nothing he had to say that couldn't speak to Fr. Hara about tomorrow morning. He'd taken the day off. He had the time. Sipping his coffee, he sat back, turning from the serenity of all before him to Fr. Hara. Shaking his head slightly, knowing he must go on, and that there was no way to start but to start, and so he did.

"Joe, the reason I asked you over tonight, and about how long you were going to be at St. Dominic's, is this house." He waved his arm in a wide arc, looking about. "I'm not going to be needing it much longer, and I thought it might make a good home for boys, orphans and the like. For the parish."

Joe Hara sat back, stunned, looking about the veranda and what he could see of the front of the house. "This house? An orphanage? My Lord! What a wonderful idea! What a *magnificent* idea..!"

From the surprise and wonder of the idea on Joe Hara's face, Jack Hennessey could see as quick the wheels turning in his head. He could almost hear them. How many rooms? How many boys? What ages? Who'd staff it? What permits would be needed? The priest turned toward him. "I don't know what to say. We need an orphanage. More than anything, St. Dominic's needs an orphanage. But there's just no money. None."

Joe Hara stood up, went out to the unscreened part of the veranda, looked around the side of the house and from the veranda into the dining room then at Jack Hennessey. "And what a great orphanage this house would make!" He looked over the railing at the front lawn, then down to it, walking backward to the willow oaks on Sixth Street, taking in the full size of it – three floors above a windowed basement. "It's perfect!" He looked up at Jack Hennessey as he walked back and up to the veranda, into the screen porch, speaking as he came. "It'd be perfect, *perfect*. But what about you, Jack? Where are you going?"

"Up, I hope…"

Fr. Hara stepped back inside the screen porch and sat down. "Up? I don't understand, 'Up'."

Jack Hennessey forced a smile as he motioned to the ceiling with his thumb. "Yes, father, you know. Up….Gone…"

Joe Hara's shoulders fell as he reached with both hands for the chair back in front of him, his head down and now turning, his eyes fixed on Jack Hennessey. Blessing himself, he pulled the chair out and sat, reaching for Jack Hennessey's hand. "Dear God, Jack…" He leaned forward, searching in Jack Hennessey's eyes, firming his grip. "Does Paddy know?"

Jack Hennessey caught his breath. "Paddy? Jesus Christ, Paddy..." He now took Joe Hara's hand in his, looking at him, then away. "No...No, I haven't told him yet...have I?" He turned back to Joe Hara. "How do I tell him, father. How do I do that? What do I say?"

Joe Hara sat back, then forward again. "How...how much time to you have, Jack? What did they give you?"

Jack Hennessey sat still, unhearing. How could he not have thought to tell Paddy Riley? He turned toward Joe Hara. "I'm sorry, Joe. Did you say something?"

"Yes." He leaned closer. "How much time do you have, Jack?"

Jack Hennessey nodded to indicate he understood the question. Yes, he thought, how much time do I have? That is the question in times such as these. How much time... He fixed on Joe Hara. "Not much. Maybe three months. It's cancer–of the pancreas." He shrugged. "I don't even know what a pancreas does, why we even need it. And it's going to kill me." He looked away.

Joe Hara sat closer still, pushing against the table. "He should know..."

"Yes, yes. He should know. He must know." Jack Hennessey was looking at the evening's last light on the wharf, electric light bulbs now bright, strings of them by the overnight packet's pier. He closed his eyes, felt his chest sink. "Gotta fix this." He thought of the others he had told, who knew, Michael Byrnes, Bill Murphy, even the priest in Baltimore, and Paddy didn't...He fixed on Joe Hara. "Can you call him for me, Joe? Ask him to come over, tonight?" He leaned forward. "Can you do that for me?"

"Now?"

"Yes. Now. Right now...Gotta fix this, get this done..."

Joe Hara nodded as he rose from the table and went into the house.

In the quiet of the evening, Jack Hennessey heard him dial the number and after a moment ask for Paddy. He could hear the sounds of more words, but not the words themselves or get any sense of what they meant. Then the sound of Joe Hara hanging up and him coming out onto the veranda.

"He said he'd be over in a few minutes. Had something to finish up."

"You didn't say anything...?"

"No. Just that you and I had had dinner and you wanted to see him about something." Joe Hara stepped into the screen porch and went to Jack Hennessey's side, resting his hand on his shoulder. "It's probably better that I go. That he sees you alone."

Jack Hennessey's eyes remained fixed ahead. "Yes, I suppose you're right." He looked up. "Thanks, Joe..." He moved to stand but Joe Hara held him down at the shoulder.

"Don't get up, Jack."

Jack Hennessey nodded. "I'll have Matt Malloy contact you about the house, getting the paper work started and all. I'm sure some neighbors will cry foul." He looked up. "But if they can run a clinic out of the Thomas Law House over there," he motioned across N Street, "we should be able to open a house for homeless boys here." He rose against Joe Hara's hand. "You'd best be going, Joe. We'll get started on all this next week."

"Fine, Jack." He offered his hand, motioning to the house around them. "I can't say how..."

Jack Hennessey took his hand. "Nothing to me, father. Just brick and mortar looking for a use." He took his hand from Joe Hara's and reached for the screen porch door, opening it for him. Jack Hennessey followed Joe Hara out into the unscreened portion of the veranda, leaning against the rail with his hands as Joe Hara went down the steps, turned to wave good bye and started toward Sixth Street.

Jack Hennessey held at the rail, thinking about his house becoming an orphanage. 'Yes, a fine use of brick and mortar.' The screen door to the house opened behind him. Thinking it was Paddy Riley, he froze, not wanting to turn around, not quite ready to speak with him.

"Are you alright, Mr. Hennessey?"

It was Mrs. Kennedy. He turned. She stood in the doorway, one hand holding the screen open the other at her chest. She seemed concerned.

"Yes. I'm fine, thank you, Mrs. Kennedy."

"Did I hear Fr. Hara ask Paddy Riley to come over?"

"Yes. He'll be here shortly."

"Would you like me to put on a fresh pot..."

"No. That won't be necessary." He motioned to the table in the screen porch. "If you could finish up in there, that'll be all for the night, thank you." He turned to the wharf, thinking of what he would say to Paddy Riley. How would he start? Why hadn't he thought of Paddy first? The screen door behind him opened again. He turned. It was Paddy Riley, filling the doorway, his eyes bright, even flashing in the failing light. 'God, he's so alive,' thought Jack Hennessey, 'so alive. The energy in him...' Mrs. Kennedy stepped out from the screen porch with a tray of dishes and serving bowls. Paddy Riley held the front screen door open for her. Jack Hennessey fixed on her and she turned to him. "Oh, Mrs. Kennedy. There is one thing. I'm having a special guest for breakfast tomorrow. Eight a. m. Serve whatever pleases you. I won't be going to mass."

"Yes, Mr. Hennessey. Eight a.m. Good night..."

"Good night." He looked at Paddy Riley quickly and then away, motioning to the screen porch. "Come on in, Paddy. Sorry to take you way from Mary and the children. Hope all's well?"

"Things'll be fine as soon as John Riley stops talking about fishing on Saturday."

Jack Hennessey smiled, thought about John Riley's eyes and the energy in them. "Yes. I'm looking forward to that myself. Saw in the paper that rockfish are full in the bay, and heavy, big. Over 40 pounds, some of them." He motioned Paddy Riley to a chair and sat down himself, looking over at him in the soft light of the veranda. "Lot of things up, Paddy. Lot of changes coming…" He fixed on Paddy Riley, leaning back, something in him telling this wasn't the time. "Wanted to give you more on this union thing…"

Paddy Riley sat up, folding his arms across his chest.

"They're big now, Paddy, and, with Roosevelt in office, they're going to get bigger. They'll be writing *all* the rules pretty soon and anyone thinks otherwise is a fool or blind or both…"

Paddy Riley sat back, nodding, his right arm now resting on the edge of the table.

"I'm not going to able to head up the Hennessey Construction forever, Paddy. And I'm too important in the getting of business for it. For the work we want it to do– 20,000 square foot and over – we need bonding and we can't get that without me. *I'm* the bond." He paused. Saw that Paddy Riley was tracking well. He leaned forward. "They're looking at my accounts, my assets. And they know I'll always find a way to get a building done, built, that I can get the crews, the craftsmen." He sat forward, pointing to Paddy Riley, nodding for emphasis. "And the last part, that's where the unions come in. As a union shop, we have call on every licensed operating engineer, iron worker, plumber, the whole lot. All of them. So that's the good of it." He paused. "But here's where its gets tough." He sat closer to the table, his chest against it.

"Last count, we had 106 on the payroll. By the deal I made with Tim Riordan, they'll let us take 25 into the

union, like that." He snapped his fingers. "In...Done
deal." Paddy Riley sat back, his head up, turned, listening
closely. "They'll see what they can do about the rest, but
it sure as hell won't be all of them. What I need from you,
Paddy, and by Monday morning, a list of the best 25
we've got. They're going to be the core of Hennessey
Construction..."

"Jesus, Jack...only 25. That's it?"

"Yes, I know, it's tough. But it's going to be your
company, now..."

"*My* company...?"

Jack Hennessey studied his reaction. "Yes. We had a
meeting of the Board just before you got here. It was
unanimous – the *aye* had it. There were no *nays*. *You're*
the President of Hennessey Construction Company.
Congratulations."

Paddy Riley stood up, backing away from Jack
Hennessey's offered hand. "Christ in heaven, Jack. How
am I going to do that?" He began to pace on the far side
of the table. "I can't be president of Hennessey
Construction..."

"Sure you can. Hell, you are!" Jack Hennessey
laughed. "Just done. Like I said, it was unanimous...Here
sit down, Paddy. Sit down. Rest your bones. You're
taking this all much too seriously. Way too seriously." He
patted the table surface in front of the chair where Paddy
had been sitting. "Here. Come here. Sit down,
now...sit..."

Paddy Riley stared down at him, wringing his hands,
then pulling the chair out and sitting down.

"It's a big step, Paddy, sure it is. I know that. But you
can do it. I know you can. And you'll have help, too.
That's why we have Matt Malloy on board. He's been
working real estate and construction for Burlington and
White for more than six years, and unions, too. He's
smart as a whip and he's yours 24 hours of any day you

want him. He knows the law and he knows the players. Thinks like a field officer, sees things and how they interact. You'll be making the decisions, now, but he'll be there to lay a lot of them out for you."

Paddy Riley was shaking his head.

"Here's what Hennessey Construction's got to do, what *you've* got to. We've got to restructure what I've built so it can survive me..."

Paddy Riley looked up...

"I started this company in houses, repairing them first, then building them. There were laborers and journeymen and craftsmen all over the city, and I could find and bring them on. Then it was ten houses at time and it still worked. I got into buildings on a fluke. Tom Brady had his building going up in Swampoodle and the Panic of '93 hit. His builder went under and Tom needed someone to finish it or lose the whole deal. We threw in together, bought what was left of the construction company, and got the bonding and licenses along with it. We got that thing built and never looked back. But it was still Jack Hennessey and his word, *my* word." Jack Hennessey sat back, his hands on the table edge, pushing back, balancing his chair.

"Well, those days are gone for Hennessey Construction. We need structure and relationships beyond what I can provide and promise. We've gotten big enough that the only way to survive is to get bigger still. We can't go back to houses. Wouldn't even know how to get it done, and who's buying houses now, anyway? All we really know is buildings. And that means bonding and playing large." He tilted his chair forward, his hands at the table's edge. "And that means linking up with the unions.

"As a union shop, the bonding companies know we'll be able to get the crews with the training we need to finish whatever we sign. As a union shop, there's no risk of pickets trying to unionize a site and slowing everything down. And then there's the unions themselves. We'll always be at one another's throat, but they can help a union shop get work. I know they're going help us on the Hecht deal, that's the wink and nod I got from Tim Riordan and you can take his word to the bank."

Paddy Riley was nodding. His breathing seemed easier and his face more relaxed.

Jack Hennessey rose. "So, what do you think? You want the job? You want to be president of Hennessey Construction?"

"Oh, yeah...Oh, yeah..." Paddy Riley rose in a rush, a smile coming to his face that soon consumed it, the whites of his eyes near sparkling. "Just came on me in a rush, that's all. When would it actually happen?"

"Monday morning. Right after you get me that list." Jack Hennessey put out his hand to shake and Paddy Riley took it, pumping hard and full.

"You'll have it." Paddy Riley gripped his hand still firmer. "Any chance of bringing in 30?"

"You give me your best 25, and five others you'd like. I'll see what I can do." Jack Hennessey started for the screen door.

"Fair enough."

Paddy Riley pulled the screen door open for Jack Hennessey who stepped out through it to the open portion of the veranda, then followed him out, speaking up. "About Saturday, Jack. Is there room for Tim Riordan? Might be good for me to get some time with you and him together."

Jack Hennessey smiled. "Good idea. I like that. Mary at the office has his number. You give him a call in the morning. If he's on, have him meet us at the Happy Harbor at 6:30 for breakfast. He knows where...And be sure to tell him we're fishing with Captain George Prenant. He'll know what you mean."

"Will do. See you, Jack. And thanks...." They shook hands.

Jack Hennessey went to the rail and watched Paddy Riley go down the steps to the front path and on to N Street for home. He turned to the wharf and the lights on it. There were fewer now. It was past ten and on a Thursday night.

It wasn't time yet. That's why he hadn't thought of telling Paddy Riley before. And that's why he hadn't told him tonight. There would come a time to tell him, and he would tell him then. But not yet...

CHAPTER TWENTY SIX
Nine Famous Irishmen

P addy Riley's walk home was short by time and distance. By the reaches of his mind, though, it spanned the galaxies. "...It's your company, now." Those were the words. "*My* company. Hennessey Construction was *my* company." He spoke this under his breath. For a moment, he forced himself to begin the list, the 25 to stay, but it was no use. All he could think of was being the president of Hennessey Construction. There was no cluttering in his mind as to its ownership. This was of no matter as his feet stepped off the 300 yards from Jack Hennessey's house to home. He was *president* of something, the boss, the top of it. "Jesus, Mary and Joseph, how about that!"

Turning into the alley to his back gate, he wondered if he should tell Mary yet. Bad luck. Keep it mum till it's done, he's thinking...

"Who's that?"

The sound of the words in the dark of the alley startled him for an instant, knowing as quick that it was Daddy Riley, coming in the alley from the south end on his bike. "'Tis me, your son, Paddy Riley." He'd do a brogue when feeling up and this was about as up as Paddy Riley had ever been in his life.

"Top of the evening to you, son, and a grand one it is."

"It is. And a little late, too, isn't it, to be out on your bike with no light?" Paddy Riley opened the back gate and made way for Daddy Riley to pass with his bike before closing and latching it.

"Just catching some time with the lads at the point." He turned back, shaking his finger in his son's face. "And sure, don't you be telling your Mary, now, neither. Don't be doing that. She'll be on me like the banshees, giving them food from her cupboard, she'd be complaining. Promise me, now..?"

"I promise."

Daddy Riley set his bike against the wall inside the shed, being careful to lock it. "And what takes you out till after ten on a Thursday night?"

Paddy Riley looked up at the house. All the lights were off and the windows he could see shut. Mary was asleep. "Well, things of a most interesting nature, now that you ask." He tried to keep a poker face but he couldn't, a smile rising. "Now I'll be needing *your* promise not to tell anyone. To keep it to yourself. Not a word to a soul…"

"Aye, aye. Not a word, my lips are sealed." Daddy Riley stepped closer, looking up at his son, studying his face. "So, what is it, now?"

"You swear, now? Do you swear?"

"Your own father, now, you're asking? Where's the trust, I'm asking me self? Well, it being so late, you have it, my word, that is. Now what's to tell?"

Paddy Riley sat down at the picnic table and motioned for Daddy Riley to sit opposite.

"Well, sitting down, now, are we? 'Tis some story to tell, you have, I'm thinking. Sitting down, now, for it and all." Daddy Riley sat tight against the table, his arms on its surface, fixing close on Paddy Riley.

"Remember, not a word…"

"Are you deaf, is it, now? Or are you wanting my oath on your sainted mother's grave?"

"Will you give it, da, then, on ma's grave?"

"Ach!" Daddy Riley part rose from the bench and waved at him, maybe it was a swing of sorts. "You have that too, you…you…It's a son's revenge, this is, the teasing I did on you as a lad. And it'd better be something, now, this thing you're to be telling me, sure worth all these oaths you got me making." He sat back, cleared his throat. "Now, then, sworn on the grave of your sainted mother, out with it for Chrissakes!"

"Shh...Jesus, da. Quiet..."

"Ach...I'm quiet, now, I'm quiet. Sure, now, tell it will ya..."

"On Monday morning, Jack Hennessey will make me president of Hennessey Construction Company..."

Daddy Riley sat bolt upright, his jaw hanging open, closing now up to speak. "The truth, now, son...'Tis the truth is it, now, what you're saying..?"

"'Tis."

Daddy Riley laid his head on the table for a moment, then rose up from the bench and came over to Paddy's side, standing behind him. He wrapped both arms around his son, laying his head on Paddy's left shoulder. "Ah, son, could a da be prouder? And if there's a happier corner in heaven than where your mother's been in, she's found it now." He stood up, turned Paddy around so he could see him full on. "President, Hennessey Construction Company. Aye, what a lad!"

"Shush, now, da, will you? You'll wake the house."

Daddy Riley sat down beside Paddy, resting his hand on Paddy's thigh, patting it gently. Looking blankly at the dark before him, he shook his head. "I didn't have shoes till I was twelve, and only then to work the quarry. They took them back each night. And reading? Couldn't at all till I was thirty years and eight. Aye, now, and here's my son, Patrick Frances Riley of Washington, DC, president of Hennessey Construction Company. Aye, such a *country* I've found...*What* a country!" He turned to Paddy. "And what a son I've got, too...But no surprise, now, neither, we being Irish and all." He rose, standing in front of Paddy Riley, motioning him to stay seated. "Did I ever tell, now, son, of the Nine Famous Irishmen? What I learned, now, working the back bar at the Black Rose in Boston?"

"No, da, you've not."

"Aye, it's the time for it, then, it's the time to tell. Sure none better time than now." He sat down, leaning back against the table top, his legs out straight before him. "Well, it seems after the rising in '48, nine of the lads were rounded up and thrown in the dock for treason. Treason!" He looked Paddy in the eyes, his index finger up. "'Twas *our own land*, now, Paddy, and the charges were *treason*! The blaggards." He shook his head.

"Their names were Meagher, Duffy, McManus, Donahue, O'Gorman, Ireland, Leyne, McGee and Mitchell. And no surprise to anyone, they're all convicted. Great shouts of 'shame,' now, all about the court, but to no effect, at all. Just more cries of anguish gone in an Irish wind. So, now, it's all done but the passing of the sentences, his lordship, from his high bench, asking if any has a word to say before he tells them what."

"I do, sir," says Meagher.

"Do so, then, and be quick about it," says his Lordship.

"I will," says Meagher, stepping forward in the dock, his shackled hands at the rail and his shoulders square to the court. "My Lord, this is our first offence but not our last. If you will be easy with us this once, we promise, on our word as gentlemen, to try to do better next time. And next time, sure we won't be fools to get caught!" Daddy Riley rose from the table, standing tall, raising his hand. "Aye, that's for him, that's for his Lordship, and from the dock, too!" He struts a step or two then back to his bench.

"Well, not taking kindly to such words, his Lordship sentences them all to be hanged by the neck until dead. Dead, Paddy! And all good men, too, none better." Daddy Riley leaned back against the table top again, his legs out and crossed, looking at Paddy with a wink. "Sure, now, the Christians of the world would have none of it. Letters and tellygrams from all about the globe poured in, thousands upon thousands of them, from princes and paupers alike, and sure doesn't her mightiness, Queen Victoria herself, commute the sentences to banishment to Australia." He winks and looks away.

"So, now, Paddy, there's the passing of 25 years and a funny thing happens, it does. A certain Charles Duffy gets himself elected Prime Minister of Australia, he does. His name striking the Her High and Mightiness as familiar, she enquires to discover it's the same Charles Duffy she banned to Australia 25 years previous. Now her curiosity's piqued, it is, and sure she's after finding out what's become of the rest, and on her command 'twas done. And this is what they found: Thomas Francis Meagher, Governor of Montana; Terrence McManus and Patrick Donahue, both Brigadier Generals, U.S. Army; Richard O'Gorman, Governor General of Newfoundland; Morris Leyne, Attorney General of Australia; Thomas D'Arcy McGee, President of the Council Dominion of Canada; and John Mitchell, prominent New York politician and later to be father of a mayor of New York City."

Daddy Riley rose, his shoulders back, his fist made and striking the air, his eyes square on his son. "Put us down, Paddy, cast us out, and we reach the heights still! Aye, that's us, that's the Irish. Them, the Nine, them's the stock you're of, Paddy Riley, them's the stock we're *all* of." He reached for Paddy's shoulder, the gleam in his eye near lighting the alley. "'Tis well for them they drove us out, now, son. Sure we'd be on the throne by now if they hadn't!" Daddy Riley, his head back and laughing, and back as quick at Paddy. "Think of it, now, son, King Dennis the First of England!"

"Shush, now dad." Paddy Riley rose, his finger to his lips like a mother to her son. "'Tis a grand story, you tell da, and what a time to hear it." He held his father at the shoulders, looking down into his eyes. "Thank you, da, thank you. Thank you for all you've done for me, for us all. I've always been proud to be your son, and never more than now." Paddy Riley wrapped his arms around his father and held him tight, breathing deep and free. What a night, he's thinking...and I'll start with the Ryan boys, the three of them...and Dennis Coughlin, too...and can't lose Fenton, that's certain...O'Leary, too...

CHAPTER TWENTY SEVEN
Morning by the River

J ack Hennessey woke to the sounds of Sixth Street wharf through the open windows of his bedroom. It was seven by the clock on his night table. He couldn't remember the last time he had slept past six. Motionless, he lay straight out on his bed, his head on the flat of it, the pillow aside, his hands joined across his chest over a light cotton blanket. Closing his eyes, he came to a sensation of rest, his body alive and full, yet still, motionless, completely at ease...

"Mr. Hennessey?" It was Mrs. Kennedy at the bedroom door. "Are, are you...are you well? Mr. Hennessey?"

He turned his eyes toward her, holding his head still. Her hands were joined at her middle and on her face was an expression of concern, even fear. "I am fine, Mrs. Kennedy. Just taking in the still of the morning."

"Yes, a lovely morning, too...It's just, well, you lying so still...all laid out...and your hands..."

His eyes now fixed on the ceiling. 'Just practicing,' was his first thought to say, but that might have alarmed her. He remembered the hurt on Bill Murphy's face when he told him yesterday at Gonzaga. Have to be careful with this sort of thing. The closer they are, the deeper the hurt. He closed his eyes. "You needn't explain, Mrs. Kennedy. I'm fine."

"I'll be downstairs, then. You've got your guest for breakfast at eight you said..."

"Yes, Mrs. Kennedy, thank you." He sought the rest he had found before she spoke, but it would not return. Putting his feet over the side of the bed, he sat up, glad for his pajamas against the morning chill as he started for the bathroom.

There was something about a working wharf that excited Jack Hennessey . Wearing his light hunting jacket, he had walked to a bench he had discovered some years ago. On a small knoll, it enjoyed the morning shade of a large magnolia tree and was set just past the joining of Sixth and Water streets, where Washington Channel turned westward and on up to the Fourteenth Street Bridge. It was here, along the Southwest waterfront, that great quantities of food–produce, rockfish, oysters, poultry, sausage–came up river from Maryland and Virginia each day to feed the Capital City.

Large scows lined the quay, some off loading onto wholesalers' trucks for shipment across the city, others selling their product to staff from nearby houses or others come down from local restaurants and hotels. For all the comings and goings, though, and all the water craft, there was less of it now. The internal combustion engine had seen to that. Forty- and fifty-mile-per-hour trucks speeding in from Annapolis and Galesville on the Bay and up from the Northern Neck of Virginia, had changed how Washington got its food. They still came to the waterfront, many of them. But for some time, now, trucks were going directly to Eastern and other markets, and to supermarket company warehouses. It was only a matter of time before the waterfront would become a backwater in the city's commerce.

From his bench, Jack Hennessey scanned the Channel left to right, breathing in the warming air, missing the small forest of ships' masts that marked each day where the water met the land when he first came. Wind and tide had powered the place then, the common denominators of all those who lived their lives on the water. You could be smarter than the next man, and work harder, too, but it was the same wind and the same tide that each and all rode and they made of the place a community, folks all bound by the same...KA-POW!

A truck back-fired to Jack Hennessey 's left, brushing him back as he looked in that direction. Oysters were being off-loaded from a skipjack on to a horse drawn cart, the horse raising on its hind legs, lifting its cart with oysters spilling behind. The teamster pulled at the horse's reins, holding it amid shouts from all sides, mothers cursed and fists shaken. The horse now settled, the teamster pointed at the oysters spilled on the ground, looking for help to reload them, the truck driver waving him off, driving away. Others nearby, though, and those on the skipjack lent a hand and soon the oysters were back on the cart, hosed off clean, and things set straight. With thanks given and taken all around, the teamster climbed up to his seat. As the horse leaned forward and the cart followed, Jack Hennessey sat up, his eye catching the cart's wheels. Large with long wooden spokes, they brought to mind the pony and trap he had ridden from Lough Ree to Galway in Ireland, more than forty years ago.

It was at Athlone, where Lough Ree fed south into the Shannon, that Jack Hennessey had over-nighted before crossing the midland of Ireland into County Galway and to Athenry. "If you'll be going to Athenry in the west, then, Jack," Liam McCarthy said, "you'll be taking the train north from here. The tracks end at Athlone and you'll be needing a pony and trap from there west to Galway. All across it now, you'll be going. That's the Ireland you need to see, Jack Hennessey, that's the west. That's where it was the worst, you know."

"Aye," said Rose McCarthy, "the west was the worst of it, and that's for sure."

His night in Athlone was quiet, with a good Irish breakfast the following morning at the hotel. The only pony and trap available for hire that day, though, was sparse–bare wooden seats with little to rest back on, and a driver to match. He was an older man, Frank McGuiness being the name, and whatever his problems, they appeared far from resolution. As the day rolled on, though, Jack Hennessey settled into a rhythm of the land, again sensing that he somehow knew it, as before. He didn't know where a river might be, now, or a hill or bog. But he knew it, like a deep, quiet throbbing in his soul, a long, low note that rose and fell throughout his body. He'd been here before, in this life or another.

On seeing the sign for Athenry at four miles ahead, the man's tongue came unstuck and he started on about the length of the trip and him needing to overnight and the expense, and this not being discussed in the price they'd settled as they should have done. Jack Hennessey had been surprised at the low price in the first place and had no interest in haggling. His only condition on paying twice the amount agreed to was that the man not stay at the same hotel as he. "You may rely it, Mr. Hennessey," were the man's parting words.

At his request, Jack Hennessey had been deposited at the inn closest to the church, St. Mary's. The room was small, its only window facing east, offering little of the late afternoon's light. Tired from the trip and hungry, he left his bag in the room and headed for the pub adjoining where mutton was offered any way he pleased, so long as it was roasted, the pratties fried, and all in a dark, heavy gravy. And he did, with two stouts before, and one with. What the fare lacked in diversity, now, it more than made up for in character and he had another plate for good measure, and a stout or two more for the taste. Having eaten his fill, he sat alone in a corner of the pub, the final rays of the July sun full on the table before him.

Reaching for the envelope he had brought from his room, he opened it up and eased out the letter he'd found in the Mary Mulholland's desk the day after she had passed. In the failing light, he focused on the name of the man who had written it, *Daniel Morrison, Country*

Galway, Athenry Parrish, July 18, 1850. This was all he had to go on. Sure Mary Mulholland's mother was gone, and by the letter, the sons as well, with only the sister maybe left, now, and she being slow. The parish records, that's what Father Power had said, there'd be some help there sure and he'd be on it first thing…

"Another, then?" The barman stood next to the table, nodding at his glass.

Jack Hennessey looked up, his thoughts broken, then to his glass and back up. "Yes, thank you. Another…And can I ask you a question?"

"And why not?'

"Good, thank you…I'm here to find a man, a family…"

"The same then, the man and the family?" He picked up Jack Hennessey's glass.

"No…" The man's manner had surprised Jack Hennessey, more cautious now. "The man's name would be Daniel Morrison." Jack Hennessey motioned to the letter. "I have this letter, written some years ago…"

"I'm sure it is, Daniel Morrison being gone altogether for Dublin twenty years or more, and gone from there, too, I'm told…" He motioned to the ceiling with his eyes and head.

"You mean dead..?

"I do and that he is, that he is." The barman ducked under the bar and back as quick with a full glass of stout, setting it before Jack Hennessey.

"Did he have any relatives here about?'

"None that I know. He was a scribe, you see, come from Galway City to write letters for the rest, and read the ones coming back, now, too. A week or two here and then on to Kiltullagh and about, writing and reading, that being his trade."

"I see…The letter was written to a Mary Mulholland. Have you…"

"Dennis, now, there's a full bar needs tending…"

The barman looked off to his left where stood an elderly gentleman, maybe five feet six inches and sturdy, his hair white and whiskers to match down the side of his face. He wore a dark tweed jacket and held in his left hand a near empty pint of stout.

"Aye, I'm on it, now, I am. Just helping this fella here with some names is all."

"Good on you, then, Dennis, and back to the bar with you." The man clapped the barman on the shoulder as he passed by to the bar, his eyes now fixing on Jack Hennessey, coming at him in an easy gait, his right hand out to be shaken. "Brendan Shanahan's the name…"

Half rising, Jack Hennessey took the offered hand. "I'm Jack Hennessey , just over from America."

"And where else?"

Jack Hennessey smiled as he moved a chair to make room at the table. "Will you join me?"

"Thank you, I will." Pulling the chair out a measure, he sat himself down. Raising his glass with a wink of the eye, he finished it off, putting it down just as Dennis returned with another. "Thank you, Dennis." He nodded at the pint in front of Jack Hennessey. "And that, one, Jack Hennessey, is on the house, you should know." He picked up his pint and raised it as Jack Hennessey raised his. "Compliments of the proprietor, that being me self, now, Brendan Shanahan, at your service."

Jack Hennessey sipped his pint. "Well, thank you Mr. Shanahan. And good health to you."

"And to you, sir." Brendan Shanahan drank a swallow and wiped the foam of the stout from his mustache and sat back. "So, what brings this Yank to Athenry?"

Reassured by the man's open manner, Jack Hennessey shrugged his shoulders and nodded. "Family business, you might say."

"Aye, 'tis always the same, with you Yanks, it is. The *auld sod* and cemeteries, and all. Have you no dead of your own, now?" He laughed as he reached for a candle off the bar, holding it close to Jack Hennessey's face, studying it, now sitting back, looking at him from head to foot. "So, you were taken out, now, were you, in the Hunger, that is?"

Jack Hennessey sipped his stout, feeling a bit of a bug in a laboratory. Returning the glass to the table, he nodded. "Yes. 1848."

"Aye, a good year, that, one of the best!" He laughed a brief laugh, his eyes bright, enjoying his words as he brought his glass to his lips for a full quarter pint draw. "Yes, I remember it well…"

Jack Hennessey stood up. "You remember it?"

"And why not?" Brendan Shanahan sat back, looking up, his face astonished. "And what do I be looking like to you, now? A school boy or a ghost?" Brendan Shanahan stood as well, turned about to give him a good look, grabbing his own forearm and banging a limp hand on the table, then biting it. "Ouuch, now! No ghost here, now, Jack Hennessey, and sure no school boy, neither!" He laughed again, his eyes bright, his voice full. "It's 67 years that I am, now, Jack Hennessey. Born in 1826, I was." He leaned forward, fixing on him, his arm on Jack Hennessey's shoulder. "Here, lad, sit down, now, won't you?" Brendan Shanahan put his pint on the table and sat down himself. "Remember it, the Hunger and all? I guess I do…" Another quarter pull on his pint.

Jack Hennessey sat down slowly, across from Brendan Shanahan, his eyes away. He had come for records, pieces of paper, buildings to see, St. Mary's church that Mary Mulholland spoke of so grandly, dates of birth, maybe a lease hold to find where her people lived… He turned to Brendan Shanahan, fixed closely on him. "But how…?"

"How? How's that, you say? How what, now?" He laughed. "I'll tell you how – by *not dying*, that's how!" He laughed again, looked at those at the bar who laughed as well, raising their glasses.

Jack Hennessey sat back, astounded by his own stupidity. It was only his own age ago, 47 years. And they *all* didn't die, now, did they? He focused on Brendan Shanahan, sitting forward. "I'm sorry, Mr…"

Brendan Shanahan waved him away. "Ach! Don't be apologizing now." He motioned about the pub with his arms and eyes. "Near six generations and counting, that's how long a Shanahan has had this pub. You don't think we'd let a little thing like a 100 year famine drive us out, now, do you?" He laughed out loud and finished his pint, putting it hard on the table for the barman to hear. "Hells bells, lad, there were famines before that, I hope you know, in the 1830s, the two of them. Not like later, now, but enough dead to count as such. I was even born in one. 'Twas how we lived, lad." He picked up his fresh pint, raised it to Jack Hennessey, and sipped it. "There was food, Mr. Hennessey, if you had the money. There was food to buy. Saints above, now, the crown was taking food out every year of it, the Great Hunger. I hope you know that, now, too?"

Jack Hennessey nodded. He did know that. He'd heard it from Mary Mulholland often enough. He sat forward. "I'm looking for the family of Mary Mulholland. Would you know any of them?"

Brendan Shanahan had his pint to his lips, and now froze. "Mary Mulholland? Aye, lad! Now she was a one! Flame red hair and spirit to match, if it's the Mary I'm thinking of and knew. Is that the one? She'd be a year or two off me, now, if she's still about."

Jack Hennessey felt the blood rush through his body. "Yes, that's her, she's the one."

Brendan Shanahan's eyes came to a squint, him thinking hard. "Yes 'Twas then that she…" He looked away, then back. "Now who's she to you, Jack Hennessey, might I be asking?"

Jack Hennessey was silent, memories of Mary Mulholland coming to him–in the house on Lemmon Street, on the stoop with neighbors, her laugh, yes, her laugh, full and freely given as things struck her. And the men that called, all turned away, all but one, he gone to war and to die in battle, at Bull Run. Jack Hennessey was thirteen at the time and there was no laughter in the home that July, only quiet and sadness all the summer through. Jack Hennessey came to a deep sense of loss, a yearning to be near her, to hear her voice.

Brendan Shanahan reached across the table and gripped Jack Hennessey's arm. "I'm sorry, son. A meddling old fool, I am. She was good woman, your mother, Mary Mulholland. More fight in her than most of the men…"

Jack Hennessey turned back to him, searching in the man's eyes, though not certain what he was searching for. Here was a man who *knew* Mary Mulholland, *before*…And he *sounded* like Mary Mulholland, *laughed* like her… "You knew her then, You *really* knew Mary Mulholland?"

"Aye, lad, I did. And why not? I knew the rest, now, didn't I? Knew them all, I did. Her da, the brothers, one gone to Australia. Aye, all gone from here, now, I'm sorry to tell you. Gone and none to see." He pushed Jack Hennessey's pint closer to him. "Here, son, have a pull. It'll do you right."

Jack Hennessey picked up the glass and took a full swallow, nodded at Brendan Shanahan, and took another. "Thank you. You've been very kind." Another drink, just a sip now, fixing on Brendan Shanahan, leaning across the table. "Mary Mulholland wasn't my mother,

225

though…She took me out and raised me, in Baltimore. But she wasn't my mother…"

Now Brendan Shanahan took a full draw of stout. "And you're saying now the name is Hennessey. Is that the name you said?"

"Yes." His eyes were still fixed on Brendan Shanahan. "Hennessey is the name. *Jack* Hennessey."

"And from where?"

"Here. Athenry."

Brendan Shanahan rose slowly, his hand on the table to steady himself. "*Jack* Hennessey, you say? As *John* in American is *Sean* here? Was that his name then, your father's? *Sean*, was it?"

"I believe it was…"

"And your mother's name, now..?"

"Bridg…"

"ARRGH!" Brendan Shanahan stepped back, his hands clenched and to his head. "ARRGH! Bridget! Bridget Shanahan Hennessey! My sister! My sister's son, you are!"

The barman came over. "Mr. Shanahan..?" He fixed on Jack Hennessey, his arm back and cocked, taking a step toward him. Brendan Shanahan reached for his arm, holding him, then turned to the bar. "Out, now, all of you! Out, I say! We're closed, we are. Take what you have and be gone. We're closed for this day…"

Jack Hennessey rose, hesitant, leaning for the door. "No, not, you. Not you Jack Hennessey. You're to stay. Sit down!...Please, Jack, sit down, stay with me…"

Brendan Shanahan went to the bar, shepherding them to the door, urging them on as they finished their drinks or carried them out, closing the door behind them, resting his head against the inside of it. After a moment, he turned to Jack Hennessey. Leaning back against the door, he looked about to faint.

Jack Hennessey was to him as quick, holding him at the shoulders. "Are you alright? Here, let me help you..." Holding Brendan Shanahan by his upper arms, he helped him to the nearest table and sat him down, Brendan Shanahan pointing to his pint on the table where they sat before. Jack Hennessey got their glasses and sat down at his side, putting his pint in front of him.

Brendan Shanahan stared at his glass. He looked at Jack Hennessey, as if to see if he were still there, then quickly away, turning with his pint and finishing it. He held absolutely still, then stood and with a full throw of his arm and shoulder, hurled his glass against the far wall where it careened off a wood brace, striking a table top, shattering a smaller glass and knocking two pewter plates to the floor. "ARRAGH!" His hands again to his head, now turning to Jack Hennessey, staring at him, breathing heavy, his shoulders falling, his whole body shaking, now slumping.

Jack Hennessey rose and caught him, helping him back to his seat, motioning to the bar. "Can I..?"

Brendan Shanahan nodded a yes, sitting weakly in his chair, staring at the table top, not moving until Jack Hennessey returned, putting a pint on the table in front of him, breaking his gaze. Looking up, he turned, fixing on Jack Hennessey. "So, here you are, now, son to my Bridget, she gone these many years..." He took several deep breaths, raised up a measure as he closed his eyes and shook his head, then reached for his pint and sipped it, looking over. "You'll forgive me, now, Jack Hennessey, I hope." Another sip. "Aye, lad, you've taken me back to hell, you have, to hell itself...the whole of it." He took a full swallow now, the workings of his mouth and throat seeming to restore him further. Sitting full up, he fixed on Jack Hennessey, his eyes coming alive and as quick, something coming to him, his head going at an angle, his eyes squinting.

"But how's this possible, now, Jack, you being Bridget's son and all? How can it be? She only had two, both girls, with a third..." he closed his eyes... "with a third on the way...and we found her with the three, now, didn't we..?" He turned away, wiped his eyes, then looked back. "I'm sorry, son. I'm afraid you've been misinformed. I found Bridget myself, now, didn't I? By a tree, with the only three children she could ever have had. Buried them all, I did, what was left of them...All dead, now, and no mistake."

Jack Hennessey sipped his stout and sat forward. "On the night Mary Mulholland died in Baltimore, she confessed to me that she had swapped her just born *dead* son for Bridget Hennessey's just born *living* son." Another sip. "It was how she kept an overseer to his promise..."

Brendan Shanahan's head raised up a measure, nodding. "Overseer..? Ah, yes. Olmstead, that'd be Olmstead...He'd be the one...Not a doubt of it...He'd be the one. He had an eye for Mary, now, that's sure..."

Jack Hennessey fixed on Brendan Shanahan, holding his eyes. "Bridget Hennessey came to Mary Mulholland's door with her children, barely able to walk, unable to nurse...Mary gave her some food and sent her on her way. Bridget Hennessey was delirious, didn't know about the switch, or was just too weak to care." He studied Brendan Shanahan's face as he continued. "She said that Bridget Hennessey had been 'put out'..." Brendan Shanahan's face grimaced at the words and he turned away. "...and that her husband had been shot for rebel, that any person found to be helping Bridget Hennessey would be..."

Brendan Shanahan nodded slightly, raising his hand to speak, his eyes blank. "Aye, that they'd be 'put out' too..." He looked over. "Being 'put out,' you see, Jack, was a special little hell of the famine. Most, now, starved by circumstance and chance. Those 'put out' were starved to death by purpose. It was an execution of the cruelest sort...and the families of those put out had to watch, now, you see...and not help, lest they and theirs be put out themselves." He looked at Jack Hennessey. "Those put out couldn't even buy food, Jack, even if they had the money." He raised his eyebrows and nodded. "Even if they had the money..."

Jack Hennessey looked across, nodded that he understood, but that was for another time. He cleared his throat. "And what about Sean Hennessey..."

"Your father, you mean?"

Jack Hennessey sat up, held Brendan Shanahan's eyes close. "Yes, my father, Sean Hennessey." Jack Hennessey felt his throat start to close but fought it off. "He was a rebel?"

Brendan Shanahan shrugged, sipped his pint. "Rebel? No, not a rebel, now. There was no time for rebelling. We was all too busy starving to death...day by day, here in the west." He turned and spat on the floor. "Ach! Well, your da, Sean Hennessey, and some of the lads got together, raiding government food stores, keeping most for themselves, but giving some to others." He looked up. "One of these, a worm named Rooney, well, his thanks to your father for the food he gave him was to inform on him to the Constabulary, to get more food, his thirty pieces of bread." He struck a hand on the surface of the table. "FOOD! Christ, it was awful, CHRIST!" He looked away, then back. "Well, they went after them, they did, tracked Sean and the others down and shot them for dogs, hanging their bodies about to be seen, a warning to others, you see." He fixed on Jack Hennessey, sipped his stout, then looked away. "And then, for good measure, they put their families out..."

Jack Hennessey sat motionless, numb.

"So, Bridget and her two little ones, and the one on the way, were shunned. No one to take them in, no food to be given." Brendan Shanahan's eyes opened wide, froze, fixing on Jack Hennessey, his mind in anguish. "Christ, Jack, she birthed you alone, she did. She must have done, now, wouldn't she? Maybe a shed she'd found...I'm guessing, I'm hoping...Like as not in a field, though...her other little ones standing by, four years and three. Girls, they were." He shook his head, fixed on Jack Hennessey. "That she got you out at all, Jack, can only be down for a miracle, all alone she was..." His eyes now away and a full draw of stout. "The bastards, the bastards, the stinking bastards..." Another draw and back at Jack Hennessey.

"She'd left the village, now, not wanting to be seen. Aye, and there might be help from strangers, too, if she could find any, them not knowing she'd been put out. It was hell, Jack, and if there's a worse place than hell, then that, too..." He leaned forward, his arms on the table. "The oaths taken and the curses made! Food stolen by parents from children and by children from parents. Ach! When you're starving, Jack, you see, you lose who you are. There's only one drive, one screaming thought– FOOD! FOOD! FOOD!" his hand banging three times hard on the surface of the table... "It's not even life, now...Sure, it's living with the snakes and reptiles...Aye, beneath the goats..."

Brendan Shanahan took a breath, his eyes closed then open again, bearing in on Jack Hennessey. "And from all of it, Jack Hennessey, of all we learned, there was only one question we never got answered..." He looked away, alone now and weary by his eyes, speaking to the blankness before him. "We...them that lived through it...we were never to know for certain which was worse– starving to death, or watching your little ones starve to death..."

CHAPTER TWENTY EIGHT
A Special Guest

J ack Hennessey checked his watch – 7:45. Plenty of time. He leaned forward to rise, and as he put weight on his feet and lifted his head, the faintness returned. He sat back, felt himself short of breath, his heart racing, his hands chilling. Letting his shoulders fall and his arms hang limp, he closed his eyes, working to find a rhythm in his breathing, slowly raising up, pressing back against the bench. His head erect, he opened his eyes. It had passed. Gripping the bench seat, he squeezed it firm with both hands, could feel the blood in them again, and their strength. Turning at the shoulders, he reached for the back of the bench and got to his feet, testing his knees – firm, even strong.

Looking to his left, in the direction of his house, he fixed on the veranda steps. He found himself gauging the distance, looking for the most level way there, how to get there in as few steps and as little up and down as he could. There was a side walk nearby that followed the curve of Water Street to where it met Sixth Street and he started for it, in short steps at first, testing his balance and then moving ahead and coming to his normal pace. The more he moved, the better he felt, looking left and right, though, for others – bicycles and the like. By the time he had crossed to the east side of Sixth Street, he was restored, his mind going back to Athenry...

He had stayed on for a while, walking the fields, sitting by places where Mary Mulholland had lived, and the tree where Bridget Hennessey had been found with her children. Brendan Shanahan had insisted he stay as his guest, in a cottage behind his house. They met and spoke each day, he telling of Athenry, Jack Hennessey telling of Mary Mulholland in Baltimore, learning to read and buying property and building her business. Brendan Shanahan would tell of her life before she left, her friends, their lives before the famine. "Well, she lived at her own speed, Mary Mulholland did. I'll give her that, now. And she got you out, too, and I'm grateful to her for that. There was naught we could do for Bridget and her little ones without risking the lives of our own. Knowing that one of hers got out and lived, that I've a nephew in America, aye, I say thank you for that, Mary Mulholland..."

And as he stayed, this thing in Jack Hennessey that had been building since he first landed, since the first smell of the place, the first sense of having been here before, was coming to full force. He would walk a whole day, find ruins and sit amongst them, stumble upon a pub in a nearby village, or be offered a meal in a home, one man thinking he was looking for work and offering him a place through the harvest. He spent one entire afternoon on a knoll by a tree, the weather coming through from sun to rain and cloud and back to sun, then it going down. As he went to rise at the dusk of that day, he put his hands flat on the earth and from his palms out to the tips of his fingers he felt a force as real as the ground he sat, a fit, a place to be...

It was just closing time when he got back to the pub that night. It was empty, Brenan Shanahan just closing up. "Lost, were you?" He poured him a stout and put it on the bar.

"Thank you, uncle." Jack Hennessey raised the pint to his lips and tasted the bittersweetness of it, felt it glide down his throat and settle below. "Lost? No, not at all...May be found..."

"Ach! None of that, now."

Jack Hennessey stood up straight, his hands on the bar, staring at Brendan Shanahan.

"Oh? You don't know, now, do ya?" Brendan Shanahan fixed on him briefly, then poured a pint for himself and come around the bar, leaning against it, nearby him and taking a full swallow. "Well, I guess it's a one-off thing, now isn't it? Them that get here don't know till they've got here and get it, and them that go back don't tell of it to them that's coming..."

"What?" Jack Hennessey sipped his pint, leaning against the bar, now fixing on Brendan Shanahan. "I'm sorry, uncle, I don't speak Irish so well, even when it's spoken in English."

The laugh again, Mary Mulholland's laugh, deep and loud and three breaths long. "Well, you got me there, lad, you do." He picked up his pint and went to a table. "Here, sit down, now. I'll translate for you."

Jack Hennessey sat down at the table, a sip of his stout before putting it down.

"You see, Jack, we're all part of the earth we come from–Brits, Germans, French, you name'em, they're part of the earth them and theirs come from. That's sure. Bank on it." He winked with a nod and took a full draw. "It's in here, maybe." He pointed to his nose. "Or maybe here." His head. "More likely, it's here." His chest. "The heart. And who's to say? What I know sure is that when you Yanks come over here, you start breathing in the land and thinking you're part of it. Aye. Hardly ever fails. Indeed, the ones that don't, well, they're not worth the trouble to meet." A draw. "But whatever it is, I call it a phantom, it's of a life long gone and never to be found, at all." Another long pull and a nod of the head to finish.

Jack Hennessey stared at the table top for a moment, then sat back. "I don't know. In the last week or so, it's like I hardly have a life other than here. I've never felt closer to my mother, both of them." He smiled. "I'd never met a blood kin..." He raised his glass to Brendan Shanahan, who raised his back. "There are things I could do here, could build. I felt it at the McCarthy's, too, in Kilkenny…"

"Ach! Kilkenny!" Brendan Shanahan turned away and spat on the floor, stomping his spit with the heel of his shoe. "That's for them, the lot of them! Kept their food, selling it cheap to their British lords and giving us their backs." He looked back, his eyes glaring, now going calm, a shake of the head. "I'm sorry, nephew. Sure, 'tis sorry I am. Things die hard, now, some of them…" He took as full draw and sat around square.

"A few things, now, Jack, you got to know. First off, this thing you got, whatever it is, comes most to them come here in the late spring and summer, and only among them lucky enough to see more sun than rain. It's three weeks you're with me now, and one in Kilkenney, and them's the best four weeks of this fifty-two, and I say that on the grave of my mother, and my wife too, saints the both of them. The best of the fifty-two, hands down. There are times in the dark of it, the winter half, when the only benefit of it turning nine in morning is there's just enough light to see that the clouds are still there, and thick as gray mud, they are, too.' He leaned forward, his arm on the table. "It's not so green here, Jack, for the want of rain, you should be knowing." He sat back.

"Then there's the 'here' of here. It's Ireland, it is, filled with the Irish who live to hate the British, and if *they* weren't here, there'd be plenty of Irish about to fill in for them." He nodded. "We weren't run down by Cromwell because we all got along so well together, now, if you take my meaning." Another draw. "And everything *new*, now, that's a *problem*, too, Jack. It's not like America, I'm told. And it's a problem to everyone now— the church, the guilds, the constabulary. You take your pick, and you're pushing up against them to get anything done, at all, at all. Build, you say? What? What's to be built? And for who? And with what? And thems what comes to mind after a full day on my feet, Dennis gone sick on me, he did…

"Thud! Thud!"

Brendan Shanahan was quick to the bar, the two pints in his hands and poured out in the sink, then to the door, opening it wide with a flourish. "Good evening Officer Murray. And how can I be of service to you this fine night?"

A large man walked in, tall and barrel chested, a club in is hand. He wore a dark uniform and a capped hat, a badge showing at its front and another on his left breast, brass buttons running up and down his tunic beside it. "Past time, Mr. Shanahan…"

"Aye, 'tis past time it is, and 'tis closed we are…"

He looked at Jack Hennessey, cocked his head. "And who's this, then?" He stepped over to the table where Jack Hennessey sat, standing close, the head of his club now resting in his left hand, at the ready.

Jack Hennessey studied him for a moment, then rose to his full height, square to him, his arms crossed at his chest.

"My nephew over from America, now. Jack Hennessey's the name."

Jack Hennessey nodded, his eyes fixed on the eyes of Officer Murray.

Officer Murray looked Jack Hennessey up and down as he turned his club in his hands. "American, eh?" He looked at Brendan Shanahan as he turned to the door. "Teach him some manners, now, won't you, Shanahan. And some respect, too, when an officer of the law enters a room." When he got to the doorway, he turned back, pointing his club at Jack Hennessey. "I've got you down for a troublemaker, Hennessey, I do. You'd do well to see that I'm wrong…" He turned again and was gone.

Brendan Shanahan lowered his head, it shaking slightly side to side and then over at Jack Hennessey.

"Then there's that, too, now, Jack Hennessey. Them. The constabulary." He started about the room, blowing out candles and turning down the oil lamps, some of them off. "We're a people of a land under a foreign thumb, Jack Hennessey. We stay apart from them for the most of it, but there are them like Murray there, aye, traitors to their own blood for the pleasure of the powers they're given. I knew his da, that one. Pat Murray. A good man, too. But his lad, there, well, he's gone with the devil, he has, walking about like a squire above his tenants, he does now." Brendan Shanahan checked the locks on the spirits locker and started for the door.

Jack Hennessey had not moved since he stood for Officer Murray, not wanting the cause his uncle any trouble. "You 'stay apart,' you say. But they're always there..."

"Aye, lad, and you'd be wanting no part of them..."

"Then all the more reason..."

Brendan Shanahan wheeled about and stared, his head up, hands clenched and ready. "To what, now, fight?" He paused for a moment. "Are you daft, lad? Taken complete leave of your senses, have you? Stay here, and fight? Hell, you're an American, for Chrissake! We pick you fellas out at 100 paces, we do... And why would you be even thinking of it, now? Like you owe it to someone to stay? Is that it, now? To fix it? Let me tell you, lad, no man owes anything to any one that would take him away from his home. You go to your home, now, Jack Hennessey...go home to America. That's where you belong. That's where you breathe as all of you seem to do, so deep and free. There'd be never the like of it here for you, I can tell you that. We've no sense of it, at all. So thank you for the thought of it, now, Jack Hennessey, and the consideration, too, but leave us to here. 'Tis our lives we're living, thank you, and we'll be getting on fine without you..."

He had tried to object, but Brendan Shanahan would have none of it. "Go, lad. 'Tis my life here, it is. 'Tis all I know, 'tis all I want. You'd die here, you would. You'd choke on the damp and the slow of the place…"

Jack Hennessey had come to the steps of the veranda, his left hand gripping the rail. The walk had taken more out of him than he expected. He rested against the rail, catching his breath. It was nine steps up and …

"Mr. Hennessey, is that you?" Mrs. Kennedy stood on the veranda above. "I was just starting to worry. It's nearly eight, and good that you're here. There's no sign of your guest, though…"

Jack Hennessey looked up, he would have been happy for her help up the steps but didn't want to alarm her. "My guest, Mrs. Kennedy, in all of our years of acquaintance, has never once been one minute late for anything…breakfast, lunch or dinner…never ever, not just once." He nodded his assurance to her, saving his breath for a moment, then looking up at her. "You may serve breakfast now, Mrs. Kennedy, thank you."

"As you wish, Mr. Hennessey."

She turned and went into the house as Jack Hennessey gripped the rail with both hands and began to pull himself up the steps, one at a time. On the veranda, he removed his hunting jacket as he stepped through the screen doorway, hanging it on the back of a chair. Reaching for the table's edge, he walked around to his chair and sat down, breathing heavier than he should have to.

Mrs. Kennedy backed out the front screen door with the breakfast tray and came to the screen door of the porch, hesitating for a moment to see if he would rise and open the door then managing herself when it seemed he would not. She placed the tray of scrambled eggs, sausage and bacon, corn muffins and orange juice on the table. "No sign of him, Mr. Hennessey."

"No sign of whom, Mrs. Kennedy?"

"Your guest..."

Jack Hennessey rose slowly, his arm out to the chair to his right. "Please, Mrs. Kennedy, do sit down. Join me for breakfast, if you would be so kind..."

She stepped back. "Well, Mr. Hennessey, I hardly know what to say..."

"Then say 'thank you,' if it please you, Mrs. Kennedy, but please *do* sit down...and have breakfast with me."

Catherine Kennedy hesitated for a moment, then pulled out the chair and sat down, looking away for a moment, then at him.

"Would you lead us in grace, Mrs. Kennedy?"

She looked at him and smiled, her shoulders relaxed, now, as she blessed herself and began. "Bless us, O Lord..."

CHAPTER TWENTY NINE
Going Fishing

M ichael Byrnes woke at 4:30 Saturday morning, before the alarm clock went off. He had trained himself in this, though was not certain how it worked. A Jesuit at Gonzaga had suggested he try it, and he found he was able to do it. Brushing his teeth, he dressed quickly and went upstairs to the kitchen. The Packard had been picked up Friday afternoon in plenty of time to take Mrs. Kennedy to her son's house by four. Generally, he dropped her off at noon on Saturday, and picked her up after dinner on Sunday. With everyone going fishing Saturday, though, Mr. Hennessey had called and asked him to get back early enough to have her to her son's home in time for dinner on Friday.

This would make the sixth time Michael Byrnes would have driven Mr. Hennessey to Deale for fishing – twice the summer before, twice last fall and once earlier this spring. Deale, Maryland was thirty-five miles east southeast from Washington on the Chesapeake Bay, about an hour's drive out across the Sousa Bridge over the Anacostia River and then through Suitland, Maryland, and on out Route 4. Jack Hennessey used Captain George Prenant when he was available, and that meant leaving the dock at seven sharp. Capt. Prenant took his fishing seriously and his boat would leave the dock at that time, with or without everyone in the fishing party onboard. Story is that a whole party was late once and he left at seven anyway, kept the deposit and refused to hire out to them ever again.

Jack Hennessey liked purpose in a man and he had found it in George Prenant. He knew where the fish were and what they were taking, especially rockfish. Some years back he had powered up his bay boat and could run on a plane at 18 knots. Didn't want other boats following him out and fishing his place of a day. Later, at the weighing and cleaning station, he'd tell them all where he'd got to. No use to them, then, though. The fish wouldn't be there the next day. It was tide and moonlight and temperature and depth of water and season and other things that George Prenant had a way of knowing and calculating. He'd also learned over the years how to do well and keep his friends at the same time–hold the bragging to a minimum, like not at all. And he never did. Being longest at the cleaning table most days said all he needed to say.

For Michael Byrnes this morning, there was ice to get out and break up and beer to chill and sarsaparilla and ginger ale, too. Then there were the sandwiches that Mrs. Kennedy had done Friday afternoon to be gotten out to the car, all wrapped in wax paper and packed neat to keep their shape. Potato salad and pretzels, too, and pickles and beef jerky, and two whole chickens, cut up and fried southern. There was just something about being on the water with a boat working under a person that brought on the hunger. It seemed to be part of the whole thing. Fishing done right is back to the basics, the hunt, knowing where to go and what to troll and then bringing them to net, and the getting back from it all. To Jack Hennessey there was nothing quite like it, all life wrapped up in the rhythm of a day on the Bay and the water.

John Riley was waiting by the car when Michael Byrnes came out with the case of beer. "Can I help?"

"Sure can." He motioned toward the house. "There's soda pop by the basement stairs. Bring it all out here." Michael Byrnes went to the freezer in the garage, returning with a large block of ice that he carried in a galvanized tub, setting it down by the beer. He motioned to John Riley to put the pop down by the beer and retrieved an ice chest from in the back porch. He opened the chest and pointed to the beer. "Put the beer in first, then chip some ice and lay it on top, and then the pop, then more ice on top of that. I'm going to start the coffee. Gotta get the muffins going, too..."

Mrs. Kennedy had mixed a batch of muffins Friday afternoon, poured a dozen in the pan, covered it over with wax paper and put the whole thing in the Frigidaire. Michael Byrnes had started the oven when he came up and now put them in. Twenty minutes in a pre-heated oven is what she said. He checked the time, 4:45. They had to be rolling by 5:20. He took the sandwiches out of the Frigidaire and carried them along with the pretzels out to the car, opening the trunk before putting them in.

John Riley had just finished packing the ice chest when Michael Byrnes had come back out. Michael Byrnes motioned him to one end of it and they lifted it up and into the trunk of the Packard. "Good job. Now, get some cups out for the coffee, four or five. Put them on the kitchen table, and some plates too. And orange juice. There's a pitcher of it in the Fridge. Put that on the table, with some glasses. You know where they are?'

"Sure do." John Riley sprang toward the kitchen, taking the back steps two at a time.

Michael Byrnes walked out to the front of the house and looked up at Jack Hennessey's window. The lights were still out. He checked the time. Almost 5:00 "Should be up by now..." He went around back and in through the kitchen, finding himself quick stepping through the hall and up the stairs, remembering how pale Jack Hennessey had looked when they left Baltimore Thursday noon. By the time he got to the bedroom door, though, there was light at the threshold. He hesitated for a minute, then knocked. "Mr. Hennessey? You up?"

"'*Are* you up?' I hope you meant to say."

"Yes, sir." 'He's up,' Michael Byrnes thought to himself going downstairs. There was a chill in the air and he got Jack Hennessey's light weight hunting jacket out of the mud room and a canvas hat he wore on the Bay along with it. Bought khaki, it was now bleached white by the sun and a hundred washings. It had a broad brim that extended and spread at the back to cover his neck. Michael Byrnes hung the jacket over the back of a chair in the kitchen and put the hat on top of it, not to be forgotten.

John Riley was standing by the back door. The cups were out and the plates as well, the aroma of the coffee mixing easily with corn muffins. He checked his watch. Fifteen minutes? No. More than that. Taking a pot holder, he pulled the oven door open, the heat brushing him back as he looked at the muffins. "Looking pretty good, there...coming along..." He closed the door and counted slowly to thirty. "That should do it, better under done than over..." He took another pot holder off the wall and pulled the pan out, resting it by the sink on a wooden cutting board.

"Good morning, gentleman." Jack Hennessey came in, going to the stove where the coffee brewed. It was a large pot, twelve cups, some for now and some for the thermos on the way out. He took a cup off the table and splashed a little in it, smelling it and then tasting it. "That's done." He turned down the heat and poured himself a full cup, sipping it as he turned around, "So, John, you ready to catch a big one?"

"Yes, sir, Mr. Jack! Sure am. Been waiting on it all week..."

"You'll have to wait your turn." It was Paddy Riley at the door with Daddy Riley trailing. "Morning, Jack." He reached for Jack Hennessey's hand as he nodded to John Riley. "Catches an eighteen pounder in the Anacostia off a scow and thinks he's a fisherman."

"You be leaving the lad alone, now." Daddy Riley stepped to the boy's side, resting his arm over his

242

shoulders. "And a full twenty pounds it was, and all of that, too." Daddy Riley caught sight of the muffins as they sat cooling, sniffing them in and then stood at the stove, by the coffee. He looked expectantly at Jack Hennessey.

"Go ahead, Daddy Riley, that's what it's there for. There's sugar on the table and cream in the ice box."

"We're all set out there." Michael Byrnes came in from the Packard, nodding out toward N Street and the car. Going directly to the muffins, he checked the wall clock. It was 5:12. Testing the temperature and feel of the muffins, he nodded at Jack Hennessey as he picked up the pan by its ends and turned to the kitchen table where an empty platter rested in its middle. Michael Byrnes flipped the pan over and the muffins tumbled out, all those there stepping forward to the table, reaching out to keep the muffins on the platter. "Muffins' up…"

Michael Byrnes set the empty pan in the sink and poured five glasses of orange juice as Jack Hennessey opened the ice box and laid out the butter. It was two muffins to a man with two more to spare, with all five of them now in the quiet of Jack Hennessey's kitchen splitting muffins and laying on the butter as the morning's first light showed itself across the eastern sky. Deale, Maryland and Captain George Prenant awaited…

CHAPTER THIRTY
The Fishing Party

The Happy Harbor Inn sat on the west bank of Rockhold Creek, the bar half of it abutting Maryland Route 256. The dining room half was on the water side of the bar, extending out over the Creek with an uncovered deck out still further. The deck had four picnic tables and an outside bar area. Running east off the deck was a narrow wooden pier where a dozen charter boats moored, including the *Stormy Petrel*, George Prenant, captain.

Jack Hennessey and Daddy Riley had left the unloading of the Packard to the others, using the plank walk on the north side of the bar to go down to the deck and into the dining room. It was 6:25 and crowded, men looking to catch some fish and maybe forget about the Depression for a few hours. Tim Riordan sat at a rectangular table set for six, a half drunk cup of coffee in his hand and the newspaper open in front of him. A lit cigarette rested in an ashtray to his right.

"You're early, Tim." Jack Hennessey nodded at the coffee cup and ashtray. "Made yourself right to home, I see."

"Well, now, Jack, you said we had Captain Prenant, and I sure didn't want to get left at the dock. Couldn't have you and the other fellas talking about me all day and laughing your self sick about it. I care too much about you, Jack, you know that..." Daddy Riley laughed as he sat down, looking to catch the girl's eye, flexing his hands on the table.

Jack Hennessey smiled as he sat down, the waitress coming over to him. "We'll have a dozen eggs, scrambled, and enough sausage and bacon for six, and potatoes, too." He caught Daddy Riley's hand coming up. "And coffee, please. Right away, on that." She nodded,

245

turning to the kitchen. "And Miss…" She stopped and turned. "One more thing." He motioned down the pier. "You should know we'll be sailing with Captain Prenant…"

"At seven..?"

Jack Hennessey nodded yes.

"That's all I need to know." She turned toward the kitchen. "Captain Prenant's party, coming up! We're going to need a dozen scrambled, on the double…"

Jack Hennessey nodded his appreciation and watched as she went to the kitchen window to call in the rest of the order before he turned to Tim Riordan, nodding at the paper. "So, Tim, what's up? Anything I should know about?"

"Well, nothing you can do anything about, that's for sure." He pointed to a headline and photograph. "Roosevelt's going to walk away from whoever the Republicans can find to run, and it's going to be four more years of fair sailing for labor…"

"And why not, now?" Daddy Riley sat back as the waitress poured his coffee, then forward against the table. "It's the working man that carries the load about here, isn't it now? And with little thanks from the bosses and their like, all grand in their striped suits and fancy cars. It's been a workingman's Depression, that's sure, now. He's the one hurt the most. It's time, I say, and I'm glad for it…" He quick looked at Jack Hennessey and then away. "Yes, sir, 'tis time, it is…"

"Time for what, Daddy Riley?" John Riley came in ahead of Paddy Riley and Michael Byrnes and sat next to his grandfather.

Daddy Riley looked at him, now noticing others in the room looking at him, as well. He looked up. Paddy Riley stepped to the chair across from Tim Riordan, looking down at him. Daddy Riley turned back to John

Riley. "Time for breakfast, I'm thinking. That's the time, time for breakfast…"

"Well said." Tim Riordan winked at Daddy Riley just as the waitress dropped a large bowl of scrambled eggs in the center of the table, fresh off the skillet, steaming and deep yellow.

Paddy Riley reached over and picked it up with one hand, ladling eggs onto Tim Riordan's plate. "Say when, Tim…"

"When…WHEN! for Chrissakes!"

Paddy Riley winked at him and turned to Jack Hennessey.

"Just one scoop, thanks, Paddy" and so on to the others at the table, with the bacon and sausage coming as quick, Jack Hennessey starting the plate around and the potatoes after that.

"So what's the weather to be?" Tim Riordan wiped egg off his chin and bit off the end of a strip of bacon he held in his other hand.

"Something that wants watching, to be sure." Daddy Riley wagged his fork at the rest. "Near ninety degrees at mid-day, the paper says. Ninety degrees coming so quick in May, aye, it can bring up some heavy weather, you should all be knowing. And quick, too." He sipped his coffee. "A squall as quick as a blink, is what. Coming up the Bay at twenty knots, and when one's on you, there's rain you can't see ten feet into and wind that'll blow a man off a boat…"

Jack Hennessey looked at Tim Riordan and they nodded to each other. They'd been caught in a squall more than twenty years past, got run down by it. The boat was barely twenty feet, and low aft. Going down the face of a wave, it broached, with water breaking in over the stern as the bow buried itself in the wave ahead, the wind rising so strong they couldn't hear each other shout. As the boat rolled over, though, it trapped air inside the hull

247

that kept it buoyant. It was all over in less than ten minutes, the sun out bright and the Bay flat. They had hung on to the overturned hull for most of an hour before being picked by a passing skipjack.

Jack Hennessey learned two things that day. One, that Tim Riordan's left leg was something he never needed to see again, broken and set crooked halfway from knee to ankle at maybe a 10 degree angle, out and back in. Two, he was careful never to go out on the Bay again without someone who knew how to run a boat in heavy weather. He leaned forward on the table, fixing on John Riley. "Well, that's why I like Captain Prenant. There's not better a man on the Bay." Jack Hennessey looked at Tim Riordan. "Real glad you could make it, Tim."

"The feeling's mutual, Jack." Tim Riordan raised his coffee cup to Jack Hennessey, and then to Paddy Riley. "Looking forward to a day with you, too, Paddy, and your boy John, here. And is this your dad…?"

"Lord almighty, where are my manners." Jack Hennessey bowed a quick apology to Daddy Riley then motioned to him with an open arm as he turned to Tim Riordan. "This is Daddy Riley, Tim, father to Paddy and over from Ireland now more than 40 years."

Daddy Riley and Tim Riordan each half stood as they shook hands across the table. "Forty-one years it is, and I'm taking you for a union man, Mr. Riordan…"

"That I am, Daddy Riley, and please call me Tim."

"I will that, now, Tim. And which union would that be, now?"

Tim Riordan smiled at Jack Hennessey then back at Daddy Riley. "Them all, in a way. I'm the man in the middle. I make things work when they don't seem to be heading that way."

Daddy Riley nodded his approval. "Well, we were denied the right of a union in the government, and that's the shame of it. But if we had the right, had a union, I would have joined, sure."

"Glad to hear it."

"My son here, now, and Mr. Jack, well, they run a non-union shop, and more's the pity, I say. They're good men, now, the both of them, and they treat their people square, too. And I know that for a fact, I do. But..." He looked at John Riley, then to Paddy and quick off him to Tim Riordan. "...But a man needs a union if he's to be his own man, just the same..."

The waitress freshened his cup and the others, looking at Jack Hennessey who motioned for the check.

"...A man's got to have more than just being some other fella's hired hand, a *skilpeen* walking about, looking for work..."

Tim Riordan raised his cup to Daddy Riley. "Well said, Daddy Riley, well said." He turned his raised cup to Paddy Riley.

Paddy Riley reached for his cup and raised it to Tim Riordan, clinking his across the table. "To being your own man, Tim."

Tim Riordan nodded, sipped his coffee as he winked at Daddy Riley.

Daddy Riley turned his eyes to the plate in front of him, fixed on it, avoided the eyes of the others at the table. "...That's all I'm saying, now, that's all I'm saying. A man's got to have a place in it all..."

Jack Hennessey's eyes moved from Daddy Riley to Paddy Riley and Tim Riordan, their eyes locked, both heads nodding. He picked up the check from the corner of the table, looked it over, all coming to $10.53. Pulling out his money clip, he peeled off a twenty and put it on top of the check, placing his empty coffee cup on top of that. As he rose, the waitress approached. "Thank you, young lady. You have a real good day, now."

She looked at the twenty. "Yes, sir, I surely will."

CHAPTER THIRTY ONE
On the Bay

As the *Stormy Petrel* cleared Rockhold Creek, Captain George Prenant pushed up the throttle of the 215 horsepower *Faegoal* bus engine to 2300 RPM. Rising up on a plane in the early morning sun, the bow of the boat rode easily over the calm of the water, clearing spray ten feet to either side with those aboard nodding and smiling to each other at the thrill and pleasure of it all. They had the fastest boat and the best captain out of Deale, Maryland...and fish were waiting.

Captain Prenant made south along the earthen cliffs of *Fair Haven* and then due east, clearing Hammond Point to starboard by 7:20 and holding east from there. Checking the engine gauges, he looked ahead toward Coaches Island on the far side of the Bay, his head up, sniffing the air, eyes alert, sweeping the horizon. Also aboard was his grandson as mate, now setting up for a day's fishing, moving gear out of the forward cabin aft. First there were trolling rods that he set in rod holders about the cockpit. Next were wire leaders and hooks, then lures, a large box of them, along with lead sinkers to take the lures deep into the Bay, all laid out, now, waiting, ready to fish.

Much of the 42-foot length of the boat was open, with the helm forward under an overhead that ran aft and shading the engine box. The hull was built for working the Bay – crabbing, fishing and bird hunting, too. The line of it started high at the bow, running aft in a clean, sweeping stroke to a low stern, near the water and the easier to handle crab traps and land fish. The engine box was in the dead center of the cockpit, high enough to work fishing gear and low enough sit on. A foot wide catwalk surrounded the cockpit at the gunnel. Sitting on the aft edge of the engine box, Jack Hennessey watched the wake stretch out behind the boat, straight and true, as it marked their way across the flat, gray-green water of the Bay.

Paddy Riley was forward with Daddy Riley, both talking to George Prenant about where they were going, what sort of lures they would troll, how the fishing's been. Tim Riordan sat on the gunnel to Jack Hennessey's left, leaning back against a stanchion, moving easily with the slight roll of the boat, his eyes closing on and off. John Riley watched the mate, asking questions, looking for a chance to help. Michael Byrnes sat on the transom, at the stern, looking forward, port and starboard, his eyes always coming back to Jack Hennessey, checking that he was alright.

In every way, Michael Byrnes had been a squire. He cared for his knight, and he learned from him, too. As he approached his own certain end, Jack Hennessey was coming to find new dimensions to the sadness of it all, it seemed, now, every day. Watching Michael Byrnes, he realized that much of the sadness he felt was never to see the completed man. Yes, the completed man. 'I am that, I guess. The completed man, or just nearly so.' He looked up, the morning calm of the Bay was such that the wake of the *Stormy Petrel* ran to the horizon, to where the Bay met the land...

"Left! Birds, off the port Bow! Bluefish up! Port bow!" Michael Byrnes was standing, pointing forward to his left. They all turned. Birds were flocking in now, diving and skimming the water's surface, it boiling with the splash of bait fish jumping and churning to get out and away from a school of bluefish up for the kill.

"Casting rigs! On the double!" George Prenant pointed to the forward cabin and the mate was there as quick, out now with three rods and loosening the drags as he handed them to those nearest the stern – Tim Riordan,

John Riley and Michael Byrnes. George Prenant spun the helm hard over, presenting the stern of the boat to the mayhem on the water's surface, the engine in reverse and backing down, the sound rising of fish and bait breaking water, the squawking and squealing of birds all around them, the sound of their wings fluttering. "Anytime, gents, anytime…"

Michael Byrnes was first to cast, a long arching throw of the shoulder and back as the bug-eye flew out maybe 100 feet, landing at the edge of the broil and struck as quickly, the fish diving now as Michael Byrnes held the tip of the rod up and set the hook. Tim Riordan was next, his fish taking him to the starboard side of the boat as he let it run and dive. The mate took John Riley's rod and cast deep into the fish, maybe 150 feet out, handing it to John Riley just as the lure was struck, his fish coming clear out of the water, maybe a ten pounder.

With three blues hooked, George Premnant put the engine in forward, keeping the boat pointed away from where the fish were running, the mate at the ready with the net. Michael Byrnes, on the port side, was first to have his fish up, but it dove beneath the boat and he had to walk his rod under John Riley's rod and hold it from crossing Tim Riordan's line. John Riley was pumping his rod and reeling, bringing his fish up close, the mate at hand and grabbing the leader as he slipped the net under it and brought it on board, its whole body slapping against the deck of the cockpit, spitting out the lure with blood trailing it as if flip-flapped aft for the length of the cockpit, the mate getting a foot on its tail and a hand under the gills and up into the fish box. Tim Riordan's fish had gone around to the port side and he brought it up close, the mate netting it quick and up, getting a gloved hand under both gills and yanking the hook through the side of the fish's mouth before putting it in the box, blood trailing over the deck and on the mate's arm and shorts.

Michael Byrnes' fish sounded again, pulling line off the star drag.

"What you got there, boy?" Captain George Prenant put the helm hard over to keep the fish aft as it tore more line off the reel. "Got to be the same as the others, only way blues run…"

Michael Byrnes walked the fish back around to the port side of the boat. "Here he is…Coming now…"

The mate grabbed the leader and netted him quick, flipping the fish into the cockpit.

"Same size…ten-twelve pounds…Sure had some fight in him…Ten pounds of bluefish'll fight like 20 pounds of anything else…" Captain Prenant swung the boat back toward the fish, but they were gone, a few birds sitting in the water picking off the surface, some diving for bigger bits deeper down, but the blues were gone. "Just as well. We come for rockfish. Blues pick up a morning, that's sure, but they don't have the taste of a rock, not even close." He pointed the boat east and pushed up the throttle as the mate washed down the cockpit deck and the catwalks, with John Riley holding the fish box open looking at his catch.

Coaches island is on the east side of the Bay and half a mile off its eastern shore. Depending on the tide, the water between the island and shoreline can run up to five knots and, when the air and water temperature's right, it was one of George Prenant's favorite spots in May. And it was here that they had landed two rockfish, neither being of remarkable size, perhaps eight pounds each. With the tide coming to turn, Captain Prenant announced that he would troll over to a hole he had found on the west side of the island whose time, he had a feeling, was due.

Michael Byrnes went forward and broke out sandwiches and the other food, laying it out on the engine box as the *Stormy Petrel* headed west around the north end of Poplar Island, the boat working now in the water as the wind had come up with the air warming. It was noon, pushing ninety degrees, and time to eat.

Tim Riordan had got himself a ham and Swiss sandwich and a bottle of beer, sitting on the starboard gunnel and looking at Jack Hennessey. "What was the name of that guy who worked for Marshall Hancock? You know, his nephew or son-in-law or something, the shithead?"

Jack Hennessey shook his head and laughed. "Yeah, what was his name? Robert something or other…"

"You ever tell that story to Paddy, here?"

"No, don't believe I did…"

"He's just got to know about that…"

"Nothing of any moment to me, one way or the other…"

Paddy Riley was sitting up now, a sandwich in one hand and a beer in the other, fixed on Tim Riordan.

"Well, Paddy, this was a long time ago…When, Jack?"

"O, I don't know…We were still just building houses then…mid-80s, I guess, thereabouts..."

"Whatever." Tim Riordan turned to Paddy Riley, pointing his thumb at Jack Hennessey. "Like Jack here said, he was still just building houses, and a lot of his work was sub-contracting for other contractors, Irish getting business on their own still a *real* problem back then…Anyway, Jack's looking to be the prime on a ten home project coming up by Charles Gessford, a big developer at the time. Trouble is, the prime contractor Hennessey Construction's just wrapping up with on a twelve house project, Hancock Builders, well, they want the job, too, see?" He took a bite of his sandwich and swallow of beer.

"Now Jack needs to be paid off by Hancock to have enough cash in the bank so he can get the bonding he's going to need to qualify for the bid. And, of course,

Hancock knows this, too. What's more, Hancock wants Hennessey to be *his* subcontractor on the deal. So Hancock's pushing Jack to sign this subcontracting agreement before he releases the check for the work he's already done. Once Jack's down for the sub, of course, he can't bid the prime. Right?"

Paddy Riley nodded.

"Sure. That's how it works. So Hancock's got our friend here by the short ones. But he's got to be out of town for some reason, so he leaves this Robert, Robert....*Ferguson*! That's the name, Robert Ferguson. Sure. Anyway, he leaves Ferguson in charge. Jesus, what a jerk, a board-certified jerk!" Tim Riordan leans back and laughs, coming forward and taking a full swallow of beer.

"So, Ferguson's in charge, and loving it. Now he's never taken a liking to Jack, here. Never did. Sees him as some uppity Mick, something like that, an Irish contractor out of Swampoodle who should know his place...You know, that stuff." Another swallow. "Anyway, he's going to show Hancock what a tough guy he is by jerking Jack here around, and getting that contract signed. Right? So, he calls Jack up...Phones were new then, so this is big deal, too...He calls Jack here up and tells him 'Jack, I got your check right here, all certified, and ready to go. Only thing you need to do is sign this here subcontracting agreement and it's all yours. Done, in my drawer, Jack, ready to go. Anytime you want it." Tim Riordan laughs again.

"Now you should know this is a Friday afternoon in the summer. Hot as hell and downtown is *empty*, hardly a soul to be seen. So Jack here says 'You calling from your office are you, Robert?' 'Surely am.' is the reply. 'Okay with you I stop by at closing then?' 'Surely is.'"

Jack Hennessey started to shake his head, a smile on his face, taking a bite of his sandwich and sipping a tonic.

"So, Jack goes over at 4:55. The building's empty. Ferguson had let his staff off early, it being Friday in the summer and so hot, you know. Anyway, Jack knocks on the door and shit for brains opens it. 'Good to see you, Jack. Thanks for coming by on such short notice. It's appreciated. Come on in.' Jack steps in, looking around, up and down, making sure they're alone." Tim Riordan's eyes flash those listening. "And they are!" Another swallow of beer. "He follows Ferguson into his office, standing in front of his desk. 'Where do I sign?'

"Ferguson can't believe this is going so easy. He can just see Hancock's face when he shows him the contract with Jack Hennessey's signature on it!" Tim Riordan laughed out loud, his head back then coming forward with another full swallow of beer. "So, he takes out the agreement, puts it on the desk, all turned around to Jack for signing. Jack reaches into his pocket and takes out his pen, looks at the desk. 'You said the check..?' 'Course, Jack, it's right here.' Ferguson opens the drawer and puts the check on the desk, right next to the agreement. Jack bends over with his pen in his hand to sign the agreement...then just grabs the check! That simple! And now he's headed for the door...!" Tim Riordan and Jack Hennessey are both laughing.

"Ferguson near shits himself, running around the desk, whining in his shitbird little voice 'But, Jack, but, Jack, you didn't sign the agreement, Jack. Jack! Come on, now, Jack, you gotta sign the agreement, for Chrissake!'

"Jack's at the door by this time and turns back. 'I already signed the agreement, last year. Remember? It was for carpentry and masonry on the twelve houses on 11th Street, and they're done, finished.' He holds up the check. 'This here's a cashier's check made out to Hennessey Construction Company for work done and delivered. Didn't I say thank you? No? Sorry about that–

THANK YOU!' He holds up the check and tips his hat. 'Now you have yourself a fine weekend, Robert.'"

Tim Riordan was laughing so hard he had to stand up. "So there's Robert Ferguson, standing there, a Friday afternoon in an empty office, nothing but dick in his hand. And Jack Hennessey? He's walking down 7th Street with a $37,585 check in his pocket." Tim Riordan does a strut walk down the deck. More laughing now, John Riley probably the hardest, Captain Prenant nodding his approval, swallows of beer and tonic all around.

Paddy Riley, done laughing, taking a full swallow of beer and pointing at Jack Hennessey. "So, did you get the deal with Gessford?"

"Yup." Jack Hennessey nodded, still half laughing. "And six more after that. Got to be his preferred contractor." A full smile came to his face, glowing. "Threw Hancock some sub work on two of them. Carpentry, I think it was...." Tim Riordan had forgotten about that and started laughing all over again.

Paddy Riley sat forward. "What happened to Ferguson?"

"What should have." Jack Hennessey shrugged. "Hancock had heard about it over the weekend somehow. Fired Ferguson's ass Monday morning. Word was that Ferguson never even got to his desk." Jack Hennessey shook his head. "A man's got to know his limits..."

"Fish on!" The mate ran aft. Two rods were bent hard over. "Big fish! Trophies, sure..." A third line got hit. The mate lifted the rod nearest to him out of the rod holder and handed it to Tim Riordan. "Keep the tip up, tip up. Let him run for a bit..." Michael Byrnes lifted the rod nearest to him and turned to Jack Hennessey to hand it to him. Jack Hennessey shook his head, motioning Michael Byrnes that he should take it.

The mate set the hook in the third fish and turned to Daddy Riley who took John Riley by the upper arm and sat him in the nearest fighting chair. "In the chair, with you now…" The mate put the butt of the rod in the gimbal of the fighting chair and John Riley took it, pulling hard on the grip of the rod and trying to reel in line. "Let him run, now, John, let him run…"

The mate turned to George Prenant. "All hooked up, captain, running out …"

"Clear the other rigs…now! They'll foul'em coming in…"

"Yes, sir." The mate pulled in the other lines, all but the trailer. It was held high off the water and out of the way by the outrigger.

"Mine's coming at us!" Tim Riordan raised his rod up and backed away to take the slack out of the line.

The mate ran to his side. "Reel! Reel in as fast as you can!"

Tim Riordan bent over the rod and reeled, his right arm cramping, taking the mate's signal to back up more toward the bow of the boat. The mate reached for the leader and put the net in the water. "Christ, a trophy sure…" The mate worked his hand down the leader and got the net under the fish, lifting it aboard in a single motion. The hook came out as the fish hit the deck, 25 pounds of frenzied rockfish, suddenly alive, and flapping on the deck boards and biting at the air.

Captain Prenant came aft, his gloved hand grabbing the fish by the tail and reaching for a sawed off base ball bat. He brought it sharply down on the fish's forehead, then threw the stunned fish into the box…

"I'm up…" Michael Byrnes backed toward the bow, giving the mate room to get to his leader. Grabbing it, the mate worked his hand down its length. "Stand back, he's a little one…" Taking a turn on the leader with his hand, the mate lifted the fish up and landed him on the deck, trapping its tail under his boot. Picking it up under the gills, he took hold of the shank of the hook and worked it free before lifting the top of the fish box and putting it in...

"Tip up, now, John, up. Hang on, lad, get some line when he gives it... tip up, now..."

George Prenant was backing the boat down on the fish, his eyes fixed on the mate who was giving hand signals on which way to turn. Paddy Riley stood behind the fighting chair, keeping John Riley's rod pointed in the direction of the fish, Jack Hennessey standing forward with Captain Prenant, watching aft and looking about for other boats.

"He's getting tired John, I can see it in the tip of the rod, I can. Keep reeling, now, keep pulling..." Daddy Riley's eyes were fixed at where the line went in the water, "He's coming up, at the boat...."

The mate stood by the transom. "I can see the leader now, keep him coming, now...pump and reel, pump and reel..."

A splash of water broke the surface and the fish sounded, pulling John Riley forward in the chair with him. Arching his back, with both hands on the grip of the rod, John Riley pulled with all his strength, the rod bending down almost to the gunnel...

Paddy Riley leaned over John Riley's shoulder. "Keep that rod off the gunnel, boy. Can't claim a fish you needed the gunnel to catch..."

John Riley fought the pull of the fish, both hands gone white with his grip as he pulled with arms and legs and back and shoulders to keep the rod from going down to the gunnel. Taking a deep breath, he laid into to it with all he had and slowly the rod tip began to rise and the fish turned out rather than down...

"That's the lad. You broke him, now, you did. Pump and reel, he's coming up, now...pump and reel...tip up, tip up..."

John Riley worked the grip of the rod in his left hand and reeled with is right, his eyes at the water, pulling and reeling…

"The leader!" Daddy Riley pointed to the leader as it came up from the water. "Come on now, lad, a few more feet… he's got the leader! Good on ya, now…"

The mate grabbed the leader and worked the fish around to the starboard side of the boat. Michael Byrnes handed him the net and he got it under the fish and lifted it up, the water churning as the fish twisted and turned, flailing against the side of the boat and then over the gunnel and into the cockpit…flapping and thrashing on the deck…

"Saints above, John, you caught a whale, you did!"

"Not a whale…" Tim Riordan backed away, giving the mate room to handle the fish. "But it's one hell of a rockfish. Must weigh 35 pounds…"

Jack Hennessey came aft. "By God, John, that's a fish. Maybe as big as your dad's last year…"

"Bigger than that." Paddy Riley stepped around in front of the fighting chair, looking at the fish, then down at this son. "John Riley, from this day forward, you can call yourself a fisherman. Yes sir, you're a fisherman…"

"Aye, that you are, lad! A fisherman, sure. Look at it now…"

They stared at the deck of the boat where the mate worked the hook out of the fish's mouth, his gloved hand going full inside its mouth with a pliers and tearing the hook out of the cartilage at the top of the fish's throat. He picked the fish up by its gills and held it at its full length, motioning John Riley to his side. Holding it against him, it came almost to John Riley's shoulders, all the others standing back now and clapping as the mate lifted the top of the fish box and laid it in.

"How many fish we have in there, Captain?" Jack Hennessey steadied himself with a grip on the overhead.

"Five rockfish..." George Prenant, turned forward to get back to the helm.

"How much by weight?" Jack Hennessey was reaching for his pocket watch.

"With that last one, maybe 50 pounds of fillet, give or take. There's got to be 25 pound on that one fish alone..."

Jack Hennessey checked the time. "I'd like to be back to Washington by four o'clock or so. Have some folks coming over..."

"Well, then, you got plenty of fish for them..."

"Trailer's on! Hooked up!" The mate grabbed the rod and reeled in the slack, setting the hook, the rod bending over. "Naw, probably just snagged the bottom..."

"Impossible." George Prenant looked about, Coaches Island to the east, taking his bearings. "There's fifty feet of water here. More than that..." He looked at the set of the rod as the mate handed it to Paddy Riley, the tip of it jerking as the fish tore off more line. "Lord in heaven, that's a fish!" He wheeled around to the others. "Stay forward of the engine box, now..." He ripped off the canvass covering the aft helm as he turned to the mate. "Get him a fishing belt..."

The mate already had it in hand and was fitting it around Paddy Riley's waist, positioning the leather cup of it midway between his waist and crotch. "How's that?"

"Fine..." Paddy Riley set the butt of the rod in the leather cup of the belt as he held the tip up. The fish was pulling line off the reel, diving deep into the Bay.

"Let him run, now, let him run. Tip up." George Prenant was facing aft, the steering wheel behind him, his hand on the clutch, slipping it into reverse and pushing the throttle up. The boat backed down, following the fish.

Paddy Riley held the grip of the rod in his left hand, tightening the drag to slow the fish, testing the tension of the line with his left thumb. "He's slowing, he's slowing..."

"Don't be rushing him, now... if you can take some line back, do it, but no more drag on that reel, sure don't want to break him off..."

Paddy Riley tried to pump and reel but the fish was still running out. He tested the fish with a pull on the rod and felt him coming in and began pumping and reeling again. "He's coming now..." The tip of the rod jerked quickly down, Paddy Riley fighting it with both hands on the grip.

"Careful, now, don't hurry...We got all the time in the world..." George Prenant fixed on where the line hit the water.

"Jesus, Mary and Joseph..." A whisper and a prayer. Daddy Riley tugged at Jack Hennessey's arm. "Mr. Jack, you should be looking forward, now, I'm thinking..."

Jack Hennessey turned and looked over the bow, to the south...all was darkness, near to black. Left and right and high, it was the leading edge of a squall. A lightning bolt flashed against it, the clap of its thunder a second later.

Captain Prenant wheeled around, saw the squall and turned back aft, nodding to the mate. "Stay under cover, now, boy." He called aft. "We got some heavy weather coming, Mr. Riley. There'll be rain and lightning and high wind likely." Paddy Riley looked quickly over his shoulder, fixed on the storm for a moment then back aft toward the fish.

"You want to cut that thing off and get under cover? There's no out running it..." Captain Prenant was shouting now, the wind and rain on them that quick.

Paddy Riley shouted over his shoulder, not taking his eyes from where the line went into the water. "Would you cut it off, a fish this big?"

Captain Prenant nodded, fixed his stare aft as the rain opened up, the wind blowing it near horizontal in gusts, twenty five miles and then gusting again, to forty or more. Paddy Riley's hair streamed off the back of his head out over his forehead as he fought for his balance on the wet deck, lurching up and down, left and right, from the rising waves striking the boat. A thunder clap broke, it seemed all around them.

"Under cover, now, son... It's only a fish! The sea's full of them...!"

"Not like this one, da. Never felt a fish near as big..."

Daddy Riley braced himself on a stanchion. "Just give it up, now, Paddy, will ya, son... give it up..."

Paddy Riley was pumping the rod now, reeling and pumping, the rain so thick Jack Hennessey could barely see him from behind the engine box, memories of twenty years ago with Tim Riordan running through his mind, the boat rolling over and them both lucky to live through it.

"He's coming up! Get a net out here!" Paddy Riley shouted over his shoulder, his body drenched, his feet apart and fighting for balance on the deck as the boat lurched to starboard.

The mate grabbed the net but Captain Prenant held him at his shoulder and took the net himself, motioning the mate to man the helm. The waves had come up with the wind, white caps breaking on the bow of the boat, and the sides of it aft, spray streaming across the stern of the boat, catching Paddy Riley high and low. The mate brought the boat back into the wind as the Captain Prenent crouched out on the deck, getting to the corner of the transom and the gunnel, bracing his knee there, the spray now lashing him. He turned back to Paddy Riley, motioning him back. "Here's the leader! He's up now..."

A burst of water from the fish could be seen even against wind and wave as the fish sounded, Paddy Riley rearing back, holding the tip of the rod up, fighting for his balance, the line slicing from port to starboard following the fish. Captain Prenant ducked under it, losing his balance and falling backward, catching himself on the gunnel from going overboard, straddling it now, his left leg and foot over the side in the water.

"Grand dad!" The mate left the helm, got his arms on Captain Prenant's shoulder and held him in.

Looking forward toward the helm, George Prenant fixed on Tim Riordan, pointing to the steering wheel, spinning freely as the boat began roll sharply in the rising sea, now near broadside to it. "Point this boat up! Get her into the wind! Point her up before she rolls over!"

Tim Riordan got to the helm and turned the boat into the wind as George Prenant got both feet back on deck. Bracing himself at the knees against the inside of the transom, he picked up the net and turned to Paddy Riley. "How is he?"

"He's tired! That last run might be all he's got!" Paddy Riley was shouting in the wind as he worked the rod and reel, the fish coming easier now, the leader breaking the water. A thunder clap struck, all heads ducking, Captain Prenant fighting for his balance, grabbing the edge of the transom to steady himself.

"Here's the leader!" George Prenant shouted over his shoulder, shifting to port as he reached for the leader and worked the fish up and along the side of the boat. The mate grabbed the net and stepped under the rod in a crouch to Captain Prenant's side, handing it to him as he grabbed the gunnel for balance. Pulling the fish to the side of the boat, Captain Prenant got the net under the fish and slipped it over his head and most of its body and lifted. "Give me a hand, quick! I can't hold it!" The mate stepped next to him, helping lift the net with his left hand as he grabbed the tail of the fish with his gloved right hand to lift and keep it in the net, "Up now…" A wave struck the stern of the boat, raising it sharply, knocking them both back on the deck, and a monster rockfish on top of them.

CHAPTER THIRTY TWO
Paddy's Great Fish

They were stunned, frozen in place by the size of the thing. It lay between Captain Prenant and the mate, each up on an arm now and looking at it, leaning away in awe. Paddy Riley stood against the roll of the boat, the butt of the rod in the cup of the fishing belt, his right hand at his side, flexing against a cramp. John Riley had moved next to Daddy Riley, while Jack Hennessey held his balance at a stanchion. Tim Riordan stood fast by the helm, his right hand gripping one of its spokes, his eyes fixed on the fish. Michael Byrnes leaned forward against the front end of the engine box, looking aft, his mouth agape, his head shaking slightly side to side, his eyes fixed on the three bodies on deck, two men and a fish.

The mate was the first to move, getting to his feet and going forward in a crouch, as if not wanting to be seen by the fish or having the fish know what he was about. Captain Prenant was next, finding his feet as the rain stopped. Rising full up, he looked about. The squall had passed, gone north of them now, moving up the Bay with sunlight breaking through its trailing clouds. The wind had fallen to a complete, dead calm. Not a breath of it.

"Aye!" was the first sound made, a roar from Paddy Riley, punching a clenched fist toward the sky. *"Aye! Look at that thing! The size of it!"* He put the rod in a rod holder and stepped to the side of the fish, bending over it, his hands on his knees, looking at its length. Turning up, his eyes fixed on Captain Prenant. "Have you *ever* in your life seen the likes of this? Ever on this Bay?"

Captain Prenant shook his head, his eyes on the fish. "No, sir, never. Never in my life…" He looked at the mate, then at Jack Hennessey and then back at the fish. "Never saw the likes of that, or ever expected to…"

Paddy Riley rose up to his full height, looked at the fish, head to tail, gauged its length with his arms. "It's five feet long, maybe more." He looked about, then back at Captain Prenant. "How much does it weigh? Sixty pounds?"

"All of that, maybe seventy. We boated a fifty four-pounder a few years back, but that looked hardly a keeper next to this..."

The fish rose now and arched along its length, flapping hard three times, shaking the deck and sliding aft to the transom, the hook coming clear from its mouth. The mate stepped forward, the bat now in hand, raising it high over his head. Daddy Riley stepped in his way, taking the bat from him. He looked down at the fish as it lay still now on the deck, its huge gills working the air for oxygen, its mouth open wide, large enough to swallow a man's boot. "He's done, now, lad, let him lay..."

Jack Hennessey stepped aft, into in the sunlight, his canvas hat keeping his face in shadow, his eyes on the fish, its gills working still... "How old, captain, would a fish like that be?"

"How old?" Captain Prenant looked down at the fish. "Wouldn't know...Hard to say...Fish and Wildlife people have done gauges by length... Some fella writing in *The Pilot* had that 54 pounder we boated at over twenty years... If that's so, it'd have to make this one over thirty..."

Daddy Riley went down to a squat by the fish, patting its side with a full hand. "Thirty years fishing this Bay, aye, and the ocean sea, too...'tis quite a life, you've lived, it is..." He fixed on the fish's head, its eye seeming to stare back at him. "Where you been to, now, you great old fish? Been to the Keys of Florida, have you?" He squinted up to the others, fixing on Jack Hennessey. "I've read they go that far south, and north up to Nova Scochie, too..." He looked down at the length of the fish. "Aye, it's a grand fish that you are, now, a fish more grand than anyone here's ever likely to see again…"

A quiet now came to them all in the dead calm of the Bay, the gills of the fish opening slowly and falling shut. Daddy Riley's head began to shake back and forth, his hand finding the fish's flank again, as a man might stroke a large dog. Still in a squat, he looked up at them all, then back to the fish. "Aye, too grand a fish this is for eating, that's what I'm thinking, by the likes of us, anyways…"

Paddy Riley reared up, his eyes bearing down on his father. "What are you saying, old man? What are you saying about *my* fish?"

"What I said, that's what I'm saying, and I've said it." Daddy Riley rose to his full height and square to his son, fixing on him, then on Jack Hennessey and then back down at the fish.

Paddy Riley looked at Jack Hennessey whose eyes were on the fish, then to Captain Prenant. "Did you hear that, Captain? Am I crazy, or did I hear him say something about putting this fish back over the side? The largest rockfish *ever* landed in this Bay? You said as much yourself…" Paddy Riley looked at them all, no eyes but Captain Prenant's meeting his. "A *record* fish, maybe *seventy* pounds! That'll last forever… Your boat, Captain, the *Stormy Petrel*… record holder!" He looked back at the others, his arms out now, incredulous. "You want me to throw back the fish of a life time? Are you all *crazy*? Have you all gone *nuts*?" All eyes were away, on the fish.

"*Stromy Petrel's* already got the record, and by seven pounds." Captain Prenant fixed on the fish. Its gills were still moving, but the color, the brilliance of the silver and black stripes that marked its length, was going flat. A drool had come its open mouth. "It's up to Mr. Hennessey, here. This boat's his hire today. Other than what's legal or not legal, it's his call." He looked over at Jack Hennessey and nodded at him.

Jack Hennessey looked from Captain Prenant down to the fish, the full length of it. He closed his eyes and took a deep breath, letting it out as he raised his head and looked at the Bay about them, the gray green of the western shore in the distance. Turning, he looked at each of those about him–Daddy Riley and John, Michael Byrnes, Tim Riordan, Paddy Riley, then back down to the fish, its gills flat. He turned to Captain Prenant. "You sure, Captain? Certain, now? You'll never see another such again…"

Captain Prenant turned from the fish to Jack Hennessey. "But I *have* seen this one, now, haven't I? That's surely something…" Captain Prenant looked at Paddy Riley. "Boating them, that's the sport of it, that's what we come to do…What comes after that, well, I figure that's up to the man who fought it…"

Paddy Riley held Captain Prenant's eyes for a moment, then looked around at the others, Tim Riordan studying him, the rest looking half away. "Christ Almighty…" Paddy Riley shook his head in disbelief as he looked down at the fish. "This is how you got so old, fish, so old and fat!" He shook a his right fist at the fish. "You're just too goddam *lucky* to die, that's what!" He looked at Jack Hennessey. "Come on, I guess. Give me a hand. *It's your hire.* Let's get this thing back where it came from…"

They all stepped forward, each getting a hand on some part of it, raising the fish off the deck and over the gunnel. Landing on its side with a great splash, it laid flat and still beside the boat, not a move, its silver and black stripes taking color in the clear water of the Bay. Soon, its tail began to move, the gills now open and pumping as it took its head and headed down, a final thrust from its great tail and gone.

Jack Hennessey's eyes fixed on it. He could feel the cool of the waters about it now, the oxygen through its gills, free and alive and safe, down into the deep of the Bay …

"Are you alright, Jack?" Paddy Riley touched Jack Hennessey's near shoulder. "Jack?"

Michael Byrnes stepped to Jack Hennessey's other side. "I've cleared a bunk for you forward, Mr. Hennessey. Maybe you should lay down for a bit. I'll ask Captain Prenant to take her back slow…Give you a rest…We've plenty of time…"

Jack Hennessey stood staring at where the fish had sounded. Rising to his full height now, he turned to Paddy Riley and nodded a smile before reaching for Michael Byrnes and taking his shoulder, walking forward with him to the cabin…

Paddy Riley's eyes followed them for a few steps then fixed on Tim Riordan, looking at them as well.

Tim Riordan seemed to sense Paddy Riley's eyes and he turned to him, their eyes locking for a moment, then each away…

CHAPTER THIRTY THREE
St. Peter the Apostle

J ack Hennessey lay still in the forward berth of the *Stormy Petrel*, breathing easy, his body calmed by the movement of the boat. Fishing was done for this day. It was a cruise home now, time to get back. He heard the clunk of the transmission as Captain Prenant put the engine in forward gear and felt the forty-two foot length of the *Stormy Petrel* move ahead, turning to starboard, heading west to Deale. He tracked the sun light through the half-opened hatch above him as it swung from the head of the berth to its foot. Jack Hennessey closed his eyes, the smell of the sea and the boat about him now...

It was so big, bigger even it seemed than Cork itself. Mounting the boarding ramp of the Cunard liner *Majestic*, Jack Hennessey fixed on the thousands of rivets that held the massive steel plates to its frame, the height of its black broadside blocking out the sun itself. It seemed half again the size of the *Umbria*, maybe twice as large. Once aboard, his eyes moved fore and aft over the full length of the ship, the decks done in wide teak planks, caulked and tarred in black, crisp lines running dead straight their full length. And the beam of the thing, maybe seventy feet wide.

People were everywhere, and going wherever their duties or needs inclined them – stevedores hoisting trunks and crates, ladies in fine dresses with broad hats and parasols taking their gentlemen's arms, business men talking, ship's officers ordering their duty gangs and everywhere the sounds of life and things getting done, steam whistles and horn blasts and the call from the bridge above – *Cast off! All lines off!* Brendan Shanahan was right enough. Ireland was out of Jack Hennessey's mind before it was out of sight. Jack Hennessey was headed home.

It was a summer crossing, sun-filled days with nights so clear the sky seemed a sheer curtain of stars, some near as bright as a distant light house and others in clusters and patterns. Beyond these were the tiniest specs of light, by the thousands upon thousands it seemed, even clouds of them against the black of deep space, so distant as to be seen only by relaxing the eye and mind, more absorbing the light of them than seeing them.

After breakfast on the first day at sea, Jack Hennessey discovered the library–and its encyclopedia. It was his first experience of one. The *Encyclopedia Britannica* filled an entire shelf, held safe against the roll of the ship in a mahogany and glass cabinet. Opening it, he removed *Volume XI – Macbeth to Osmosis*, feeling its heft as he took it to a reading table and laying it open. Here, as never in his life, the world opened before him. All he need do is read about it. Each of the next seven days would begin with the *Britannica,* starting with the *Milky Way* and the mid-night sky that he was to now learn and feel some part of.

At the entrance to the *Grand Salon* of the ship was a map of the North Atlantic and on it the ship's position marked at the change of each watch, every four hours. As he passed the map at meal and other times, he found himself increasingly anxious to get home, to see his friends, Tom Brady and Tim Riordan, Fr. Power and the rest. And business. How was business? There were men on board the *Majestic* who spoke of markets and railroads and interest rates and equities, all things that Jack Hennessey knew of by effect only, not by cause. This he would fix.

These men, or who they were in Washington, anyway, he would meet. He would understand them and what they were talking about, and how they thought.

Being Charles Gessford's preferred contractor was fine as far as it went. But they were all houses, grander now, to be sure, every project, but houses just the same, three stories or four, each with a lady of particular tastes, only some less intolerable than the others. Jack Hennessey wanted to build buildings now, of six or eight stories, housing whole companies and firms, and he was looking for landfall so he could get on to doing it.

The *Majestic* landed at Pier 90 on the Hudson River at 8 am of an August Tuesday. The pier was where Forty Second Street met the river, not ten blocks up and four over from Pennsylvania Station. He had paid a premium to have his trunk amongst the first off the ship and he was through the crowds on the pier and customs in less than an hour. And it was less than that to a window seat on board the 10:38 am Atlantic Flyer for Washington, DC, as it began to roll west for New Jersey and points south. He had bought his first copy of the *Wall Street Journal* in the station and this was where it was to begin.

He sat on the right side of the train to have the shade on the trip south, holding the paper against the wind of the open window. His eyes ran down *The Journal's* columns and then, inside, to its tables of stocks and bonds and puts and calls and Kansas City Red for ninety day delivery and on to the editorials, his enthusiasm soon bearing the full weight of his ignorance of such things. After an hour of it, he put the paper down and went to the dining car for a sandwich and cup of coffee and back at it as quick, re-reading an article on New York real estate, the losses in the Panic of '93, the bankruptcies and the auctions, and the fortunes made by some coming out of it. These were verbs and nouns of which he had some experience in Washington and could sense an understanding in himself of what the article was about. He didn't know all the verbs and all the nouns, but came to a comfort with it, nonetheless, and a continuing enthusiasm to learn more.

Trenton had passed by the windows of the train and the stop in Philadelphia hardly turned his head. But as the train crossed over the Susquehanna River, seventy-five miles north of Washington, he put the paper down. Breathing the full summer air, he smelled the ground of his home. He could not speak of a particular flower or type of tree, but he knew it to be where he had come from. Memories of his travels in Ireland came back to him, the sense of having been there before. But this was different. This was not a sense of some time past, this was the reality of his life today, Jack Hennessey coming home.

As Brendan Shanahan had said, a man comes out of a ground and it is this that is his home, the place he is of. He can leave if he may, but it being of where he's from never changes. And then came back to him what he had learned in Ireland of the Hunger and what it had done to those who got through it, and now the conductor walking the aisle announcing *Baltimore! Baltimore in three minutes!*

Jack Hennessey sat bolt upright, it all now so real again, the years he had lived there, in Baltimore, the years that Mary Mulholland was his mother, the night he learned that she was not, and his leaving as quick for Washington, for anywhere to be away from it. He rose and caught the conductor between the coaches.

"Excuse me, excuse me, but will you be getting off the train at Washington?"

"Yes, sir, I will…"

"Can you see that my trunk is taken to the freight station? Here's the claiming ticket…"

The man hesitated. Jack Hennessey reached for his money clip and pressed a ten dollar bill in the man's hand. "Here, for your trouble."

The man stood back, his head up. "I am sorry, sir, that would not be proper…"

Jack Hennessey looked out the window of the door of the coach, then back at the man. "Then for a charity you might support…Do you support a charity?"

"Yes, sir, I do, but…"

"Here, then, here's twenty dollars for your charity. What could be the harm in that?"

"None, I suppose…"

"Exactly, none…" Jack Hennessey pressed the money and the claim check in the man's hand. "Thank you, thank you. Just make certain the trunk gets off the train in Washington for holding at the freight office." He pointed at the ticket in the conductor's hand. "The name's there, Hennessey , Jack Hennessey. It's on the check. I'll pick it up tomorrow."

"Yes, sir…"

The train had slowed to a near stop. The conductor reached past Jack Hennessey for the door handle, ready to open it. Jack Hennessey's fixed on him for a moment. "And what is your charity?"

The conductor stood erect, his head up. "St. Patrick's Orphanage, on Tenth Street, corner of F…"

"Yes, I know it, on Tenth Street… Thank you…"

"It's where I'm from, Mr. Hennessey."

"I see, now. Yes, of course. And your name?"

"Martin Boyle…"

Jack Hennessey took his hand and shook it firmly. "Thank you, Martin Boyle, thank you…" He turned back toward the door. 'An orphanage, St. Patrick's Orphanage…'

He hired a hansom cab at the station in Baltimore, directing the driver to St. Peter the Apostle Cemetery. It was half of an hour west of the city, in open farmland, trees rising in clumps across its hills and meadows. Asking the driver to wait, Jack Hennessey entered through an arched fieldstone gate, turning to a small building to his right, also of field stone and with a slate roof. It was unattended. No help. Where to start? Where to look?

It had been thirty years since he was last here, a summer's day then, as this, hot and him in a heavy wool suit. 'All part of the service,' Mr. Crilley had said, the high starched collar cutting at his neck as he had struggled that day with the memory of Mary Mulholland's final confession, haunted by one thought and one thought only: *Who am I?* And now, since getting off the train in Baltimore, other words, fresh in Jack Hennessey's mind, and for this all the more real 'Don't be judging us, now, don't be doing that...' Rose McCarthy's eyes on him, her head nodding.

He started up the long slope of the place, a pebble walk wide enough for a hearse and two. There were more trees, now, and more grave stones as well, tall and grand, some of them, angels at prayer and stones cut in square towers, coming to pyramid shapes at their tops. His head was down and his arms at his side, like that day thirty years ago, remembering now that he was alone, leading a line of mourners trailing behind the hearse pulled by two black horses, high black plumes affixed at their foreheads. There was no stone the day they buried her. That was to come, and he couldn't remember any of the stones nearby, if there were any at all. The stones he passed now, though, were both old and new, some lettering still sharp, others with their limestone faces showing the wear of wind and rain.

It was more than three hours past noon, now, and high summer, the sun full on Jack Hennessey's head, his hat left on the train. And as with the stars in a midnight sky at sea, he stopped looking for a particular stone and let his mind settle, not trying to remember as much as feel. The slightest of airs rose from his left and he looked that way, his eyes now fixing on the curve of the ground as it turned against a meadow beyond. "Yes...over there..." His eyes fixed on a stone with fresh flowers laying before it. Walking down a slight incline, the pebble path registering his steps, there was a sense in him of having walked this path before, drawn now to the stone with the flowers, his mind saying 'There'd be no flowers.' When he came to stand before it, though, the name was clear–*Mary Mulholland, Mother to Jack, Born in Athenry, County Galway, died July 12, 1864.*

Jack Hennessey covered a gasp from his mouth with his right hand, his legs weakening. Letting himself down, sitting askance, his eyes fixed on the words *Mother to Jack...* Mother *to* Jack. "Yes, she was that, she was mother *to* me, the only mother I ever knew." His eyes fixed on the flowers. They weren't three days old. 'Who would be putting flowers at Mary Mulholland's grave?' He looked about. No other graves had flowers, then noticing that most of the graves were unkempt, weeds at the stones, bushes uncut and the grass as well. Mary Mulholland's grave, though, was manicured. Who would keep her grave? Rising, he looked back to the gate house. Its door was still closed. He checked his watch. The rectory at St. Peter's would still be open.

An expectation of an uncertain origin grew in him as the cab found its way to St. Peter the Apostle rectory, his mind wondering who would be keeping Mary Mulholland's grave after all these years with memories of his life with her rising... There was the good and bad and all the in-between, in his mind coming to see her, now, as a woman, and one of merit and substance on Lemmon Street and in the parish, as well. It was late afternoon, the sun still high in the west, the rectory door on the south side of the building, and at the back of the church. Jack Hennessey sat in the cab, his eyes fixed on the door of it, the one he had left through the night he went to Washington...

"Sir? You alright, sir, Mr. Hennessey?"

Jack Hennessey opened the side door to the cab and let himself down to the street, looking from the rectory door to the driver. "I'm fine, thank you. Can you wait again? I'm not sure how long I'll be..."

"Don't be troubling yourself, about me, sir. A fine day for a wait-about."

Jack Hennessey started for the steps of the rectory, noting just now that the driver was English. Looking up, there was a large, cast iron knocker in the middle of the door, gloss black against varnished oak. Reaching for it, he raised it and knocked three times, stepping back to the street level, waiting. There was no response.

"Give it another go, sir..."

Jack Hennessey turned back to the driver.

"My time's your time, sir. Just don't want to be wasting any of it, now, do we?"

Jack Hennessey nodded and started back up the steps when the door opened, slowly, a man bent at the shoulders in a monk's garb, brown and tied with a cincture at his middle. The voice was strong.

"Yes, young man. How can I be of serv..." The priest rose up a measure then forward, his eyes squinting and his hand to his forehead in a quick sign of the cross. "Is that you, now, Jack? Is this Jack Mulholland come home to St. Peter's?"

Jack Hennessey froze, stepped back, blessing himself as quick at the chest. "Fr. McColgan?"

"The same, and let me give you the welcome!" The priest opened his arms and Jack mounted the steps and walked into them, the priest's shoulders back and near straight up now.

"Come in, come in, now, won't you, lad, and tell where you've been..."

Jack Hennessey woke, now. Lying for a moment in the forward berth of the *Stormy Petrel*, savoring the memory, the arms of Fr. McColgan about him. Sitting up, he swung his legs over the edge of the berth. The boat was working easily in the waters of the Bay, the whole of Jack Hennessey's return from Ireland as clear in his mind as if it had happened just that morning.

He closed his eyes, his mind reaching back. They had spent the evening and dinner, he and Fr. McColgan, talking about whatever was to come to mind, Jack Hennessey telling of Christine McCarthy and his time in Ireland, and his business in Washington. It was *Monsignor* McColgan, now, and retired at St. Peter's, and him telling of the times since Jack Hennessey had left, the families gone and come, and the trust Mary Mulholland had set up for him. Lawyer Larkin had managed it well, giving the parish funds from the proceeds for things Fr. McColgan knew Mary would approve, and the flowers each week to good Mary's grave in thanks, all done proper and waiting for the return of Jack Mulholland.

The houses had tripled in value, earning good rents, and the balances at Alex Brown doing near as well, even with the Panic. They had agreed that night that Mary's house would be kept for the memories of her and the rent it could earn, with the other houses to be sold and the proceeds put up, along with the balances, for security against the building of an orphanage, the *Mary Mulholland Home for Boys.*

Jack Hennessey stood now in the forward cabin of the *Stormy Petrel*, leaning against the berth, checking his watch–2:30. In the working of the boat through the water, the sound of the waves against the hull, he remembered Mon. McColgan's parting words the next day. "Now, Jack lad, I knew your mother better than all the others here from Galway. She had more spirit and fight than any woman I ever met. And, truth be told, in my priestly musings, when tempted of another life, it was Mary Mulholland I saw myself with, and none other. And she loved you Jack, as much as any mother could love a son, and it was me putting the words on the stone, *Mother to Jack*. I did that, now, because that's what she was, Jack–mother to you. You were first in her mind and first in her heart. And I know that to be true by knowing the woman she was, no question, none at all…"

Jack Hennessey snapped the cover to his watch closed and started aft, making his way through the companionway, passed the small galley, and stepping up on deck beside Captain Prenant, standing his helm. "Well, Captain, that's a fine berth you have there forward, and I thank you for the use of it. But I believe it's time get on home. You can take her on up any time you please."

Captain George Prenant nodded as he winked a smile and reached for the throttle. "Hang on folks, we're going up top…"

CHAPTER THIRTY FOUR
Good News and Bad

"**M**a! Ma! Come quick...wait'll you see..." John Riley burst through the screen door of the kitchen.

"What have I told you...."

"Ma, you *gotta* to see..." He grabbed her hand and led her out on the porch, down the stairs to the alley and on out to Jack Hennessey's Packard on N Street. Jack Hennessey smiled and nodded from the front passenger seat with the rest of them by the trunk of the car, Paddy nearest to it and holding a thirty-eight pound rockfish, his face beaming.

Mary Riley smiled at Jack Hennessey as she slowed to a stop, her eyes on the fish and then the rest of them. "And what's all the commotion? Sure last year's was as big, maybe bigger..."

"It's *mine* ma! *I* caught it! Didn't I, dad?"

"Sure did. Nearly took him out of the chair, but he caught it. Held that rod up and brought..."

"Aye!" Mary Riley's hands went to her face. "What a fish you've caught, John boy! The size of the thing!" She brought him close, her eyes now on the fish. "Give me a look, here." She took the fish by its gills and held it up against John Riley. "Near as big as yourself, now, it is!" She handed the fish back to Paddy Riley and in a motion hefted John Riley off the ground with a full mother's hug that he took and as quick pushed himself down from.

"There's more, now, too, Mary." Daddy Riley motioned to the ice chest, the head of one the eight pounders sticking up, its eye staring blankly about.

"That's right." Paddy Riley laid John Riley's fish back in the chest and closed it. "And Jack's having us all for a roast..."

"And everyone's coming, ma...Fr. Hara, Mrs. Kennedy, Mr. Riordan...and they're not going to cut up my fish until everyone's seen it!"

"And the dinner I've been doing...?"

"Save it for tomorrow." Paddy Riley closed the trunk of the Packard. "It's not every day a lad gets to show off a fish like this." He waved to Jack Hennessey and started toward the alley, his arm over John Riley's shoulders.

"And ma, there was this storm, too, wind and rain..."

Paddy Riley gripped the boys shoulder to silence him. "Run up ahead now, John. Get yourself a bath and a fresh set of clothes. I want a picture of you next to that fish of yours."

John Riley looked up beaming, then broke down the alley and through their gate.

"Storm?" Mary Riley looked up, fixing on Paddy Riley as they walked.

"A squall, is all. To small eyes, a squall's a storm. It was on us and gone in ten minutes, if as long as that." He held his eyes ahead, silent until they got to the gate. Gripping it, he turned to her. "Things are happening, Mary. Things are happening." He motioned her through and followed her up the stairs to the deck.

Mary Riley stopped at the screen door to the kitchen, not looking at him. "And what sort of things would these be?"

"Good things, bad things, sad things." He opened the screen door to let her pass.

She turned, looking up at him, not moving out of his way until he had looked down at her. "What's going on, now, Paddy? What's the bad, that's what I want to know..."

Paddy Riley put his finger to his lips and motioned her upstairs, following her in silence through the kitchen and hall and on up to the upstairs hall and reaching ahead to open the door to their bedroom. Facing east over

Fourth Street, the windows were in the afternoon shade, their curtains working slightly in a breeze. He closed the door behind them and she turned back, her eyes up, afraid. He put his hand to her mouth and spoke softly.

"The good news first." He smiled. "Jack's going to make me president of Hennessey Construction on Monday morning…"

Her eyes opened wide, a gasp getting through his hand. "Jesus, Mary and Joseph, and God in his heaven, too." She flung her arms around him and held him close, her head at his shoulder, stifling a sob, speaking softly. "Paddy, dear Paddy, I'm so proud of you, so proud." She leaned back against his arms and hands at the small of her back, her eyes bright in the shade and quiet of the room, at him, in him. Holding his face, she gave him a full kiss and held him again, now against him, still and unmoving. "And the bad..?"

He loosened his hold of her, stepping back, taking her hands in his. "Jack's sick I think, real sick…maybe…"

She froze for an instant, her hand up to his mouth to hold him from saying more. She stepped back and sat on the edge of the bed, looking fixed ahead. "How do you… Has he said anything …? Why do you …?"

"I don't know for sure, not really." He looked away. "All last week, at the Board of Trade, it's like he's stepping back, out…" He looked at her. "And today, today we caught this fish, a giant fish, huge, a record sure. But Jack went queer on it, wanted to put it back…Daddy Riley started it all, but Jack did it, it was his decision…He's fished that Bay his whole life…I sure never saw him put one back. And the one he did? A monster, a record fish…Then the way he smiled at me after we'd done it, like a good-bye, his shoulders slumping…He looked so weak, even frail…Then Michael Byrnes helping him to a berth forward, Jack leaning on him, taking these little steps…Tim Riordan saw it, too. I tried to speak with him about it later, Tim, but he turned away, like he knew something and didn't want to talk about it." Paddy Riley turned away. "Then this taking Hennessey Construction into the union, and bringing on Matt Malloy…All sorts of papers, something about a trust in *Baltimore*, of all places…It's like he's taking care of things before he goes…" Paddy Riley covered his mouth with his right hand and caught himself, sitting next to her on the bed.

"Oh, Paddy, now, it's not like you to be thinking the worst…"

He turned to her, nodding. "I know. That's what really scares me…It's like I know something inside, something no one's told me, just somehow know and know it more all the time…That's what scares me…"

She sat closer and put her arms about him, leaning against him.

"And tonight, the roast. He's been planning this, Mary, I bet, all week. Like it's his…his farewell party, maybe…" Paddy Riley turned away for a moment, then back at her. "Whatever it is, he's invited a whole bunch of people. He was setting it up yesterday. Had Mary calling people all over. Charles is coming over to do it…Been setting it up all day, I think. Mrs. Kennedy and her son and his family, Joe Hara, the pastor…Matt Malloy and his wife…others too, Tim Riordan…."

He sat up now. Held her eyes. "It was my idea to invite him today. Jack really liked it, though, like me getting close to Tim was really important…"

She looked back at him, not understanding.

"Like I was saying, this whole union thing looks like he wants to make sure the company gets on. Like he's not going to be here…He doesn't *want* the union, not at all. He built Hennessey Construction on his own crews, everything. He doesn't need anyone to keep it all going…He can get the business and do the building…But just no way I could do all that... It'll be easier to get work as a union shop, surer. This is what Wednesday was all about, but it's clearer to me now, what's going on..."

He stood up, started to pace. "And Tim Riordan's key to the whole thing..."

Mary Riley looked away.

He stopped. "What's that?"

She looked at him. "What's what?"

"That." He looked away as she had, then back down at her. "You looking away, about Tim Riordan?"

"Is *she* coming tonight?"

"If you mean Esther, his wife? Yes, she's coming..."

Mary Riley turned away.

Paddy Riley stood still, staring at her, waiting for her to turn back to him. She did not. He closed his eyes, opened them and she was still looking away. He went to his right and got the chair from her dressing table, set it down before her and sat facing her. "Mary..."

She now turned, her eyes on him, impassive.

"I can't believe you have this problem with her, Mary, can't believe it." He shook his head. "You don't know anything about her. I can't remember you ever even speaking with her..."

Mary Riley's eyes looked away, then back, stern, determined.

"She's a good woman, Mary, and married to a man we're likely to be needing. A good friend of the company, and Jack Hennessey's *best* friend...." He moved from the chair to beside her on the bed, reaching for her hand, holding it. "It's not right the way you feel about her, Mary. It's not right..."

She smiled at him. "And the Jew jokes you're on with all the time, now, Paddy, you and all your mates?"

His eyes froze on her, his grip of her hands loosening. "They're jokes, Mary, that's all. Just jokes. I tell as many about the Irish..."

"Sure you do, now, Paddy, dearest. Sure you do." She patted his hand as she looked away.

The room went silent, only the sound of a car rolling slowly over the brick surface of Fourth Street to be heard. 'Where does this come from? So deep and hard? This loving mother?' Resting his hands on his knees, his head bowed slightly, he spoke into the empty space of the room. "Esther Hodin was the daughter of a High Orthodox Jew in Richmond, a rabbi. Her uncle, Maurice Hodin, had taken Tim Riordan off a train platform years before, at the age of eight, and gave him a home, gave him a home when his own wouldn't take him in. Tim grew up in that house and learned the lumber business. He met Esther and they fell in love. Her father, the rabbi, forbade it. He was a partner in the company and threatened to have Tim fired. They stopped seeing one another for a while, but picked it up again, in secret. The rabbi found out. He threatened to shun her unless she promised never to see him again. She refused and he threw her out of his house."

Paddy Riley took Mary Riley's hands again, not speaking until she looked at him. "They were married by a justice of the peace and moved to Washington. Her father disowned her. He forbade her mother ever to speak with her again, and her brothers and sister, too. Not one blood relation, not one person she grew up with and called friend, ever spoke to her again. Not ever. Never once." He held Mary Riley's hands firmer. "She did that for love, Mary. That's who Esther Riordan is." He looked down at their hands. "So when you see her tonight, and she says hello to you, or sits at your table, or just smiles, try to remember what that woman did." He held her eyes. "She gave up her entire life for the love of a man, a *Christian* man…"

Mary Riley's face was blank, without expression, saying nothing.

He rose after a moment, still holding her right hand, bending slightly at his waist, his eyes away, speaking at her ear. "And if you can't take her for the good woman she is, Mary, try to find the kindness in your heart to be pleasant to the wife of Jack Hennessey's best friend."

He kissed her on the forehead, looked at her, then kissed her again before letting himself out in to the hall…

CHAPTER THIRTY FIVE
The Fish Roast

C harles Ramsey was a young man when Jack Hennessey purchased the house on Sixth Street. The previous owner had employed him as a part-time handyman and Jack Hennessey had kept him on in this capacity. While he rarely spoke of it, Charles kept a home and family in Port Tobacco, Maryland, some thirty miles down river. It was to here that he went when not cutting lawns and fixing sheds and cleaning gutters for Mr. Jack and others along the waterfront. Temperate in all things, Charles Ramsey was a man largely in control of his life, as far, that is, as nature and convention would allow.

In the years he had worked for Mr. Jack, Charles had become a first rate barbeque chef, fashioning his own grill from a 55-gallon oil drum. He'd had it split down the middle, from top to bottom, and hinged the two pieces together making of the two halves a top and a bottom. When set on its side in a wooden frame, it was a barbeque oven with a top that kept the heat in and on whatever was being cooked. Charles Ramsey's particular contribution in this was to always keep the inside top of it scraped and clean. It was his thinking that this would radiate more heat to the top of a steak or a rockfish, though he might not have chosen that word to describe the effect.

Mr. Jack had spoken to Charles on Thursday morning about doing a barbeque, asking him to bring along a bushel of steamed crabs from the docks. It was just before five when Mr. Jack and Michael Byrnes drove up, the Packard coming to a stop on N Street and Charles going over to it, opening the front door for Mr. Jack.

"Good to see you, Charles."

"Yes, sir, Mr. Jack."

"I appreciate you being available on such short notice."

"Yes, sir, Mr. Jack."

Jack Hennessey stepped out of the car and stretched, looking about his front yard. Three wooden picnic tables had been set in the shade of the trees along Sixth Street, with Charles' oven on its stand by N Street, the coals already started. Several card tables had also been set about with folding chairs, four to a table. The two Adirondack chairs normally on the open side of the veranda had been brought down with a bar set up by the front path, Charles' workbench out of the garage skirted in dark green cloth. Jack Hennessey turned to Charles.

"Looks like we're all set to go, Charles. Good work."

"Yes, sir, Mr. Jack. Thank you, sir. All we need now is rockfish. You folks catch any rockfish?"

Jack Hennessey turned to Michael Byrnes. "What would say, Michael? Did we catch any rockfish?"

Michael Byrnes went to the back of the car and opened the trunk, taking out John Riley's 38-pounder and holding it up for Charles to see.

"Lord Almighty, Mr. Jack, you sure did catch some rockfish. Yes, sir..."

They walked around the back of the car. "Got some blues, too, Charles. Why don't you start cleaning them up? Be careful, though, to leave the big one whole. We want to get a picture of it with John Riley and his dad."

"Yes, sir, Mr. Jack, I surely will." Charles lifted the chest out of the trunk of the Packard and started for the outside wet board he'd built against the back of the house for cleaning fish and game, nearby the back stoop.

Jack Hennessey turned to Michael Byrnes. "And Michael, why don't you put what's left of the tonic and beer out by the bar, and whatever's worth keeping of the food on up to the kitchen?"

"Yes, sir."

"After that, get yourself a quick shower and on up to your folks' place in the Packard."

Michael Byrnes stopped where he stood, looking at Jack Hennessey, not understanding.

"They're coming to dinner, Michael. I spoke with your father yesterday. They're expecting you a little before six." Jack Hennessey checked his watch. "That gives you exactly thirty-eight minutes. Think you can do that?"

"Yes, sir, Mr. Hennessey. In a walk. Thank you…"

"Get going, now. We'll see you then."

Jack Hennessey went to the back porch and up the stairs to the kitchen. Mrs. Kennedy was there with her son, Brian, and his wife Mary. They were standing at the counter on the far wall, just off the pantry, shucking corn. Three children, two boys and a girl, stood around the kitchen table breaking string beans.

"Well, looks like we're all here…"

They looked over, Mrs. Kennedy nodding as she shucked the last ear of corn. Brian stepped forward, offering his hand. "Good to see you, Mr. Hennessey, and thanks for having over us to dinner."

"For Christ's sake, Brian, it's *Jack*. When are you going to get that straight?" He took Brian Kennedy's hand. "Suppose I spent the whole night calling you *Doctor* Kennedy? How would you feel about that?"

"*I'd* feel pretty good about it." Mrs. Kennedy laughed. "I just never tire of hearing it said, *Dr. Kennedy*." She lifted the shucked corn and piled it near the sink for rinsing, stopping at the sound of water running outside. "Do I hear Mr. Ramsey setting up at his wet board? Did Captain Prenant find you some rockfish?"

"You wouldn't believe it if told you, Mrs. Kennedy. *No one* would believe it. Let's just say there'll be no wanting for rockfish on Sixth Street this night." Jack Hennessey smiled at Mary Kennedy, nodding as he took off his hat. "I'm going up and get a shower, maybe lay down for bit." He looked at Brian. "Michael will be up getting his folks. If anything's needs getting, could you…"

"At your service, Jack."

"There, that wasn't so hard, was it?"

Brian Kennedy smiled as he began gathering the corn husks and stuffing them in the garbage pail.

Jack Hennessey turned to Mrs. Kennedy. "Matt Malloy and his wife will be along earlier than the rest. Could you send him up as soon as he gets here, and make her comfortable?"

She nodded. "Yes, sir, as soon as he gets here…"

Jack Hennessey motioned her out into the hall and she followed him through the swinging door, standing before him. He spoke in a lowered voice. "Have you thought over what we discussed at breakfast the other morning?"

"Yes, sir, I have." She spoke in a near whisper, lowering her head for a moment then looking up at him. "I was raised mostly in an orphanage. I think you know that, Mr. Hennessey…"

Jack Hennessey nodded.

"…And I can think of no better a thing to do than finish in one." She stood up straighter. "I'd be proud to be cook and mistress here, if and when the time comes."

"Have you spoken to Brian about this?"

"I have. He'll be watching to make sure I can keep up with them all, but he's for it as well…So long as I get my weekends like now."

Jack Hennessey nodded, offering her his hand. "If it happens, that is how it will be." In the hall shadows of the coming evening, he caught the sparkle of her eyes in her smile. "I've been blessed with such friends as you, Mrs. Kennedy. Truly blessed." He kissed her hand and turned to the stairs.

Catherine Kennedy walked back through the kitchen, going directly down to her room, closing the door behind her, leaning against it, her hands to her eyes. "I must not cry, must not." She raised herself up straight, taking a deep, full breath, holding it for a moment before letting it out slowly as she opened her eyes, fixing on her kneeler. She went to it, blessing herself as she knelt, softly speaking three *Hail Marys* and a *Glory Be*. There was a knock at the door

"Mom? Are you alright?" It was Brian.

"I'm fine, son. Just need a minute, that's all…" She could hear him go back upstairs as she gazed at the crucifix before her on the wall. Reaching to it, her fingers touched Christ's feet. "Thank you, Lord, for the knowing of Jack Hennessey , for bringing us to him in our hour of need, and for the life we've lived with him since. In all your heavens, there's no finer man." She bowed as she blessed herself quickly again and started back up the stairs.

Brian Kennedy and his two boys stood outside the screen door at the top of the back stoop. They were watching Charles Ramsey at his wet board, honing his knife on a whetstone under the running water from the faucet. Shaking it dry with a flick of his wrist, he tested the edge of the blade with his thumb, nodding to himself. He took one of the eight pounders out of the fish chest and laid it out on the counter in front of him. Holding it flat with an open left hand, he glided the knife into and along the underbody of the fish, slitting it open, his right hand moving inside and pulling out the entrails, tearing them free and dropping them in a bucket set beneath the end of the wet board.

He held the fish under the faucet as he opened the cavity he had just cleared and let the water run in and through, washing the fish free of blood and loose scale before laying it flat before him. Holding the head of the fish firmly in his left hand, he cut across the flank of the fish, just behind the gills, down to its spine. Here, he turned the knife flat against the spine and then ran the blade of it along the spine's length, through to the tail fin, lifting the freed fillet and laying it on the galvanized steel surface of the wet board. He turned the fish over and repeated the process, holding this fillet in his left hand as he pushed the carcass of the fish off the end of the board and down into the bucket with his right.

Laying the fillet on the surface of the counter, he held it firm with his left hand and, with his right hand, guided the blade of the knife between the meat of the fillet and the skin for several inches, enough to get a firm grip on it. Holding the fillet on the surface of the counter with his left hand, he gripped the skin with his right and tore it off in a single motion that finished with the dropping of the skin into the bucket. Repeating the process with the other fillet, he rinsed each under the faucet, his fingers working the meat clean of all traces of blood and bone before laying them on a large pewter platter at his right...

"Good evening, Charles." Matt Molloy approached the stoop, his wife Elizabeth at his side.

Charles Ramsey turned and nodded, a bright smile coming to his face showing a gold incisor tooth. "Well, look who's come to dinner. Mr. Matt Malloy himself. How are you this fine evening?"

"Couldn't be better, Charles" He turned to Elizabeth. "Charles, this is Elizabeth. My wife."

Charles nodded a deeper nod. "Good evening, Miss Elizabeth. I am so pleased to meet you."

Elizabeth Malloy went to offer her hand but Charles waved her back. "No need for that, now, Miss Elizabeth. Cleaning fish, you'll understand." He smiled again and turned back to his work.

Catherine Kennedy was at the screen door. "Come on inside, boys. Leave Mr. Ramsey to his fish." Her eyes fell on Matt Malloy. "And Matt Malloy. So good to see you again, and so soon." She came out on the stoop. "And this must be…"

"Elizabeth." Matt Malloy took Elizabeth by the arm and walked her up the back steps as Brian Kennedy pulled his boys close and out of the way. Matt Malloy smiled at his wife. "This is Mrs. Kennedy."

Elizabeth Malloy offered her hand with a slight courtesy, smiling. "It's a pleasure to meet you, Mrs. Kennedy. Matt speaks of his year here so often."

"Did he tell about all the food he ate?" They all laughed. "He was the first budget buster. Never had I seen a boy eat like that. Never needed worry about leftovers when he was here. There weren't any. And never put on a pound…Even now, look at him. Thin as a rail." More laughter as Mrs. Kennedy ushered them in, introducing the Malloy's to Mary Kennedy and her daughter, fixing on Elizabeth. "We have iced tea made. Would you like some?"

"Yes, that would be nice."

Mrs. Kennedy started for the Frigidaire. "Matt, Mr. Hennessey asked that you come up as soon as you got here. He's in his room. Be sure to knock if the door's closed."

Matt Malloy nodded to Mrs. Kennedy, kissed his wife on the cheek and started for the hall, taking the stairs two steps at a time and finding Jack Hennessey's door open. He was on his chaise, dressed for the evening and lying in the mixed shade of the trees on Sixth Street and the muslin curtains.

"Ah, Matt. Come in, come in. Sit down, over here, close by."

Matt Malloy picked up the chair at Jack Hennessey's desk and set it by the chaise.

"You might want to get a pad and pencil, too. On the desk."

Matt Malloy got the pad and pencil and sat down, his legs crossed, ready to write.

Jack Hennessey sat up a measure, fixing on Matt Malloy. "How are you doing on all this, Matt?"

"Well, Jack, quite well. Quicker than I expected, in fact. Mid-day Monday should do it."

"The will, the trust, the house...?"

"Yes, everything. I've brought in an estate partner from Burlington and White. He's a grinder. A lot of its boiler plate."

Jack Hennessey smiled, nodding. "Yes, I expect it is." He cleared his throat. "The orphanage, though, that's got a lot of angles and corners to it, Matt. It's not going to be simple. Mrs. Kennedy wants to do it and I don't want it done without her. So she's got to be part of the deal. And it's physically located in St. Dominic's parish, so they have to get it, no matter that I've been going to mass over at St. Peter's on C Street. And I'm sure St. Peter's will be expecting something, too, for all the praying I've been doing there. So we're going have give them some money, especially when they find out St. Dominic's is going to get this house. I'm guessing $10,000 will lessen the pain sufficiently to stay in their prayers when...when... whatever..."

Matt Malloy made a note on the pad as Jack Hennessey took a deep breath, opened his collar.

"Now the orphanage is going to need some sort of legal status, a trust or something. Has to be separate from the general holdings of the parish. If we're not careful, *Monsignor* Ryan might take a fancy to it, make it his summer rectory or something..."

Matt Malloy smiled as he made a note.

"...A board of directors and all that..." Jack Hennessey took a deep breath and pushed himself up a measure again, fixing on Matt Malloy. "This is going to take some time to get it all straight, Matt, more time than

I'm likely to have. You're going to be doing most of the thinking and talking." Another deep breath. "Be sure that's in the papers you're working up, now, you know...that you alone have the authority. And when I introduce you to the Monsignor tonight, I'll make that clear to him. I'm also going to suggest to him, and in the clearest words I can manage, that Joe Hara is to be the point man in the rectory on this. I want it under him and run by him."

Matt Malloy was making notes, underlining words, sitting back, checking what he'd written.

Jack Hennessey leaned to Matt Malloy. "I've stopped telling people, Matt, about all this, you know...Seemed to hurt them more than I wanted to watch." He looked away, toward the river, then back. "The only ones here tonight that know are you, Mrs. Kennedy and Fr. Hara." He took another deep breath. "And get to know him, too, now, Matt, Fr. Hara. He's a good one. He's Paddy's best friend. They're a pair for life..."

"Then Paddy doesn't know..?"

"Not from me. Don't know how I'm going to handle that, yet. I'm writing a letter to him. Going to leave it with Joe Hara. That might be the best way to do it...We'll just have to see..."

Jack Hennessey's eyes lost focus, his right hand went to his chest, then his left. "Get me some water, Matt, quick."

Matt Malloy stepped quickly to the bathroom and came back with a glass of water, putting to Jack Hennessey's mouth as he held his head forward to drink. "I'll get..."

"You'll get nobody, you'll tell no one..." Jack Hennessey took the glass and drank some more water before putting the glass on the reading table. He felt his head, wiped the sweat from his brow on his pants leg. "It's called arrhythmia, and something else. We read all about it in the Merck." He pointed to his desk. Matt Malloy started to rise. "Don't bother. Nothing you need to know anything about, and there's nothing to be done about it, anyway. Hell, could be the first break I've had since this whole cancer thing started..."

Jack Hennessey wiped his brow again, looking at his hand. "Less now. Likely it's passed." He looked at Matt Malloy. "That's how it works. Dizziness, sweating, your heart going like sixty, then it all settles down again. You get tired after, but it's all fine again, normal." He closed his eyes for a moment then opened them, fixing on Matt Malloy, reaching for his hand. "You're my executor, Matt. It's on you to get the right things done with what I've got...making things a little better around here." He nodded at Matt Malloy. "You spent a year with me as a squire and you've known me since, know me about as well as anyone. Just get the right things done, Matt, that's all I'm asking you."

Matt Malloy pulled the sheets of paper on the pad back over and uncrossed his legs. "I'll do my best, Jack."

"You're best will be good enough, Matt. Now get on downstairs with everyone. I'm going to rest for a bit longer. First thing when I get down, though, is we have a drink with Fr. Hara and monsignor what's his name."

"Yes, sir."

—————

Matt Malloy went down the front stairs into the foyer and on out to the veranda. He recognized most of whom he saw. Tim Riordan and his wife, Fr. Hara and Monsignor Ryan. Mary Smith, Jack Hennessey's secretary, and her husband Harold, just arriving with what looked to be their four children, huddled close, looking at Brian Kennedy's children who were looking back, wondering, curious. Paddy and Mary Riley were by the bar fixing themselves a drink with John Riley over by the barbeque, watching Charles Ramsey. Mary Catherine Riley was at a picnic table picking at a steamed crab with a friend. Daddy Riley was nearby them with his other son, Edward, his wife Patricia at his side, her arms folded across her middle. Michael Byrnes was walking from the Packard with what must be his parents, headed toward Mrs. Kennedy who sat at a picnic table with Elizabeth Malloy, newspapers spread across it and the two of them working on steamed crabs.

Heading for that table, Matt Malloy reached out to Michael Byrnes and shook his hand. "Good to see you again, Michael."

"You, too, Matt." He stopped, turning to his parents. "These are my parents, Matt." They formed a small circle.

Matt Malloy shook their hands, Mr. Byrnes a man of average height with a quick smile, and his wife curtseying slightly as she offered her hand.

"Very happy to meet you, Mr. Malloy…"

"It's 'Matt', and very nice to meet you, as well." Matt Malloy gestured to the table where Elizabeth and Mrs. Kennedy were eating crabs, all standing and helloing as they approached with Michael Byrnes taking his mother to Mrs. Kennedy. "Ma, this is Mrs. Kennedy. Mrs. Kennedy, this is my mother." They shook hands then gave each other a brief hug.

Mrs. Kennedy stepped back. "I was just telling the others that Matt here broke the food budget when he was a squire. But your son, here, Michael, well he just *shattered* it. There were never any leftovers, and some nights I found myself going back to the pantry to get enough food in him so he'd sleep the night through…"

Mrs. Byrnes smiled, nodding that she knew, that she was proud of her son beyond speaking.

"I'll get some iced tea." Matt Malloy left and they all settled at the table, Mrs. Kennedy lifting up some crabs from the bushel. "Got to eat all the crabs before we get to Mr. Ramsey's rockfish. That's the rule!"

Now there's a leveling element to the eating of steamed crabs, banging the claws with wooden mallets and breaking the shells off the body of the crab and then breaking the body in half to get at the meat. In this, pretense is impossible. Mrs. Byrnes wiped her face and hands with a paper towel, fixing on Mrs. Kennedy. "We don't see Michael much these days, Mrs. Kennedy, but whenever we do, he speaks so highly of you. We are so happy he's had this chance…"

"It's been just wonderful for him." Mr. Byrnes reached for another crab. "The people he's met, what he's learned…It's as good as a year of college by my thinking, maybe two…"

"Do you have children, Mrs. Kennedy?" Mrs. Byrnes smiled, leaning forward against the table.

"Two sons." Mrs. Kennedy sat up, looking about, motioning to Brian Kennedy, by the bar with Paddy Riley. "That's Brian, speaking with Mr. Riley." She fixed on Mrs. Byrnes. "Brian was my student. Got full scholarships out of Gonzaga, to Catholic University and then Georgetown Medical School. His father would have been so proud."

"Yes, so proud, I'm sure." Mrs. Byrnes sat back, her hands clasped and against her chest.

"My younger one, Stephen, he went to Gonzaga, too. Like Brian and your Michael. But he struggled. Quick as a whip, that boy, but book-learning just came hard to him. He was class of 1916. Hennessey Construction was full up busy with war coming on and Mr. Hennessey brought him in as an office boy. After a bit, though, he started to drive Mr. Hennessey around to meetings, parking being a problem and all, and pretty soon that's most of what he did, that and running errands. Plenty of work, all hours. Brian was finishing up at Catholic University and pushing

Stephen to apply, but there was no chance of that. Like I said, war was coming and there was just no way on God's green earth that Stephen Kennedy was going to miss a war if one came up." She sat back, her eyes on the table.

"And it did...and he joined the Marines." She looked up, pointed at Mrs. Byrnes. "Now, *they* knew what to do with a boy like Stephen Michael Kennedy, let me tell you that...And they did it! My word, what they did with that boy. Well, he wasn't a boy any more, now, though, was he? When we got him back?" Mrs. Kennedy nodded at Mrs. Byrnes. "No, ma'am. He may still have smiled like a boy, and such a nice smile too, but he was all *man*, hard as stone and sharp like a knife. He'd found a place, that boy had, and he knew what to do in it, too. Never was that boy happier..." Her eyes went back to the table, still now, vacant.

"And then they sent them off, my Stephen and the rest. The Marines like to be the first in, you know, and my Stephen was all Marine, all Marine...Then...then he...then Stephen...was killed...They called it Bellow Wood...in France...Bellow Wood..." She fixed on Mrs. Byrnes. "In my entire life, Mrs. Byrnes, I never imagined such a hurt. Did not know there was such pain, that it was possible, so deep, so long..."

Mrs. Kennedy looked around the table now. "They gave him a medal for bravery, and then, later, they sent us a letter saying where he was to be buried in France... And the hurt came all over again, my boy in a foreign land, never to be home again... There was a mix-up, is what. They thought I wanted him buried there for some reason. I didn't know what. But I wanted him here, near me, *here*...I didn't know what to do..." She sat up. "Well, let me tell you, Jack Hennessey, he knew what to do! And quick, too. He went off to France, himself, on his own, and he got it fixed, got my boy, my Stephen, got him home. There and back in three weeks. And we buried

Stephen in Arlington National Cemetery..." She raised her head, looking to her left, across the river. "That's where my Stephen is..."

Mrs. Kennedy looked around the table, the eyes of each on her. She waved them off. "Oh, it's alright now. Really it is." She shook her head. "The hurt's passed, now. I don't know how, but it's passed. But not the love...No, never the love..." She looked over toward the bar. "Here's Mr. Hennessey. You'll have to excuse me, now."

Jack Hennessey was talking with Paddy and Mary Riley. He had a whiskey in hand, Paddy a beer and Mary a wine. Mrs. Kennedy nodded to the Rileys. "Mr. Riley, Mrs. Riley." She looked at Mr. Hennessey. "We're about done with the crabs. You wanted a picture of that fish with John and Mr. Riley?"

Jack Hennessey stood erect. "Yes, yes. Need that picture." He looked around. "We have to get the whole fishing party in on it." He looked at Paddy. "Can you get to that?" He looked around again, "We'll do it over by the barbecue."

"I'll get the camera." Mrs. Kennedy went up the steps to the house.

Tim Riordan had just walked his wife to the steps, she going inside. "Jack...Jack..."

Jack Hennessey turned to him. "Yes, Tim. Good to see. Just down from a nap. Long day on the Bay. How about that squall?"

Tim Riordan nodded, sipped his beer. "Hope never to see another like it." He fixed on Jack Hennessey. "Are...you alright, Jack?"

Jack Hennessey looked away, then back. "Alright? I'm fine. What do you mean?"

"Nothing, I guess. Nothing." Another sip of beer. "Paddy said something about a picture?"

"Yes. Over by Charles. I want to make sure Michael Byrnes is in it. Got to have Daddy Riley, too…"

Jack Hennessey started for the barbeque when he saw the Byrnes at their table and turned, smiling as he stepped to them.

"Mr. Hennessey…" Michael Byrnes rose. "Mr. Hennessey, you remember my mother and father."

Mr. and Mrs. Byrnes rose and stepped around the table toward Jack Hennessey, offering their hands. Mr. Byrnes reached furthest out. "It's an honor, Mr. Hennessey."

Jack Hennessey took Mr. Byrnes' hand in his left hand and hers in his right. "The honor, I assure you, Mr. and Mrs. Byrnes, is mine. To have raised such a son, what more can be done than that?" He paused, thinking of what he had just said, then fixed on them. "I tell you, *nothing*…There is *nothing* more important than that. *Nothing*." He nodded at Michael Byrnes then turned back to them. "May I borrow Michael for a minute?"

"Certainly."

Jack Hennessey rested his right hand on Michael Byrnes shoulder and started toward the barbeque where the others had gathered. Mrs. Kennedy had given the camera to Matt Malloy and he stood before them, pointing to each in the fishing party where to stand, arranging them around John Riley in the middle, holding the fish across his chest. Then another picture, this with just John and Paddy Riley, and then one with them and Daddy Riley. The fourth and last was of John and Paddy Riley and Jack Hennessey.

When the picture taking was done, John Riley handed the fish to Charles Ramsey who took it to the wet board, they all following. In the quiet of the evening light, he sharpened his knife and filleted the fish, hefting each fillet under the water to clean it of blood and scale, then taking the fillets back to the barbeque for seasoning. The pair was then set together on the grill, Charles leaving the top open at first. "That sure is the biggest rockfish I seen this season…"

The fishing party stood in a circle, surrounding the grill, all eyes on the fillets and the glow of the coals beneath. On Charles' words, they had nodded their heads in silent unison. Theirs had become a brotherhood, a shared knowledge that somewhere in the deep of the Bay there roamed a monster bull rock that, before one year was done, would fish the ocean sea from the north end of the continent to its south, and they each and together had a place in the wonder and majesty of it all…

CHAPTER THIRTY SIX
Sunday Mass

J ack Hennessey woke early on Sunday despite a late evening and more to drink than he'd had in some years. Lying in bed, he thought about the party – John Riley's fish and Michael Byrnes' parents and how Mrs. Kennedy's grandchildren had grown. It was full light outside. Sitting up, he checked the clock – 7:00. Plenty of time before eight o'clock mass. He laid back down, his right hand covering his chest, feeling for his heart. Normal. Closing his eyes, his mind drifted back to the night before, and Tim Riordan asking him how he felt. 'He knows...He knows...Yes, Tim Riordan...Yes, he would know.'

Michael Byrnes had dropped Jack Hennessey at the front entrance of St. Peter's, driving off to park the car. Jack Hennessey stood on the side walk, looking up at the façade of the church and then at the steps, easily as many as to his veranda. Looking right, he took a deep breath and reached for the hand rail, taking it firmly as he mounted the steps. He was early, only a few others about. Going in, he approached the altar, stopping half way down the aisle, there genuflecting before stepping into the pew. He sat on the aisle, laying his hat beside him, resting his left arm over the end piece of the pew.

Looking at the altar, bright in the morning sun, a smile came to his face. 'Further up, now, Jack, further up. You should be sitting further up.' Christine had always been on him to sit further up. 'Nearer the front, now, Jack, is where you should be, with your contributions and place in the parish. A close friend, now, aren't you to Monsignor Power? And sure, now, isn't he always looking to you for ideas on this and that, and to help with the fund raising?' She never had in mind herself, he remembered. To her, it was just the way things should be, less confusion among the others at a mass wondering whether they should be sitting in front of him.

An altar boy came out wearing a white surplice over a black cassock, a candle lighter in his right hand. Crossing in front of the tabernacle, he genuflected as he made the sign of the cross, then mounted the steps of the altar and lighting the candles on either side of the tabernacle and returning to the sacristy. Jack Hennessey's eyes turned back to the altar, closing now to pray, the faces of those at the party last night coming to mind, all smiling, saying their 'good nights' and 'thank you's' and then the thought that there would be no more such events in his life... No more trips to Deale, no more fishing parties, his mind going to the warmth and the quiet of an evening by the river with crabs and rockfish and corn on the cob and Mrs. Kennedy's muffins and on into the cool of the night...

The rhythmic recital of the Latin mass had lulled Jack Hennessey into the twilight of a near nap from which he was roused by the priest mounting the pulpit and reading the gospel. It was the parable of the laborers in the field and the discontent of those working a full day and getting the same pay as those who worked only the last hour of it. 'Bargain hard and keep your word,' Tom Brady had said. 'It's as simple as that, now, lad.' Tom Brady's face was as clear in Jack Hennessey's mind as if he had been sitting next to him in the pew next to him, and his voice in the memory clearer still. 'You're getting them work, now, Jack, something they couldn't find on their own or they wouldn't be available to you, now, would they? No, not at all. You're bringing it to them, now, don't you see? And isn't it your name that's writ on the line, on the contract? Sure it is, now. And if you can't keep your men to the deal they made with you, then you'll be gone as quick and back here looking for work yourself.'

And that was how it had begun. Learning masonry and brick laying around Swampoodle and finding work with contractors nearby in Northeast and Southeast, then getting better and faster at it than those he was with and signing the odd contract on his own and then on up from there. The Panic of 1873 was the ruin of many about and he stepped up when it was done, and before anyone knew it he was running three crews of brick layers and looking to know carpenters and stone masons to bid with, building houses in Washington as the city grew. 'Common sense' is what Jack Hennessey would say when someone from *The Rose* would ask how he'd done it. 'Common sense, and keeping your word' is what he'd tell them.

By the tone and rhythm of the sermon, it was coming to a close, all about labor and unions and a man being worth his wage and in need of his pride and dignity, too. Jack Hennessey had no trouble with any of this. What he'd never liked was the sense of the thing, organized labor and unionism, being told that he wasn't fair to his men, and an organizer coming between him and the crews. He'd got by by paying union scale and keeping them busy and being sure they knew how to do what they were being paid to do, that they were competent–that was *his* job.

It was after he'd got back from Ireland and into bidding office buildings and putting them up two and three at a time with iron workers and stone masons and plumbers and steam fitters and subcontractors for a lot it, with more than 100 on his own payroll, that he'd lost close touch with the crews. With Paddy Riley, and others like him, he was able to keep staffed and get the business. Without himself to get the business, though, there'd be no business, and no Hennessey Construction Company, neither. Unthinkable…

Those kneeling in the rows in front of him began to rise for Communion. Two or three rows and up to his right, Jack Hennessey caught sight of Esther Riordan and then Tim just behind her. He hadn't seen Tim at St. Peter's in some time. Before he could turn away, Tim Riordan caught his eye and nodded. 'Too late.' Jack Hennessey nodded back and rose, stepping into the aisle and the communion line. 'If he knows, he knows. We'll talk.'

He stepped forward toward the altar, the woman in front of him of the size and posture of Christine, the raven hair under her black lace veil, the shoulders square. Memories flashed by of their time together, the Sundays they went to mass here at St. Peter's. He knelt next to the woman for communion, stealing a glance at her face, her head back to take the host. Pretty enough, but not Christine, not at all. The memories, though, yes, the memories, lingering as he took communion, rising to return to his pew…

It was more than forty years that she was gone. The memory of last week at Mt. Olivet, of her walking its grass and picking the plot, her laughter, the sense of her presence, her smile. It was a Tuesday that she died, their last mass together the Sunday previous, in this pew perhaps, sitting beside him, her hands resting on her middle, her eyes closed in prayer and quiet anticipation. She never once had seemed fearful, of the pain or it going badly. For Christine McCarthy Hennessey, life was to be lived and she lived it as it came…

"Jack?"

Tim Riordan's voice startled him, Jack Hennessey leaning away, now, and half rising.

"I'm sorry, Jack." Tim Riordan's hand gripped Jack Hennessey's shoulder to steady him. "Didn't mean to scare you, now, Jack. Just wanted to say hello."

Jack Hennessey rose from the pew, fixed on Tim Riordan, found himself looking about for Esther, then back at Tim Riordan. "That's alright, Tim. Just day dreaming I guess." He looked about, then settled back on Tim Riordan. "And how are you, this morning, Tim?"

"Good, well. Good...Got a minute Jack? Can I sit with you?"

The church was empty now and Jack Hennessey nodded, moving back into the pew to make room as he sat down. "Sure, Tim. Here, sit down." He eased his hat further into the pew.

Tim Riordan stepped into the pew and sat down, looking about before he spoke. "Jack, got to ask how you're doing, here...Gotta tell ya, you looked a little off, there, on Saturday..."

Jack Hennessey sat up. "I'm fine, Tim... good as gold..." He looked up at the altar, then back at Tim Riordan, shaking his head, his right hand moving to his chest, not in pain but to reassure, comforted by the beat of his own heart. He took a deep breath then fixed on Tim Riordan. "No, Tim, that's not true. That's a lie, and I'm sorry for it." He fixed hard on Tim Riordan, reaching for his arm. "I'm not well, Tim. Not at all." A deep breath. "I'm dying..."

Tim Riordan stiffened, his eyes wide and fixed, his right hand going to Jack Hennessey's shoulder. "Christ, Jack...Whatcha got? How long you known? Christ..."

"Well, the sure thing is pancreatic cancer..."

"The *sure* thing? What the hell's *that* mean? How many things you got, here Jack, for Chrissake? The '*sure*' thing..?"

Jack Hennessey chuckled to himself, 'God I love this man...'

"It's complicated, Tim. Give me a minute." A deep breath, a pause taken. "The cancer is going to do it in six to twelve weeks, maybe a little more, but not much. The cancer's where the weight loss is, the skin color a little off..."

Tim Riordan nodded. "Yeah, that's what I'm seeing, why I come over..."

"But I've also got arrhythmia, too, heart going like sixty every now and then, dizziness, the sweats...That could take me any time..."

"Can they do anything about that?"

"Yes, if I check into Providence or somewhere, they can manage it, keep it under control, you know, keep me alive, make sure I get the full course of the cancer...the pain, the wasting away inside, not able to eat..."

Tim Riordan nodded again and raised his hand. "Spare me, Jack, spare me. I already know where going, and it's not to the hospital..."

"You got it."

Tim Riordan looked away, fixing ahead, now swallowing hard before turning back. "I'm sorry, Jack..." Tim Riordan's shoulders sank. "You're my best friend...my best..."

Jack Hennessey gripped Tim Riordan's arm. "Don't, now Tim, please don't...None of that..." He looked at the altar and then the stained glass window above it. "Christine loved that glass. In the late spring, like now, she'd come up here in the afternoon, to see the sun full through it...I could see it in her eyes when she got home from it, what it did to her inside...God, I loved her, Tim, I loved her so..."

Tim Riordan put his arm across Jack Hennessey's shoulders and held him close.

Jack Hennessey sniffled and shook his head, looking back at Tim Riordan, sitting up a measure, a bit away. "Well, now, Tim, soon I'm going to know the answer of the ages...What's on the *other* side? *Is* there an 'other side'?" He nodded at the altar, motioning to the inside of the church with his arm. "Is there anything to this at all, the prayers, the sacraments, the saints, the *all* of it? Or is it all just something we make up to get by, to help us through the hard parts of a life until it's all over, *really over*...a big fat ZERO... *Nothing*..."

"*Jesus*, Jack..." Tim Riordan sat up, laying his hand on Jack Hennessey's arm to quiet him, now looking around to see if anyone was nearby, then back. "Got to be careful, here, Jack talking like that, now. They'll have us up on felony sacrilege for Chrissakes...Could make kicking the bucket look like a day at the beach..."

Jack Hennessey held his breath against a laugh as Tim Riordan took his arm and helped him up and out of the pew. Genuflecting together toward the altar, they turned and started for the vestibule, hands over their mouths to keep from laughing out loud.

Jack Hennessey was first to the door, and he held it open for Tim Riordan who stepped outside to the top of the steps. As Jack Hennessey was about to step through the door, he froze in place, fixing on Tim Riordan. "Did you hear that..?"

"Hear what?"

Jack Hennessey looked at Tim Riordan, then about and above them. "Nothing, nothing..." He turned toward the altar, his ear cocked forward, a smile now coming to his face, a slight nod of the head. "Give me a minute, Tim. My hat, got go back for my hat..."

CHAPTER THIRTY SEVEN
Born American

M att Malloy parked his car on N Street, just behind Jack Hennessey's Packard. Reaching for his briefcase in the back seat, he got out of the car, going around front, scanning the front lawn. It was empty. The picnic tables and the bar and Charles Ramsey's oven, all gone, the lawn raked clean. Mounting the steps, he could hear Jack Hennessey speaking. Matt Malloy cleared his throat to announce himself as he crossed the veranda, reaching for the screen door and letting himself in.

"Good afternoon, Matt." Jack Hennessey remained seated. Paddy Riley rose, moving the chair he was sitting in back to make room for Matt Malloy then extending his hand. "Matt."

"Paddy." Matt Malloy shook his hand and turned to Jack Hennessey, nodding. "Jack..."

"Here, sit down. We're just getting started. Iced tea?" Jack Hennessey was pouring a glass. Matt Malloy took it as he sat down, resting his brief case against a corner leg of the table. "Thanks for coming over, Matt. Especially on a Sunday, and even more on one such as this." Jack Hennessey sat back, his arms out at the afternoon sun breaking through the tall poplars beside the house in great shards of light, yellow on the green of the grass and the shrubby.

"Not a problem. Happy to be here." Matt Malloy raised his iced tea to the others and sipped it.

Jack Hennessey put his drink down and motioned toward Paddy Riley. "Our first order of business is making Paddy here President and CEO of Hennessey Construction Company. Pretty simple, I expect, me owning eighty-five percent of the company and all. But I think we should give some notice to the other shareholders. There's only four of them, and I'll call them all first thing. But Matt, I want something couriered over to them in the morning, too. Mary Smith has their address and numbers. Make it official. Can you work that up?"

"No problem." Matt Malloy reached for this brief case and took out a pen and legal pad, making a note.

"Next...the unions." Jack Hennessey looked at Paddy Riley. "I had breakfast with Tim Riordan this morning after mass. Nothing I planned on." Jack Hennessey looked away, then at Matt Malloy. "...Anyway, we had breakfast." He fixed back on Paddy Riley. "Paddy, just how hard did you hit that son of a bitch Conley, anyway?"

"Just as hard as he needed hitting." Paddy Riley pushed back from the table. "He still crying about that? Pissant..."

"He's all of that and less. Problem is, he may be having second thoughts about our agreement, about Hennessey coming into the union..."

"Didn't they sign the letter? I thought you said they signed it?"

"They signed it, alright. Matt's got it with him. All notarized." Jack Hennessey sat back. "That doesn't mean that son of bitch Conley can't be a son of a bitch about it..."

"What's he want? An apology, for Chrissakes? That's what he was whining about ten years ago. Gonna press charges against me, he said. Have me thrown in jail for assault and battery. Wouldn't apologize then, won't do it now..."

"That's what I told Tim. Told Tim you wouldn't, and that I wouldn't let you even if you were inclined. No way to start with a union, especially with Conley running it...."

"So...?"

Jack Hennessey looked at Matt Malloy then back at Paddy Riley. "So here's what we're going to do. We – the three of us – we're going over to the hall tomorrow afternoon. Tim's getting it set up for 3 o'clock. By then, it'll already be out that you're the President of the company. We go over to the hall to make the announcement, Hennessey Construction is going union, come to sign the master agreement, right then and there. Apply for membership in the AGC, sign their master agreement, all of it." He looked at Matt Malloy. "That's your homework for tonight. I want a draft announcement we can bring on in, make it easy for them when Paddy and I go in at 3…"

Matt Malloy nodded, making notes, looking up.

Jack Hennessey fixed on Paddy Riley. "Now Paddy, I want you in your best suit, hair combed back, smiling like some Mick at a squire's hanging. The trade press will know about it, we'll make sure of that." He looked at Matt Malloy who made a note. "A photographer, maybe two. Anyway, the key is that you and me go into Conley's office all smiles and happy and just thrilled that the largest non-union general contractor in the city is signing on. That's when you get that big Mick hand of yours across the desk, all smiling and hoping that bygones can be bygones and let's be getting on. Tim will have already told him that the Hecht warehouse deal is done, and it's ours…"

Paddy Riley and Matt Malloy sat up, looked at one another, then at Jack Hennessey.

"Yes, that's right. It's done. Hecht got their financing committed with Hennessey Construction down as contractor. It'll come out Tuesday morning, but it's done, and it's ours." Jack Hennessey winked at Paddy Riley. "Know your banker, Paddy, know your banker. One way or another, everything goes through the banks. They know things ahead of just about everybody else. Yes, sir, gentlemen, the largest non-government project in the city and Hennessey Construction's got it..." Jack Hennessey picked up his iced tea, raising it to the others.

Paddy Riley raised his glass. "Incredible, Jack, incredible..."

"What? You didn't think we'd get it? You *doubted*?"

"No, I knew you'd get it. What's incredible is that we're sitting here toasting a deal like that with iced tea!"

Jack Hennessey laughed, shrugging as he raised his glass a little higher, smiling at them both. "So that's done. There's no way Conley can keep us out if we make the gesture to go there, shake their hands on it with flash bulbs popping."

Jack Hennessey sat back, fixing on Paddy Riley. "And now, Paddy, there's you being President of Hennessey Construction Company, Inc." He paused, nodded. "You *are* the President of Hennessey Construction Company, Paddy, from now on. Done. I'll be down as chairman, but that's it, that's all. I'm going to chair the board meetings, which is you and me and Matt here as Secretary. We're going to have monthly meetings and all, and I'll be around and available in the first few months, but that's it." He looked at Matt Malloy, then at Paddy Riley, winking.

A ferry whistle sounded and Jack Hennessey turned toward it, fixing on the side wheels of *The City of Richmond* as it backed out of its slip before he turned back to Paddy Riley, motioning to Matt Malloy. "Paddy, I want you looking to Matt for any help you need. Might be a good idea to give him the title of General Counsel, but I leave that to you. He's available twenty-four hours a day. I want you leaning on him, especially as we go union. They're a tricky bunch. They get paid to be pushers and we're the pushees, so stay close."

Paddy Riley nodded, looking at Matt Malloy and nodding to him as well.

Jack Hennessey cleared his throat. "There'll be others, too, folks and hangers-on looking for favors and contributions, offering you kick backs on deals, the low lifes of the city. I know you're an honest man, but you're going to be tempted now as never before. Keep your friends close, Paddy. I know most of them, and they're good people. Hold them close and watch the new folks. If you don't like a person right off, put high stock in that. You're probably right about him. Most of it's instinct, and it's really important. People will be wanting to get to know you, and a lot of them you'll want no part of. Trust me on that. Keep your distance and watch who you're seen with. And remember this above all else, at the end of the day, all you really got is your *word*. 'Bargain hard and keep your word,' that's what Tom Brady told me once, and it's the best advice I ever got."

Jack Hennessey sipped his tea. "Now you being of an Irish-born father and the head of an Irish-named company that's doing well, there's a special caution. Likely as not, you'll be getting a call from the boys back home. *Finians* is what we called them. They'll be on you for money, and whatever else they think they can get from you – for the 'Cause'."

Paddy Riley nodded.

"They get their claws into you, Paddy, there's no making them happy. Trust me on that, too. A year or two after I got back from Ireland, back in '94 or '95, a certain Martin Flaherty called on me. I learned from Tim Riordan that his real name was Flynn, Michael Flynn, and that he was wanted in Dublin for bombing a railroad station or two. Real pushy fella, telling me my 'duty to home' and all that." Jack Hennessey sat up.

"Now I'd been giving money to charities over there that Monsignor Power linked me up with. Scholarship programs, too. But this Mr. Flaherty, he wanted help to make trouble, and I wasn't inclined." Jack Hennessey nodded at them. "Wouldn't been even if I had taken a liking to him, which I didn't, pushy son of a bitch that he was..."

Jack Hennessey sipped his drink and looked away, then back. "Tells me I have this 'obligation,' he said. Real slow and important. A 'sacred calling' he claimed that I wasn't honoring. Speaking in a way like I'd be regretting it if I didn't sign on. Tells me I'm tied to the land I was *born* to, like he knew something he wasn't supposed to know about me. Like he knew Monsignor McColgan at St. Peter's in Baltimore had entered me as born at sea, making me a natural born American and citizen, rather than born in Ireland, which in truth I was...that sort of thing.

"Anyway, I told him 'We're men, not salmon. Where we end up is on us. Home is where we call it.' Jack Hennessey sat forward, sipped his iced tea. 'Blah!' he says, waving me off for a fool. Like I said, it wasn't going well, this little talk we were having, and right from the start. Then he treads sacred ground. 'Your Christine, now,' he starts, 'she living in Ireland till near thirty years, sure she'd be seeing the need to help...'"

"He was getting real close now, talking about my Christine, like he knew her, like she'd pay him more heed than a passing gnat, trying to use it to his advantage. I leaned closer to him. 'Christine McCarthy,' I said, 'was *born an American*. She just didn't know it till she got here,' that's what I told him." Jack Hennessey sat back, nodding his head for emphasis before sitting forward again.

"Then he starts on me how awful it was in Ireland–all about how they couldn't own land, had no vote of any use, that it was the last colony in Europe, Cromwell had stolen it and how he and his lads were going to take it back. 'And mark my words, Jack Hennessey, we'll have it back, we will. We've got the lads. It's the guns we're needing.'"

"'If life's so bad in Ireland,' I told him, 'why not come over here? Hell, it's not exactly a new idea. There are more Irish-born in New York City than there are in Dublin, for Chrissake. And there's still plenty of room. They're pining for good men all over the west...'"

"'Blah!' he says again. 'Slave wages for slave jobs,' he says. 'Who'd be wanting to come to a place like this, now, Mr. Jack Hennessey. Kept out of where we're not wanted, and all just for being Irish-born or bred?' And he goes on. 'So grand over here, now, is it, Mr. Hennessey, in your *wonderful* America. *Irish Need Not Apply.* You've seen this, I'm sure. 'Tis on every doorway and window, keeping us from jobs and a place to live. And I'm told, now, Mr. Hennessey, you're familiar with *Swampoodle,* and sure wasn't that a fine bit of hell after a summer's rain, the stink of the place with Irish at every corner, begging work or food?'"

Jack Hennessey made a face, winked at them. "Well, now, this got me to my feet. Here was a man looking for trouble and was just that close to finding it." Jack Hennessey held his hand up, his thumb and index finger near touching, now sitting up in his chair. "'Course, now, he's up, too, head back, chest out, taking my measure, getting close. "Careful, now, Martin Flaherty,' I cautioned, 'Careful, now. Watch yourself...'"

"Well, now, that was all he needed to hear, staring at me, his eyes aflame, stammering something as came with a fist so slow I had to wait for it to grab. 'Christ,' I'm thinking, 'why's this fella not dead, slow as he is with his fists.' Anyway, I grabbed his fist and got it and his arm up behind his back before he even knew what was happening and started him for the door. Shoved him out on First Street, over some whiskey cases stacked at the curb, and into the gutter. Splat!" Jack Hennessey smacked an open hand on the table. "Well, now, there he is, In the gutter, sitting up, wiping mud and horse shit from his face, looking at me, no idea at all of what had just happened to him.

"'So, Mr. Flaherty,' I said, 'We're agreed then...'"

"''Agreed?' he roared, struggling to his feet, reaching for a light pole for balance. 'Agreed are we? Now in what particular way would that be, Mr. Hennessey, that we're *agreed*?'"

"Someone had handed me his hat from the bar. 'This is how we're agreed' I said. 'I'm going to let you save Ireland, and you're going to leave the saving of America to me!' I threw his hat at him. 'Now you stay away from me, you son of a bitch, or you'll end up worse than in a gutter!'"

Paddy Riley and Matt Malloy laughed out loud, their eyes fixed on Jack Hennessey, him breathing easy and well. They each reached for their glass in a toast. Jack Hennessey bowed modestly, a broad, full smile on his face, his eyes wide and bright.

Paddy Riley sipped his drink and put it down. "So, Jack, did he ever come back, this Mr. Flaherty?"

"Not yet..."

CHAPTER THIRTY EIGHT
Friends

M rs. Kennedy found him at the top of the stairs. "Michael! MICHAEL BYRNES! Come quick! Quick as you can!"

She had sat down beside Jack Hennessey by the time Michael Byrnes had gotten to her. "He's alive, Michael...just asleep it seems. He's breathing alright..."

"I guess I am, if I'm alive..."

"*Aye!*" Mrs. Kennedy sat up, her head and shoulders aback, hands at her chest, staring at him, mouth agape.

Jack Hennessey rolled over on his back and gripped the baluster, pulling himself up to a sitting position with his feet on the second step of the stairs. "Can't a man catch a nap around here without getting screamed and yelled at?"

Michael Byrnes stepped up next to him, helping him to stand, holding his arm, positioning himself between Jack Hennessey and the stairwell. "What happened Mr. Hennessey? Are you alright?" He was looking in his eyes, raising Jack Hennessey's right eyebrow, looking and feeling about his head for a bruise or a cut.

Jack Hennessey leaned away, turning his head. "It's nothing, it's over..." He started for his bedroom, his right hand sliding along the wall for balance.

"We should get you to the hospital, Mr. Hennessey, get Dr. Lynch in to take a look..."

"We're going to do no such thing. They get me in that place, I'll never see the getting out of it." He was at his door and let himself in. They followed as he went to the side of his bed and sat down, looking at Michael Byrnes. "It was the same as up in Baltimore, Michael, and Friday on the wharf. Dizziness, heart racing. I got down on the floor before I fell, then just laid there..." He looked about. "What time is it?"

Mrs. Kennedy looked at the alarm clock. "Four-thirty-five."

He closed his eyes, thinking, his fingers moving. "Paddy and Matt left about three forty-five, maybe later. I read the paper for a bit and was coming up to get a nap..." He looked at Michael Byrnes. "Laying there for maybe fifteen minutes. I was never really out. Heard Mrs. Kennedy coming up the stairs..." Jack Hennessey looked to a bookshelf. "Check the Merck, Michael. It's called *arrhythmia*, a-r-r-h-y..."

"-t-h-m-i-a. Got it." Michael Byrnes picked up the book, balancing it in his left hand as he searched for the entry, going to the foot of the chaise lounge and sitting down. Mrs. Kennedy helped Jack Hennessey off with his shoes before he stretched out on the bed, she fixing his pillow for him, he waving her back, smiling to reassure.

"You got it?"

"Yes. Read it before, just scanning through once..."

"Good. When you have it all straight, be sure and tell Mrs. Kennedy here what it's all about." Jack Hennessey looked at Mrs. Kennedy. "It's an irregular heart beat, is what it is. Comes and goes. There not much anyone can do about it. Happens to folks who get as old as me. It's sure nothing worse than the cancer..."

Catherine Kennedy caught her breath, blessing herself as she nodded.

Jack Hennessey turned to Michael Byrnes. "We can talk about this later Michael. I want to nap if I can, just to lay here. But one thing you must understand. There's a meeting tomorrow afternoon at 3 pm at the union hall and I am going to be there, with Paddy Riley. Nothing is going to get in the way of that. Do you understand?"

"Yes, sir...I do..."

"Good, now, if it's alright with everyone, I'd like to get back to my nap."

Michael Byrnes turned to the door, pausing for Mrs. Kennedy to go before him. She waved him on by, stepping closer to the bed. Jack Hennessey 's eyes opened, fixing on her, uncertain.

"May I sit here with you Mr. Hennessey …?"

Jack Hennessey looked about, seeing that Michael Byrnes had left. "Yes, if you wish." He smiled at her. "That would be nice…Pull up a chair, if you like…"

She smiled at him. "That won't be necessary, Mr. Hennessey . I'll just sit in the wing chair by the window, if that's alright…"

He smiled at her, curious by her tone. It was almost playful.

She went to the wing chair and sat down, bringing one leg underneath her, leaning comfortably into the back of the chair, her form framed by the window beside her, its muslin curtains moving easily in the afternoon air. Her eyes turned to him, smiling and soft, at rest…

Jack Hennessey rose up on his elbow. "I must say, Mrs. Kennedy, you take very comfortably to that chair…"

Her smile broadened, like he had guessed something.

"Is there something you want to say, Mrs. Kennedy?"

Catherine Kennedy lowered her head for a moment then looked up, the smile gone, the eyes warmer still. "I have a confession, Mr. Hennessey…"

"A confession?" He sat up on the edge of the bed. "What do you mean, a confession? You want to confess something? To me?"

"Yes…" She turned away, as if suddenly aware of something that frightened her. She swallowed hard and then turned back to him. "There were times, times when I was so lonely, missed Mr. Kennedy so deeply, that I would come up here after you'd gone to sleep. I'd sit here in this chair…and listen to you breathe, hear you move in your bed, think of...him. Always him, only him." She paused, closing her eyes for a moment and then fixing on him. "...In time, though, a long time, you and Mr. Kennedy, well, were just the same to me. Now, I don't know how this came to happen, or when it did...I know, though, when I first realized that it had..."

She sat forward a measure. "It was the night you got home with Stephen, from France. You were so tired, so tired. You came up here after we'd taken the coffin over to Arlington to await burial. I had never seen you so tired, just spent. You came up here, and collapsed in bed, I guessed. I was downstairs. Didn't hear you moving about for the longest time. It worried me, so. So I came up. You were sound asleep when I got here. I removed your shoes, and your jacket. Then I covered you with a cotton spread.... and then I held your hand..."

Jack Hennessey sat up, his eyes away for a moment, than at her. "Yes, I...I seem to remember that now, I do..." He rose from the bed, steadied himself on the bedpost. "You...you kissed my hand and then...then you went to that chair...like now...I remember that..." He went to her, reaching for her hand. He took it to his lips and kissed it.

Catherine Kennedy looked up at him, smiled.

He reached for her face, cupping it in both hands, kissing her on the forehead. Standing back, he took her hands, held them firm and smiled, nodding. "Thank you for all our years together...Catherine..."

Catherine Kennedy caught her breath, smiling as she settled deeper in the chair. Kissing her hands and, for the briefest moment, holding them to his face, Jack Hennessey returned to his bed, looking at her as he lay down, smiling, the room in the full spring light of a May afternoon, his head back now, his right hand finding the beat of his heart...

CHAPTER THIRTY NINE
Done Deal

J ack Hennessey walked down the steps of the union hall, gripping Paddy Riley's upper arm, whispering "Steady, now, Paddy, steady...Eyes forward, steady...Get me to the car..."

Michael Byrnes' was out of the Packard, leaning against the front right fender. On seeing them come down the steps, he fixed on Jack Hennessey and sprang to the back door, holding it open as Paddy Riley walked Jack Hennessey to it.

"That's good, good..." Jack Hennessey bowed his head and eased his way in to the back seat. Michael Byrnes closed the door, taking Paddy Riley by the elbow and leading him around back of the car to the left rear door and opening it. "Get in, Mr. Riley, quickly..." Michael Byrnes closed the door behind Paddy Riley, got in the driver's seat and started the car. Looking over his left shoulder he started to make a U turn...

"What are you doing?" Jack Hennessey was wiping his forehead with a handkerchief. "*Where* are you going...?"

"Georgetown Hospital..."

"The hell you are! You're going to Sixth Street, that's where you're going. And now, right now!"

"What's going on?" Paddy Riley was sitting forward in the rear seat, looking to Michael Byrnes and Jack Hennessey as each spoke. "Jack, what the hell's going on here?"

"He's got arrhythmia..." Michael Byrnes straightened the car on K Street, the acceleration pushing Paddy Riley back in the rear seat.

"What the hell's that?"

"He's got a bad heart..." Michael Byrnes shifted lanes, passing a large truck, pressing through a yellow light.

"You listen to me, now, Michael Byrnes, and you listen good. You get this car turned around for Sixth Street, and you do it now!" Jack Hennessey had pulled himself forward with his right hand and gripped Michael Byrnes shoulder with his left. "Do you understand? Michael? DO YOU UNDERSTAND?"

Michael Byrnes shoulders lowered a measure as he sat back in the driver's seat, the car slowing as he signaled for a left turn on 13th Street. "Yes, sir, Mr. Hennessey , yes...I understand..."

"Jack, for Chrissake, you gotta tell me what's going on..." Paddy Riley gripped Jack Hennessey's forearm, fixing on him until Jack Hennessey turned to him...

Jack Hennessey looked into Paddy Riley's eyes, then away. "I'm sick, Paddy...I'm...sick." His head nodded slightly, as if affirming to himself what he had just said. He turned to Paddy Riley, patting him on the arm. "Pretty sick..."

The car pulled over to the curb on 13th Street. "What are you doing now, Michael?"

"Calling Dr. Lynch. Going to have him meet us at the house..."

Jack Hennessey nodded. "Yes, okay. Good idea...Good idea..." He looked back at Paddy Riley, his head lowering as Michael Byrnes jumped out of the car and quick stepped to a phone booth, reaching in his pants pocket for change. "Didn't know how to tell you, Paddy...didn't know..." His head shook from side to side slowly before he looked up, a forced smile. "It's not good, Paddy, it's not good...I've got pancreatic cancer. It's a killer. Sure thing. The best I'm good for is three or so months." He looked ahead. "Then last week, up in Baltimore, this arrhythmia showed up." He looked back.

"Makes me dizzy, gives me the sweats some times, heart racing like I don't know what…"

Michael Byrnes got back in the front seat and started the car, pulling out on to Pennsylvania Avenue for Southwest, shifting lanes, following close…

"No need to push it, Michael. It's passed, I'm fine." Jack Hennessey sat up, straightened his shoulders, shook his head. "Did get you him, Dr. Lynch?"

"Yes. He'll meet us there."

Jack Hennessey nodded, watched the street signs as the Packard crossed Eighth Street and moved to the right curb to turn at Sixth Street. He reached for the grip on the door jamb to hold himself against the turn. "Sorry you had to learn this way, Paddy… Was going to tell you Wednesday night. That's why I called you over. Just didn't seem right at the time, though." He looked at Paddy Riley and forced a smile. "Seems for some things, there's just never a *good* time." He looked ahead, the car now headed south on Sixth Street, the late afternoon sun on his face, warming him. "So, now you know, now you know…"

Michael Byrnes signaled for a left turn on N Street, and pulled over to the curb, setting the brake and getting out to open the rear passenger door for Jack Hennessey .

Paddy Riley was out as quick, motioning Michael Byrnes away, offering his hand to Jack Hennessey. "Here, Jack, take my hand…" Paddy Riley was bending over now, both hands in to help, Jack Hennessey looking up, unsure. "Hold the door full open, Michael…" Paddy Riley reached further in, his shoulder against the inside of the door, helping Jack Hennessey shift his weight, getting his legs out onto the curb, then to a near standing position. "Get his other side, Michael…"

Michael Byrnes moved quickly to the other side of the car door, getting his hands behind Jack Hennessey's shoulder, helping him up straight.

"Thanks, Michael, standing back now..." Paddy Riley got to Jack Hennessey's side and lifted him up in his arms, cradling him as he kicked he door shut behind them. He started for the house, taking the front steps one step at a time, making way for Michael Byrnes to pass and open the front door, and then up the stairs to Jack Hennessey 's room, laying him on the bed, looking down at him. "How you doing, Jack? You okay?"

"I'm fine, fine. Like I said in the car, it's passed." Jack Hennessey smiled up at him. "Didn't know what you had in mind, then figured, what the hell, let's see if he can do it..."

"Do what?"

"Carry me all the way up here. Might really need it some time." Jack Hennessey sat up, put his legs over the edge of the bed, leaning forward to stand...

"Not another move..." Dr. Terry Lynch came into the room, Ms. Kennedy just behind him. He set his bag on the floor near the bed, motioning Paddy Riley away. "Mrs. Kennedy, can you get his shoes off, please?"

"Yes, doctor."

"Exactly what do you think you're doing, Jack? You know suicide's a mortal sin, don't you?" He reached for Jack Hennessey's wrist and took his pulse, then felt his forehead. Taking off his own jacket, he ordered Mrs. Kennedy to remove Jack Hennessey's, and his tie and dress shirt as well. Lifting his bag, Terry Lynch placed it on the desk and removed his stethoscope, fitting it his ears and going directly to Jack Hennessey. Placing one hand on his shoulder, he put the stethoscope on his chest...

"Yo! That's cold! You trying to kill me right now? Murder's a sin, too, you know..."

"I'll put your sensory reaction down as excellent. Now, let me have a listen..." Dr. Lynch breathed heavy on the cup of the stethoscope and rubbed his hand over it to warm it before placing it at different areas across Jack

Hennessey's chest, and then his back, thumping here and there, feeling his hands and ankles, checking his eyes, then their focus. Standing straight, he fixed on Jack Hennessey. "Well, the good news is that it's passed. The bad news is I didn't get a good look at it."

Leaning closer, he put a hand on each side of Jack Hennessey's neck, working it, looking at his eyes. "I want you in the hospital, Jack." He focused on him closely. "Do you remember having rheumatic fever when you were young?"

"When I was young? Well, when I was young I remember seeing Abraham Lincoln on his way back to Washington, from Gettysburg for one thing. I was fifteen then. Don't remember much before that...No idea on rheumatic fever..."

"Well, no matter. From what Michael here tells me about today and, where? Baltimore? Last week? You have arrhythmia, arterial fibrillation, and that can kill you just as sure as the cancer, and a lot sooner if there's no one around who knows what to do about it. We can treat it with digitalis..."

Jack Hennessey nodded. "Michael here and me, we read all about in the Merck. Read the section on pancreatic cancer, too. A laugh a minute, that is." Jack Hennessey sat up in his bed. "I don't want to die, Doctor. I want to live forever, even tried to get some of my millions of days indulgences shifted over to this side of the ledger. You know, down here rather than later? Talked to Bill Murphy at Gonzaga just the other day about it. No help. Can't do it. Said the Pope can't even do that." He opened his arms, motioning to the room and the outside beyond.

"Doctor, I've lived in this room for near forty years. I slept in this bed with the only woman I ever loved. She died in it. So, I'm not going to your hospital. I'm staying put. Happy to have a nurse about if it will make you happy, and take some of the load off Mrs. Kennedy here and Michael. But everything I had to get done before I go is done, finished this afternoon." He motioned with his hands, level and out. "Done." He shrugged. "You tell me I'm dying, two ways at least, and that you can't really do anything thing about it. Right?"

Dr. Lynch nodded, fingering his stethoscope. "Yes, that's correct, pretty much…"

"So, I'm going to live as normal a life as I can until it is over, lived out. Just leave it to mother nature to see who gets me first, the cancer or the arrhythmia. Is that alright with you?"

The room went quiet, a silence that blocked all sound from the street and the river. "Yes, of course…Of course…" He looked about the room. All eyes were on Jack Hennessey , fixed and down. "I'm at Providence most mornings this week. I'd like to stop in when I can, see how you're doing…"

"Glad to have, you, Doctor. Anytime."

Dr. Lynch nodded, put his stethoscope in his bag as he winked at Jack Hennessey then turned to Michael Byrnes. "You'll call me, Michael? Keep in touch?"

"Yes, Doctor. I have the numbers."

"Good." He nodded for emphasis. "Anytime, now, you call at anytime…"

"Yes, sir…anytime…" Michael Byrnes reached for the bedroom door and opened it full for Dr. Lynch, leaving it open behind him to catch the afternoon air…

CHAPTER FORTY
On the Veranda

T he first thing they did was come up with some rules. Jack Hennessey would not be going up or down stairs alone. Either Mrs. Kennedy or Michael Byrnes would walk up or down with him so that if the arrhythmia came there would be someone to help him hold his balance. Next was setting up a spare bed outside Jack Hennessey's room. Michael Byrnes would be sleeping there now, with Mrs. Kennedy in the bedroom adjoining. And they all would be eating together, as well.

"I won't be baby sat. *Normal*, that's the idea, that's the deal, and I'm not *normally* baby sat."

"Let's just try it out for a few days." Michael Byrnes had somehow caught the exact balance of authority and common sense and Jack Hennessey had nodded, not able to think of anything sensible to say against it. They had wanted him to carry a bell, to ring if he needed anything, and to this he had said "No," and this with sufficient authority to win the point. "If I can't shout loud enough for you to hear me, hovering as it seems you are so determined to do, then I'm a goner anyway. No bell's going save me, that's for sure."

The first dinner together had been that night. Jack Hennessey found it awkward, as if he was not in charge of the dinner, not the head of his own table. More guest than host. Though he knew they meant well and had only his interest in all that they did, there was a sense of being a patient and in this a dependency of which he became increasingly resentful. The others seemed to sense this in him, Michael Byrnes announcing as dinner ended that he would be reading in the library if Jack Hennessey needed anything. Mrs. Kennedy picked it up as well, making a point of saying she would be in her room downstairs.

It was now past 7:30 with the mid-May sun still up and Sixth Street wharf already changed from the day's commerce of freight and drayage to the evening's trade – entertainment. Jack Hennessey could hear piano music from an open air bar and, more distant, the band on the top deck of a dinner boat making its way down Washington Channel to the river. He sat in one of he Adirondack chairs on the open side of the veranda, a glass of beer at his side, taking the pleasure of a steady and warm breeze that both comforted and cooled him.

To his left, by the finger piers off Sixth Street, his eye caught Daddy Riley at his scow, and John Riley now out from behind him. They had just tied up the boat and were making their way along Sixth Street, fishing gear in hand, each with the other as one together. Jack Hennessey marked their progress as they came to across from where N Street abutted Sixth Street. Here they waited for the traffic to clear, then crossed, coming to the corner of N and Sixth streets, John Riley looking up and waving. "Mr. Jack!"

Jack Hennessey sat forward in his chair, waving back, feeling the joy of a smile come to his face. 'Something in that boy. It just comes out, doesn't wait from worrying about what others might think, or if it's allowed. It's electric, is what it is.' Jack Hennessey waved the two of them over, rose from his chair and went to the railing.

"Evening, folks. Out fishing?"

"Not really." Daddy Riley started across the front lawn, John Riley trailing now. "Mainly bringing the scow back from Buzzard Point. Had it out for spring caulking and painting." He looked across the lawn in the direction of the boat. "Had her more than twenty years, now, and she's good for another twenty."

"You take care of her like that, she will…"

"Yes, sir. That's the plan. Another twenty…" Daddy Riley stopped himself, looked up at Jack Hennessey, his mouth stuck, his eyes locked…

"Come on up, Daddy Riley, and John there, too." He turned toward the front screen door. "Mrs. Kennedy…" He spoke up, without shouting. "Mrs…"

"Yes, Mr. Hennessey." The screen door opened and she stepped out.

"We have guests, Mrs. Kennedy." He turned to Daddy Riley and John Riley. "Gentlemen, what's you pleasure?"

Daddy Riley raised his hand. "I'm afraid we must be off. I promised Mary Riley, I did, that I'd have young John here back by now, and she's a woman who watches the clock like a hawk. There'll be no peace on Fourth Street tonight if he's not there straight away."

Jack Hennessey looked at John Riley, smiling. "Well far be it from me…" He turned to Daddy Riley. "Then you stay, have a beer with me." Back at John Riley. "Any boy who can land a 38-pound rockfish can surely find his way two blocks along N Street in the daylight."

Daddy Riley looked at his grandson, then away…

Mrs. Kennedy came nearer the railing. "We've had some *Harp* in the ice box since noon, Mr. Riley, fresh in from Ireland, all chilled and ready to be had…"

"*Harp* is it, now…?" Looking down at John Riley, he handed him his rod. "Off with you, now, lad. Straightaway home, you go. You'll be there by 7:35 if you step lively. Tell your ma I'm with Mr. Jack Hennessey, himself, Chairman now he is of Hennessey Construction."

John Riley took the rod and bowed his head to Mrs. Kennedy and Jack Hennessey, quick stepping to the sidewalk and gone for home.

Jack Hennessey sat down, motioning Daddy Riley up and to the other Adirondack chair. "Here, have a seat.

Rest your bones." Jack Hennessey leaned back in his chair as Daddy Riley sat down. "How far rowing is it to the landing at Buzzard Point from here?"

"I make a mile and three quarters." Daddy Riley settled in his chair, taking the Harp from Mrs. Kennedy, a silent nod of thanks. "A good pull of the oar." He fixed on Jack Hennessey. "And I'll tell you, Mr. Jack, if there's a finer way to spend an hour on a spring evening such as this with your grandson, I'm not aware of it." He raised his glass and took a full draw of beer, drinking near half the pint, wiping his mouth with his right hand and resting his head back.

Jack Hennessey had raised his glass, sipping his beer as he watched and listened. There was still a hint of red in Daddy Riley's grayed hair, likely as full and bristled as when he left Ireland. The sweat of the row showed through his heavy cotton shirt, buttoned in front and tucked into his dark wool pants. He had the large, knuckled hands of a life early to work and long at it, a thin frame wrapped tightly in muscle and vein with not a speck of fat to be seen. It was with men like Daddy Riley that Jack Hennessey had built his company, men who worked a full day and took their wages home to a wife who ran the place and raised the children and never looked back. Sean Riley owned his own life, all of it, like Skeets Skilleen, like them all...

Sean Riley took another draw of his beer, rested it on the arm of the chair and looked out across the lawn. "Paddy told me your news, Mr. Jack, and sorry I was to hear it...Sorry indeed." He turned to Jack Hennessey. "I hope you don't mind me speaking of it now, and not being asked...It's just that I never see you, just you and me, like this." He sat up, leaned closer. "I wanted to thank you, now, for some time, for all you've done for my boy, for Paddy, and for us all." He raised his glass and smiled.

Jack Hennessey raised his glass and smiled back. "When you and John came up N Street just now, him waving and calling my name, well, I just couldn't not think of Paddy the first time I saw him... It was just after you and I sat together at a Communion Breakfast...at St. Dominic's. You were bragging on about your boy, 'Six foot two inches and hard as stone, made sergeant in the Army Engineers, just back from France.' I'd given you my card and told you to send him on over..." Jack Hennessey looked to the river, picking up his beer, sipping it, putting it down, turning to Daddy Riley.

"What astounds me, Daddy Riley, is that I've only known him for 16 years. I was 72 when he came on with us. Most of my friends, what I had left, were retired by then. I could have. But I just kept on at it. Didn't know what else to do. And then Paddy came on. I watched him from the day he started. I'd make a point of going to jobs he was working, just to watch him. He made the others around him better. When I brought him along sooner than others there longer, there was some resentment. But I knew..." He looked at Daddy Riley, reaching for his arm. "It was like on Saturday, Paddy fighting that fish...rain driving on him...wind...lightning and thunder...the boat pitching in the seaway...rising and falling...And Paddy there like a rock, like his feet were glued to the deck...What a sight!"

Jack Hennessey sat back, still looking at Daddy Riley, smiling now. "So you were thanking me for what I've done for Paddy." He shrugged. "Well, for that you are most welcome." He raised his glass and sipped his beer. "Now I want to thank you for what Paddy has done for me. He has made these last years so much more than they might have been...He recharged my life is what he did, with his spirit and fight, and his Mary and then the children..." Jack Hennessey looked away, then back. "I'm so glad you are here tonight, Daddy Riley, so glad I can say this to you, just the two of us." He fixed on him. "I've meant to do it for some time, but the time just didn't come till now." Jack Hennessey raised his glass and took full swallow, feeling the liquid wash the inside of his mouth, excite his taste, and then down to settle below.

Daddy Riley raised his glass as well, emptying it, looking out toward the river, then across at Jack Hennessey, nodding.

"But there's more than that, Daddy Riley." Jack Hennessey sat forward. "I need to thank you for Saturday, too, on the Bay, for knowing that we had to put that fish back, for speaking up and saying it...Such a beautiful thing, it was, the size and the grace of it...to have let it die, far worse to have killed it...What a terrible thing that would have been to do." Jack Hennessey's eyes were away, toward the river but not fixed on any one thing. "...And to see that fish swim down and into the deep of Bay, safe and free...away..." He turned to Daddy Riley. "Thank you, Daddy Riley, thank you for that. Somehow, seeing that, having that, has made all this so much easier..."

CHAPTER FORTY ONE
Afternoon

M ary Riley sat in the armchair in Jack Hennessey's bedroom, the windows open, the early afternoon air bright in the room. It was Tuesday. Mrs. Kennedy had gone with Michael Byrnes to do the week's shopping and Mary Riley had come over to be with Jack Hennessey. She'd brought her book to read but had put it down, her eyes falling on things in the room, pictures and brick-a-back, a life's collection, each piece set where he may have first put it, or where he later thought it needed to be.

Jack Hennessey lay on his bed, his shoes off, him propped up to read, a book at his side, now, and him asleep. He looked small to her, there on his bed…and old. He'd gone thin in recent months and with his weight sunk in the bed, he looked frail, even gaunt, his mouth open slightly, his reading glasses down on his nose. Mary's mother, Norah Coughlin, she had known. Yes, she had known, and had told Mary so. It was Saturday night, on the walk back from the party. 'He's dying, don't you know…

"He is, now, is he? And who's this that's dying?"

'Who else? 'Tis Jack Hennessey, himself, now.'

'And how would *you* be knowing such a man as Jack Hennessey is dying?'

'Well,' said she, 'him being a man like any other and needing to die some time, you can see it in them when they know it's coming…And they know, you know. Sure they do. And, sure, Jack Hennessey knows it's now.' She had looked up at Mary Riley as they stepped along N Street, Paddy staying longer at the party. 'It's an Irish thing, I'm thinking. There being so much of it, the dying, I mean, and so fast. Whole villages…There being so much dying, we come to be expert at the watching and the knowing of it...'

"Oh, so it's 100 years old we are, now, Norah Coughlin? Memories you have of the Great Hunger and all, do you? Away with you, now! You weren't born yourself till it was done, and done for years."

''Tis true, what you say, 'tis true enough. I wasn't born till after it was done. But it came to be part of who we are, don't you see, watching people die, that is. We can see it in a man's eyes. Don't know what it is. Nothing specific, now, so don't be asking me the particulars of it. Just the way they look, or maybe don't look." She thought about what she's just said for a few steps, continuing. "Don't know just what it is, but I saw it in Jack Hennessey's eyes tonight, and mark my words, daughter, the man's dying and he knows it." She'd reached for Mary Riley, gripping her forearm. "And it'll come quicker than you think..."

And right she was, too. 'Jack Hennessey's dying,' and that from Paddy Riley himself getting in Monday night from work. A cancer it is, and something else, too, that Paddy couldn't pronounce. Sitting, now, in the armchair, Mary Riley looked at Jack Hennessey, lying in his bed, still. 'Looks at death's door right now, fast asleep in his bed on a bright afternoon.' A curtain moved beyond the desk, to her left. Mary Riley turned, her eye catching a photograph framed in forest green leather, gilded at its edges. Rising, she went to it, picking it up, holding it at an angle to deflect the glare of the glass.

It was the same as a thousand she'd seen in homes all over Brookland and here too, and in her own house, as well. A white cottage with people about, all staring at the camera's eye, as they might regard a stranger. And why not? Sure strange it was to be looking at a man known to no one in the village and him crouching behind a black box, shouting everyone deaf not to be moving and covered all over at the shoulders with a shroud.

There was a picnic table in the picture, by a tree. An elderly woman sat at it, a younger man at her side, something telling Mary Riley it's her son. Workmen were beyond, eyes fixed on the camera, their shovels held in front like rifles at parade rest. At the table, to the left of the woman, another man sat, his eyes at the camera, but smiling. Jack Hennessey it was and none other. "Handsome you were, Jack Hennessey, and handsome you are, too." Beyond them all was the cottage, and a large one, with a high thatched roof and windows lining its front, all marked by flower boxes filled to overflowing. "High summer, it looks..." She squinted to read the inscription. *So grand to see you, Jack – God's blessing and good fortune to you. Always, Rose McCarthy.*

Another picture. The same look about it, but of an earlier time. She picked it up. A cobblestone street before a town house. Here? Baltimore? Eight, nine of them, all but a boy of eight or so fixed hard on the camera, and he smiling. "That'd be Jack, again, a smile like that..." Next to this, a picture of a woman, maybe thirty, her eyes bright and at the lens, the trace of a smile on her face and beside her the boy of the other picture, now maybe ten and sure, now, Mary Riley can see Jack Hennessey in him. "Mother and son..." Putting this down, she looked up. On the wall behind the desk was the picture of an ocean liner, the name *Majestic* emblazoned on the frame. A dresser was next, to the left, five drawers high and atop it the things a man wants to hand – a pocket knife and change, a fountain pen and a money clip, keys and a comb.

Turning, she fixed on the chaise. She had noticed it coming in. Not the sort of thing she'd expect in the bedroom of Jack Hennessey. Beside it, on a reading table, was the photographic portrait of a woman. Going to the near side of the chaise, she fixed on it, struck by the woman's eyes, clear and focused at the camera, engaging it, as if expecting it to look back. "Jack's Christine, no doubt...Aye, and beautiful, too...So alive, even now...Such a shame, such a shame, poor man..."

Drawn to it, she sat at the foot of the chaise, turning to Jack Hennessey to be certain he was still asleep, then reaching for the picture, holding it. 'Expectation' was the thought that came to her mind, 'hope', so much more than just getting on. Life and living, that's what Mary Riley saw in the face, the eyes. She turned to the picture of Jack and his mother. It was the same in that as well, his mother, eyes at the lens, claiming a place, 'Here we come, ready or not...' Yes, that's why they come, the why *we* come, Da and Ma and the boys and me...' Mary Riley's mind going back to the crossing and them landing in New York, Christmas, 1908. And it was down as quick to Washington, they were, where there was work to be found. Three of a kind we are, she's thinking, over from Erin, never to return, not one known to either of the others, but of a kind nonetheless.

She turned back to the picture of Christine, her eyes, then about the room...It was a room a woman would have done. It was Christine's room, not the same room she had died in, now, but the things of hers that were in that room...the chaise, yes, it was *her* chaise, and the armchair and the four post bed where Jack Hennessey lay. They were a couple...but nothing to be left when he's done. Raising up, she looked about the room, the walls, the bureaus and the tops of the tables. No pictures of children, none but of himself as a boy. She thought of her own room, hers and Paddy's, and the pictures about of John and Mary Kate and Michael – on a night table or jammed into the frame of a mirror...

No children, none at all. Living now 88 years and leaves none of his own to follow. Sad, so sad. All he's done and he dies alone, gone. A sadness came over her. "All he's done and none to follow…" She'd spoken the words of her mind, now, and they affected her all the more, bringing her hand to her mouth to cover it, to hide the words and the thought with them, fighting a need to cry…

"Why so sad, Mary?" Jack Hennessey's hand rested on her shoulder. She jumped at his touch, looking up, fumbling with the picture of Christine as she moved to stand.

Jack Hennessey's hand held her seated. "Sit, Mary. Don't get up." He looked down at her. "I didn't mean to startle you." He reached for the picture, taking it and returning it to the reading table. Turning, he pulled over the desk chair and sat down. "Tell me, Mary, why so sad?"

Mary Riley wiped her eyes and nose with her hands. Jack Hennessey took a handkerchief from his pants pocket and gave it to her. She wiped her eyes and held her hands to her chest, avoiding his eyes. "I'm sorry for picking up the picture…I had no business to… shouldn't have done…" She looked at Jack Hennessey. "She's so beautiful…I just wanted to see it closer, don't you know…So beautiful…And to die so young…Aye, I'm sorry for speaking such, now, Jack…"

"Don't be upset." He looked at the picture. "I guess you'd never have seen that. I keep it up here…always near. I can see it from my bed, you see, and it's nearby here when I read, sitting in her chaise…And yes, she was beautiful, and so alive, beyond any other woman I ever met – before or since." He looked from the picture to Mary Riley. "You remind me of her, in a way, Mary, you know. You do. Your fight and your spirit, it's what I love most about you…you and Paddy, both." He took her hands. "You're so lucky to have to have each other.…"

Mary Riley's eyes teared. "Oh Jack, we'll miss you so. How will we…" She rested her head on their hands in his lap. "I was just thinking…thinking that you'll leave none of your own…It's so sad…."

He raised her head, fixed on her. "So that's what's saddened you?"

She nodded.

He smiled at her, motioning to Christine's photograph. "Christine died and left no one…but she's as alive to me now as the day we met…I breathed in her last breath, Mary…I still feel her by me, in me, as much as ever, it seems, these last few days…The love we shared…" He turned to the desk, motioning to the picture of himself standing next to a woman. "That's me on my twelfth birthday. And that's Mary Mulholland." He half rose, reaching for the picture and bringing it close, showing it to Mary Riley.

"She took me out of Ireland, you see. Raised me as her own." He paused for a moment, looking at Mary Riley then back to the picture. "My blood mother had died in the Hunger, you see. So Mary Mulholland left none of her own, either." He looked at Mary Riley, shrugging. "I loved them each – Christine and Mary Mulholland–as they each loved me, and not a drop of blood among us, and none to follow a one of us, either." He smiled, returning the picture to the desk and taking Mary Riley's hands.

"Blood and kin's where life starts, Mary. It's where we begin our life's journey. But we each must become our own person, make our own way…with the people we come from and the people we gather, and those who gather us, family and friends and those we come to love." He fixed on her, firming his grip of her hands. "I can't imagine a son meaning more to me than your Paddy. It's impossible to me…He seems even more than a son might be, though there's no real way for me to know that, now, is there?" He looked away for a moment then back at her. "It's love, Mary, that's what gives the greatest happiness, the truest meaning…It's the most we can get in a life, and most we can give…Love…Blood's just part of it…"

There was the sound of the Packard's door opening and shutting on N Street.

Mary Riley rose quickly, wiping her eyes and handing back Jack Hennessey's handkerchief before smoothing the front of her dress. "I've got to go, to be downstairs…" She found herself avoiding his eyes…

"Relax, Mary, relax…"

"Ach!" She stood erect, looking at him up and down, from head to foot. "You're up, now, Jack! Walking about, you are…"

"Yes, it would seem…"

"Yes, but…Aye, yes. That's good…That's good…" She turned about, fixing on her book, picking it up and holding it against her chest, looking at him. "Well, then, Jack, I'll be on, I will, with Mrs. Kennedy and Michael…Michael…back from their shopping…"

Jack Hennessey nodded and smiled, taking Mary Riley by the elbow and walking her down the hall, and the stairs as well, and then on through to the kitchen where they helped Mrs. Kennedy and Michael Byrnes put away the shopping.

CHAPTER FORTY TWO
Confessional

F r. Joseph Hara had decided to walk the eight blocks to Jack Hennessey's house. As he crossed M Street, the waterfront came into clear view, the calm at the close of the work day and before the bars hit their stride. Joe Hara's eyes tracked west along Water Street toward the Jefferson Memorial, ferries and fishing boats laying by for the night, cars and taxis stopping at the restaurants and bars. Across Washington Channel was Haines Point, and to his left the Channel flowed south to where the Potomac met the Anacostia. All before him was wonder and light, a crystal clear spring evening and memories of another time, of him and Paddy Riley at Buzzard Point swinging off a rope into the Anacostia, running and racing on the river bank and talking about Walter Johnson and the Senators and Daddy Riley getting tickets to a game against the New York Yankees on a Saturday afternoon.

Jack Hennessey had called that morning and asked him to stop by after dinner, that he'd be waiting for him on the veranda. Crossing Sixth Street to N, Joe Hara looked up at the house. Jack Hennessey sat in one of the Adirondack chairs on the veranda, his head back, but not asleep, his hand on his chest...Looking quickly to his left to check for traffic, Joe Hara broke into a run, then a sprint. He was closer now. Jack Hennessey was pale, both hands on his chest and leaning forward. Breaking across the lawn, Joe Hara took the steps three at a time and up to his side, taking a knee and gripping Jack Hennessey's hand and arm. "Jack, Jack what is it?"

Jack Hennessey opened his eyes, focused on Joe Hara, then pointed to a water pitcher on the table. Joe Hara quickly poured a glass and brought it to him,

347

holding his head forward and putting the glass to his mouth. "Mrs. Kennedy, Mrs. Kennedy..."

Jack Hennessey drank the water, taking the glass in his right hand and waving Joe Hara quiet with his left, swallowing the water in his mouth. "No need for that, Joe. She's fine... I'm fine...It's passed..."

Joe Hara rose, standing by Jack Hennessey's side. Mrs. Kennedy came to the screen door, opened it. "Did you call, father?"

"No, it's nothing..."

Looking at Jack Hennessey, she came out on the veranda, going to him, taking the glass from his hand. "Is there anything I can get for you? Iced tea? A Harp?"

"No, no...I'm fine, thank you." He looked at Joe Hara. "Can we get you anything, Joe?"

"An iced tea would be nice, thank you."

Mrs. Kennedy smiled at him and left as Jack Hennessey sat up and motioned Joe Hara to the chair beside his.

Joe Hara sat down, looking at Jack Hennessey. His color was off and his chest sunken, his legs somehow seeming weaker. Joe Hara checked the screen door to be sure they were alone then fixed on Jack Hennessey. "Are you alright Jack...I mean, I know you're...But is something..?"

Jack Hennessey waved him quiet, smiled. "Got something new for you, Joe. It's called *arrhythmia*." He pointed to his chest. "A heart thing. It starts dancing a jig when the rest of me's doing a waltz. Pretty scary, really. It's pumping so fast nothing's coming out." He sat up another measure. "That was the worst it's been so far, just then...couldn't breathe for a bit there..."

The screen door opened. Mrs. Kennedy came with a tray and on it a glass of iced tea and a bottle of Harp with a chilled glass. She placed it on a short table between them, nodding at the Harp. "Just in case." She smiled at Jack Hennessey and went back in the house.

Joe Hara watched Mrs. Kennedy go in the house and pull the screen door closed behind her before turning to Jack Hennessey. "I've heard of arrhythmia, can be pretty serious…"

"That's what they tell, me." Jack Hennessey looked toward the river.

"Shouldn't you be in the hospital?"

"Nope." He turned to Joe Hara. "The only reason to go to a hospital is to get better. Any man going to a hospital to die is just wasting his money and their time."

"Never thought of it that way…" Joe Hara picked up his iced tea and sipped it, sitting back in his chair. Jack Hennessey had followed his reach to the tray and fixed on the Harp.

"I went to the Chancellery today. About the orphanage…"

"How'd that go?"

"Try to imagine Dante's *Inferno* with a heavy edit by Franz Kafka…"

Jack Hennessey laughed. "I expected no less." He laughed again then looked at Joe Hara. "You going to be able to get this done?" He motioned to the house. "Make an orphanage out of this place?"

Joe Hara shrugged, smiling. "I'll get it done. Spoke to the assistant pastor at St. Patrick's. We were in the seminary together. He's on the diocese's committee that oversees the orphanage program. They've been looking to do something in Southwest. Getting this place is perfect, solves all of their problems at a stroke. It'll take time. Permitting, fire code…whatever, but it'll happen…"

Jack Hennessey's hand stopped him. "And Mrs. Kennedy? She's…"

"Yes. She'll be part of the deal. No problem. She becomes an employee of the arch diocese…"

Jack Hennessey nodded, waving Joe Hara quiet as he sat forward, reaching for the beer and pouring it in the glass. Lifting it, he looked at Joe Hara, a smile coming to his face. "Sure you wouldn't want a Harp. Fresh over, you know, chilled to perfection...?"

"No, Jack. No, thanks."

"Suit yourself." Jack Hennessey sipped his beer and sat back in his chair. "I've got something for you." He reached beside his chair and picked up an envelope, handing it Joe Hara. "This is a letter for Paddy. I left it open so you could read it."

Joe Hara held the envelope up. Lifting the flap, he looked inside and then to Jack Hennessey.

"I want you to read that after I'm gone, and then seal it up. You and Paddy being so close, I figure you'll know when to give it to him..."

Joe Hara nodded, checking the screen door. They were alone. He sat closer. "Is there anything else I can do, Jack? Something you want to say? To do, maybe, to *make*...?

Their eyes met, Jack Hennessey not understanding at first, then nodding and shrugging a smile. Blessing himself, he sat up a measure, sitting forward in the chair, leaning toward Joe Hara whose head was turned, now, his eyes away. Blessing himself again, Jack Hennessey began.

"I've tried to do the right thing, and mostly I believe I did...I think. There's not much I regret, not that I can think of. Can't remember firing anyone who didn't need firing, or said hard things to someone who didn't need telling, hearing them. Maybe a couple of fights, years ago, when I was young, that I should have stayed out of...or enjoyed winning too much. Some business, I got, too, I guess. Yes, I'm sure...Not caring so much about the other fella...And I've seen men headed for trouble that I might have warned off. Didn't know if it was my place. Don't know now...I stopped worrying about such things some time ago...Then there was the loneliness after Christine...about overwhelmed me...things done that shouldn't have...I stopped worrying about that, too... Just don't know, it's so long I've been coming to now...years and places and things and people...Of what I would change, though, father, what weighs on me still, is how I thought about Mary Mulholland for so many years, for too many years..."

Jack Hennessey paused, swallowed hard, his hands joining, working together. "I was her ticket out of Ireland, you see, away from the Hunger. Once she got here, though, she could have left me at a parish stoop, or somewhere else...been on with her life in America. But she didn't. No. She kept me and raised me as her own, her son. Blood was everything to her, you see...She said that and believed it to her core. But she raised me just the same, like I was blood to her, and she loved me, too, like a son, and maybe more for all of that. So I hope to see her again there, if there is a 'there', to thank her for bringing me here, to America...for saving my life...for making my years with Christine possible, for having and knowing the love we shared...for learning what love is..."

Jack Hennessey sat back in his chair and Joe Hara opened his eyes, blessing himself and turning to him. Reaching for Jack Hennessey's forehead, he made the sign of the cross...

"Fr. Hara...Fr. Hara..." Mrs. Kennedy's voice came from the front hall before she opened the screen door and stepped out on the veranda. "Fr. Hara, it's Mrs. Baker from the rectory. You're needed there right away."

Joe Hara rose from the chair. Looking from Jack Hennessey to Mrs. Kennedy. "Did she said what it is?"

"No. Wouldn't. Said she couldn't say. Only that you're needed there right away..." Mrs. Kennedy turned inside, speaking over her shoulder. "I'll get Michael Byrnes. He can take you right on up…"

"Thank you…" Joe Hara looked from the screen door down at Jack Hennessey. "I've got to go, Jack…"

"Yes. Duty calls…Do you have the letter?"

"Yes, right here." He showed it to him. "I'll take care of it, Jack. I'll get it to him…you can count on me."

"I'm sure I can, father." He smiled, nodding easily. "Keep me in your prayers, will you…"

"I will, Jack." Fr. Hara made a quick sign of the cross over Jack Hennessey and was gone…

CHAPTER FORTY THREE
Evening Time

J ack Hennessey woke with a start, sitting forward, his hands gripping the arms of the Adirondack chair, the day gone dark. "Where...?"

"You okay, Jack?"

He looked to his right. Paddy Riley sat in the Adirondack chair beside him, an open bottle of Harp in his hand as it rested on the arm of the chair, his teeth showing bright in the dark of the evening. Shaking his head, Jack Hennessey looked about, then focused on Paddy Riley, looking away, waving him off. "Yes, yes. I'm fine...fine. What time is it?"

"Pushing 9:30..."

"Late... Dozed off." He turned back to Paddy Riley. "How long have you been here?"

"An hour, maybe more. A beautiful evening, though. You missed an incredible sunset. Almost woke you for it, but figured you could use the sleep..."

"Yes, thank you. Been so tired these last few days." He looked at Paddy Riley. "Who's here?"

"Michael Byrnes is in the library, and I think Mrs. Kennedy's in her room...Can I get you anything?"

"No, not...Yes, a glass of ice water would be nice."

"Coming right up." Paddy Riley set his beer on the arm of the chair and went into the house. Jack Hennessey sat back, the lights of the waterfront ranging before him under a black sky marked by several bright stars. He breathed deeply, his eyes closing as he exhaled, slowly, his entire body calm, relaxed.

"Here you go." Paddy Riley handed him a glass of ice water and sat beside him.

Jack Hennessey sipped the water to taste it, then took a full swallow before setting the glass down. "So, how was your first full day?"

"First full day..?"

"First full day as President of Hennessey Construction..."

"Oh, yes. That." He smiled and sat back, taking a swallow of Harp. "Pretty uneventful, really. Some friends called to congratulate me, that sort of thing. Finishing the clean up of the Ag site..."

"What about the deal, Hecht..?"

"Yes, that, too. It was in the paper, that we got it. Anyway, the signed contract came by courier just before noon..."

"Well, that's something, I guess..." He looked at Paddy Riley who was smiling, reaching over to push his forearm.

"Relax, Jack. It's done. Biggest deal in the city this year and we got it."

Jack Hennessey nodded. "And how do you like it, being president?"

Paddy Riley sat back. "Well, I woke up this morning, a little earlier than usual, thinking about it. What I was going to do...what I was going to do *different*." He looked at Jack Hennessey, waiting for him to look back, their eyes meeting. "Then I got up and did it. Pretty simple, really..."

Jack Hennessey held his eyes, smiling as he nodded. "Yes, I guess it is in a way, for the right fella. Pretty simple..." Jack Hennessey took a deep breath, exhaling as he turned to Paddy Riley. "I was thinking the other day about all the buildings Hennessey 's put up." He paused. "It's more than fifty, you know." He turned toward the river. "Anyway, I was thinking which of these I liked the best. You know, by the look of it. And then I was thinking that you spent a year in Europe, after the war, the rebuilding and all, and told me once you'd been to Paris and London, even Rome." He turned and fixed on Paddy. "So, tell me, of all the buildings you've seen, is there one above all the rest. I mean of all the buildings you've *ever* seen?"

"Yup." Paddy Riley sipped his beer, putting it down, joining his hands at the finger tips as he sat back. "But it wasn't over there. No, sir. It's here, right here." He motioned over his shoulder with his right hand and thumb. "The Capitol building. It's the first building I remember seeing as a building, as a separate, distinct thing." He sat forward, leaning toward Jack Hennessey. "I was with Joe Hara. We were ten, maybe twelve, not sure about that. Anyway, we were walking up to the Mall, along Fourth Street. It was just past noon on a spring day, like this. Just as clear, maybe even clearer. As I came to Independence Avenue, I looked to my right – and there it was, above us. White beyond white, and it seemed all around us, the width of it, and rising up off the Hill, the grounds and trees about it in full spring green. And then the dome of it, glistening in the sun, maybe just painted. It took my breath away, Jack, stopped me cold in my tracks, just the sight of it…Yes, sir, that's the one above all others…to me, anyway…" He sat back, reaching for his beer.

Mrs. Kennedy was at the screen door, Michael Byrnes beside her, both looking out on the veranda. She pushed the screen door open, its spring squeaking faintly and turning Paddy Riley's head. "Ah, you're still here, I see, Mr. Riley."

He nodded at her, his eyes going to Michael Byrnes behind her.

She stepped out on the veranda, to beside Jack Hennessey 's chair, looking down at him. He was asleep. She turned to Michael Byrnes and motioned him to the other side of the chair then looked at Paddy Riley,

speaking softly. "We should be getting him upstairs now."
She pointed to her wrist indicating time. Paddy Riley
nodded and rose, moving his chair out of the way.

"Mr. Hennessey, Mr. Hennessey…" She touched his
shoulder. "It's time to go up now." She touched his
shoulder again, looking at Michael Byrnes who touched
his forearm. They spoke together. "Mr. Hennessey…"
Michael Byrnes' hand moved toward his wrist…

"Yes…What..?" Jack Hennessey looked up, first to
Mrs. Kennedy then to Michael Byrnes. He seemed
confused, half sitting forward. "Where…"

"It's time to go up, Mr. Hennessey, to bed…nearly
ten o'clock."

Jack Hennessey nodded, sitting back for a moment
then forward, gripping the arms of the Adirondack chair
to pull himself up, breathing deeply. Michael Byrnes
helped him at the shoulders with Mrs. Kennedy taking his
hand. "Here we go, up…"

Jack Hennessey couldn't lift himself up on his feet.
He looked at Paddy Riley, afraid. "Paddy, I..I can't…"

Paddy Riley stepped closer, moving Michael Byrnes
away. He bent over, looking at Jack Hennessey, smiling.
"No problem, Jack, none at all. He reached his arms under
Jack Hennessey's legs and across his back and lifted him
up, holding him at chest level and starting around the
chair for the screen door. Michael Byrnes stepped quickly
ahead and opened it, standing aside as Paddy Riley
carried Jack Hennessey into the hall and up the stairs,
Mrs. Kennedy following closely. She got around Paddy in
the upstairs hall and opened the door to Jack Hennessey's
room, going in ahead and turning down the bed quickly,
standing away. Paddy Riley stepped to the bed and laid
Jack Hennessey on it, Mrs. Kennedy working the pillows
under his head and Michael Byrnes untying his shoes and
putting them on the floor.

Jack Hennessey looked up, fixing on Paddy Riley. "Good thing we were sure you could do that, Paddy." They all smiled, nodding. "Thank you...There's just nothing like a freshly turned bed when you're really tired." He looked at Mrs. Kennedy, standing on the other side of the bed. "I'll be fine, now, thanks." He reached to her and she took his hand in hers, her eyes tearing. "None of that, now. All I need is a good night's sleep." He took a deep breath, looking about the room. "Is Michael here?"

"Yes, sir, Mr. Hennessey ." Michael Byrnes stood forward at the foot of the bed.

"Ah, Michael. Good. Glad you're here." Jack Hennessey shook his head slightly. "No need to trouble Dr. Lynch about this tonight, now. Understand? He'll be by in the morning."

Michael Byrnes nodded silently, gripping the footboard of the bed.

Jack Hennessey looked up to his right, at Paddy Riley. "Can you sit with me for a bit, Paddy?"

"Count on it, Jack."

Michael Byrnes moved the desk chair to behind Paddy Riley who pulled it up, sitting down, taking Jack Hennessey 's hand.

Jack Hennessey looked at the others. "I'll be fine here with Paddy. You two get off to bed. I'll see you in the morning." He fixed on Michael Byrnes. "Michael, you can sleep in tomorrow. We'll do the noon mass at the Cathedral."

"Yes, sir."

Jack Hennessey turned to Mrs. Kennedy. "Good night, Mrs. Kennedy. Keep an old man in your prayers, will you?"

"I surely will, Mr. Hennessey." She moved about the room, turning out the lights, all but the one on the reading table by the chaise. Going to Michael Byrnes, she took him by the elbow and out into the hall, leaving the door open.

Jack Hennessey's eyes followed them out of the room then looked up at the ceiling before turning to Paddy Riley. "It's good to have you're here Paddy, so good." He closed his eyes, breathing in. "Paddy…"

"Yes, Jack…"

"Can you finish the story about the Capitol Building, seeing it that time..?"

Paddy Riley pulled his chair closer, holding Jack Hennessey's hand in his own, speaking softly, thinking to remember how he had told it just before. "Well, I was with Joe Hara. We were ten, maybe twelve, walking up to the Mall, along Fourth Street. No memory at all of why. Anyway, it was just past noon on a late spring day, like this. Just as clear, maybe even…"

Jack Hennessey's eyes had closed. He was asleep. Paddy Riley sat for a moment, holding his hand, feeling its warmth, its pulse. Leaning forward, he spoke Jack Hennessey's name, softly. "Jack?" Nothing. And again "Jack?" Nothing again.

Paddy Riley rose, laying Jack Hennessey's right hand on his chest. Reaching over for his left hand, he laid that on his chest as well, covering them both for a moment with his own. Turning, he was struck by the calm of Jack Hennessey's face, and the strength of it, too. Among those dearest to him, Jack Hennessey stood alone, untitled–not father, not wife nor child, more than friend… Bending over, he kissed him softly on the forehead, not to bless, nor to comfort, but to touch, to share. "Good night, Jack Hennessey…"

Rising, Paddy Riley looked about the room, dark but for the light on the reading table, Christine's picture clear to be seen from Jack Hennessey's bed. Crossing the room to the wing chair, Paddy Riley sat down, his head back, his eyes on Jack Hennessey and then to sleep…

'Mr. Hennessey, Mr. Hennessey!
Wake up, now, won't you? He's come, he has!'

Jack Hennessey woke to first light on the park
summer bright and full in the house.
In strong, full strides he took to the stairs
up into their room, struck still where he stood.

Christine McCarthy Hennessey
eyes bright, clear and blue
a child at her bosom, held sure in her arms.
'You've a son, now, Jack Hennessey!
'Tis a strong healthy son that you have!
One done, says I, and nine to go!'

Acknowledgements

A great many people were helpful in the research for this book including Carl Cole, whose father was a piano player on the Southwest Waterfront during the timeframe of the story, and Kevin Traver of the National Marine Heritage Foundation. Others include Jim Donohoe of Donohoe Construction, a fifth generation Washingtonian, and Maurice Cullinane, life-long resident and former Chief of Police in the District of Columbia. Jim Nalls, a graduate of Gonzaga College High School, provided useful background on the Swampoodle area. Also helpful was Paul Warren who has written two books about Gonzaga and its graduates. Of particular use in learning about the history of the Swampoodle area was a paper by Kathleen Lane *The Construction of Irish-American Cultural Identity in the Swampoodle Neighborhood of Washington, DC: 1859 -1907*. Other background sources on the Irish in Washington DC included *Washingtonian* magazine articles by Terence Winch (*A Bit of Ireland*) and Tom Kelly (*I Knew I was Irish as Soon as I knew Anything*). Mike Brant was generous in providing information on Swampoodle as well encouragement throughout. Christie Hughes, *restaurateur extraordinaire* and a leader among in the Irish-born community in Washington, DC, was exceptionally helpful in sharing his knowledge and the experiences of his early years in the west of Ireland. I want particularly to thank Drs. Kevin Nealon, Tom Fleury and Doc Martin for their technical support, though any errors of a medical descriptive nature that may occur in the book are mine alone. The following were kind in reading manuscripts and offering advice and encouragement: Hank King, Paul Warren, Jackie Kane, Dan Donohue, Jill McNamara, Michael Belford and Pam and Mike McCarthy. I would also like to thank Pat Leibowitz whose cover art captures brilliantly a May afternoon in Swampoodle of 1936. Sue Hamilton, and especially Lot Ensey, provided invaluable assistance on line editing. And finally I want to thank Peggy Carr for her assistance and support. The generosity of her time and the keenness of her insights contributed significantly to the final manuscript. A fellow writer, Peggy's encouragement over the years has been invaluable and is greatly appreciated.

Beyond all these is my wife Michaele Anne. In nearly forty years of marriage she has been friend, partner, lover and mate. A native of Washington, she has been a constant source of information on the area and people. Over the years, she has developed a knack for seeing things in the paper or just around town that are useful in whatever I may be writing. Having her nearby, knowing that she understands, makes writing possible. And then there are our children, David, Claire and Peter and Peter's wife Quincy and their children – Storm, Lawson and Barrett. To have meaning, learning must be shared, and it is through writing that I hope to share and pass on to them what of value I have learned in my time here.

P. D. St. Claire
Kensington, Maryland
March 2010

P.D. St. Claire is the pen name of Paul Belford, a Washington DC-based executive recruiter. Made up of the first letters of his children's given names – Peter, David and Claire – he first used it for *Notes from a Passage,* a collection of stories that capture the values learned in his early years and later experiences. "You want to be careful about putting your name on a collection of *values,"* was his thinking at the time. "It may incline others to hold you to them."

A native of Long Island, New York, he has lived in the Washington, DC area since 1968. His great grandfather, Michael Moran, landed in New York harbor in 1850 aboard the *William Hitchcock,* one the hundreds of 'coffin ships' that evacuated more than a million starving refugees from Ireland during the Great Famine of 1845-52. Michael Moran was later to found the Moran Towing Corporation whose tugboats ply New York harbor to this day.

Paul, a product of Boston College, earned a MA in Economics at Fordham University in the Bronx, New York. Between BC and Fordham, he spent a year teaching Economics Al-Hikma University, in Baghdad, Iraq, another Jesuit institution.

Breinigsville, PA USA
21 May 2010
238451BV00001B/1/P